Saint Brenda

Shall I abandon, O King of mysteries, the soft comforts of home? Shall I turn my back on my native land, and turn my face towards the sea?

Shall I put myself wholly at Your mercy, without silver, without a horse, without fame, without honour? Shall I throw myself wholly upon You, without sword or shield, without food and drink, without a bed to lie on? Shall I say farewell to my beautiful land, placing myself under Your yoke?

Shall I pour out my heart to You, confessing my manifold sins and begging forgiveness, tears streaming down my cheeks? Shall I leave the prints of my knees on the sandy beach, a record of my final prayer in my native land?

Shall I then suffer every kind of wound that the sea can inflict? Shall I take my tiny boat across the wide sparkling ocean? O King of the Glorious Heaven, shall I go of my own choice upon the sea?

O Christ, will You help me on the wild waves?

Also by Cynthia Rinear Bethune

The Family Tree

BRENDAN'S CROSS

Cynthia Rinear

Brendan's Cross

First Edition, May 2018

DEDICATION

To *my father*

Berman Maurice Rinear

&

To *my sister*

Becky Rinear Magowan

And to my beloved progeny, Kendall, Devon, & Iris.

And to all the family I know and love, as well as to those whose names and dates I see on my family trees, people I wonder about but will never know ...

CONTENTS

Prologue

Off Bermuda's Northeastern Shore
March 1865

THE SHIP WAS IMPALED on the jagged reef, her starboard sidewheel slowly rocking in the ebb and thrust of each wave, cargo escaping from the gaping tear in the hold. Shattered timbers drifted to shore or were caught up in the currents of the Gulf Stream as dawn's pale saffron light gradually suffused each swell and crested wave with a soft pearlescent glow.

Summoned by the sunrise, a single gray-mantled gull landed and hopped from planks to casks to the tangle of fallen rigging, giving her high squeaking calls with each jump, stopping now and then to peck at some small morsel. Now, perched upon a small, tarpaulin wrapped rope-bound bale, she was fascinated by the frayed strands of rough hemp, tugging and pulling until the bundle bobbed, sending her into the water.

Raucous calls soon rang out and the floating detritus discovered, some gulls diving towards crushed barrels of dried beef and broken cases of bacon, others drifting along on bits of debris or soaring high above for a wider view.

On the junction of a fallen mast and spar, a lone crewmember lay supine. His eyes were closed as though in sleep, his dark hair ruffling lightly in the gentle breeze. The first rays of sunlight glinted on the bands of gold at each cuff of his dark blue uniform.

The little gull, back aboard her bundle, was once again enthralled with the knots and tugged persistently, squawking with each attempt until at last, the rope surrendered its hold and the bundle opened.

The tightly folded blankets loosened in the gentle swells, and as they drifted towards the depths like manta rays, a shower of golden coins fell from each fold, settling among the coral reefs and sandy bottom.

PART I

LILLIAN

Annapolis, Maryland

*"It is in our nature to travel into our past,
hoping thereby to illuminate the darkness
that bedevils the present."*

Farley Mowat
Aftermath: Adventures in a Post-War World

Chapter One

What's in a Name?

ONCE THE NURSE FINISHED her fussing and left the room, Tom opened the letter. He bypassed the familiar property description, his gaze dropping to the current figures on the enclosure, where a significant rise in property values, moderate expenditures for reasonable improvements and expected maintenance to the old buildings, investments, and savings and interest accumulation were all reported. For the first time in years, the contents made him stop and consider…

Dear Mr. Cherrington,

Per our agreement, please see the enclosed official notification and annual financial statement regarding assets in Talbot County, Maryland.

In the event you now wish to take possession of the above-referenced property, I will be pleased to meet with you at your earliest convenience.

As always, I remain your servant,
Alexander Reynolds, Esq.

… consider the contents of the report which illustrated that he was a wealthy son-of-a-bitch … and one damn fool.

This new kid was a crackerjack, Tom thought, chuckling at the formality he knew was sincere yet tongue-in-cheek. Young Alexander was nothing if not persistent, just like his grandfather, Tom's childhood friend and sailing mate, Jake Reynolds.

Alexander's father had allowed Tom to ignore the white elephant of a skeleton in his closet, but once the youngster had taken over the law firm he had faithfully contacted Tom annually, and supplied the facts and figures, which, annually, made him feel guilty as hell.

Upon receipt of the first letter, Tom had promptly called and demanded to be taken off the mailing list. Reynolds had laughed and said people usually like receiving good news and this was like Publisher's Clearing House, only true. No doubt he would find it a great joke to learn that when Tom stopped at the post office before checking into the hospital the day before, the only contents of his mailbox were "the letter" and a notice from said clearinghouse, its bright red script proclaiming: '*You may have already won two million dollars!*'

He smiled, imagining the young lawyer's expression if he finally made that call. The smile faded when he remembered those medical bills mounting at an alarming rate, and leaving his daughter to struggle alone, still getting her bearings after recently becoming a single mother. He knew just how hard that was, having become a single father when Lily was ten years old.

When his grandfather had died and bequeathed the estate to Tom, he *wanted* to accept the inheritance for his wife and daughter's sake. Now, he wanted the relief from financial worries for himself and for Lily and knew she would treasure knowing her family history. But, even with his worries about the future and the old secrets of his past weighing him down, he could not overcome the revulsion which overtook him at the thought of walking across its threshold again. Every inch of it, every stick of furniture, the smell permeating the air, all reminded him, made him feel physically sick with the fear and shame and anger he experienced every day of his childhood.

He leaned back on the pillows, looking out at the hot afternoon sky and thunderheads forming far in the east across the Chesapeake Bay, towards that old home of his near Easton.

"*You'll never amount to a damn thing, just like that Rebel uncle of yours. You'll bring this family nothing but shame and hardship…*" He could still hear the old man's typical stream of invective thundering through his memories louder than ever…and feel the pain…

A northwesterly wind, fresh off the Chesapeake had put a chill in the air and scattered scarlet oak leaves across the muddy trail. Running home that bright, crisp October day, he knew he was late, but he was happy, and still smiling from winning the last sailboat race of the season. He and Jake Reynolds had triumphed over the Johnston boys in their fancy new sloop. Money isn't everything, he thought smugly as he turned towards home.

He stopped when he saw his grandfather rounding the corner, stomping his way down the backyard path towards the beach, a fierce expression on his stern face and the wide leather strap clenched in his hand.

He tried to turn and run but the old man was on him, the strap biting and clawing through the thin cloth of his shirt and into his skin, like Jake's mean gray cat after too much teasing. Each hateful word, each brutal stroke drove the pain deeper.

And then Grandma Claire was running towards them, screaming, as ferocious as a mother lion, "For God's sake, Ernest, stop! It's not his fault!"

He remembered the dear woman wresting the strap out of his grandfather's hand but had never known why the old man had beaten him that day. Tom rarely knew what set him off. Usually, it had to do with Tom's desire to be a sailor or some problem with money. These two things, somehow, linked Tom to an ancestor, a man whom he had never met, who had died nearly a century before Tom was even born and was blamed for every misfortune that ever befell the family.

The visible scars the strap had scored into his flesh had faded, but after sixty years he could still feel the rough wood as he braced himself against the fence post, hear the pleading echoes of his own cries and his grandmother's murmurs of comfort, and see old Mr. Crawford's grim expression as he helped them home, as clearly as he did that autumn day.

Was part of his aversion due to the fear his grandfather had been right about him all along? Shame? No, Tom thought, he was proud of the way he'd lived his life, but hardship…

The hardship came from having been so determinedly unconcerned about the accumulation of money and possessions. Each day since he had left home at fifteen was a new beginning with a clear horizon and contentment that had never faltered. Until now…

Any money he had ever earned had gone into their sailboat, the Gulfstar 50 ketch *LilyRose,* which had been his home for over thirty years or to help with his daughter's education. He had counted on Social Security and a small nest egg for his retirement, and he had only ever bought insurance for the boat because it was their home.

His annual tradition after reading "the letter" was a swift sacrifice over the galley stove, followed by tossing the ashes overboard. Today, however, the ceremony had to be adapted for circumstances. He shredded the damn thing while searching the hospital room until his eyes fell on the bright red box on the wall.

Biohazard.

Very appropriate, he thought, slipping it piece by piece into the narrow opening of the plastic container.

He lay back on the pillows and closed his eyes, the now familiar foreboding overtaking him once again each time he thought about dying—not the fear of death itself, but of leaving so much unsaid and his family in need.

The boat was safely docked over at the Annapolis harbor, but Tom felt adrift on the open sea. The sanctimonious and useless hospital chaplain had told him terminal patients often felt uncomfortable about making end of life decisions.

End of life decisions?

God Almighty! He cursed at himself, his jaw clenching again as another wave of dread washed over him. He imagined Lily's sadness when she learned he had kept such a painful secret from her and the betrayal she would feel when there was no way he could ever fully explain or make amends.

LILLIAN CHERRINGTON RAN HER fingers over the rough edges of the sediment encrusted artifact, one of the museum's latest acquisitions from the brigantine *HMS Cirencester* which sank near the Chesapeake Bay during the War of 1812. By its size and shape in the recent x-ray, she knew that hidden inside the gray clump of coarse sand and tiny shells was a gunpowder flask. After snapping on tight latex gloves, she prepared the solution to begin the long process of conservation and set the flask gently into the liquid.

She went on to finish cleaning a challenging bit of etched design along the broad silver band on an enameled snuffbox, where she had been delighted to discover a distinct Ashford family coat of arms emblazoned upon its side.

In her research on the *Cirencester*, Lillian had discovered that her captain, Aidan Ashford, fifth Earl of Soudley, had inherited the earldom in the midst of the Peninsular Wars. He had refused to abandon his ship and men to return to the safety of his great estate in Gloucestershire but went on to face action in the renewed hostility in America. In June 1814, after sustaining heavy damage during an engagement, they retreated to safe territory but were caught in a heavy squall and the ship sank. Still, Captain Ashford was valiant even in those dire circumstances, remaining on board until all his men were accounted for, despite his own life-threatening injuries. Only then did he allow his executive officer to assist him to a lifeboat.

Before its recovery from the Atlantic the previous year, this had last been in its owner's hand before it had been in hers, and she felt the usual satisfaction in restoring this snuffbox to its full beauty. If not purpose, she thought, wrinkling her nose.

The work itself was its own reward, and yet…

She glanced at the clock and out the windows towards the large soaking tubs to make sure she was alone before giving in to temptation and removing her gloves. She held the snuffbox and closed her eyes, cool metal against her cupped palms. Yes, there it was, the warmth, the fascinating little tingle of being connected just as she felt the familiar tightening of her diaphragm.

Lovely, she thought, keeping her eyes closed, trying to hold on to the sensations, the images of … richly patinaed dark wood, a desk, with an opened ledger, and a neat stack of white paper nearby, along with a quill pen, crystal ink bottle, and silver handled blotter. A three-branched silver candlestick, simple but elegant scrollwork etched along its base. Diamond-paned windows behind the desk were mottled with color, a blend of the greens of grass and trees and the blues of skies bright with golden sunlight. And there was some movement to the colors, too. Wherever and whenever this was, it was a bright, breezy day.

Then it was gone, leaving behind the residual warmth and a prevailing sense of tranquility and contentment. And, before even opening her eyes again, a headache. But she would take the headaches for the privilege, as she believed that often any energy she perceived was from the last moments of the owner's existence. Sometimes death and loss of the artifact where simultaneous. Not so in others, as Ashford died an old man, over thirty years after the sinking of the Cirencester. If her theory held true for the snuffbox, it appeared that Aidan Ashford had died quite peacefully.

In her experience, the energy always came through metal. The best from silver. The most frightening so far, from a gold locket. She didn't understand the miracle of psychometry, nor was she always tempted to test it. Even when she was, there was often nothing beyond the simple sensation of touch. Sometimes, much more, but only once had she ever seen a person …

The gray clump had been rough beneath her bare fingers, coarse bits of concretions made up of sand and tiny shells encasing the seventeenth-century silver tankard were breaking away with a bit of effort, and the usual questions were already crowding into her thoughts. Who had been the last to hold it? Had it held ale, cider, something stronger? And *where*? Found in the submerged ruins of Port Royal, Jamaica, had the tankard been in a tavern or inn near the water's edge, or on one of the ships sunk in the tsunami which followed the catastrophic earthquake of June 1692?

After she'd donned her protective gear and used the air scribe to loosen the thick encrustations, a large chunk broke away from the handle.

She had slipped off a glove, touched the patch of silver and closed her eyes. Warmth suffused her finger, her hand, and arm and when the warmth reached her chest, the vision appeared. A memory…the memory of the last person to have touched the tankard.

A man's hand was all she had seen at first, his left hand, fingers through the handle, which appeared somewhat delicate, fingernails clean and well-manicured. Light glinted off the dusting of fair hair, and a ring, yes, a gold signet ring on the pinkie finger, but no hint of its design. A ruffle of white lace covered his wrist and fell over the back of his hand.

The vision widened, and Lillian had seen the dark green of his embroidered coat sleeves, his right arm stretched across the table, an emerald and gold ring on the middle finger of his right hand. This hand held a woman's, clean but bereft of jewelry and with nails cut close to the fingertips, a simple ruffle of gathered muslin at her wrist.

The vision disappeared when Lillian jumped at a sound from outside the lab, and, as though she had been caught spying, she guiltily let her fingers slide off the artifact. Along with the vision and breathlessness had been a subtle but unmistakable sensation of desire, and the headache which followed much worse than the usual.

Now, she pulled on her gloves once more and examined a different silver tankard, nineteenth century and also from the Cirencester, from another tub and began the tedious task of removing the last remnants of softened sediment. Artifact conservation was good work when you had something to worry about, she thought, gently picking her way through the concretions still embedded around copper inlays and deep in the embossed oak-leaf pattern.

And what wasn't there to worry about? She looked up as pictures of last summer's trip with her father and children aboard their sailboat *LilyRose* scrolled slowly across her computer screen. Her children looked so like one another, though they would never see it themselves, with hints of their father in the shape of their eyes and the way they smiled. Both had inherited her dark brown eyes and hair, in the sun Miranda's glinted with gold. Ryan had those enviable long eyelashes, and he rolled his eyes whenever she teased about them.

What their grandpa called their stubborn jaws were all her fault, though. *His* fault really, she thought with a smile, looking up at the strong features in her father's tanned, weathered face, his clear blue-eyed gaze as bright as the sky behind him.

Nothing worried her more than when he suggested he forego his usual fall cruise. Six months passed since he finally admitted to feeling ill and docked the boat in Annapolis for the winter to be close to Lillian. Now he was in the hospital, undergoing new procedures and awaiting test results.

Miranda, just fifteen, had recently completed the metamorphosis to sullen, arrogant teenager who was always at her worst after a weekend with her father. The kids would be going to their father's place tonight. Lillian sighed, already dreading the Sunday night transition. Miranda and Ryan needed time with Aaron, she knew, but hated the back and forth that fragmented and unsettled their lives as much as the kids did.

Lillian went back to work as the next photo scrolled past, Miranda standing at the wheel of the *LilyRose*, smiling up at her grandfather as he signaled twelve-year-old Ryan to pull the jib sheets. Miranda had dreams to join the Navy and was excited about her upcoming two-week cadet camp, which would certainly help, or worsen, her recent attitude, Lillian thought. Ryan hadn't shared his dreams for the future, though he did have uncanny instincts when helping her with artifacts. He had questions about almost everything. Reassuringly normal for a kid his age, but he just seemed lost lately, she thought, sighing again, tracing the fine, stainless steel pick along the edge of the coat-of-arms, eager to please but not very happy himself.

Sometimes life was rather like a hopscotch game, and she was teetering precariously on single squares of marriage, kids, finances, father. Work had been a double square, even with the unpredictable nature of psychometry, both feet solidly on the ground. Until now.

Recent contributions from Voyagers International now soaked in tubs of various shapes and sizes. Several swords, a sextant, and many items still unrecognizable because of sediment, soaked in diluted sea water, antibacterial solutions, citric acid, or were hooked up to electrolysis units. Larger pieces, including a vividly painted and very buxom figurehead, waited in the large seawater storage tanks outside.

The brigantine had been quite a find, and the first wreck discovered so close to the Chesapeake Bay for many years.

The expedition had been led by Duncan Scott, former Coast Guard commander and now a maritime archaeologist with Voyagers International, in partnership with his father-in-law, shipping magnate and philanthropist Vic Andrastus.

She checked the connections on each of the electrolysis units and went back to her workstation, turning her back to the clock over the door and tried to keep working as though she didn't know what was happening in the next room. What Lillian consciously tried to ignore was manifesting in one of the worst migraines in recent history, aggravated as always by the close work and chemical smells hovering in the air, not to mention her brief psychometric indulgence.

All on its own, artifact conservation could often be a tedious, headache-inducing business. "Two months in the field, two years in the lab," was an expression often heard in their profession.

But now, the museum was closing. They all knew it was inevitable. The recent disabling stroke of old Josiah Prentice had started the process, and his death the week before had sealed its fate, and the fates of the few employees as well. The only question now was how much time they would be given to close the place down properly.

The Prentice House Museum of the Nautical History of the Chesapeake Bay had been home to an impressive collection, the family having settled in the area and been involved in naval history, merchant shipping, and maritime exploration from the time of the Revolution.

In 1928, young Jared Prentice became an archeologist and went off to the Middle East on far-flung digs until he returned to work on digs located in Maryland, near or within the Chesapeake Bay.

On a dig near the Patuxent River, Jared met and married Adelaide, fledgling archeologist, whose true love was conserving the artifacts he loved to find. The old house became a museum and the lab, such as it was, was added. Josiah, their only child, after a short but distinguished naval career, had carried on with enthusiasm, never married, and poured all of his time and energy into the museum.

Even when Lillian first applied for the job, it was evident the museum's days were numbered. The lab could not afford or fit all of the newest conservation and safety equipment. They were skating on the edge of OSHA violations at every turn, but the Prentice money and social connections had kept them limping along. Still, his personal resources and the support of patrons had dwindled over the years, until Vera had joked that their equipment needed conserving almost as much as the artifacts. In between projects, Lillian did just that, sanding and sealing rust spots on metal shelves, painting workbenches, cabinets, and desks to help keep up appearances.

Soon, however, the house and land would go to a great-nephew, who had no interest whatsoever in maintaining the museum. His plans were more practical, sell and pocket a substantial amount of money, or renovate and open the house as a hotel. Its size and location were sure to make it a very valuable enterprise. Three years before, at age eighty-five, Josiah had even told them with his usual good humor that he had optimistically made a five-year plan, to gradually find buyers for the current exhibits and close the museum. Josiah had seemed content with his decision and had told Lillian he was happy to have carried on his parents' legacy and do what he loved all his life. Still, she was sad that he was gone and would miss him, and working for him, very much. For Josiah, though, perhaps it was fortunate he didn't have to see the work of a lifetime undone.

Financial worries of the museum's last years had been eased by the patronage of Josiah's longtime friend Vic Andrastus, who was here today, at the meeting which had been called by the nephew's attorney to expedite the closure of the museum.

Andrastus was a generous soul with a quirky passion for anything to do with the sea and the history of the United States of America. His father, the owner of a successful shipping business in Greece, lost everything when the Andrastus family emigrated from Crete on the eve of the Axis occupation in World War II. Not long after the war ended his father returned to become one of the richest men in Greece. Vic had lived between the two countries all his life, settling in Annapolis to run the family's American business interests before inheriting everything twenty years later.

Voyagers International was a sideline to his shipping business, his way to give back to his second home and country which had sheltered his family during the war. Together he and Duncan Scott were responsible for the recovery and restoration of several ships and their cargos that told priceless tales about their time and place in history.

Lillian set her tools aside and rinsed the tankard once more, tracing her gloved finger over the delicate oak leaf pattern and the intricate design of the family crest before setting it into a gentle citric acid solution to soak. She peeled off her gloves before unlatching the old window, opening it wide to let in the warm, Chesapeake Bay-fresh breeze. She leaned on the sill, closed her eyes and rubbed her temples.

Though she had not heard him come in, she was not surprised to feel Mark's presence behind her or his hands fall gently on her shoulders.

She tensed at his touch but relaxed as he massaged her neck and scalp, pausing to apply gentle pressure at certain points and her migraine immediately began to ease. Mark had just the right touch. And not just to ease migraines, she thought, tipping her head back to look up at him. Even upside-down Mark Seaton was a very handsome man.

He smiled down at her.

"Better?"

Wanting to savor his touch, she paused. Many months had passed since they had last made love and she missed him. But, at least for today, he was still her boss, she reminded herself as she perused the individual features making up such a very attractive whole.

His hair had grown out a bit into slightly unruly curls of dark burnished gold. He had somewhat severe features, but his mouth was relaxed in a questioning smile. Vera called him a 'thin-lipped Limey', which was perhaps technically true enough, but it had certainly never hindered him. And if it had, the deep, mellow voice and cultured English accent would more than make up for any deficiencies.

A smile was in his gold-flecked green eyes as they met hers.

"Better. Thank you," she said, finally, instantly missing his touch when he moved away and leaned on the counter next to her place at the window.

"I thought you were leaving early," he said.

"And I thought you were gone all day…the reason you had to miss the meeting?"

"I knew Vera would jump at the chance, and I would sooner sift dirt for potsherds all day. Beautiful," he said, glancing down at the tankard, "It's not Ashford's. Any idea of the family?"

"Not yet," Lillian said, immediately regretting the accompanying shake of her head, wincing at the pain. "I will, though. You know I have to find out about everyone else's family tree since I don't have one of my own."

He noticed, pushed away from the counter and massaged her neck again.

"I'd share mine if I could."

His deep voice was as gentle as his hands and she didn't quite know how to respond. Voices in the hall signaled the end of the meeting, the end of their time alone. He left the lab only seconds before Vera came in with the full report.

"Golden Boy survived, *no* surprise there," she said sitting at her desk, adding her usual finger down the throat gesture when referring to Mark.

The year before, they had been surprised when a new position had been created and the young Englishman was hired. Vera had taken an immediate dislike to him, even given her unabashed fascination with handsome men. Mark was also intelligent, with an acerbic sense of humor which could be all at once cruel, extremely funny, and bulls-eye accurate. Unfortunately, he had also proved to be...duplicitous.

Dr. Moulton, longtime friend of the Prentice family, had been head conservator and museum curator for, well, far too long, and threatened retirement each year but remained like some stubborn bit of calcification in a delicate engraving. He and Lillian had developed somewhat of a system over the years. He would prescribe the methods she use to conserve an artifact, she would ignore him and proceed using the correct methods and modern technology at their disposal. Vera had designs on his position and Lillian knew better than to even tease about competing for it.

Mark had asked Lillian out once her divorce was final and after two casual, friendly, and very enjoyable dates, he invited her to dinner at his place...and she had stayed for the weekend. Only days later, while he was away on some temporary assignment, Prentice had announced Mark's promotion to replace Moulton. A vast improvement, no matter what Vera said, but the conflict of interest, not to mention his duplicity, effectively ended their brief relationship.

A crying shame it was, too, Lillian thought often enough in the past year, since Mark had been a vast improvement on her last and only other lover, as well. She had not expected, or even wanted, permanence from him, but the deception had hurt. Still, after a somewhat awkward transition, they managed to work well together again and become even better friends.

Vera's animosity had only increased, of course, as well as her suspicions, speculating he was a smuggler one week, or on the run from some sordid incident in England the next. When Vera surmised he was an undercover agent, Lillian laughed, as the only thing likely to be uncovered within the museum's administration was Josiah's unfortunate tendency towards fiscal freewheeling.

"Hello? Are you *listening*?" Vera snapped her back to the present. "That shark of a lawyer said his client chose *him* 'due to his superior training and breadth of experience in maritime archeology and nautical artifact conservation' but if you ask me, its because he's scared of me and mad at you—"

"Mad at me? Why?"

Vera laughed, "Remember what Josiah told us, the creep thought you were using your *wiles* on him to keep your job."

Lillian remembered, and she remembered the merry twinkle in Josiah's eyes when he shared that with them. She rolled her eyes.

"Wiles? Visiting before work in the morning, sharing homemade bread or chocolate chip cookies? He was just lonely."

"More likely the little whippet has the hots for Seaton," Vera laughed again but then sighed. "Whatever the reason, I'm afraid we did not, survive, that is. We have two weeks."

"Two weeks?" Lillian could hear the bleakness in her voice, her head throbbed again, "I'm not really surprised, but…"

Vera paused, and looked at Lillian with concern before adding, "Duncan's in town… he has a new project. Vic made the announcement. He said Duncan's new ship is nearly ready and he'll be hiring extra crew."

"Oh."

"Sorry, sweetie. I thought maybe you wouldn't want to go."

Lillian turned away and dropped the tankard into the boiling solution, brusquely flipping on the timer.

Wouldn't want to go?

"*Please* stop pretending not to care about him —"

"I've barely *seen* Duncan lately. *Please* stop pretending there's anything between us."

"Listen to me, Lillian, since your dear husband took himself out of the picture, the only thing between you two is Victoria Scott –who's a bitch! Don't look at me like that, everybody thinks so, even if she is Vic's daughter. Duncan's bound to divorce her one of these days. Till then, keep a professional distance and enjoy the view, like I do!"

"Professional distance?" Lillian tried to smile but winced instead at the stab of pain behind her eyes. "Don't you usually address him as 'you tempting bit of man flesh' or something as equally shy and retiring?"

"Shy and retiring are your specialties, besides he would think something was wrong if I didn't make a lot of him. Here's the new ship," Vera said, waving her hand dismissively before entering something on the computer and turning the screen towards Lillian.

"At least he wasn't whipped enough to name it after her," Vera added, diverting Lillian's glance towards the bow of the ship.

"Wow —" Lillian's exclamation caught in her throat when she saw the ship's name in large, delicate blue script along the portside bow. She turned back to her workstation to hide her face, which surely must be red if the heat surging through her body was any gauge. The sudden pounding of her heart did nothing to help her head.

Lillian fussed with the electrolysis clips as Vera pulled her purse from her desk drawer and stood up. "So, my dear, *is* your name going on the roster?"

"I can't." Lillian didn't look up from adjusting the clip on the encrusted steel of a surgeon's amputation blade until she saw a fine stream of bubbles rising.

When she did, it was to see Vera giving her a shrewd smile.

"Don't give me that look. You know I can't leave the kids and go on a long assignment. Besides, Dad's not doing well and something weird is going on with Aaron."

Her ex-husband was acting guiltier than when he had routinely cheated on her during their marriage. She assumed the worst.

"Then do me a favor? Take one of my two weeks?"

"What? No, Vera…"

"Just listen now and don't interrupt! I *am* taking the assignment, and I'll need the time off before we head out. I'll have a chance to finish most of my own projects, and you'll have a little more time before you need to find another job."

Vera hurried out before Lillian could argue or even say thank you.

True, Vera did wear her out sometimes. A non-stop

talker, when she was excited, talked too fast to be clearly understood—a trait which Lillian was often grateful for as Vera never shied away from relating explicit details of her life, no matter how private. Still, they had been through a lot together over the years, and Vera was a good friend with a true heart of gold.

Mark may have briefly been her lover, but the love of her life was Duncan Scott. Single when she was married, married when she was single. They were ships passing – not even in the night, but in the harsh light of day. And speaking of ships...

He had christened his new ship *Fleur de la Mer*.

Flower of the Sea.

Thankful for the quiet, Lillian stood at the sink preparing a final boil in sodium hexametaphosphate. She held the tankard under the streaming faucet, mesmerized by the bubbling water distorting the intricate silver pattern, wanting Calgon to take her away, too.

It couldn't be...

Setting the tankard aside, she dried her hands and sat at Vera's desk, resting her chin on the damp towel in her hand, looking at Duncan Scott's new ship still on the computer screen. Twin-hulled, *Fleur de la Mer* was nearly two hundred feet long, with three upper decks and all the latest technology.

Lillian glanced up at the pictures taken three years before, during her first expedition as the newest assistant conservator at the museum when she and Vera had been assigned to the Voyagers research ship, *Jupiter*.

The kids would spend the time sailing on the *LilyRose* with their grandfather, while Aaron had a long-planned business conference in California. Everything had fallen into place so remarkably well she had not felt the least bit guilty for taking the assignment.

THE EXPEDITION TO RECOVER a late eighteenth-century brigantine off the coast of Virginia had been underway for weeks, the pre-disturbance site plan and photo mosaic complete and teams of archaeologists were in the process of exposing, tagging, and mapping hundreds of artifacts. This atmosphere of controlled chaos was a sharp contrast to the usual day-to-day realities of the exploration team, which consisted of monotonous, endless searching within the grid of a specific area, while side scan sonars of anything remotely resembling a wreck were investigated.

Duncan Scott had arrived on board a few days later. Photographs had not prepared her for seeing him in person, truly one of the most handsome men she had ever met, a walking cliché Vera called him, among other more descriptive phrases. Tall, dark-haired and in an otherwise perfectly symmetrical face he had a slightly crooked and rather mischievous smile, which went right to his blue eyes. Single, too, although the rumor was he was dating Victoria Andrastus.

Happily married though she was, Vera was always an incorrigible flirt. Much to Lillian's embarrassment, Vera teased Duncan about how they should leave their significant others and run off together. Falling right in stride with her, by the end of the week, their plan was firmly in place to run off to Mexico when the time was right.

And, though she was happily married, at least most of the time, Lillian couldn't help noticing Duncan's still military-trim body, the certain scent of him that quickened her heart whether he was fresh from his morning shower or working on deck with the rest of the crew, and, she had never met anyone who could make her knees go weak just by looking into her eyes and smiling.

Hurt by her husband's recent cold and antagonistic behavior, she was flattered Duncan Scott seemed to single her out to spend time with, to talk with at lunch, and dinner, and afterwards. Only her imagination, she told herself at first, but Vera confirmed her suspicion without asking and begged Lillian to go to bed with him, just so she could live vicariously.

On their last afternoon, the *LilyRose* rendezvoused with the *Jupiter* as planned, and Duncan gave her family a tour of the ship. As they were all heading to port in Annapolis, Duncan and Vera joined the family on the sailboat for the afternoon.

Both men were passionate mariners, and her father and Duncan bonded immediately. At the end of the day, Duncan had stood next to her, his arm lightly over her shoulders as they posed for the last photo of the afternoon.

Back aboard the *Jupiter* gathering her things, she turned to leave the crew cabin to find him leaning quietly against the door frame, a slight smile at the corner of his mouth, and his dark hair still tousled from the afternoon sail.

"Goodbye, Lily." Using her father's pet name for her, his eyes met hers before his gaze fell to her mouth and he leaned very slightly towards her. Before she could panic, protest, or succumb graciously, he whispered, "Goodbye, *Fleur de la Mer,*" turned and walked away.

At the time, once her heart rate returned to normal, she had thought it was more of his light-hearted flirting. But she had never told anyone, not even Vera. *Thank God,* she thought, imagining Vera's reaction in the meeting at the sight of the new ship. The entire street would have known.

But, why on earth would Duncan have named his new ship for her? She *hadn't* seen much of him for months. No, she thought firmly, placing the tankard in its final distilled-water rinse, the flower in the *Flower of the Sea* was not necessarily a *lily.*

And as sweet as Duncan's flirting had been, it was such a small thing compared to what happened so soon after. About to leave for work one morning the week following the trip, she received the call. Still, now so long ago, the memory brought tears to her eyes.

"Mrs. Lindsay?" a stranger's voice had asked. "I don't like doing this to you, but I'm desperate." He paused briefly, and she heard him take a deep, shaking breath. "My wife and your husband are having an affair."

The beginning of the end, she thought, remembering how cold her hands had felt as she stood silently, listening to the details of how Aaron and this man's wife had planned their California rendezvous for over a month.

"She wants a divorce. She actually thinks this guy is going to marry her…"

This guy? Aaron—he's talking about Aaron, a voice in some far-off place in her mind was insisting while the frost worked its way into her core. From his behavior, she had known something was wrong, but he had blamed his foul mood on work, as he had done in the past, several times before.

She called in sick, and felt, even while standing in a steaming hot shower, as though she would never be warm again. Aaron, still in Los Angeles, had not denied the affair but refused to rush home, telling her the woman, his "friend", had already left. Lilian had relaxed, agreeing it might be better to have some time to think things through. That is, until the husband had called again, stating that his wife was not rushing home because she needed time to think. Her "friend", she said, had already left.

Would she, could she, ever forgive him? She wondered both of those things throughout the week, often wishing she were still blissfully ignorant. During the days she waited for him to come home, she forced herself to keep up appearances, driving to practices and cheering at games, helping, encouraging, even kissing owies and reading stories at night, fighting to stay on an even keel no matter what she felt inside.

Having been out sick for two days, no one was surprised she was pale and less than her usual friendly and efficient self. Vera was, however, shocked at the language she used when reminded of their annual family museum day on Saturday, especially when she saw who she was paired up with on the schedule.

"He doesn't work here!"

Vera laughed. "He might as well since Voyagers just donated several lovely pieces from the recovery to us, didn't you notice? They are now an official patron of the museum—and we must be nice to our patrons!"

She had *not* noticed the contributions or much of anything else. The nights had been a misery of loneliness and insecurity. That morning, however, she had woken with the vivid memory of a dream, her heart hammering, mortified by the vision of Duncan Scott's eyes and a tingling sensation on her lips from a kiss she had never experienced.

Now she was faced with spending an entire day with him…

"Lillian?" Vera was snapping her fingers in front of her eyes. "Listen, I know you're thinking of how he looked in those swim trunks, but like me, you'll just have to—" she stopped her teasing when Lillian turned away. "Hey, what is it?"

Lillian heard the concern in Vera's voice and apologized and got on with work. She said nothing more about Museum Day, only promised herself she would avoid looking into Duncan Scott's blue eyes.

Before and after was the way she thought of their marriage. Before, when she didn't know about her husband's affair, and after when she did. She soon learned it was not the first time, only the first time anyone else, in this case, the cuckolded husband, had been willing to tell the cuckolded wife.

Adjusting another clip of the electrolysis unit connected to a silver, eighteenth-century medallion, she watched the tiny bubbles stream to the surface for a moment and then checked the powder flask. Soon she would start working her way through the sediment to find exactly what lay beneath. Another good worrying project, she thought, slipping off her lab coat. Now, along with worrying about her kids, her father, and the mortgage payment, she needed a new job she didn't want and needed to refuse the one thing she absolutely, wholeheartedly wanted.

On Museum Day, Duncan was not overtly flirtatious and was surprisingly at ease with the crowds of children. As theirs was the most popular table of the day, with a line always in front of them, there was no time to worry about anything except helping youngsters practice a bit of artifact conservation.

The annual event attracted kids of every age, color, and background, all of them excited about discovering treasure. At their table, treasure was cheaply made pieces-of-eight submerged in mineral-laden water long enough to acquire a thin layer of calcium on their lumpy surfaces. Using a soft bristle toothbrush, a few drops of vinegar and a pinch of baking soda for a frothy effect, the delighted mini-conservators worked away at revealing a coin with a gaudy gold or silvery shine.

For the first time since finding out about her husband's affair, Lillian found herself forgetting for several minutes at a time, at least until he brought the kids halfway through the day. When she first saw him, she felt the initial happiness, as always, before the memory hit like a punch to her stomach.

She finally left the lab for home. Now, auras flickered around her field of vision as she got into the oven-like heat of the car. Her head throbbed again when she remembered she needed to pick up her prescription before reaching the soothing quiet of home. What had the naturopath recommended for her headaches – cool, dark, quiet? Empty your mind of troubling or exhilarating thoughts? Hot, bright, noisy, and worries about work were definitely not helping. As for exhilarating thoughts…

By the end of Museum Day, she was convinced of two things. First, she had completely imagined Duncan's flirtatiousness of the week before because, while he was polite and fun and helpful, he acted no differently toward her than anyone else. The second was, well, she had fallen in love with him.

Pragmatic as she was, she reasoned it was a simple infatuation, an inevitable reaction rather like vinegar and baking soda, because of Aaron's betrayal, Duncan's attractiveness and their recent closeness, and Lillian's vulnerable emotions. Still, the irony of it seemed to restore her equilibrium to face what needed to be done to get her marriage back on track.

Duncan was often at the museum in the following months and while there had certainly been a chemistry she couldn't deny, there was never anything inappropriate in his behavior towards her. They talked about his years in the Coast Guard and what had led him to become involved in maritime archaeology, everything, really, except his relationship with Victoria Andrastus. Lillian told him about how she grew up on the *LilyRose* and her 'family with no past' led her into a profession where she could delve into her passion for history. She talked frequently about Miranda and Ryan and her father, everything, really, except about Aaron and the problems in their marriage.

Beyond her physical attraction to him, there was an ease and comfort to being with Duncan, compatibility for work and sailing and history and, well, a hundred other things they shared during the brief times they worked together. Another before and after, Lillian thought, the way she always thought of their friendship, remembering the time before, when they hadn't acknowledged how they felt about each other, and after.

"This is *not* the sword of a British naval officer!" Vera insisted to Dr. Moulton late one snowy, December afternoon six months after that first expedition.

"We'll simply disregard the insignificant detail about it being found in the crumbling remains of a British ship, shall we?" Lillian had smiled at Moulton's perfectly confident and well-enunciated dismissal of Vera's, correct, opinion.

Duncan walked in from the cold, stomping wet slush from his boots. "Sounds like a job for your resident history detective."

Although he grudgingly admitted she did have uncanny gut instincts, Moulton was annoyed at Duncan's reference to Lillian's knack of identifying artifacts. Bristling, he turned to Duncan. "Congratulations on your impending nuptials, Dr. Scott."

"Impending *what?*" The young intern asked, giggling.

Lillian looked up from the chronometer she was polishing.

Duncan met her eyes.

"Dr. Scott and Miss Andrastus have announced their January wedding date in this morning's paper." Moulton used the obsequious tone he always took with large benefactors to the museum. Vic was oblivious to that type of sycophancy, Duncan annoyed.

"Thank you," Duncan said, acknowledging Moulton after a long pause, an uncharacteristic coldness in his voice.

"Well, Duncan, I suppose running off to Mexico won't happen for us after all," Vera said, the first to find her voice after Moulton left the room.

"Funny you should mention that," he said, handing her the brightly wrapped package he carried. "I brought you a little something to remember me by."

The chronometer forgotten, Lillian looked at Duncan as he sat on the edge of the table across from them, watching Vera unwrap her gift.

Snowflakes were melting on his dark hair and gray jacket and he smiled, but today it did not reach his eyes. His smile faltered as their eyes met again. His eyes were more gray than blue today, recalling how they changed depending on what he was wearing, the weather, or his mood. Today they seemed to mirror all three.

Vera held up a Talavera sun plaque. Within its gaily painted edge was a face with plump rosy cheeks and a saucily winking eye, bearing such a distinct resemblance to Vera they all laughed.

"*Gracias*, Duncan, it's beautiful and of course I will think of 'us' whenever I see it." Vera set the plaque back in its box and stood up. "Sarah, could you give me a hand with something?" she ushered the intern out of the lab, closing the door behind her.

"Obviously, we talked shop way too much," Lillian said, trying to keep her voice light and her eyes on her work. "I should congratulate you, too."

"*Should*? Don't you want to?"

She looked up at him and tried to smile. "Of course, I do, I just never knew you and Victoria were…officially engaged." Not quite finished with the job, she stood up and carried the chronometer to its place on the shelf near the window, hoping the tremor in her voice was only in her imagination.

Outside, wet, heavy snow fell across the beam of a street lamp. She saw his reflection in the glass as he stood up and walked over to her.

"I've always known you were married," he said quietly, turning her to face him.

Holiday music played softly from the radio on Vera's desk and the copy machine hummed in the hallway. His hand rested on her shoulder and she had reached up, covering it with her own.

Only seconds passed as they stood together silently, and too soon Vera was talking, loudly, to Moulton as they approached the door.

"I'm sorry," Duncan had said, before leaning down for one quick, gentle kiss. He left the lab as the door opened.

Lillian remembered touching her tingling lips with shaking fingers, remembering her dream, Museum Day, and many days since when she had convinced herself he did not have romantic feelings for her. To avoid Vera's inquiring glances over Moulton's shoulder, Lillian turned back to the window, watching Duncan walk away and listening to the continued dispute about the origin of that eighteenth-century sword.

Not quite a year later, she was out shopping for Aaron's Christmas present when she saw him walk out of a nearby restaurant. She started towards him with a smile but stopped when she saw him take a woman into his arms.

Lillian watched as they kissed passionately, as Aaron draped the wool scarf Lillian had recently bought for him tenderly around the woman's shoulders, as he opened the door of a waiting taxi, as he helped her in. When the cab pulled away from the curb he looked in Lillian's direction, his smile quickly fading as their eyes met.

NOW, THE APRIL SUN was hot and the daffodil beds along the sidewalk were such a blaze of yellow that Lillian kept her sunglasses on as she walked into the store, compiling a very short grocery list in her aching head.

"Hello, Lillian."

Lillian snapped out of her reverie. Aaron's current girlfriend was taking in her appearance. Behind her sunglasses, Lillian rolled her eyes. In her wrinkled khakis, navy blue, museum-logoed tee shirt and running shoes she was a sharp contrast to Meg, who looked like she just left a department store makeover.

"Hi, Meg," she said, wanting to be polite but not wanting to get into a conversation, she resumed her walk into the store.

"I'm glad I saw you," Meg said. "Aaron has to go to Orlando tomorrow afternoon but said we'll still have the kids tonight. And…"

Another weekend cut short, Lillian thought, the familiar annoyance enhanced by the fact it was Meg passing on the message.

"…and if they can, we'd like to have them come to Boston for the wedding."

"Wedding?"

"Yes. We're keeping it very small. Just family." Meg's pale eyebrows rose at Lillian's expression. "You didn't know? Oh… I guess he hasn't told you!"

"When?"

"Next month. We wanted to have the pictures done before I start to show too much," she said, smiling, laying her hand below the waistline of her crisp linen slacks. "Oh, I suppose he didn't tell you about that, either!"

Mystery solved, and why he was acting so squirrelly, she thought, now sick from more than the headache. The kids saw so little of him now; would he have any room in his life for them once he had a new family?

Finally home an hour later, her headache immediately began to ease as she parked in the cool shade of a pair of old white oaks. Home was a sea green Arts and Crafts bungalow, with a wide front porch and foursquare white columns, and gray stone in the chimney and along the walkways. Her first real home on dry land, not counting the college dorm, and it had been comfortably settled in the quiet Annapolis neighborhood for over a century.

Reaching to unlock the back door, she was startled to discover it already open and paused before stepping inside. Music. Miranda's music. She dropped the grocery bags onto the kitchen table and went through to the living room.

The drapes were partially closed, and the afternoon light diffused by the pale green sheers. A bottle of wine and two glasses sat on the coffee table, and there on the couch was her precious little girl necking with a boy Lillian had never seen before.

Lillian's gasp was only audible because of a brief pause in the music. Miranda saw her mother standing motionless under the living room archway, sprang from the boy's lap, staring at her mother for a moment before scrambling to pull her iPod out of the stereo.

Fumbling his way off the couch, the boy knocked over a glass and they could only watch it fall, shattering against the hard tabletop, the dark red liquid soaking through newspapers and magazines before finally spilling down onto the very new gray carpet below.

"Oh no!" Miranda moaned, cupping her face in her hands and running into the kitchen.

The boy, a very red face and panicked look in his eyes, had not moved another muscle.

"Get out," Lillian said, as calmly as she could.

"Mom, it's not Jason's fault—it…it was my idea." Miranda was standing in the arch, paper towels in her hands and trailing on the floor behind her.

Jason looked from Lillian to Miranda, not knowing what

to do.

"We have a lot to talk about then, don't we?" Lillian was struggling to keep her voice in control. "Get out," she repeated to Jason.

He sped past them both, the bang of the screen door punctuating his departure. Miranda threw the paper towels on the floor and ran upstairs.

"Miranda Christine Lindsay, come back here! Now! Do you—"

Pictures rattled on the living room wall when she slammed her bedroom door.

Lillian stood rooted to the spot until waves of pain and nausea collided with the pungent odor of the wine and it was her turn to run from the room.

Back in the kitchen, she saw the bottle of Beaujolais, a gift from friends for their last anniversary. They had split up soon afterwards and the wine remained in its gift basket on top of the refrigerator, dusty and untouched for two years. Hoping the stupid kids had choked on the strong, bitter stuff, she dumped what remained down the sink and tossed the bottle in the garbage.

She also saw that the hastily dropped grocery bags had toppled, chocolate ice cream now oozing from its container and seeping onto the tablecloth. Plucking the bottle of painkillers from the puddle, she turned her back on the mess and let herself cry.

Her tears had dried, groceries were put away and the kitchen table was clean. She was just kneeling down to work on the carpet when Ryan arrived home from school.

"What happened?" Ryan said instead of hello, the screen door slamming closed behind him. "Phew! What stinks?"

"Everything's fine," she said, giving him a kiss before he started up the stairs. He paused, and Lillian followed his gaze, her eyes meeting Miranda's for a moment before Miranda turned and ran back to her room. A moment later Ryan pounded on his sister's door, shouting at her to turn down her music.

HEY, LIL."

Aaron walked in an hour later when she was on her knees again, trying one more application of stain remover on the carpet. "What the hell happened?"

"I hope you enjoy Disney World," she said, not bothering to look up.

"The meeting was changed and I couldn't do anything about it," he said, adding, "I *am* the one supporting everyone."

What a man, she wanted to fire back and defend her own income which usually did its part quite respectfully. Knowing it was gone, even temporarily, only made her head throb harder at the humiliation she felt knowing his remark would soon be true.

"Yes, and soon there will be another hungry mouth to feed." She stood up and gave him the look before going into the kitchen.

"Randi! Ryan! Time to go!" Aaron called, following her. "Meg told you?"

"You know, you could be a daddy again and a grandpa all at the same time."

She washed her hands and drank another glass of water while she waited for her comment to register. Closing her eyes, drowsiness began to settle over her brain like a fog, unsure if it was the medication taking effect or the stress of the day.

"*What?*"

"Let me put it this way, I'm glad I came home early today."

"Randi? Oh, come on, Lil, she's just a kid…"

"Do you remember how old we were?" *Not all that much older,* she added to herself. Aaron was silent, turned and left the kitchen as the kids came downstairs. *No, you don't remember us at all.*

Chapter Two

Fleur de la Mer

FRIDAY AFTERNOON'S WEATHER CHANGED rapidly from record heat and humidity to the afternoon thunderstorm which ended work on the new ship for the week.

Duncan was alone on the *Fleur-de-la-Mer.* He leaned on the chartroom table, looking down from the pilothouse to the main deck far below, remembering the afternoon aboard the *Jupiter* when he had first seen Lillian.

AFTER A SERIES OF TEDIOUS meetings with the company's business manager and the project coordinator for their next contract, he had flown out to the *Jupiter.* His mind was on future logistical challenges at their next site and the penchant for both men he had just met with to be micromanaging penny pinchers. Less than enthusiastic about having a group of interns and trainees aboard, he stood glowering down from the bridge without paying much attention.

"Who is *that?*" he said, standing up straight and reaching for the binoculars.

First Officer Trey Munro heard the swift change in tone and laughed.

They had met during their Coast Guard training, but their reasons for joining were as diverse as their backgrounds. Duncan wanted adventure, the maritime lifestyle, and an escape from a dysfunctional household in the high desert of Southern California. Trey grew up in a dismal suburb of Chicago, where, as he put it, drugs and gangs had put most of his family and friends into a more contemporary form of slavery. After a dozen years stationed along the Great Lakes, he was also ready for something new and readily joined the crew of the *Jupiter*.

"What's this? Mr. Freeze thawing out?"

Beyond throwing him an annoyed glance, Duncan didn't respond.

"Let me guess, red shirt, long brown hair?" Trey followed his gaze and nodded. "You definitely have good taste, my friend, but bad timing. She's married."

Three conservators worked at measuring and logging artifacts as they were removed from site to surface mesh bags and storage boxes, while three others tagged the pieces and loaded them into smaller bins that would keep them stable in seawater until the conservation process could begin. Trey read the roster, pointing out those who were busy on the deck below, but Duncan had kept looking back to Lily.

Delicate features but not a delicate face, he thought, oval, with the slight cleft in her square chin, and expressive, wide-set dark eyes.

Each day she was aboard he made excuses and opportunities to be near her.

"You have women literally — *lit-er-al-ly* throwing themselves at you, married or not. Hell, some men throw themselves at you married or not—" still laughing, Trey ducked when Duncan threw a clipboard at him. "We travel in your wake, salvaging the disappointed and horny women you leave behind—and not that I'm complaining about it or anything, but now *you're* throwing yourself at *the one* woman on the ship who *won't* sleep with you?"

Duncan admitted his first reaction to her was purely physical, but it didn't take him long to fall in love, or to realize he would never be the same again.

He walked down to the second deck below, to his new home away from home.

Gray light filtered in through the Fleur's small windows aligned along the bow and port side of the main living area, empty except for the built-in cabinets and bookcases and the large flat screen and entertainment system set in amongst them. The master stateroom to starboard had larger windows than the original design had called for and a slightly raised ceiling over the bed, all because Lily mentioned her claustrophobia caused by too many years sleeping in the bow of a small sailboat. Empty, too, except for the built-in bed, dressers, and closets, the cabin had no stamp of personality or design, not yet.

Trey had been right, even if he had phrased it crudely. Women did come on to him, a lot, sometimes because of his looks, sometimes because they thought he was rich, sometimes both. He had gotten over the thrill of the easy conquest a long time ago. Now he just wanted to feel connected with someone. And he was. With Lillian.

Married Lillian. Married with two young kids Lillian. What had Trey said, that day he'd first seen her? Very beautiful but very bad timing. Well, the bad timing had been reversed. She was married when he was single; now she was single and he married.

Still, he imagined how the rest of the deck might be modified, someday, creating two staterooms for her children and across the narrow passageway, the conference room might be shifted to the lower deck to make room for guest quarters or even a small private galley and dining area with windows that looked down on the main deck below. For family time, he thought, something he had not truly experienced since his own parents divorced.

The week he met them on board the *Jupiter*, he had overheard Vera talking to Lily about their Family Museum Day event and volunteered, hoping for a seat at Lillian's table. An excellent excuse to be near her again and an opportunity to continue the flirting game. *She is married*, he reminded himself quite regularly, and to absolutely no effect.

Vera was knowingly amused when Voyagers donated the artifacts and even more knowingly amused when he volunteered for Family Museum Day. She was not so amused when she called him back the morning before the event and said without preamble. "Whatever did you do to Lillian, Duncan?"

"Nothing…" he had answered slowly, remembering that last look as he leaned on the cabin door, wanting to kiss her, wanting to kiss her more than he had wanted to do anything in a very long time. Lily had known it too, he had seen the surprise and then the uncertainty in her eyes before he turned away. "Why?"

"Lillian was very upset when I told her you had volunteered for Museum Day and I couldn't think why that would be, unless…" The knowing tone was back in her voice.

"Unless what, Vera? Don't be shy." Even knowing Vera for a few short weeks, Duncan knew *that* was a risky thing to say and took a fortifying swallow of his morning coffee.

"Unless you let one head overrule the other."

Once he had stopped choking on the inhaled coffee, he had assured her nothing untoward had occurred between them, annoyed by how obvious he had been if both Trey and Vera were giving him shit about it.

She had changed in the short time since he had seen her last. Beautiful, of course, but pale and drawn, and she greeted him with a definite reserve. While he didn't think he was the cause, he was careful to be friendly but professional.

From the moment the doors opened they were surrounded most of the day by children of every age, helping them to brush baking soda and sprinkle vinegar onto their fake coins, and enjoying every moment of the delighted laughs and smiles as the chemistry worked its magic and restored the luster to their pieces-of-eight. All the activity did not keep him from being observant, however, watching Lily smile at each child as they came to the table, how she seemed to instinctively know the independent spirits from those who needed a bit more help, those who needed an extra touch or even a brief hug before moving to the next table.

She was more herself during the flurries of activity, but during the few brief lulls, he saw her mask slip a bit, never more so than when her husband brought their kids to participate in the fun.

Even with the steady din of the crowd, he heard the small gasp she gave and glanced over the curly blonde head of the little girl standing between them. Before she turned away he saw tears in her eyes. A moment later the mask was back in place, and she introduced them before calling a volunteer over to take her place and left the table.

A few weeks later he was on his way to visit her father on the *LilyRose*. He had visited before, insisting to himself it was not only because of Lily but because he genuinely enjoyed trading sea stories with the Captain.

He remembered the glorious summer day, and the feeling of, well, buoyancy. Happy and in love, willing to wait for Lily, no matter how long. He had convinced himself, if Vera's recent remarks and Lily's tears on Museum Day were any indication, he would not have to wait long. In the meantime, he had his work to keep him busy and at least somewhat involved in Lily's life. He had paused before starting down the stairs, enjoying the cool breeze from the Chesapeake glittering in the bright sunlight, wishing he could take her out on his sailboat, alone, some afternoon just like it.

And then he looked down the dock towards the *LilyRose*, where he saw the Captain hugging Lily and Miranda and ruffling Ryan's hair as they came aboard. Duncan observed with some satisfaction that the captain gave Lindsay a brusque sort of nod as the man stepped aboard.

Lindsay was about the same height as Lily, and the guy was good-looking enough, in a characterless, urbane, and perfectly outfitted for sailing kind of a way. But there was just *something* about him, Duncan thought, the same something that might keep him from making business deals or diving with someone.

From a discreet distance, Duncan had watched from above as they prepared to set off. Lily was laughing and helping Miranda and Ryan release the lines and pull in the fenders, her long brown hair tied back for sailing, tanned skin glowing against her white tank top, sunlight glinting off her necklace and gold wedding band. The gauzy veil of infatuation and denial lifted abruptly with the sudden awareness of how foolish, how selfish he was to hover like some vulture, waiting for the death of a bond Lily considered sacred.

He had lived through the divorce of his parents when he was just the age of Lily's son, had seen the impact his father's affair had had on his usually assertive and nurturing mother and remembered losing both parents, even though it was only his father who moved away. He could not wish that experience on anyone, especially Lily.

Not long afterwards, he became more seriously involved with Victoria. She understood the business, and in the early years had often been involved in the expeditions, and they had always enjoyed a playful, flirtatious physical attraction. In his mind, she had always been off-limits, not only because she was Vic's daughter, but because she had a way about her that came from always getting her way, and assuming she always would.

While he knew it was no basis for a marriage, he was attracted to her and did truly care for her. The union made Vic ecstatic. He had always called Duncan his son, and this made it official and sacrosanct—at least in Vic's eyes. Very soon after their marriage, he learned Victoria never considered it so, did not care about him, about anyone but herself and getting whatever she wanted at any given moment. Before they were married it was him; only a few months later, it was the man she was with when Duncan had walked in on her one day.

Outraged, he had expected apologies, tears, excuses, but her only significant reaction was scorn that he was annoyed. When he said he would file for divorce, to his surprise and confusion, she refused. Not only refused but dug in her heels and threatened to run to Daddy with excuses and her own accusations against Duncan.

Vic would never have believed her, but it was not worth risking enmity between them; there was too much at stake, and not just in their business relationship. When Vic left for an extended stay on Crete, Duncan moved onto *Callisto*, his sailboat at the city harbor. With no sense of urgency, he worked at broadening his business contacts and income opportunities. No sense of urgency, that is, until several months later when Lily's new co-worker Mark Seaton spent a week on the *Jupiter*. Recovery operations on the wreck of the sixteenth-century Spanish ship *Santa Lucia* had begun out in the Gulf. Seaton had worked for a week before weather moved in the day before he was due to fly back to Annapolis. The night before his departure, playing cards in *Jupiter's* dining and lounge area off the galley, they discussed the possibility his return to Annapolis could be delayed.

"I sincerely hope not. I have a date worth swimming back for," he said, leaning back against the galley bulkhead, contemplating his cards. "I'll get there somehow."

"Sounds impressive," Trey said, tossing a few chips onto the pile, "anyone we know?"

Roused from distracting thoughts and a bad hand by the long pause, Duncan glanced up to see Seaton looking over the top of his cards at him.

"Lillian."

A significant silence followed the single word.

"Lillian?" Startled, Trey glanced quickly at Duncan and back to Mark, "You don't mean...*Lillian?*"

"Lillian Lindsay has divorced her cheating little weasel of a husband and is now, officially, a free woman—"

Seaton had broken off with a hint of a smirk when Duncan dropped his cards and abruptly left the table. As he opened the hatch, he heard Trey behind him.

"You have a death wish, boy?"

Leaning against the rail in the shadows beyond the harsh beam of the stern floodlights, oblivious to the heavy wind and salt spray, Duncan took deep lung-filling draughts of the cool, damp air, only one thought in his mind.

God Almighty, Lily is free!

TEMPTED AS HE WAS to lock Seaton in his cabin and commandeer his seat back to Annapolis, Duncan took the high ground and let him leave with thanks for a productive week's work, stopping well short of clapping him on the back and wishing him good luck.

Vera took his place on the crew and Trey wasted no time. Surprised, she looked from Trey to Duncan, and while clearly wanting to elaborate, said only, "I am not at liberty to confirm or deny, but how the hell did you know?"

When Trey told her what Seaton had said about a date, she scoffed, reassuring Duncan immediately. Vera was a tough person to keep a secret from. "As though Lillian would be likely to go out on the rebound with some…" she paused, not able to come up with reassuringly negative terms for the young man she had taken such an immediate dislike to.

"…young, handsome, educated, English, successful, *young*…" Trey supplied adjectives helpfully, breaking off at the glares he received from the others.

Duncan left the table, not wanting to intrude further on Lily's privacy. Vera neither 'confirming nor denying' had to be Lily's direct order not to talk about her private life.

Left to her own devices, Vera had no discretion, and had always broadly hinted Lindsay had big problems. But Duncan doubted any man would be fool enough to mess with perfection, and once he had recovered from his blinding infatuation, never thought she would divorce. These past months must have been very difficult for her and her children.

If Seaton was telling the truth, it was understandable if she wanted to go out with a friend and co-worker, it would be good for her, he reasoned, fighting to keep on an even keel and not let his imagination run amok.

From personal experience, he knew she would need time before she was ready to be involved in a committed relationship; time to grieve the loss of her marriage, as well as time to help her children through the transition. His own father had been distracted from his family once too often, leaving Duncan on his own with a mother who did not allow herself or her son time before jumping from one intense relationship to the next. He may have missed out on a 'normal' childhood, but he had learned much about the right and wrongs of honor, manliness, and commitment from what he witnessed during those formative years.

No, once again and for entirely different reasons, the very last thing Lily needed was him hovering too near too soon.

After two more weeks of solid recovery operations, heavy weather set in again and Duncan set course for Annapolis ahead of schedule. There was time enough left in the season for another short expedition to recover large timbers and hardware that remained.

Only an hour out of Annapolis, he received a frantic message from Victoria. Her father had suffered a heart attack. Duncan went directly from the harbor to hospital and arrived to find his old friend and partner weak, pale and in and out of consciousness. Uncharacteristically nurturing, Victoria refused to leave his side.

Vic recovered. Doctors said the attack was an early warning to a man wearing himself out with worry and work. George Andrastus, Vic's nephew and second in command took charge of the business while Vic was forced into a temporary retirement.

Except for Voyagers. Victoria's vehemence that Voyagers should be kept from her cousin's influence had surprised both Duncan and Vic. George did not understand, she had insisted, did not approve of Vic's philanthropy, or appreciate his passion for history. While all true, Duncan wondered if it was some way of making amends, although a business decision could hardly repair the damage done to their marriage.

ON A WARM MAY morning, almost a month after his return, he stopped by the museum on his way to Voyagers. He found Lily alone, outside in the back storage area where several large pieces were soaking in vats of diluted seawater.

Hidden by the cool, deep morning shade of the building,

he watched as she crouched next to the largest, ground level pool. Not working with any toxic solvents or solutions, she was barehanded and barefoot as she worked at filling tubes to test salinity levels. He saw her flutter her fingers in the water, playing with the resident goldfish who helped control the bacterial growth in the tanks.

A post-divorce hairstyle framed her beautiful oval face perfectly, her tank top was the same pale pink as the azaleas blooming in the hedge behind her, and the khaki shorts showed the muscle definition of her legs as she stretched to hang the water hose back in place. She was thin, he noticed, too thin and with an uncharacteristic tightness to her mouth and slight creases in her forehead he knew would relax with a smile.

Finished, she finally caught sight of him, her expression both revealing and immensely gratifying.

"Good morning"

"Hello, Duncan."

"Nice hairstyle, Lily. Suits you."

"Thank you," she said, capping the last of the tubes, "it was time for a change."

"I hear that's not all that's changed, Ms. Cherrington." Vera had at least told him she had taken back her maiden name.

She looked up, meeting his eyes.

"Before Seaton left the *Jupiter* last month, he said he had a date worth swimming home for."

"Flattering, but that would have been quite an effort for dinner and a movie."

"I have to admit, when I found out it was with you, I very nearly let him," he said, reaching out and taking her hand in his. "How are you, Lily?"

She had deflected the question with a bit of a shrug and gently drew her hand away, asking about Vic. Before he could answer, Vera arrived, the atmosphere changed dramatically, and Lily disappeared inside.

When Vic was stronger, Josiah Prentice and his staff

hosted an appreciation dinner for Vic at the nautical history museum.

The museum's main gallery was transformed to a warm and friendly taverna, modeled after a favorite of Vic's on Santorini, lush pink and red-flowering vines climbing up each post and along each beam in the room, and candles on each white linen covered table. Lily had conferred with Vic's cook and housekeeper Sophie on Vic's favorites, while significant and valuable maritime artifacts escaped their glass displays and became centerpieces on each table. A relaxing and unpretentious event, where nothing was asked of him, press not invited, and speeches kept brief. Duncan knew Vic enjoyed the evening and was touched by the effort.

And Lily was stunning in her off-the-shoulder gold-threaded dress of shimmery green and blue, emeralds sparkling at her ears. He watched as she worked on some last touches, spoke with caterers, and laughed as she sat through dinner with her children on either side.

Seaton, recently promoted to head conservator, was always somewhere close by as well, but that had not bothered him as much as the scene they both witnessed from the front steps later in the evening. The guest of honor had gone home, Victoria had left in the company of her oily cousin George shortly thereafter and he and Seaton had been standing outside near the front entry, discussing plans to return to the *Santa Lucia* the following week. They had fallen silent and watched when Lily's ex-husband arrived to pick up the children.

"Isn't Mom pretty tonight, Dad?" her daughter, Miranda, had said as they transferred backpacks and sports gear from one car to another.

Lily thanked her daughter and hugged her goodnight.

"You bet, kid, like a million bucks." Her ex-'s sarcastic tone and dismissive glance were not lost on either of the men watching. Lindsay had slammed the door after tossing in a backpack and got into the car without another glance or word.

Duncan saw a fleeting look of hurt confusion cross her son's face, something Duncan could remember feeling often at his age. He couldn't hear what Ryan said as he hugged his mother but did hear Lily's answer before kissing the top of his head. "I love you, too, sunshine." She watched and waved as the car pulled away and avoided the men on the front steps by slipping through the shadows to the lab entrance behind the museum.

After a moment, Seaton had said, "Bloody moron." He spoke quietly, but still opened the door wide enough for Duncan to step through.

"Still seeing each other?"

Seaton shook his head. "Regretfully, my lovely underling has principles."

"An excellent argument for declining a promotion."

Seaton shrugged as Vera's strident laugh reached them. Duncan shrugged back in sincere sympathy. Vera was a good conservator and fun to have around to a point but as a supervisor? A week with her on board was about as much as he could handle.

"Is she seeing anyone else, do you know?"

Seaton looked at him for a long moment before answering. "I think she's given the lot of us up as a bad job, at least for now."

Duncan couldn't believe the words were forming in his mind. He had seen Lily's face before she had walked into the shadows, hurt and embarrassed by her ex-husband's rudeness in front of her children, in front of them.

"If it was me, just for tonight, I would invite her out for a drink or something."

"She wouldn't…not even to celebrate the triumph of the evening."

"Even if you told her you quit?"

Startled, Seaton laughed, making him seem even younger. "While I may have no scruples about doing such a thing, with all the very best intentions, of course, I rather thought you did. At least in regard to Lillian Cherrington."

Seaton had given him another measuring look and slipped inside when Vera came out. Minutes later, Vera's husband Tony, inexplicably suffering from some mysterious pain, said he couldn't possibly stay to help with the cleanup as promised and asked Vera to take him home.

Lily had assured Vera that she and Mark could restore order in the gallery on their own. After an initial sense of satisfaction, Duncan tried not to think about what he had done.

NEITHER OF THEM HAD ever brought Lily up in conversation again. Not until today.

Back in *Fleur de la Mer's* master cabin, Duncan lay back on the still plastic-sealed mattress and closed his eyes, chilled, and still disappointed he had missed her earlier when he stopped by after the meeting.

When Vera had told him Lily was not able to sign on to the project, his own expression revealed his disappointment, he knew, because Vera gave him another of her thoroughly knowing looks. He knew Lily couldn't leave her kids for the summer, but he had hoped she would be part of the team, at least for a while, at least at the beginning.

Seaton was unusually brusque when he interrupted Vera's tirade about the abrupt closure of the museum. When she ignored him and started in again, Duncan watched, surprised and amused, as Seaton straightened to his full height and looked down his rather aristocratic nose at her until she grew silent and walked away. If she had been the little terrier she sometimes looked and sounded like, she would have whined and rolled over on her back.

"You'll need help at your lab with everyone away, won't you?" Seaton said, once Vera was out of range. "Given she's just lost her job but can't join your crew…?"

Not only was it a great suggestion, he was annoyed he had not thought of it himself.

He would make the offer, tonight. Not only a way to help, less altruistically, it would be an ironclad excuse to see her immediately.

Chapter Three

What Shall We Do with a Drunken Sailor?

OPENING HER EYES TO a house now cool, dark, and quiet, Lillian lay still, uncertain if it was late night or early morning, listening to the drumming sounds of rain on the old tin roof and the whisper of cars driving past on wet pavement.

The storm had been only dark clouds in the distance when she had kissed the kids goodbye. Too warm earlier, all the windows stood open and now the cool, damp breeze flowing in was as soothing as the sound of the rain. The headache was gone, replaced by the usual fragile sense of relief. Chilled, she pulled the throw over her, closing her eyes again.

Her stomach rumbled with hunger, reminding her she hadn't eaten anything except painkillers since breakfast. She finally reached for her phone to check the time and was startled to see four hours had passed since she lay down. She hoped her father would call soon, with good news, Lillian prayed, the very best way to put the horrible day behind her. She sat up slowly and waited until the dizziness passed before starting a fire in the fireplace, a treat for herself on a cool, quiet evening.

As she closed the last of the windows, the telephone rang.

"Hi, Lily."

"Oh!" she said, surprised to hear not her father's voice but Duncan Scott's.

"I'm sorry I'm calling so late, but I have a proposition for you."

"I heard," she said, sitting abruptly on the window seat. "It sounds great, but I can't leave town right now."

"Vera told me. This proposition doesn't involve going

out of town," he paused for a moment before adding, "Invite me over?"

Definitely *not* a good idea after thinking about him most of the day.

"I can't."

"Hot date?"

Startled by the question, she laughed. "No such luck."

"I do have something important to talk to you about, Lily. When I saw Vera today she told me you're not signing on, but this is something else." His voice lost the teasing tone and was serious. "I'd stop by the lab, but I leave again before you'll be back to work on Monday."

"You don't know where I live…."

"Of course, I know where you live. Vera told me that, too."

Curious, she capitulated, acknowledging to herself that resistance, if not futile, was certainly undesirable. She hurried to change out of her work clothes, tidy the house, pull the coffee table over the damp spot in the carpet, pace, and look out the window. In between everything, she changed twice, flinging clothes willy-nilly around her bedroom until finally changing back into her favorite black sweater and blue jeans.

Name your feelings, Lillian, it's all right to feel what you're feeling and to share them.

The marriage counselor had said that during their last appointment. She had never quite found the words to express the depth of her humiliation and profound disappointment she felt about Aaron as a husband and father. Naming her feelings about his great potential and sad reality was like mentally untangling knots in a bundle of intricate gold chains.

Tonight, however, there was no ambivalence, no problem naming what she was feeling, despite the fact that light-hearted anticipation was something she had not felt in a very long time.

YOU LOOK GOOD," HE SAID, handing her a bottle of wine.

"Feeling better?"

"Thank you, and yes, I am better. Is there anything Vera doesn't tell you?"

"No, but there's lots she probably shouldn't tell me," he said, following her into the kitchen, he set a large box from the whole foods deli on the counter. "I didn't get a chance for dinner…hope you don't mind."

"Perfect, neither did I."

"Nice house, Lily. It suits you."

He opened the box and removed two small platters, one with a variety of small sandwiches and crudités and dips, another ready for the microwave.

"After years on the boat or in a dorm room, it was love at first sight," she said, reaching into the drawer for the corkscrew. "But it would probably fit in your living room," she added, referring to Vic's Colonial mansion across town.

"Well, that's not my house. I just live there." He put the platter in the microwave and punched a few buttons. As it warmed, Lillian detected the wonderful aroma of crab cakes. Duncan looked at photographs and some ancient children's artwork attached to the refrigerator with homemade seashell magnets. "This one has your personality all over it, outside too, from what I could see in from the street lights."

Good thing you didn't see it earlier, she thought, reaching into the cupboard for wine glasses and plates. "My favorite wine, too. Vera again?"

"Of course," he said, after carrying the platters to the living room he came back and accepted a glass of wine with that very inconvenient, knee-weakening smile. "Besides, I thought it might make you more receptive to my proposition."

"This *was* about a job, wasn't it?" Wanting to be receptive to just about anything he might suggest, she led him to the living room before he could see that written all over her face. "I think you better tell me how this proposition differs from what Vera told me about today."

"I do want you to come to work for me," he said, grabbing the bottle off the counter and following her, sitting down on the couch, across from where she had settled herself in one of the wingback chairs.

"With my Dad so sick right now…"

"Vera told me about your Dad and I'm sorry the captain has to weather that particular storm. No," he added, shaking his head, taking a plate and handing it to Lillian before taking his own, "we need a conservator at our lab for the summer, to finish up with artifacts from the *Cirencester* before we start sending back anything new. With most of my team on the ship with me for the expedition, we're stretched pretty thin. Make your own hours, come and go as you need to. Our office manager will be there to help you get settled."

"Oh." She selected a mini croissant sandwich and a few of the crab cakes, ignoring the vegetables. The first bite of croissant reminded her how hungry she was, but she wasn't too hungry to notice Duncan was talking as though she had already accepted the job.

"I'm sorry about Josiah, of course, and I know the museum is closing, but this is more a favor for me than for you, Lily, and the job is yours as long as you want it. I wouldn't ask if I didn't think you were great at what you do, you know that, I hope."

She paused, trying to look away from the eyes looking at her so directly. "It sounds perfect, much more than I could have hoped for earlier, but…"

Except for the casually mentioned proviso that he would be away much of the time, she could not have considered the offer, but this was the best of all worlds. Added to the relief she felt at the rescue, Duncan's lab was state-of-the-art and would be her first experience working in her profession without the headaches of tight budgets and bureaucracies.

"Thank you, Duncan. I…accept."

"What, no salary demands or benefit packages to negotiate?" he teased, pouring more wine into their glasses.

"I'm sure anything you might suggest will be an improvement," she said, adding with a smile, "besides, I trust you know what I'm worth."

He lifted his glass to her and said seriously, "I do. I just don't know if I can afford you."

"Something tells me you'll manage," she said, wryly, raising her own glass. She had a vague idea of the company's net worth and knew the pebble of her salary would not create a ripple in that pond. "Now, tell me where you disappeared to after the *Cirencester*?"

"Government stuff, mostly. Nothing very exciting."

"What kind of work?"

"Routine, really, identification of artifacts, sometimes investigating—"

"It wasn't the case I recently read about, in Nassau? I didn't see your name mentioned."

"Sometimes my role is, as they say, discreet," he said, with a wink.

He told her about some of his recent adventures, from diving on the site of Port Royal, Jamaica, submerged since the seventeenth-century earthquake, to helping prevent looting from shallow World War II era wrecks off Virginia.

Surreal, she thought, being alone together, sharing the meal, hearing him talk so naturally, so unguarded and laughing. The physical aftermath of her migraine, the emotional turmoil of the day faded away, replaced with the warmth of the fire, sustenance of good food and wine, and his presence. A powerful combination.

"Along with the new recovery, I have another assignment next week."

"I imagine Victoria doesn't care for that much."

Oh my God, did I say that? Lillian panicked, swaying as she stood too quickly to add wood to the fire.

"I imagine Victoria doesn't even— whoa, steady on sailor!" Duncan was on his feet easing her back to her chair. "Let me take care of the fire, Lily," he said, adding with a smile, "you just relax and…ah… have another glass of wine."

She tucked her feet under her and watched as he took his time stirring the coals, adding more oak to the fire and watching the flames consuming the dry wood. She watched him move in the sure but graceful way he had, wondering if the rumors were true, recent snippets in the local gossip column hinted at trouble on the horizon for his marriage.

Apparently, the young Mrs. Scott had recently been frequenting a local nightclub in the company of someone other than her husband, no doubt lonely because of all his long absences, a columnist speculated the week before. Vera's opinion of the speculation was heard throughout the lab the morning it was in the paper.

"If she's lonely it's her own damn fault! Her father has one of the largest shipping fleets in the world and she can't arrange to meet up with her husband once in a while when he's on assignment? Shit, if I had the chance to be in a stateroom alone with him, I'd—" At that point, Lillian put on ear protection and turned on the air scribe.

Now, she watched him and tried *not* to wonder about his lonely stateroom and caught herself before reaching out to touch the soft heathery blue sweater. *That would be a very bad idea,* she thought, with a quivery little sigh she couldn't suppress.

He replaced the screen and sat back on the couch. "You said you'd had an interesting day. I take it there's even more than the worry about the job and your dad."

Lillian told him of her concerns for Ryan, as well as her run-in with Meg and Miranda's afternoon escapade.

"Very good thing you caught her, especially the first time. My mother told me those were the moments that make kids believe Moms have eyes in the back of their heads."

"Aaron seemed to think it wasn't anything to worry about, but, well yes, a very good thing I came home early."

"So, he's getting married again. How are you with —"

The house phone rang, and she stood up, carefully, to reach for it on the side table, this time glancing at the ID and turning away before answering.

"Hey, Dad. Did the results come back?"

"I'm sorry it's so late, honey, but the doctor's just now been here."

"And? … Dad, what is it?" she asked during the long

pause. Wine and worry combined compelled her to sit on the couch.

"It's damn rotten news, honey, and keeps me on the binnacle list a bit longer, pretty much what I expected."

"What's the plan now?" Duncan heard her ask before closing the bathroom door. He could tell she was struggling to keep her voice steady.

Fighting battles on every front, he thought. Of all the nights to force his way in and ply her with wine. He smiled, remembering how she had reached out to hold onto the chair as she stood.

She was still on the phone when he came out of the bathroom, and he didn't want to eavesdrop on news he could tell was anything but good.

The old-fashioned living room was an all-purpose family room, with the television and fireplace, comfortable sofa and chairs, the family computer in one corner. Photographs and books, movies and mementos filled several bookshelves. The woodwork was dark, aged oak, soothing but warm with the blends of pale green and dark gray in the understated English botanical upholstery. He could imagine Lily curled up on the couch reading a book, or with her kids watching a movie.

Photographs of the family ranged along one wall and Lily must have taken most of them because she wasn't in many. Photos around a door frame were from the expedition when they had met, including the one of him and Lily on the deck of the *LilyRose* before they said goodbye.

Fleur de la Mer.

She hadn't said anything about the ship or its name tonight, but then, neither had he. He had thought seriously about christening her *Lily*, telling some cover story to explain it away, but woke up one night with the answer. In the picture, she was laughing at something Vera had said to them. It had been a way to get Lily's picture, and an excuse to put his arm around her.

He glanced into the room beyond the pictures. Lily's

room. Walls were a restful shade of blue and white lace curtains fluttered at the open window. Simple, elegant and comfortable, with floral prints and seascapes on the wall. A small lamp on the bedside table spilled a golden pool of soft light across her bed.

Stepping inside, he imagined it to be his one day, too, until he turned to see large, framed pictures of reality. School photos of her children.

Favoring their father in looks, with well-defined features, both had Lily's dark brown hair and eyes. Her daughter radiated confidence in the way she leaned forward, smiling, looking directly into the camera. Interesting, Duncan observed. The look in Miranda's eyes was all about her, declaring her own outgoing, determined personality. Ryan's was about who he was looking at. Not smiling, not frowning. He had something of the captain's direct gaze in those eyes.

He could still hear her talking quietly as he stepped out of her room, and smiled, noticing their picture again. Placed at her eye level, she would see it each night as she went to bed.

Has to be a sign, he thought, *a very good sign.*

Back in the living room, he sat near Lily on the couch and poured himself a last glass of wine, amused to see her holding the phone slightly away from her ear. He could hear the Captain's hearty voice quite clearly.

"We'll plot a new course when the doctor comes back in the morning, Lily, and then I'll be able to cut and run in the afternoon. I know you wanted to come visit, but it's too late now. Crew home with you tonight? I don't want you to be all alone worrying about me."

"No crew. An extra hand, though," she said, looking at Duncan with a teary smile, "Duncan Scott is visiting."

Duncan saluted.

"He says hello."

"Great guy! Tell him hello for me, will you? The nurse is fussing, so I'll say goodnight."

Lily sat holding the phone for a moment after saying goodbye.

"What is it?" Duncan asked.

"He didn't say exactly, only that it was what he expected, and he expected the chemo wasn't helping."

"I'm sorry."

"The doctor will be back in the morning 'to plot a new course.'" She smiled at him through her tears, set the phone aside and used the cuff of her sweater to wipe her eyes. She pulled one of the couch pillows towards her and wrapped her arms around it. "I hope the doctor has passed his basic seamanship, or someone will have to translate."

"The Captain's a great guy."

"Well, he's been sick quite a while, probably much longer than we knew.…"

"You know he'll put up a hell of a fight, Lily." Duncan reached over and put his hand on her shoulder. She closed her eyes at his touch and he saw a tremor cross her face. As she had once before, she reached up and placed her hand over his. "I know I should go, but I don't want to leave you alone feeling like this."

"I'm going to see him tonight," she said, pushing the pillow aside and standing.

He smiled at Lily's little white lie, but then she surprised him. She leaned over, put her hands on his shoulders, and looked into his eyes. "Besides," she said smiling, "I don't need a guilty conscience and one more thing to feel bad about in the morning."

Before she could escape he pulled her onto his lap.

"Duncan!"

"The Captain's voice was loud and clear. And, even if it wasn't too late, as a friend, I couldn't let you drive anywhere tonight."

"Let me up—oh—!"

He kissed her neck and laughed softly at her gasp, mostly because it masked his own sharp breath when she moved, and he had felt the warmth of her against him.

God, he wanted to kiss her, wanted her so much. She lay in his arms looking up at him with those panicked, tipsy brown eyes until the fact this was to be a reconnaissance mission only completely left his mind. He leaned towards her.

"Blue!"

"Pardon me?" he sat back, confused, and amused at the fresh alarm in her eyes.

"Your eyes…Vera said they were gray and I said…"

"You and Vera have discussed my eyes?"

"Well…" she started, as he traced his finger over the blush coloring her cheeks.

"I'm flattered."

"You know Vera's in love with you."

"No, Vera wants to have sex with me."

She laughed but acknowledged the truth by rolling her eyes.

"What about you, Lily?" he asked, his own voice now seductive. What would she say, he wondered, about being in love with him or wanting to have sex with him? Her heart beat against his. Her pupils expanded as her smile faded and their eyes met again.

"I…I said they were kind of a gray-blue," she said, in a quick, breathless rush, "like the sea on a stormy day."

"Well then, I guess you win." He covered his disappointment with a wry smile. "You are also *very* clever, even when you are three sheets to the wind."

She gasped as he kissed her neck again, this time nipping gently with his teeth. "You know, Lily, I would have thought an old salt like yourself could hold your grog a bit better, and not say things that could get you into trouble."

"Duncan, please…please let me up…"

"*What shall we do with a drunken sailor…*" he held her tighter and whispered the melody slowly, "*What shall we do with a drunken sailor…?*" punctuating each line with kisses from her forehead back down to her neck. "*What shall we do with a drunken sailor…?*" She started to relax in his arms and he wished he knew all twenty verses, "*early in the morning?*"

Her eyes were closed, one hand rested on his chest and the other had found its way into his hair at the back of his neck.

"Lily?" he whispered.

She opened her eyes.

"What about all we'd have to feel good about *before* morning?" He moved closer to kiss her lips, ready to carry her to her room and lay her in that pool of golden light on her bed, ready to forget all of his good intentions. His lips brushed her cheek when she turned away.

"Don't tease me, Duncan." If he had still been in doubt, the longing and need she betrayed with the tremulous whisper dispelled them completely. No doubt as to her integrity, either. "You know we can't."

He sat back, holding her for a while longer and she made no move to escape although her body tensed and he saw her eyes widen when he stood with her still in his arms.

"I'm sorry, Lily, truly," he said, setting her down gently and while still holding her close, he added, "but, if we *ever* find ourselves in a situation like this again, it is *not* going to end with me saying I'm sorry."

After a long moment, she said, "Promise?"

"I promise."

Chapter Four

Better the Devil You Know

BY THE TIME LILLIAN arrived at the hospital the next afternoon her father was very eager to leave, and an elaborate bouquet had been delivered to Tom's room. Lillian read Duncan's lengthy get-well note to Tom, thick with technical nautical terminology.

The night before, all of it, from the moment he stepped into her home to the surreal memory of being in his arms, was now like a dream. Rumors about his marriage had to be true or he would never have held her the way he did or suggested what he did. She had tried to avoid thinking of the implications since she woke up. She smiled as she tucked the note back into the bouquet, her emotional pendulum still swinging widely between relief nothing more had happened and being sorrier than she had ever been about anything in her entire life.

"Is that yeoman trying to kill me with hay fever?" said Tom, sneezing theatrically into a tissue. "Better take them home with you, Lily."

"You don't have hay fever," laughed Lillian, caressing the creamy pink petals of a rose.

"I will if you put that monstrosity inside the *LilyRose* with me. Very nice of him to think of me, though," he said, giving her a wink.

She smiled. "Duncan's offered me a job at his lab, while he and most of his conservators are away on assignment through the summer. What do you think?"

Tom paused in the process of buttoning his shirt, watching as she inhaled the heady scent of a dusky pink lily.

"Do you know that's just how you came to be called

Lillian?" he asked suddenly, smiling at her puzzled expression and resumed his buttoning "Well, your mother and I were both so sure you were going to be a boy, you see, we didn't have one girls name picked out. We were admiring you one afternoon and trying to come up with a name other than Charlie or Bob and then a big, mixed bouquet like this was delivered to her. Katie and I looked at one another and said 'Lily!'" He added with a chuckle, "Damn good thing for you she didn't get gladiolus!"

"Do *you* know," she asked, gathering his book and his few essentials, "that is one of the few stories you've shared from our past *not* about sailing?"

"Well," he said, his smile slowly fading, "the past has been on my mind a lot lately." He lowered his voice adding, "And, to answer your question, I think the same reasons the Commander sends flowers to me instead of you are ones that could get you involved in a real mess if you spend too much time together. I think you know that, too."

Startled by the direct hit, she blushed but acknowledged his words with a nod.

"Working in close quarters, you could lose your bearings and get lost in the fog."

"I only accepted knowing he'll be away most of the summer."

"Where is he off to this time?" Tom turned away to tuck in his shirt. Lillian handed him his belt without his needing to ask.

"A Civil War era merchant vessel. It's been charted for years but now Atlantic Energy plans to drill in the area, somewhere between Hatteras and Bermuda, I think Vera said."

"You can tell me all about that new ship of his on the way home," he said, picking up his overnight bag and heading towards the door.

Stopping mid-reach for the bouquet, Lillian's stomach flip-flopped when she realized the fleur in *Fleur-de-la-Mer* really *was* a lily.

Duncan pulled the new car onto the highway, still unaccustomed to the near silence of the hybrid's engine, its fuel-efficient stealth mode in direct conflict with the unique sports car look, not to mention the adrenaline still coursing through his body.

He had assigned Cal, head of Voyagers security team, to a bit of freelance surveillance. On Victoria. Four times in the last few months Cal had caught his wife out with other men and photos would appear, via an anonymous source, in the local gossip column starting today. Duncan realized with annoyance his picture would be included in one of them, confronting his cheating wife and her lover; tawdry, but it would help get him out of this marriage while preserving his business and his relationship with Vic.

Ironically, it was Vic who had helped provide the strategy; Duncan had merely helped to embellish the story.

The year before, at some fancy philanthropic event Vic was involved in, Duncan gave a speech and presented a short video about Voyagers most recent recovery. It caught the attention of the local gossip columnist and 'Newsy Nancy' became obsessed with him, the kinder critics said, and wrote frequently about Duncan and how it appeared that Mrs. Scott had been on solo expeditions of her own that had nothing to do with maritime archaeology.

With Victoria's infidelity exposed and his financial resources diversified, he could finally ask Lily to marry him. He wasn't waiting the months the legal process of the divorce would take to make it clear to her how he felt; he had waited long enough.

His cell rang and lit the digital display on the dash. His office manager Mariah, texting in her personable, secretary-of-the-month kind of way, "*WHERE THE HELL ARE YOU? INA'S HERE FOR YOUR MEETING!* The team from Texas A & M's Institute of Nautical Archaeology had scheduled the meeting weeks ago and he'd forgotten all about it when Cal had called. He hit the code seven reply, "*Be sweet and make coffee, I'll be there soon!*"

JOSIAH PRENTICE MIGHT NOT have had many family members to attend his funeral, but every seat in the old church was filled with long-time friends and colleagues. Doors were thrown wide and windows opened to let in the light and the warm, fresh breeze off the Bay.

Lillian had been preoccupied with her dad's telephone call before leaving for the service. The doctor was proposing new treatments and Tom was trying to sound positive, but Lillian could tell he was troubled.

She was sad, too, and fighting another headache, not to mention a severe case of annoyance. Vera, undaunted by the solemnity of the occasion, talked as though they would never see each other again, although they were still, essentially, working together. During their short drive up Duke of Gloucester Street to the church, she vented about the rushed closing of the museum, about Mark "bossing" them around, which led to a sudden detour into gushing her excitement about working for Duncan. If Lillian had been in a teasing mood she would have asked Vera if she had been skipping her medication.

Even at the church, Vera continued, whispering close to her ear, peering through the crowd, keeping up an annoying stream of commentary during the beginning of the service.

When the Navy Hymn ended, the final words of the hymn reminded Lillian of her father and his own peril on the sea. Her worries for him and her grief for Josiah wrenched at her heart. As she searched through her purse for a tissue, Vera started up again.

From Lillian's other side, Mark stopped her with the simple gesture of handing Lillian a fine linen handkerchief. Vera shot him an annoyed glance and leaned towards Lillian again, and he silenced her for the duration of the service by casually draping his arm over the back of the pew behind Lillian. Grateful, Lillian found herself relaxing against him, finally allowed to give attention to the tributes paid to their old friend and boss.

After the service, she and Vic offered each other

condolences, perhaps, she thought, recognizing they would be the ones to miss old Josiah the most. She was touched when he took her by the shoulders and kissed her cheeks in his traditional Greek manner, the scent of Old Spice bringing Josiah instantly to mind.

She knew it was odd for a kid his age, but Ryan liked going to work with her. With Miranda still grounded and at the boat with her grandfather, on the weekend after the funeral Lillian took him to the lab to check on some of the artifacts they were preparing to transfer to other labs.

Ryan had always displayed a natural talent for the work, a true intuition for the history of an artifact and its connection to the people that made them important. She had meant to stay only long enough to change some solutions on their way to a movie. Ryan had been excited about seeing the latest blockbuster for months, and it promised to be a fun, loud and chaotic evening. But Ryan had questions about everything, and their usual guessing game took so long they missed the late afternoon showing entirely.

At the lab working late on one of his own projects, Mark listened to them.

"What exactly is it you do for fun, Lillian?" he asked.

"Isn't this fun?" she asked, first Mark and then Ryan.

Ryan gave his usual half-smile and shrug.

"What is the last fun thing you did with your Mum?" Ryan had met Mark a few times before but still sized him up before answering with a question.

"Fun or funny?"

Oh dear, Lillian thought, bracing herself.

Mark smiled. "Either."

"She sat down in the bathtub with me with all of her clothes on!"

Mark raised his eyebrows at her.

"I was hot!" she protested, laughing, "And you were what, five or six at the time?"

Ryan giggled, a sound she remembered from that day, too, a sound she didn't hear nearly enough anymore.

After a short pause, she added, "Well, if that was the last time I was fun *or* funny, I think it's time to stop work and get to the movies!"

In the process of turning off her computer, she heard Ryan say, "Want to go with us?"

Mark glanced her way, uncertain.

"What, you have something against *fun?*" she asked, smiling.

"Do you like the Avengers?" Ryan added, his way of sweetening the deal.

Mark set aside his air scribe and reached over and turned off the magnifying lamp. "As a matter of fact, some of my best friends are Avengers."

On Monday morning, the last day when all three of them would be working together for the foreseeable future, Mark thanked her for including him and they laughed at something Ryan had said about the movie. After he left the lab, Vera glared.

"What?"

"Cavorting with the enemy?"

"Cavorting? Movie and pizza with a twelve-year-old hardly qualifies," Lillian laughed, snapping on her gloves and turning her back on. "Besides, Mark's not my enemy," she added, lifting a sediment-encrusted artifact out of its vat and set it on the counter in front of her, hoping Vera would just let the subject drop. "If it makes you feel better, I might as well not have been there at all. Ryan sat between us, and afterwards, Mark treated for pizza and they played every arcade game in the place. Ryan's been more cheerful ever since, and was thrilled to have something very cool to goad his big sister about."

"Whatever," Vera said, dismissively, finally ready to move on, Lillian thought but, unfortunately, Vera continued on the same subject, just a different theme.

"Now, *listen* to me, Lillian. You need to take advantage of this new opportunity to encourage Duncan."

"He's married, Vera," Lillian said, not even bothering to glance up from her work.

"*Listen* to me, Lillian, strike while the iron's hot this time. Don't wait—"

"Duncan is *married.*" Lillian tried not to let Vera get to her, truly, but she was pushy to the point of rudeness. Nothing seemed to jar her out of her obsession with Lillian's love life.

"But listen—"

"But *you* listen! I don't encourage married men, and Duncan wouldn't, he *wouldn't...*" the memory of his eyes and his voice, *but just think of what we'd have to feel good about before morning...* intruded and she paused.

Mark walked into the lab from his office. He smiled and raised his eyebrows, waiting for her to finish. Vera, not noticing, unaware of his presence, not that it would matter, continued.

"The night of Vic's party? He didn't look like he needed much encouragement."

Mark nodded in agreement, but Lillian didn't want a reminder of that night at this particular moment. She turned her back on both of them, picked up her chisel and started working on the lumpy mass of concretions in front of her, within which the x-ray showed some sort of lock mechanism and length of chain.

Vera's deep, gravelly chuckle should have warned her. Lillian knew from nearly four years of experience that it was unreasonable to believe that Vera was quite finished. "Married or not, Lillian, if you ask me, he looked like he wanted to take you to some secluded location and have you up against—"

"Ow!" Lillian cried when the chisel glanced off the lump, passed through the thin layer of latex and into the fleshy part of her left palm. Perfect.

"Ladies," Mark said, joining her at the sink where she was flushing the wound with cold water, "such improper talk. I'm shocked."

"So sorry to offend your delicate sensibilities," Vera said.

He met Lillian's eyes, his own smiling, a muscle in his jaw twitched and she didn't know if it was possible to blush anymore without fainting. She put her head on her arm.

"Listen, Lillian—"

"*Vera*! It doesn't matter what I might want, what Duncan might want, or what you so obviously want. Duncan is *married*. He is *not* the kind of man to be unfaithful. I am *not* the kind of woman to have an affair with a married man – not to mention my boss!"

"That certainly is true," Mark said, as he set her hand on a clean towel and patted it dry, "sad, but true."

Finally silenced, whether from Lillian's vehemence, Mark's presence or the letting of blood, Lillian didn't know, but she was relieved to hear the door close behind Vera when she left the lab.

"How ironic. You seem to have impaled your Mount of Venus."

"Please don't talk about that night…."

"Uncanny what she said about the wall, though, isn't it?"

"Mark…"

He laughed softly, a sexy kiss on the back of the neck kind of laugh that made her toes curl, but didn't tease her about their one-night lapse of protocol.

"She's like a schnauzer, don't you think? Even looks like one, or would if she had a set of muttonchop whiskers to go along with all of her wild, wiry salt and pepper hair."

Lillian laughed at the apt description and turned, finally looking up at him as he applied a band-aid. He glanced towards the door before leaning down and applying a kiss on her palm.

"She even yaps like one, but instead of rats, she sniffs out the truth. Or Vera's own interpretation of the truth."

"Just because something may be true, doesn't mean it's not private," she said, sitting up and leaning forward for a real kiss. She didn't care who saw. "Thank you."

TOM THREW THE NEWSPAPER down. "Don't these damn people have anything better to write about than the miseries of others?"

"Shhh… the whole harbor can hear you!" Grace turned off the boiling kettle and filled their cups. "What is it?"

Grace Lynd, his long-time sailing pal, whose ancient Beneteau sloop, *Windsong*, was currently docked next to the *LilyRose*, sighed as she read the local gossip column.

Recently, Newsy Nancy had renewed her fixation on the Scott's marriage. The incident at a local nightclub where Victoria was seen with another man had been covered in minute detail. In another, a candid shot of Victoria and another man not her husband included quotes from various so-called friends filling in any gaps. In yet another, Duncan confronted his cheating spouse and a young man trying to blend into the background.

"If you're reading Nasty Nancy's column, you must be bored. Poor Duncan Scott. Why she would want to cheat on him is beyond me!" she said emphatically, slipping on her glasses to more closely examine the picture.

"And beyond my daughter as well, madam," Tom said, one eyebrow raised. "I just don't want her offering him any tea and sympathy, if you … ah, know what I mean."

"Yes, dear, I know what you mean," Grace said, smiling at his grim expression. "But Lily is a grown woman and she'll make her own decisions. Besides," she added, "you said Duncan's leaving soon, paying her twice what she made at the museum, and she's already engrossed with new research into some artifact. She has a sparkle I haven't seen in quite a while."

"Ha!" he said, skeptically, "Sparkling, is she? Well, maybe with him away and other things to keep her occupied, she won't let herself get too involved."

"She's delivering your grandchildren *and* dinner from Maria's very soon, isn't she? You can repeat your tea and sympathy warning to her."

His expression lightened at the reminder about his grandchildren and take-out from his favorite Italian restaurant, but he glowered again at her teasing and gestured to the paper, "Get rid of that damn thing away before she gets here!"

ALREADY WORKING LATE?"

"Just trying to impress the boss," Lillian said, smiling as Duncan entered the lab. "Although, Mariah was sure you'd be out at the *Jupiter* tonight."

"I was hoping to see you before I left, to make sure you have everything you need," he added, smiling back. "And I am impressed."

"Everything I need, and projects already chosen," she said, moving towards the long row of small tubs lining the windowless side of the lab. Soaking in one was what appeared to be a candlestick, and the other was a mystery ensconced in a substantial gray clump. The x-ray was intriguing but inconclusive as to what exactly was locked inside.

As they stood by the tubs and talked about the recovery site and conservation techniques planned, the awkwardness of their attraction dissolved. Until the conversation turned to the new project, due to begin the following week.

"Maybe we can bring you out to the site—for a day or two, if you'd like."

"Maybe." She turned away to adjust the clip on a nearby electrolysis unit.

"Lily..?"

She looked up, surprised at the change in his voice.

"Come out and see her with me."

"Tonight?"

"I'd love to show you around," he said, softly, taking her hand.

She looked up at him, examining the face she had recently been able to savor surreptitiously to her heart's content, and discontent. His voice and his character, too, as he worked with his office manager and conservators, or talked with contractors on the telephone, hearing the honesty, humor, and intelligence in each exchange. In the brief time she had worked at Voyagers, she had learned far more about him than in the three years she had been infatuated at a distance.

"I can't."

"Hot date?"

"Very," she answered without hesitation and was touched by his reaction. She clarified the hot date included kids, father, and good Italian food aboard the *LilyRose*. "Why don't you join us?"

LILLIAN CLOSED THE BOOK and her eyes.

A character in a novel, she thought, easy for him to be noble. Still, she wished Aaron had made even a trifling attempt at nobility when she had asked for details of his affair.

You will have to kill me, the character said when facing his nemesis, who demanded intimate details of a compromising situation. *I will tell you nothing.*

He had stammered a bit and looked sheepish, but he had told her. Everything? She would never know. It had been enough, but she was never sure whether it was the details or the guilty excitement in his averted eyes that crushed her heart even much more.

With typical "grace" she thought wryly, she had blamed herself for asking. Grace and dignity. Which had been one of the jibes Aaron had hurled at her, lack of passion, lack of emotion. She admitted a distinct lack of passion *after* she knew about his affair, but certainly never a lack of emotion. His sister summed him up succinctly as a "needy bastard."

She sighed, and set the book aside, leaving her favorite character in imminent peril.

Ryan had been even quieter than usual since he found out his dad was getting married and Lillian worried about him even more. Recently, while sorting clothes for washing, standing at the bottom of the laundry chute that opened near the kids' rooms when she heard them talking.

"I thought he would move back home sometime—"

"They didn't just have a fight, they've been divorced for over a year!" After a short silence, Miranda added, "You goof, don't cry, there's nothing we can do about it anyway."

"But *why* did they get divorced?" The laundry chute amplified Ryan's choked whisper.

"Well…" Miranda paused, and Lillian waited, dismayed by the fact Miranda had a ready answer. "You know how many girlfriends dad's had since they broke up—he probably had a girlfriend *before* they broke up…I don't know for sure, but that's what Brianna thinks. Why else would Mom get divorced?"

How naïve she had been to believe this had never been a topic of speculation for the kids—and their friends. She wanted to shake the precocious Brianna by the neck.

Miranda shrugged when Lillian had asked her how she felt about her father's marriage.

"Mom, they *do* live together," she said, rolling her eyes and adding with a smirk, "even though they pretend to have separate rooms."

For several days leading up to their departure, Miranda had been in full rebellion about the dress she was supposed to wear and her role in the wedding party. Ryan had always been uncomfortable in new situations and with new people. Now the wedding had grown into a much larger event, and he was expected to wear a tuxedo and usher strangers to their seats. He began to complain about going at all and had asked if he could stay home with her.

"It's only for a few days, and really, it can't do any lasting harm," she had promised them at dinner the night before, dutifully chastising them both and reminding them their favorite aunt, uncle, and cousins would also be there. She told them to make the most of the time they got to spend with their dad, and wasn't it nice they were asked to be a part of the ceremony?

Blah, blah, blah, she thought, sick to death of hearing her own upbeat pep talks, especially now, knowing they understood far more than she ever imagined. She should have known, thinking back to one of the last times she had started to justify some disappointing change of plans and Miranda's eyes had met hers. The look of resignation, a mature acceptance of the situation, broke her heart far more than a tantrum or tears.

WHILE THE *FLEUR DE LA MER* was being prepped for her first expedition, the *Jupiter* would go on her last official Voyagers mission to Jamaica, where recently recovered artifacts needed to be transported to their lab.

George Andrastus told him the *Jupiter* was needed for an urgent shipment to and from the Caymans. Vic now left his business in the hands of a network of deputies, some in Annapolis and others based in Greece, and somehow or another connected to the family. It wasn't the first time since George had taken over in Annapolis he had elbowed his way in and used the *Jupiter* for small, emergency shipments.

Duncan's involvement with Vic's shipping business was minimal. He preferred it that way, hoping to ensure Vic's investment into Voyagers was independent of the broader concerns of the company. Along with his own gut instinct, he had heard things that concerned him about George, but Vic trusted him, and Duncan had no concrete reasons not to.

He could have promoted Trey for this assignment but decided being out of town for the release of the latest photo would be preferable.

Lily had not expected him to accept her invitation to dinner with her family, but after her initial surprise, he could tell she was pleased. It had been a delightful evening in the intimate cabin of the *LilyRose*, talking, laughing, and playing a noisy game of gin rummy with Tom and the kids.

When he returned, he would tell her exactly how he felt and propose before anything else could stand in their way.

The night before reaching the Caymans, Trey called him down to the cargo hold.

Duncan looked at the neat stacks of US currency and swore, vehemently and colorfully enough to raise even Trey's eyebrows.

"Nick?" Duncan asked. Another of Vic's nephews, Nick Pandarus, acted as company representative and supercargo for any shipment they carried.

"Indisposed." When Duncan looked at him questioningly, he added smiling, "passed out in his cabin. When I saw him leave the hold earlier, he was slipping something in his jacket; made me curious. After he drank himself to sleep, I came back and checked it out."

From their days in the Coast Guard, they both knew what they were looking at and exactly what it meant.

"Anyone else…?"

Trey shook his head. "Hugh, earlier, but not since I saw Nick leave the hold." Hugh was Gordon Hewitt, a maintenance tech and helicopter pilot, relatively new to their crew but Duncan had no reason to suspect him, especially not over Nick.

"This one was already sliced open; he'd slipped it further down under the stack."

"You don't think all of this is money?" Trey asked.

Duncan shook his head and glanced over the six fully loaded pallets lined up in the hold, "Most of it probably *is* electronic components. The rest is someone sending their ill-gotten gains out for cleaning."

"What do you want to do?"

"Close it up and put it back exactly the way you found it. No one else knows and *you* don't either, for that matter. I'll take care of it."

"But what…?"

"You and I will watch Nick as closely as we can, and if the opportunity for his… in disposal presents itself on the way back, we'll try to find out what we're taking in. When I can be sure it won't be monitored, I'll make the call."

He watched as Trey put the carton back and re-secured the metal banding.

"*Fuck*," he repeated.

DUNCAN KNEW IT WAS inevitable. Between an open box in the first shipment and the confiscation of the second, he knew George would follow up. He hadn't expected such an immediate, public confrontation.

Duncan's call to a DEA contact had led to the second shipment, a hold full of steroids, being tracked and intercepted far away from the *Jupiter*. But George wasn't stupid, and now he was angry, suspicious, and stood in front of Duncan, waiting.

"Computer components, wasn't it, six or seven pallets? What did Nick say?"

"Nick said all of the boxes were sealed when he checked them in, one was discovered unsealed by the receiver," he lowered his voice, his eyes menacing. "The inventory shows some…computer components are missing. We want them back."

Laughter from across the room gave him an excuse to glance over at Mariah, Vera, and Lily talking at the far end of the lab and then back to George, answering casually.

"Sure thing, George. I'll keep my eyes open," he said, turning to walk towards the hall, "What should I look for?"

George grabbed his arm. "You'll know it when you see it," he growled, releasing him with a shove and pushing past him.

"What the hell was that about?"

Duncan jumped at the sound of Mariah's voice close behind him.

"I have absolutely no idea," he said, rubbing his arm, and answering loudly enough for George to hear him as he walked out. "Having a bad day, I guess."

How bad a day depended on the shipper and receiver of the laundered money, and just how much the thief had helped himself to that night. If George was having a bad day, anyone he caught being a thief or snitch would have a worse one.

"What's so funny back there, anyway?" he added.

"Oh, nothin'," she said, innocently, "just girl talk."

About to ask if it had to do with his eyes, he thought better of it. "You do girl talk?"

"Lillian's sweet," Mariah added, ignoring his comment and winking at him. "I like her."

"So do I," he whispered. "You keep your hands off!"

THUNDER RUMBLED IN THE distance as Lillian ran through the downpour from Voyagers to her car at the end of the parking lot. Traffic was light on her way home, and as she drove, her mind turned inevitably to the column she had read.

Duncan and crew had now been on the *Fleur de la Mar* for a week, on the site of the *SS Rhiannon* and preparing the photomosaic of the area prior to diving. She knew he was on the *Fleur*, knew he was working but she was still annoyed at the columnist, and more annoyed at herself at getting drawn into the web. The columnist now speculated that the lovely Mrs. Scott was only looking for love because her handsome husband was a man with a girl in every port he visited on his mysterious missions.

Funny, how you come to understand the origins of a cliché, Lillian thought, remembering the sensation of her stomach dropping as she had read the article.

Nope. No other way to describe it.

Waiting at the traffic light near her street, she watched a pack of the neighborhood teens run across the road, all looking like drowned rats, screeching with laughter and punching at each other as they ran. Lillian recognized a couple of the kids' friends in the bunch, and hers would have certainly been among them but were overnight with their dad.

The stupid woman was just sensationalizing, she thought, her mind going back to the article. Remembering the pain and emptiness of the existence on the other side of a spouse's infidelity, her hands tightened on the wheel. Bad enough even when no one knew, how much worse it must be having photographs made public and bloggers speculating on this most private part of his life.

An e-mail was waiting for her when she finally sat down at her computer:

"Don't believe a word of it, despite my recent, feeble attempt at lechery. Vera and company are doing a great job…and so, I hear from my other spies, are you.

Chapter Five

A Perfect Storm

THE OLD PLACE WASN'T the same, she thought, looking around the museum's conservation lab. After regular working hours, late-afternoon sunlight streamed in through the western windows, heating up the lab even more than usual.

She slipped a lab coat over the new blouse. The soft, filmy yellow fabric with its subtle floral print clung to her body but wasn't too tight, and its softly gathered V-neck was sexy but not too low. Just right. A way to put on a brave face while seeing her children off with Aaron, remembering his appraising glance and Miranda's very unusual request, "Wow, Mom, can I borrow that?"

After the kids had left on the afternoon flight, she went to Prentice House to help with preparing some of the artifacts for transfer to Voyagers or for shipment to other facilities, hoping the work would keep her distracted until the kids called to check in.

The sun had set by the time she finally finished. She slipped off her gloves and lab coat and opened the windows. While she stood enjoying the cool breeze and reflections of the floodlights on the water, her phone vibrated once from the depths of her pocket.

A text from Miranda. "BMA.AMUCDC&e.TTYL.XO .M&R." After deciphering the code, she decided they had arrived in Boston, and were now with their Aunt Marcia and Uncle Chris, and their cousins Deanna, Christian and baby Emma.

She texted back a return XO and felt herself relax. Marcia had been her friend before she met Aaron. She was grateful to know the kids were in good hands amid the wedding chaos.

Hearing the clock in Mark's office chime the hour, she looked up at the old clock, surprised. As she was getting ready to leave, her phone buzzed again. A new email from Vera, with an attachment and several exclamation points in the subject line. Now what, she wondered.

"*No.*"

Bold black letters burned the words into her brain.

Victoria Scott was pregnant.

In the latest society column, Victoria herself was quoted, saying both her husband and father were thrilled, even helping to choose nursery colors and baby names. Victoria laughed away the recent gossip, the columnist wrote, explaining she had been out with a cousin and her husband only upset because he did not want her overexerting herself.

"It's just… not… possible," Lillian whispered, closing the article, ignoring the second email from Vera. The columnist was known for printing, if not lies, extreme exaggerations… still, there had to be *something* to the story if Victoria was being quoted.

At the sound of footsteps, she turned toward the door as Mark hurried in.

"Lillian!" He had been out in the sun most of the day, she noticed his fair skin was flushed, his hair even more golden. He looked gorgeous and very happy to see her.

She tried to smile back.

"Hey, Mark. What are you doing in so late?"

"Just stopped by for something, and I probably should ask you the same," he said, his deep, usually mellow voice seemed higher, agitated. "Are you all right?"

"Another headache coming on, unfortunately."

"I know an excellent remedy for headaches," he leaned against her desk, only inches away. "You know, now that you're not officially working here there's no chance for a conflict of interest. Have dinner with me?"

Lillian looked up, surprised. "Mark…" He began tracing his fingers lightly over her bare arm. "I was surprised to hear you passed on going out on the expedition with the others."

"Couldn't leave town …" he said, moving closer. "Will

you? We won't even call it a date. We could go somewhere, have dinner, and talk *intimately* about the newest conservation technologies, or have a *stimulating* discussion about the structural and intrinsic integrity of reconstructed artifacts." His voice, his eyes, his touch became even more seductive, "or we could just go to my place."

She sat at her desk, closing programs and shutting down her computer, ignoring her tears.

Just for tonight…it would be great, wonderful. Yes, remembering the way he had made love to her made her lips tingle and toes curl. She did like Mark, and he was here, now, and *wanted* her. She was free to do as she pleased, but …it wouldn't be love. It hadn't been *love* their first time, either, her brain reasoned helpfully, and, really, what did love ever matter for her? One man she had loved could never be faithful, and she had now found out the man she did love could never be hers.

She stood up, meaning to walk away from him, but Mark moved closer. His eyes were even more disquieting tonight and looked into hers as he gently wiped the tears from her cheeks.

"Were you thinking of another one-night stand?" she said, remembering the sense of rejection she had felt after their one weekend together.

"Brilliant idea," he said, with a very wicked smile, "but I thought we were meant never to refer to our one late night lapse of protocol in my office." His arms now closing around her, he added, "You know, I've kept that stretch of wall clear, just in case—"

"No!" She started to push away from him, but he held her tightly.

"Our first, then? But that was *two* nights and *two* days and I remember very little standing involved, except for that enchanting interlude in the shower…"

His body radiated heat and when he pulled her closer she could feel a shiver, an undercurrent, as though she were standing too near high energy wires. Aware of her heartbeat in several areas of her body, she wanted him. Desperately. Wrong, though, on the rebound from a failed marriage the first time, and now the door shut so forcefully between her and Duncan?

Would Mark *care?*

She couldn't...could she?

His kiss was not brutal, but she felt a controlled ferocity which, combined with the heat and trembling of his body, began to frighten her.

"I can't, Mark," she tried to pull away, but he held her tight against him and didn't seem to be listening. "What's going on with you tonight?"

"I need you," he whispered.

"I'm sorry, Mark. I *can't.*" He was kissing the vulnerable spot at the base of her neck. *I need you, too.* "I... love someone else."

He laughed softly. She felt the warmth of his breath and the vibration of his words against her skin, "You've been in love with *someone else* since we met."

She pushed gently against his chest as a familiar ringtone echoed through the lab.

Mark drew back and looked at her for a long moment, the warmth in his eyes fading as he released her, his hands slowly sliding down the length of her arms before he finally turned away. Her throat closed tight, and a rough, strangled sob escaped her when he left the lab, slamming the door with enough force to rattle the old windows.

She was tempted to turn off her phone, which she never did when she was away from the kids. Instead, she silenced the ringtone and pushed it away from her and went back to work on the last of her notes, striving for some degree of coherence against the tide of chaotic thoughts, physical need and emotional surges bludgeoning their way through her mind and body.

Again, the phone lit up and again Duncan's name was on the display. She pushed it further away and began to tidy up her workstation, to keep her hands busy, to keep from answering.

He's a married man, he'll be a father soon, you have to let him—the idea *of him, go,* she corrected herself, having never actually *had* him, and remembering her mother's long-ago counsel about maintaining one's grace and dignity in the face of disappointment.

A sobbing scream seared her throat and then a stand of chisels and picks was in her hand, in the air and scattering throughout the lab, breaking glass, rattling into metal cabinets, and sinking into vats of both caustic and benign solutions. Next was the tape dispenser, satisfyingly heavy but she dropped it onto her desk with a thud, and turned, startled by a sound behind her. Duncan was slipping his own phone into his pocket.

"How did you get in here?" she demanded, slamming her desk drawer shut and walking past him to the door.

"Lily—" he reached out to stop her.

"Shouldn't you be on a boat somewhere, or at home picking out nursery colors?"

"I *didn't know*. Please believe me …"

"That night…," she said, looking up into his eyes, full of anguish and she could see the struggle he was going through but didn't care, "these past weeks …you made me think—"

"Made you think what? That I care about you? That's no secret, from anyone. Or that I want you?" Their eyes met again, and she felt as though the air was being drawn from her lungs during the long pause. "That can't be much of a secret either," he added softly.

Their eyes were locked, holding them motionless until Lillian had to turn away, hiding anger, disappointment, sadness all combined with an aching physical hunger stronger than she had ever felt before.

"Lily, I am so sorry."

"Don't say that!" she cried out, slamming her fist on the old metal cabinet. "You promised you wouldn't say that —".

When he turned her roughly and pulled her into his arms, her instinct to struggle against his kiss lasted only until his mouth forced hers open and at the touch of his tongue to hers, an agonized moan rose from deep inside. Her hands were under his shirt, over the taut, warm length of his back, drawing his body even more tightly against hers.

Facing her disappointment and ending whatever it was

that existed between them with grace and dignity would have to wait. She wanted to memorize the taste of him and the scent that triggered a physical response every time he was near. Headier than any cologne, more intoxicating than any wine, she breathed him in. Each new sensation heightened her desire unendurably, the strength of his arms, his hands exploring and the instinctive way their bodies moved together. Electricity pulsed through her when they pressed together, and she felt him hard against her.

"God, Lily," he gasped, eyes narrowed in passion, as they stood, trembling and panting, clinging to each other.

Under the glare of the harsh fluorescent lights, reality gradually returned. She dropped her head onto his chest, wanting to beg, demand he make love to her, to leave his wife, a wife he didn't love who treated him horribly, but was now having his baby.

All she could do was cry.

He stroked her hair, whispering words she couldn't hear and didn't want to if it meant he was leaving. She listened to his calming heartbeat until, with a long, shuddering breath, he finally loosened his arms. In the harsh light, his usually smiling and teasing eyes were dispirited and sad.

"I'm not sorry," he said.

"I'm not sorry," she whispered, "and I don't want to let you go."

"I don't want you to let me go." He stroked her hair, pressed his lips to her forehead.

A sound from the office startled them and they separated. When no other sound followed, they stood apart, each looking as lonely as the other felt.

"Goodbye, Lily."

Standing outside, Duncan heard her subdued sobs through the open window.

What had he been thinking, coming here tonight? Leaning on the railing above the saltwater storage tanks, he could see little through the murky water, only the distorted feminine outline of a figurehead in the tank below. He cursed himself for not letting this outrageous piece of fiction put further distance between them, distance he now needed to help keep her safe.

If only he hadn't looked through the window and seen her in Seaton's arms. Now she was more hurt and confused because he had impulsively, selfishly needed to tell her it was not, could not possibly be his baby. But he knew telling her the truth about the baby meant he would have to tell her everything, and that he could not do, not yet.

From his place in the darkness, he saw her leaning against the same metal cabinet she had slammed her fist into, that he had wanted to take her up against. Gripping the guardrail to keep from going back to her, he watched as she wiped the tears from her face.

"Lillian?"

"Mark? I thought you'd left…"

"Would you come into my office, please?"

Oh, my God, what else? Even without a mirror, she knew how she must look. Her body still trembling, her lips felt bruised, her heart broken. She stalled, going to her desk for a tissue.

With each step, she felt as though she were slogging her way through knee-deep water, sand shifting and slipping away beneath her feet.

He was sitting on the edge of his desk, his small office lit only by a small amber-shaded lamp. The look in his eyes when they met hers left no doubt he had seen them.

"Busy night for you."

"As they say, when it rains it pours. What do you want?"

"I thought we could finish what you two started out there." The wicked smile was back, "or were you trying to finish what *we* started?"

"Whatever you saw is none of your business."

Before she could turn to leave he held up his cell phone.

"You might be interested to know this tasty bit of *in flagrante delicto* I just witnessed will hit that absurd gossip column tomorrow." On the screen was proof, she and Duncan clearly in each other's arms.

"*What* ...?" she gasped, stepping towards him.

"Don't you just love modern technology? Don't you wish you'd gone out with me tonight? But no, you were saving yourself for a special shag up against the old storage cabinet, with your new *boss*, no less!"

Oh, my God.

Lillian sank down in the chair opposite his desk, closing her eyes. Miranda and Ryan would be so embarrassed. "What have you done?" she whispered, more to herself than him.

"Just my luck to get a good shot when the local rag will pay good money."

"But we've never –" Lillian choked, now thinking of her father.

"Oh, I'm sure everyone believes that... until tomorrow, that is."

"But—"

"But what about his lovely wife? Poor thing, no wonder she's shagging her way up the eastern seaboard. What about his doting father-in-law, *Lily?* Will he take away his millions when the *video* goes viral? You'll be the main event on YouTube by this time tomorrow."

Mark paused as he set the phone on the desk and stepped towards her.

As Seaton taunted her, Duncan moved silently to the door, fury replacing every vestige of sadness that had gripped him only moments before.

Five minutes, Duncan's thoughts raged, for five minutes he had allowed himself to be completely unguarded and now this fucking son of a bitch had plunged them into a scandal with the potential to devastate Lily and her family and to ruin everything, every intricately laid out plan he had for extricating himself from a ridiculous fraud of a marriage. Only her presence kept him from kicking in the door and shoving Seaton through the concrete wall.

From the angle where he stood beside the door, he could see Lily, pale and trembling, tears once again streaming from her eyes.

Lillian stood up and Mark left the desk and moved towards her, his eyes traveling slowly over her body.

"Why would you do this to me? Mark…" her lover and coworker, but also a true friend, someone she often felt knew her better, inexplicably, understood her more than anyone else. Something was wrong with him, terribly wrong, but she knew he couldn't be reasoned with tonight. She just needed to get away.

"Let me go, Mark," she said when he placed his hands on the wall behind her. She pushed her hands hard against his chest, but he didn't move and she felt the shiver of heat and energy she had noticed earlier still radiating from his body.

"There is *one* way you might convince me not to release the video," he said, taking the hem of the new blouse in his hands and pulled, slowly and deliberately, looking into her eyes as the little pearl buttons gave up their hold all too easily. She heard them, one by one, drop and bounce along the floor with hollow little clicks. "It's not like we haven't before, after all."

"Mark, *please* don't…" she whispered, clasping her hands tightly against his when he reached the top button, knowing she had to turn the moment, somehow. She pushed his hands away and moved against him, reaching up to cup his face in her hands. If he wouldn't let her escape, and she wasn't strong enough to fight, she *couldn't* allow him to force her. She would never forgive him, and she knew he would never forgive himself.

His eyes widened in surprise, softening, and she felt the tension leave his body. It was something, she thought. *Thank God.*

"Lillian," he whispered, his arms went around her again, cautiously, gently. "I'm sor—"

Seaton caught sight of him and pushed Lily aside as

Duncan kicked in the door. Before Seaton had a chance to defend himself, Duncan slammed his fist into his face. Photo or video, sent or not, no longer mattered. Lily's soft, pleading voice and hurt, vulnerable expression ignited a blood-red rage that surged from the deepest part of him and flared behind his eyes.

Lamp and light shattered; computer, books, desk accouterments flew in every direction. Amidst the sounds of cracking fists, grunts of pain and effort, splintering wood and furniture scraping across the floor, he was vaguely aware of Lily recoiling through the darkness. Frenzied movements were strobe-like in the shard of harsh white light from the lab.

Caught at a disadvantage, Seaton scrambled to fight back, threw a punch or two but Duncan fought with out-of-control fury, desperate frustration pulling reserves from him, giving an out of body detachment to every blow. Finally, he dragged Seaton onto the desk, one hand pinning him down by his throat. Seaton gasped for air, his trachea slowly being compressed.

"This is nothing, *nothing,* to what I will do if you ever so much as look at her again," Duncan said between his own rasping breaths, tightening his grip so that Seaton couldn't even struggle. "Do you get that?"

Not waiting for a response, Duncan loosened his grip on Seaton's throat and slammed his fist down ferociously one last time.

Panting, he wiped blood from his lip with the back of his left hand while he flexed his right, now bleeding profusely. He reached over and switched on the overhead light, ignoring Seaton's limp body while he searched through the wreckage for the cell phone. He grabbed it up off the floor, shoved it in his pocket and then reached over and roughly felt Seaton's neck for a pulse. Satisfied he wasn't dead or dying, Duncan turned to Lillian, standing pale and motionless against the wall, clutching her torn shirt around her. She slowly moved her gaze away from the supine, bloodied body on the desk in front of her up to Duncan's face. Even in the brightly lit room, her pupils were so large he could barely see the dark brown of her irises.

DESPITE HER PROTESTS, HE took Lily home. Once back on the *Callisto*, he removed the blood-soaked layers of cotton gloves Lily had used as a very effective bandage and showered before sitting down to check out Seaton's phone.

He had to know what damage had been done. He downed some Advil with a beer while scrolling through the pictures, not surprised to see several snapshots of Lily, leaning over her work in serious concentration or smiling or laughing with Vera. Nothing too provocative, but obviously from a hidden vantage because he could tell she was unaware of his presence. *What a slime*, Duncan thought. In the midst of taking another drink, he stopped, choking, almost dropping the phone.

The intensity of their few moments together flooded over him; her body arched into his, the tightness of her blue jeans when he pulled her closer, the scent of her, the silkiness of her skin and her beautiful, filmy blouse against his arms. Urgent, kneading caresses, her anger, frustration, desire in each touch, the press of their hips, the nip of her teeth on his lower lip, and it made him hot and hard all over again, and angry as hell at the thought of others seeing it.

He'd also keep a copy in his wallet for the rest of his life.

Another drink, a deep breath and he tried to examine the three pictures objectively. Only those who knew them would clearly recognize Lily, and there was no indication Lily's name had been sent along with the picture. They were kissing, passionately but Lily's hand was resting on the outside of his shirt, her nails no longer etching their way down his bare back. His hands were somewhat south of her waistline, but thankfully not caught when he'd cupped his hands under her bottom and pulled her tight against him.

Taken in rapid succession, either Seaton hadn't a chance to take others or was too busy watching. One picture had been sent, but he found exactly what he had hoped to find. Nothing. There was no video.

THE CITY HARBOR WAS QUIET by the time Duncan walked down the pier where the *LilyRose* was docked. He was determined to talk with Tom tonight, before he saw the picture or heard about the incident from anyone else, especially Lily.

The main cabin light was on. At his light tap on the gunwale, the boat shifted and the cockpit light flooded the deck.

The hatch opened, and if the Captain was surprised to see Duncan, he didn't show it.

"Evening, Commander."

"Captain," Duncan said, "Permission to come aboard?"

Tom gestured and Duncan stepped into the cockpit and offered his hand. Tom accepted with a whistle but shook as firmly as ever and Duncan forced himself not to wince.

"I hope the other guy looks worse," Tom said, assaying the blackening eye and split lip.

"Aye, sir."

Tom offered Duncan a cup of tea. "Nothing stronger, I'm afraid. I gave up all spirits nearly thirty years ago, after the midwatch when I nearly fell overboard and left Lily an orphan in the middle of the Pacific."

Duncan's stomach clenched in sympathy at the very idea and shook his head.

"I've been through a lot in my life, Commander, but it took me years to get over the PTSD. I'd wake up clinging to my berth like I'd clung to the lifelines that night. Didn't go offshore again without another crewmember for a few years after that. How I met Grace," Tom said, pouring hot water into two mugs He pushed one towards Duncan, adding, "but that's a story for another day."

When they settled in at the wide, main cabin table, the Captain said, "So, what brings you skulking around here close on to midwatch?"

"Two things. The first is that I need an ally in you, Tom, because the second is that I want to ask your blessing to marry Lily."

Tom's brows drew together. Duncan saw storm clouds

on the horizon.

"I know how Lily feels about you. It's a damn sad situation, but you're a married man, and if the recent gossip is to be believed, about to become a father."

"*If* a baby does exist, I am not and cannot possibly be the father."

"The trash this woman's been printing about your wife is true?"

"For a long time."

Tom waited.

"I had come back from the Alexandria expedition to find her... well, let's just say... keeping the home fires burning. I left almost immediately on the Florida trip and rarely saw Victoria for the next year. Soon before I came back, I found out Lily was divorced.

"I put a plan in action to get out of my marriage, but I very recently discovered certain other elements of this mess which has kept me from starting divorce proceedings against Victoria, or giving anyone any indication I plan to. I can't share the details with you tonight. If my plans don't work, I'm not convinced I, or possibly those I care about, wouldn't be in danger..."

"By 'certain other things' I assume you're talking big league? Something to do with those old things you dig up? Or worse?" Tom's gaze sharpened. "Got yourself tied up in some kind of overhand loop, Commander?"

A harsh laugh acknowledged the accuracy of the captain's metaphor and Duncan continued, lowering his voice, "Months ago, I hired someone to follow Victoria, and he's been feeding the photographs to the media. I wanted to build a case publicly for divorce, so it can be independent of any connection Vic and I have."

"It's all true? Not inventing anything or setting her up?"

Duncan shook his head.

"I'd say that's damn clever of you."

"Before today, I would have agreed with you," he said, grimly, adding. "Are you up to more tonight, Captain?" which he regretted at once, seeing the swift change in expression.

"Start mollycoddling me now and you'll have another black eye!" Tom barked, brows drawn at a sharp angle over the vivid blue eyes. "You haven't told me anything that couldn't have waited till forenoon, or explains the condition you're in. Get on with it!"

"I'm afraid cleverness and seeing freedom on the horizon made me careless."

"What happened? Lily…?"

"She's okay. She's home." After a long pause, he continued. "The night I was visiting Lily, it was to offer her the job, but also a reasonable excuse to see her. It had been months since I had seen or talked with her at all, and I took the opportunity.

"And…well, nothing…much happened," not meeting the captain's steady gaze, Duncan smiled involuntarily at the memory of a sea shanty and soft brown eyes. Tom cleared his throat.

"And nothing was said, but I knew I had given her reason to believe something might be possible between us. I meant to, frankly, because how ironic would it be for me to be free only to find out she was in love with someone else? In any event, I knew she would be very upset when that article appeared today."

"You've never told Lily your marriage is over?"

"No," he said, quietly. "And I won't tell her about this other situation, not yet, not until I know what I'm dealing with. About the marriage, all she knows is what everyone else knows through the paper. And…" he paused, forcing himself to meet her father's gimlet eye again, "and, well, I'm sorry to admit it, Tom, but I thought if she knew, it would be too easy for us to justify an affair."

"Lily would never—"

"She was working at her old lab when I found her tonight. She had seen the article and was very upset. I was very upset. What we didn't know was that Mark Seaton was lurking in the shadows with a camera. she had turned him down again earlier tonight and, well…"

He took the phone out of his pocket, opened the photo, and handed it to Tom.

Duncan looked away, out of the cabin's narrow portlight towards the lights of Annapolis, thinking of her heartbreaking sobs that twice tonight he had caused and could not comfort. *Please trust me, Lily.*

"I take it you're showing me because it's going to be made public?"

"Yes," he said, facing Tom again. "Seaton emailed it to Nancy's column before we could stop him."

"Hoisted by your own petard," Tom grunted, handing the phone back.

"Quite."

"And my daughter along with you."

"Yes, sir. As much as I would be willing to try, I think attempting to stop it now would create even more attention. In those few minutes, I've put Lily in a very difficult position."

"You have Seaton's phone, is that how you earned your colors?" When Duncan didn't answer immediately, Tom prompted, impatiently, "Well?"

"He sent the picture, but also claimed to have a video he would release." Tom's brows drew down ominously as Duncan hastened to add, "All a video could show is a very passionate kiss and a very sad embrace. The picture caught us somewhere in between the two.

"Seaton tried …to get her to do something to keep him from releasing the video onto the Internet. He suggested she, well…" his voice dropped, and he grimaced, both from the memory and the pain as both hands tightened into fists remembering Lily's expression. "I had to…"

"*GOD ALMIGHTY!*" Tom roared, outrage etched in every feature, his own hands clenched into fists and slamming onto the galley table, making mugs, spoons and everything else on the surface rattle. "You're goddamned right you had to! Lily's all right? You're sure he never…?"

"She's fine, upset, about everything, of course, but she's okay."

"What kind of fool does that to a woman with a man who loves her standing near?"

"He didn't know I was still there." Duncan ran his good hand through his hair, relieved the worst was over. "I had started to leave, but the lab window was open, and I was waiting…waiting to go back inside to her or just waiting to know she was okay… I'm not really sure. I heard Seaton ask her to come to his office. I think he was high as a kite on something and very jealous. But he was bluffing. There is no video. I *am* sorry, Tom. I do have a plan. Something, I hope, that will mitigate the impact of this on Lily."

"Given the facts, it seems to me you didn't do anything to apologize for. You kissed a woman you love and were intruded on in the most contemptible way. What if you hadn't shown up tonight and she was alone with that S O B? There might not have been a picture of you two, but he might have tried something she couldn't stop!" He shook his head again, "You say you have a plan and I believe you.

"Anyone could see you two were meant to be together. I saw it the first day I met you. So, if it helps, you don't have to convince me of your feelings for her."

Duncan nodded, gratified by Tom's straightforward honesty, and hoped he would stay in the captain's good graces. Duncan stood, now tired to his core, and sorry to have to leave the camaraderie he felt with Tom to go back to his own boat alone.

"Commander."

"Sir?"

Tom held out his hand. "You keep Lily's blessing, and you'll have mine."

Chapter Six

Fight or Flight

A PICTURE OF DUNCAN and Lillian appeared on the columnist's page the next day, as well as a new photograph of Victoria. For avid readers used to Victoria's dalliances, a picture of Duncan with someone else was a treat and comments ran the gamut from cheering support for Duncan, sympathy for Victoria, sympathy for or speculation about the baby, and a few *who the hell cares?* Lillian's flight or fight response was triggered alternately as she read each one.

What was he doing with another woman when he and his wife were expecting a baby?

The comment echoed in her own mind, as did his own plea. *I didn't know, Lily. Please believe me.* How could he *not* have known? And if the child was *not* his, why bother to come to her if not to tell her the truth?

After her divorce, she had always felt it was a matter of *when* not if for her and Duncan, no matter what she denied to Vera. Not romantic, wishful thinking, but a gut-level certainty they were meant to be together which had been confirmed by his recent behavior, repeatedly showing how much he cared about her, wanted her, loved her. Now her gut instinct was proved wrong and everything had changed. There was a child to consider.

Her relationship with Mark had changed as well. Angry at what he had done, and tried to do, and frightened by his jealousy, nevertheless, she was worried about him. She had gone back to the lab early in the morning to find order had been restored. Broken glass had been cleared away, chisels and picks had been fished out of the tubs and vats they had flown into after her burst of temper. Even Mark's office was clean. Very clean, his few personal effects gone.

At midnight, she had received an email from him.

I'm sorry I let you down.

And a song. Their song. In all their years dating and married, she and Aaron had never had a song. In one April weekend together, she and Mark had *February Song*. She hit play and listened to the words, hearing the apology in the lyrics.

He could not have sent a more meaningful message about their friendship and his regret, and a reminder of sometime during the small hours of their second night together, drifting in and out of conversation and sleep as music played softly in the background.

"Who would write a song about February?" he said after a long silence. "February is one of those months where nothing happens."

"You happened," she reminded him sleepily. Intimacy had revealed birthdates and astrological signs, territory heretofore not covered during small talk at work.

"That is true, of course. Otherwise, it's …"

"After winter, before spring, a kind of limbo," she said, "like—"

"Like loving someone who's in love with someone else."

"JESUS CHRIST, LIL, I didn't think you ever had anything hot in you," Aaron said instead of 'hello' when he called later that morning from Boston.

"I haven't." At the first words out of her ex-husband's mouth, all of her carefully rehearsed responses were gone. "*Yet.*"

A significant pause followed, and then he laughed softly. "Ouch and touché!"

"It's the day before your wedding, don't you have anything better to do?"

"Not better than talking to you about what I saw in that picture," he said, still laughing. "I couldn't believe it when Curt called me. What the hell were you thinking?"

Wouldn't you both love to know? Aaron's friend Curt had been after her to go out even before the divorce was final; yet another reason to be grateful there was no video.

She recited the "script" Duncan had proposed when he called her early that morning. "It was a stunt. Duncan was annoyed at Victoria for partying with her friends again and getting her picture in the paper. I said something like 'how would she like it' and before I knew it, he'd set the timer and grabbed me. He emailed the picture in as a joke."

"Don't tell me you didn't like it."

"Okay."

Another thoughtful pause before he said, "but the kids—."

"I've already talked to the kids about this," she cut him off impatiently. "and they know it was a joke and that Duncan never meant to embarrass me, or them. Miranda couldn't believe I could do anything so cool, and all Ryan said was, 'Ick'."

"Meg and her mother are aghast—"

"I'm sure they're just jealous," she said, wished him felicitations on the happy occasion of his marriage, hung up and exhaled, the highest hurdle cleared. She'd been afraid he could use this against her somehow and the thought of possibly losing custody kept her awake most of the night. But, he'd bought it, as her father would say, hook, line, and sinker.

It wasn't long before Vera emailed from the *Fleur de la Mar*: "You must tell me everything or *I WILL NEVER SPEAK TO YOU AGAIN!*"

So worried about her children's feelings and her father's reaction, she was finally able to laugh when imagining Vera's face when she'd seen the picture. Lillian wasn't laughing later, however, when she glanced up while walking back from the mailbox to see old Mr. Giovanni from next door, smiling and winking and giving her the thumbs up sign.

"WHAT?" TOM GLANCED UP from the pile of Veteran's

Administration health insurance paperwork spread out across the galley table in front of him, feeling as irritated about the delightful inefficiency of an agency that was a combination of insurance company and federal bureaucracy as he was about hearing from his doctor that he was soon to be admitted to the hospital for more tests.

"Lily," said Grace, pouring a glass of water for him, "she mentioned she was thinking about selling her mother's jewelry. She said she never wears it, and Miranda was never likely to either."

"Oh, to hell with that. I know what those old things mean to her," said Tom, taking off his glasses and rubbing his eyes. "I've been thinking about selling the boat."

In the long pause, Tom fidgeted with the edge of the soft cotton blanket.

Grace took his restless hand in hers, the weathered skin dry and cold. "You're not ready to sell the boat," she said, searching through the rack near the galley sink for a tube of lotion. She squirted out a palmful and began massaging some into his hands "She would never stand for that, especially, and you know it. Besides, I know she and the kids love to have you for extended visits, but I'm not sure she's ready for you to move in permanently!" she added with a twinkle in her eye, and a smile as warm and comforting as her touch, "And, honestly, do you really think you could live permanently on dry land?"

Tom sighed, closed his eyes and gripped Grace's hands.

"Tom? What is it, dear?" alarmed, Grace removed her hands from his grasp and felt his forehead. "You've gone so pale."

He had a choice and it was time to make it. He could come about and head for the island he knew was in range or let the current carry them all towards the storm.

He looked up at Grace's worried face. "Lily won't need to sell her jewelry."

Chapter Seven

Clear for Running

AFTER EARLY MASS ON Sunday, her father said he had a surprise and was treating for breakfast.

"And no, they are not one and the same, missy," he said, rather gruffly, though he caught himself and smiled, chucking her under the chin. The old tavern was near the city dock and the *LilyRose,* and a favorite place for Tom when he wanted to be sociable.

One of the oldest buildings in Annapolis, Stewart's Tavern had a recently remodeled interior displaying all the visual charm of the eighteenth century with all the comforts and conveniences of the twenty-first. On the far side of the room was a row of slightly raised booths, intimate nooks with age-darkened oak and heavy Jacobean upholstery. The tables near the large bay windows had the harbor as a backdrop, and the same upholstery was brightened by the natural linens and buttercream walls that caught and reflected the sunlight.

A man, about her own age and dressed in a nice gray suit, stood near a large table slightly set apart from the busiest section of the dining room.

"Lily, meet Alexander Reynolds. Alexander, my daughter, Lillian," Tom said, as they approached. At her look, he added, "My attorney. I've asked him here to discuss my will."

"*Will?*" Lillian couldn't help the startled reaction, but smiled and nodded politely, and Alexander Reynolds did the same, as they shook hands.

"How do you do, Ms. Cherrington?" He didn't wait for an answer but held a chair for her. As soon as they were seated, the waitress was standing by. After ordering coffee, Tom didn't waste time. And no wonder, Lillian thought, how much was the handsome Mr. Reynolds charging per hour to meet with them on a Sunday?

"This prolonged stint in sickbay has made me face up to some decisions I've made in my life, Lily, far more than I've ever had to before," he added, after Alexander handed them each a copy, Last Will and Testament bold across the top of the document. "I want you to be angry at me now, and you *will* be, and forgive me before I die since I am determined to hang around awhile."

Lillian glanced down only briefly before asking, "Who is Ernest Bonneau Cherrington … the fourth?"

"And so it begins," Tom said. "Are you ready, Reynolds?"

"Aye, Captain," he answered, smiling "readier than you are, I'm sure."

"To answer your question, I am Ernest Bonneau Cherrington…the *fourth*. My grandfather renamed me when I was two years old. My parents, Ernest the third, of course, and Ada Caldwell, died. My father in the Normandy invasion on D-Day, my mother a year later, in a car accident on her way home from a trip to Philadelphia.

"My parents named me Thomas Wilson Cherrington. Apparently, it was a last request from *his* grandmother, and from what Grandma Claire told me, my father was of the opinion that three Ernests were two too many and the world didn't need a fourth. Grandfather did not agree. Two birth certificates exist, somewhere, so both names are included on the will to avoid any possible legal confusion.

"Against orders I gave to young Mr. Reynolds's family, they have retained and maintained an estate I inherited many years ago—"

"An *estate*?" Lillian asked, not sure she heard correctly.

"As far as I'm concerned, it's some dirt, a couple of sheds and a bunch of junk," he said gruffly, not meeting her eyes.

Lillian was remembering long, isolated trips across lonely

oceans and her bedroom in the cramped, damp bow of the sailboat, never having real friends, not even being able to collect anything as she grew up.

Her father's heartiness faded as he realized there was no putting off a full explanation. He cleared his voice and continued.

"I ran away from home when I was fifteen, the day of my Grandmother Claire's funeral."

"You said you didn't know your family, Dad," she said, struggling to keep the hurt she felt out of her voice. "Why?"

"For me, there wasn't any family. I told myself I would never go back and with Grandmother Claire gone, there was never any reason. I've had misgivings over the years—serious misgivings," Tom added, shaking his head, "when you wanted to know about our family history or when you chose your profession, Lily, trying to get those old things into your life because I had nothing to hand down to you.

"The truth is I had too much, too much old stuff around me, and too much grief from a cruel, domineering old man who wanted to mold me in his own image and live my life for me."

Tom closed his eyes for a moment. Lillian could see his grip tighten on his coffee cup.

"My grandfather was, what would be called today, an abuser. I was thrashed when he was in a bad mood, a good mood, if there was too much rain or not enough. My grandmother tried to stop him and succeeded a time or two, but I knew I couldn't stay after she died. I didn't want to stay since she was the only thing about the place that made it a home.

"So, I left, determined never to go back. I stayed in Baltimore for about a year. My friend Jake," Tom paused and nodded towards the attorney, "Reynolds's grandfather, was a year older than me and had gotten a job in Baltimore. We bunked together in the dorms at the Old Central YMCA and worked as laborers in the shipyards. When Jake went on to college, I joined the merchant marine and lit out to see the world.

He paused, a faraway look in his eyes, as though he was scanning the horizon as she had seen him do all her life.

"The old man found me once, about a year after Katie and I were married, only weeks before you were born. His letter was pleasant, very formal, but from him, it was like getting flowers." He shook his head but kept on. "So, I went back, curious about what he could want with me after so many years.

"From the tone of his letter, I let myself believe the visit could lead to forgiveness on my part, but it was only a matter of hours until his cordiality evaporated. He demanded I return, to give up sailing and work with him at the goddamn bank. He didn't care that I was an adult, or even that I had a wife expecting his great-grandchild. He'd alienated everyone from his life and was a lonely old man. All he wanted was someone to take care of him; someone to inflict his abuse on. It wasn't difficult to turn and leave that house a second time, with him hurling every curse known to man at my back as I walked away. I was afraid if I let that old man into our lives, he would have tried to dominate our every move, and I had no interest in fighting with him, no desire to see him at all.

"The stubborn old son-of-a-bitch lasted another dozen years and died alone in that huge old barn among the junk he treasured so much. I was the only heir, so it came to me whether I wanted it or not. That was when I told you I went fishing with Troy, remember that, when you stayed with Gracie on her boat for a while? I was supposed to be gone for a week but came back after three days? I tried to want it, for you, Lily, but I couldn't …

"Truth is, months, years sometimes went by when I never thought about it, except times when Katie would get impatient with life in a small apartment, or later when you started asking family questions. I was ashamed I couldn't get past my feelings for your sakes.

"I'm sorry."

Lillian's irritation dissolved as his voice faltered and she reached out and took his rough, weathered hands in hers. She was seeing those hands on the wheel of the *LilyRose*, pointing out over the water towards a breaching whale, or up to the constellations in the night sky. She knew it was true; some dirt, a couple of sheds and a bunch of junk could never compare to all he had given her.

"For all that," he continued, "selling and taking the money for it didn't feel right to me. Young Reynolds's family had been swindled by my grandfather decades before, and when I realized I couldn't take it and didn't want any part of it, I gave the place to them, the whole nine yards…or intended to, at any rate. But I'll let Reynolds explain that to you."

"I can't very well imagine living anywhere but on the boat and I know you don't want to leave Annapolis. At least now," he added, gruffly, "well, now you'll have a choice."

That's what this revelation was all about, thought Lillian, not only to ease the financial hardship but to protect his own legacy of the *LilyRose* and all their life had meant to him.

"The long and the short of it is, you won't have to worry about money, girlie. You're clear for running."

TOM ABANDONED SHIP SOON after his confession, declaring his need of fresh air and a nap, but insisted Lillian and Alexander stay to talk over the details of the estate. After they ordered, Alexander handed her a heavy, russet-toned legal folder. She opened the first leaf to see her first glimpse of the Cherrington estate. Far more than "dirt, sheds, and a bunch of junk," the classic Federal could not be considered a mansion, and yet the five-bedroom Adam-style house seemed like one, compared to anywhere else she had lived.

"What's been done with it since my great-grandfather died?" she asked.

"Rented, soon after your father made his decision. The current tenants have been there five years with no plans to leave, unless of course, you want to move in."

Alexander gestured to the next page of the folder. "Grandfather Reynolds was adamant. All good furniture and personal belongings from the main house, like the paperwork and small items I brought today, would be moved into the small beach cottage for safekeeping."

One of the photos was of a small Victorian-folk style

house facing the cove. "That sweet little place, a storage shed? All this time?"

"My grandfather felt storing your family's belongings anywhere else would make them vulnerable to the elements or other people who didn't have the same degree of loyalty to your father. Namely, I'm afraid, my grandmother and my mother," he smiled apologetically. "They never understood why he didn't sell, but he never would."

Built for John and Evelyn Cherrington, who moved from Philadelphia in the early nineteenth century, they raised their four children in the house. The small beach house had been added after the death of their eldest grandson, Edward Cherrington, in the 1880's. His widow, free after years of his penny- pinching, had wanted a place to hold parties at the beach like some of their more fashionable friends.

Preoccupied with not only the physical inheritance but the realization she could now trace her own family history back centuries, she reluctantly closed the folder and set it aside as the waitress served their lunch. They ate in silence for a while and distracted as she was, it was impossible not to enjoy the lump crab quiche Florentine.

"So, what do you think about all of this?" he asked.

"I'm not sure, to tell you the truth. It's really…quite a shock, and so unlike my father. Before today, I would never have believed he had a secret in the world. Now, almost everything I thought I knew about him has changed, including his opinion of lawyers," she laughed, raising her glass to him before adding, "He once swore he'd never hire a lawyer for anything."

Alexander contemplated her quietly, the voices of other diners and soft background music filling the silence. He had truly lovely gray eyes, she thought, like smoky quartz crystals.

"I don't know your father well, of course, but it seems everything you know about him as a father is still true. As for the *lawyer* part," he smiled, "there has never been, nor will there ever be, any fees charged for our services to your family."

"Oh?"

"Our family owes your father an enormous debt of

gratitude," he said. "You see, everything he said about the old man was true, generous even, given what I've heard, and I didn't even know the full story until I started working with my father ten years ago.

"The rift between our families happened back in the mid-1900's, not long before World War II. The Reynolds family had a period of severe financial difficulty. My great-grandfather requested a loan from Cherrington, using their home as collateral."

"What happened?"

"Payment came due. Cherrington refused to allow him more time and took everything." He paused while the waitress filled their water glasses. "He generously allowed them to remain on their own property while charging rent they could barely afford."

"Until they repaid the loan?"

He shook his head. "Permanently, and according to the unfortunate language in the contract, he was within his rights to do so. My great-grandfather died soon after, devastated.

"That property," he continued, "was part of the estate your father inherited, which he deeded back to my grandfather immediately. And, as he said, when he determined he couldn't take the original Cherrington property for himself, he gave that over as well and wouldn't hear any argument or take any payment. But my grandfather was absolutely sure Tom would change his mind one day. For you, if not for himself."

"He probably didn't expect it would take quite so long," Lillian said.

Alexander smiled. "I know you haven't read far enough into the folder for details, but for the interim, my grandfather made the decision to use one-half of any monies collected from rents for our family, one-quarter for taxes, insurance and maintenance, and the rest has been put into savings, for you.

"So, here's to the Captain." Alexander raised his glass, smiling at Lillian's stunned expression. "He may disdain us poor lawyers along with the rest of society, but his generosity made it possible for me to go to law school."

Lillian smiled and raised her own glass again, "Now, *that* sounds like my father."

ALTHOUGH SHE ARRANGED WITH Alexander to visit the estate later in the week, Tom had asked him to bring along a peace offering.

Lillian shared the story with Miranda and Ryan when they arrived home that afternoon. Discovering hidden treasures in the artifacts she conserved, no matter how exciting, there was always a professional distance in the work. Now, she was about to investigate her own history and she felt a tingle of anticipation as she lifted the lid.

After glancing inside, she ordered everyone to put on white cotton gloves.

"Look at this—Charles Dickens!" she opened the first, automatically assessing its condition and searching for a publishing date, "And a journal of the Lewis and Clark Expedition… published in 1820!" She gasped and reached in to pick up another.

Miranda protested.

"Mom! They're just books! You can do that later, what else is there?"

The expression on Ryan's face showed Miranda had an ally. Lillian, very reluctantly, set the books aside.

A delicate turquoise and silver paisley-patterned box, cracked from age along its seams, held several framed photographs and small albums. Stoically, often grimly countenanced subjects were pictured standing or sitting in formal poses with Grecian columns and potted palms behind them and their old-fashioned costumes had the kids giggling, Miranda teasing Ryan about how he would look in wide collars and bow ties.

"Okay, that's enough you two," she said, laughing when Ryan nodded towards his sister, holding up a picture of a young girl in a heavy wool and many-layered bathing costume, floppy hat and all. "We'll look through these later, too."

The last item was wrapped in an intricately hand-embroidered pillowcase. She set it on the coffee table and moved it towards Miranda to open and all of them held their breath while she uncovered a wooden keepsake box, adorned with intricately carved flowers and with inlaid beads of mother-of-pearl at each center.

"Wow!"

"Open it!"

"It's locked. Is there a key?" Miranda asked, searching the pillowcase and now empty cardboard box.

Lillian picked it up and turned it around, examining it carefully from all sides, anticipation heightened by the intriguing rattling and shifting of things inside. "Hold on a minute."

She went to her office for her portable toolkit and pulled on her headlamp with the magnifying glasses to more closely inspect the box.

"Aha!"

She poked a long metal pick into a small hole in the center of an inlay, and a small drawer in the back sprang open. Inside was a tiny brass key.

"Wow, Mom—that was cool!" said Ryan.

She was now considered cool by both of her children. *How cool is that?*

"Because it's your turn to open something and…" she paused, turning off the headlamp and setting it aside, "for saying I'm cool, you may do the honors!"

She held the key out and he started to reach for it but shook his head, glancing between the key and the lovely old box. It didn't surprise her; he was always the cautious one, watching before he would try something, although usually, it was bigger things, like roller coasters or water-skiing. She turned and offered the key to Miranda, who had no such qualms.

Miranda slipped the little skeleton key into the hole, wiggled it a little—and even expecting it, the little click was like a firecracker, making them all jump and laugh.

Miranda slowly raised the lid and peered inside.

"Mom! It's your name!" Miranda drew out a ribbon-tied

bundle of letters.

"What? No, look at the spelling, she must have been French, it's Lilién," Lillian said, adding a slight French inflection to the name. Lilién Bonneau Cherrington. Whatever would her father say when he found out he named me after some long-lost ancestor?

Lillian drew out a small, white satin bound book with tiny golden fleur-de-lys embossed on the fabric and gently opened the cover. "Her diary," she said, looking up at Miranda. "1857 is the first date. April 25, 1857."

Ryan reached in for the next and last treasure, a handful of coins scattered on the velvet-lined bottom of the box and Lillian had him put each one into a separate little zip-lock bag. Only adding up to eighteen dollars and sixty-one cents at face value, the coins were a disappointment to the kids but not to Lillian. Not a coin expert, still, some appeared unique enough to make her want to run to the computer or consult her reference books.

"Well, the books and the photos, the box and letters are treasures themselves," said Lillian. "We can't expect too much for one night."

Miranda was looking closely at the lid, tracing a gloved finger over the inlays. "It's kind of dirty, Mom, can I clean—?"

"No!"

The kids jumped, and Lillian laughed at their expressions.

"Sorry. What I meant was, yes, of course, you can clean it, as long as you let me show you what to do." Kneeling next to her, the box on an old towel, Miranda listened carefully to her step-by-step instructions.

Now she sat and watched the thoughtful expression on Miranda's face as she worked.

Holding both children when they had arrived home hours before had finally helped to dispel the fear shivering through her chest at the very idea of losing them.

At first, she could tell Aaron had wanted to tease her again about the picture, instead, he asked, "Everything okay,

Lil?"

"It is now," she had answered.

"I CAN STILL HARDLY believe this is real."

"I hope you're not too upset," Grace said when she stopped in for tea. "You know your father is a very practical man. If he didn't want any part of it, his memories must be very bad."

"I'm not angry, really, but having all of this and …"

"Poor Grandpa," said Ryan, who was leafing through a small album of more informal photos, "but he must have liked this place. Look," he added, pointing with a floppy finger of the white glove, "there's a sailboat a lot like the *LilyRose!*"

She sat on the couch with him, looking through the envelopes of pictures and visiting with Grace while Miranda cleaned the box. Ryan was snuggled in close, his warmth comforting. She breathed in the little boy scent of him and kissed the top of his forgetful twelve-year-old head.

"Look, Mom," he said, pointing out a tree fort high in a huge old oak tree, "that's cool!" He pointed to something on top of the beach house, "What's that?"

She leaned closer. "Wow, good eyes, sailor. I can't see the design, but that's a weathervane, like our old rooster weathervane up on top of the house. You know, a fancy type of wind indicator like on top of the mast."

"A rooster would look funny on the boat, wouldn't it?"

They all laughed, even Miranda. A sweet, natural little giggle and so engrossed was she in her work, she didn't notice the others exchange glances. Her mercurial temperament lately meant they never quite knew what kind of attitude to expect from her. Watching her daughter tend gently to the artifact that may have belonged to a long-ago great-grandmother, Lillian felt another rush of gratitude. Miranda brushed the hair away from her face and saw her mother watching.

"Beautiful job, sweetheart," she said, smiling. Now Miranda seemed surprised, making Lillian wonder if Miranda automatically expected criticism the way Lillian expected attitude. "The inlays are almost glowing."

Miranda continued with her work, looking thoughtful. "Mom, you're the one who always says *things* don't matter. Like when you said that about your job and the things you do whatever you do with, it's not the things, it's the people who once owned them that matter."

Silence followed, and Miranda glanced up to see the others looking back at her.

"*What?*"

"Wow," Lillian said, smiling, "you listened to me once." She did not add that often when she said *things* didn't matter, she couldn't afford to buy them the things they wanted.

"*Whatever.*" Miranda rolled her eyes. "But I don't blame Grandpa for not wanting to live there." She gently turned the box on its side. At the sound of a distinct rattle from inside, she looked up guiltily.

Lillian slid down next to the table and grabbed her headlamp again. "The coins were decoys!" she said, lifting the lid and tilting the box gently from one side to the other.

A muted rattle again emanated from below a false bottom, and Lillian began searching for the clue to opening the secret compartment. "In an old diary I read, there was something about a false bottom in a jewelry box. Coins and less valuable jewelry were put in the box to make noise. If someone had picked this up and shaken it, they would have heard the rattling, seen letters and the few coins and not looked further."

"Can you see anything, Mom?" asked Ryan, peering over her shoulder.

"No…," she said, taking off her gloves and feeling along the inside for subtle differences. "Maybe …" she lifted the old cloth away from the bottom, the dried paste at the corners broke away with slight encouragement. "There is something!"

Beneath the dusty swatch of black velvet were two very old letters. She slipped on her gloves again and took them out of the box. Neither were postmarked in any way, and both were addressed to Miss Lilién Bonneau, Fleur-de-Lys Plantation, Kershaw County, South Carolina.

Lillian set them aside with the others and went back to the box. Without the velvet, she could clearly see it would open, but how? Scrutinizing the inlays once again, she pushed the pick into a small hole at the base of the box, goose bumps rising on her arms even before the compartment opened with a soft *clunk*.

Without looking beneath the panel first, Lillian held out the box to her daughter.

"*Oh, my goodness*," Grace whispered, and the others gasped as well as Miranda slowly drew out a long, double strand of luminous, shell pink pearls that had slipped from their velvet pouch. Colors danced as the bright light from the headlamp hit the diamond-encrusted clasp. Passing it hand to hand they all oohed and aahed at the luster of the pearls and the sparkle of the diamonds.

Who was the last to wear this? Lillian thought, *which one of her living, breathing ancestors had last hooked the clasp, appraised herself in a mirror, received admiring glances at a ball or soiree?*

Ryan pulled the heavy strands through his gloved fingers and moved the diamonds under the light to see the colors flash.

"Now that's more like it!" he said for all of them, making them laugh.

Lillian found its black velvet pouch and held it for Ryan. When he slipped the pearls inside, she gestured toward the box and said, "Your turn, sunshine."

No hesitation now, he reached in and drew out another pouch. Inside was a heavy gold chain and pendant set with diamonds and deep violet amethysts.

"It looks very old," said Grace, tracing a finger over the gold filigree. "What do you think?"

"Early eighteenth century. My first guess, anyway, given all the clues."

Lillian held the box out to Grace, who hesitated but looked tickled to be asked.

The last pouch was not quite as heavy and held a brooch. A giardinetto, a lovely bouquet of sapphires, rubies, and topaz with delicate emerald leaves. Instead of examining the shimmering stones, Lillian turned it over searching for hallmarks, tempted to take off the cotton gloves, to see what she might see...or feel.

"Mom?" Miranda said, glancing into the box, "looks like you get the last—unless there's another compartment you haven't found yet."

One very old document was all that remained at the very bottom of the box.

"What is it?" Ryan asked.

Lillian gently unfolded and scanned the brittle parchment. "It's in French. I think we need a translator. Where's my phone—"

"I can dust off my college-era French and give it a try," Grace offered, but when she glanced at the old document, her first words were not French, but, "*Oh my.*"

"What's wrong, Grace?" Miranda asked.

Grace began to read. *"Extrait Du Registre Des Audiences, Du Tribunal Revolutionnaire, Establi au Palais—"*

"Grace, *s'il vous plaît?*" Lillian prompted.

She continued slowly, haltingly translating the text into English.

> *"In Paris, '19ᵗʰ Ventôse, Year II of the French Republic,... one and ... indivisible, by judgment rendered ... in a public hearing of the court at which Citizen Robespierre--*

She broke off, meeting Lillian's startled eyes, *"Robespierre?"*

"Good God," Lillian said, scanning the document for the familiar name.

"Who?" Ryan asked.

Grace read through the rest of the document silently so she could translate more smoothly. After a few tense moments, she continued aloud.

> *... Citizen Robespierre filled the function of President, Arnaud and Vachel, Judges and Jury Clerk. The court decrees that on the report of the jury, Louisa Felicianne Desjardins, aged thirty-nine years, has been condemned to death. Born*

at Beauvais and having resided in Paris from the
age of thirty-eight years, her property has been
declared confiscated for the profit of the
Republic."

"Condemned to *death?*" Miranda whispered the question.

"*Why?*" Ryan asked.

"The French Revolution," Lillian answered, grateful she had not followed her impulse to remove her gloves to handle each piece of jewelry. Did she dare, *ever*, to attempt using her gift of psychometry on this ancestor's possessions?

"Maybe someday we can find out why, honey."

Subdued by this revelation, Lillian shared what she knew of the history while they looked at the jewelry again. Had she been a cruel, heartless aristocrat? Had she done anything to deserve such a fate? Or, was she simply one of the innocents murdered during the Reign of Terror?

Wearing the headlamp, Ryan listened while examining the box, peering into the inlays and deep inside searching for other hidden switches and compartments.

As they began to look at the old letters found beneath the velvet lining, Miranda said, "We've all gotten to open something, we should let Grandpa read the diary and letters first."

"Yeah," chimed in Ryan, agreeing with his sister.

Grace and Lillian exchanged glances.

"That's very sweet," Lillian said, patting her shoulder, "but Grandpa said he didn't want to see any of it. This was for us—"

"I think Miranda's right," Grace said, as Miranda placed the diary and letters back inside the box, "It may be a way to take his mind off his grandfather and consider some of the other family members, some of the other history."

Miranda made the decision for them. She closed the box and turned the key.

Chapter Eight

La Ruse De Guerre

SO LATE, BUT IMAGES of the day crowded into her mind and would not let her rest. Her father's revelation, Alexander's kindness, the discovery of family treasures with her children, Grace's visit and the knowledge of the existence and unjust death of her unknown ancestor.

Her silenced cell phone lit up the dark room. She glanced at the screen and paused only briefly before answering.

"Hello, Duncan."

"How are you, Lily?"

"My kids are home safe and my father still loves me. Are you—?"

"Okay?" he asked. His voice sounded different, and a long silence followed before he continued. "Okay about what exactly? Finding my *wife* with lover number …hmmm… I do believe I have lost count. Or… seeing you with …whom exactly?"

"Duncan, are you drunk?"

"Not…quite…yet." She heard liquid pouring in the background. "You're not cleverly avoiding another question, are you, Lily?"

"Maybe I don't understand the question," she said, softly, remembering another question she had avoided while looking into his eyes.

"Who is he?"

Hearing his voice through the darkness, she remembered the sadness in his eyes as they stood together, and the urgently whispered *please trust me* when he left her that night.

"If you saw me with a man today, it was Alexander Reynolds, my father's attorney. We had lunch at the tavern to talk family business."

After a long silence, he said, "I'm sorry."

"Let's not go there again."

"Lily?"

"Yes?"

"Don't miss the column tomorrow."

THE PHOTO HE HAD found of Lily and Seaton together presented him with a stark choice.

Drink or cry.

He hadn't sat alone at a table with a whiskey bottle for company in a very long time.

Even without glancing at the date, Duncan knew the picture had been taken on the night of Vic's appreciation dinner.

Wearing her classy dress, she was standing against Seaton, who had removed his suit jacket, loosened his tie, and rolled up the cuffs of his dress shirt. They stood in front of one of the displays, a recently restored figurehead and shining brass chronometer. His hands rested on her shoulders and he was looking only at her as she smiled for the camera. And, if ever a man looked to be in love with a woman, it was Mark Seaton.

Fucking Limey. Duncan could almost hear theme music.

"Perfect. Absolutely *fucking* perfect," he said aloud.

They were like some posed wallet couple meant to sell thousand-dollar Bulgari wallets or on Fifth Avenue billboards advertising Clive Christian perfume. He fought the impulse to take the goddamn phone topside and toss it into the harbor.

Instead, he took another drink before scrolling through the rest, dreading what he might find but driven. Driven by what? Love, jealousy, or just good old-fashioned prurience? Probably all three, he answered himself honestly, combined with a very unhealthy dose of masochism.

The headline read "Same Port Different Girl?" She stared at the photograph. On the deck of a sailboat, Duncan stood smiling down at and with his arms around a woman, a tall woman with short, spiky blonde hair in a very short, very tight black dress.

Why had he told her about this? She wanted to turn away from the image until she saw the tattoo on the woman's shoulder. The very same as Mariah's, and she knew immediately it was Alexis, Duncan's secretary's wife.

She received a brief text from him. *'Well, that was a first— for both of us. One more for good measure.'*

"OUCH!"

"Oh, hush. That was just a nibble," Vera purred, she actually *purred* against the place on his neck where she had applied her teeth, "I've got to get into the spirit, you know."

"Biting is off limits." He moved away. She moved closer. Vera was proving to be what she always claimed to be, one lusty armful of woman.

"You want this to be convincing, don't you?"

Convincing was one thing, exchanging fluids quite another, Duncan thought, wishing he had posed with Zach and let Vera take the damned picture.

"You're supposed to look horny, not sceered," Zach drawled in that low, slow drawl of his, obviously enjoying the show while trying to position himself for a good shot.

"My God you smell good, Duncan," Vera whispered, wriggling closer, again.

He *was* a bit scared, frankly, and it was a matter of both pride and self-preservation that she not either provoke her desired reaction, or God forbid, become aware that she had provoked the desired reaction, so he made every effort to keep a buffer zone between his pelvic region and Vera's obvious attempt to suck every possible bit of enjoyment out of this opportunity.

He shouldn't have even *thought* the word—

"*Vera!*"

Lips, teeth, and tongue were busy now and she laughed that throaty laugh of hers when he tried to move away but didn't release her latch.

"Jesus Christ," Zach drawled again, "like a sea lamprey on a mackerel."

Vera laughed, sputtering wetly against his neck. Duncan, too, and God it felt good to laugh, he couldn't remember the last time he'd laughed so hard he cried. But, afraid once he got started he wouldn't be able to stop, he wiped his eyes and lifted Vera off her feet and up onto the counter behind her.

"Now, behave yourself," he scolded, resting his forehead against hers.

The next thing he knew, her legs wrapped, tentacle-like, around his waist.

ALL LILLIAN COULD DO was stare at the screen.

Somewhere aboard the *Fleur*, Vera was sitting on a counter with her legs wrapped around Duncan's waist, each of them with a caught-in-the-act expression on their face.

She knew Duncan wasn't faking the panic in his eyes. My God, she thought, Vera must have been in seventh heaven.

I promise I will fix this. Please trust me, Lily.

Duncan had done what he promised that night, and, of course, Vera would certainly have made the most of her opportunity.

The columnist still hadn't caught on and her avid speculation was followed by even more avid comments from obsessed readers. The first woman in the series wasn't even mentioned.

Her fifteen minutes of fame was, thankfully, over.

LILLIAN FELT THE BUTTERFLIES as they passed the ornate, wrought-iron gate.

'Cherrington House.'

The narrow, graveled lane was dotted with small puddles and lined with huge oak trees, their thick, sprawling branches reaching down to the ground. Beyond them, the tops of tall pine trees were shrouded in fog.

"Wow," said Ryan, already impressed, and pulling on his jacket, ready to explore. Lillian was thinking the same thing as she parked in front of the house.

Alexander opened the front door as they got out of the car.

"Well, what do you think?" he asked Lillian after she had introduced him to Miranda and, with a wave towards the trees, Ryan.

"I think it's unbelievable!"

"The tenants are away for the day, but Loretta said to make yourself at home and tour around all you like," Alexander said, opening narrow French doors into a front parlor, where the windows faced west, out over a courtyard and the cove beyond."

Adjoining the parlor was a small library, an old-fashioned bath was along the corridor which also led to the dining room and kitchen. The large Colonial kitchen at the back of the house still had its wide fireplace along one wall, its hearth and mantle now artfully displaying a collection of eighteenth-century kitchen implements and a lush array of houseplants.

"Where does that path lead?" Lillian heard Miranda ask.

"To the beach and beach house, and, over there is the path leading to our house, where my mother, sister, and her family still live. All of us have kept the path to the cove well-trod since we were old enough to come and go on our own."

Illuminated by the gray light from the east windows, the wide plank floor was covered here and there with braided rugs and cast-iron skillets and copper pots hung on a sturdy wrought-iron frame above the center island. The tingle came back to her full-force as she ran her fingers lightly over the rough bricks, wondering about the generations of women of her own family who had raised children in this very place.

They walked up the narrow servant's stairway, which emerged at a landing bordered on all sides by bedrooms. Miranda broke away to investigate.

"These old bedrooms are all rather small, except this one. This was your great-grandparents' room, Lillian."

Lillian walked around the room, appreciating the vintage detail in cut glass doorknobs, old light fixtures, intricate woodwork, not to mention the views outside. The large bay window looked south towards a meadow of wildflowers bordered by hedgerows.

"My grandmother Reynolds and your great-grandmother Claire were good friends, even a generation apart in age." Alexander stood next to Lillian as they watched Ryan jump to the ground from the limb of one of the huge old oaks. "We have some of Claire's letters; I've asked Mother to find them for you, though I think you'll have enough to look at for a while."

"They wrote letters, living so close to one another?"

Alexander leaned against the window frame and crossed his arms. "Part of the fallout from your grandfather's swindle. They had to continue their friendship from a distance."

"Could I have given this up?" she said, more to herself than Alexander, looking past the tenant's tasteful décor, touching the dark, cherry wood wainscoting.

"From what my father heard, old Cherrington branded your father a bad seed from the start, especially when he started talking about becoming a sailor and going to sea."

"Does the other stairway go to an attic?" Miranda peeked into the room, snapping a quick picture of the two of them standing near the window.

"Yes, go ahead up if you like."

As her footsteps echoed on the stairway, Lillian said, "A young boy with dreams of being a sailor and going to sea must have been common enough, especially around here."

"Well, there were two factors that worked against your father. First, old Ernest was jealous of his brother Emil, who was a sailor and died late in World War I. He was a favorite of everyone's it seems, except his brother. But all the troubles of the household had originally been caused by a black-sheep ancestor of his who was also a sailor. That was your Bonneau side—your Rebel side, according to the old man. Apparently, Bonneau had served aboard a blockade runner and made off with the family fortune sometime during the Civil War."

"According to my…" Alexander paused, counting on his fingers and then shook his head, "three or four times great-grandfather, Thomas Crawford, it is absolutely *not* true. Bonneau was held up as one of the most honorable men he'd ever known. Thomas had been a very young crewmember on that blockade runner and had been sent by Bonneau to look after his sister. He ended up marrying a Reynolds, Sylvia, and settling here. Their granddaughter married a Reynolds cousin from Baltimore sometime during the Thirties."

As Lillian moved towards the door, he added, "With your interest in history and knowledge of antiques, I think you might find the best is yet to come, the personal items and furnishings still in the beach house. Shall we follow Miranda to the attic first before we go down?"

Octagonal windows on either end let in dim, gray light to reveal open rafters, a few stacks of boxes, a sheet-covered artificial Christmas tree and an assortment of small, forgotten furniture. Rain was falling again, drumming hard on the roof above them. Three small rooms once belonged to the female servants. Cook, housekeeper and maid, Alexander explained. "Men servants were housed over the old coach house."

As they walked down the main staircase leading to the large foyer and entrance, a soggy Ryan peered in the front door.

"You missed the tour," Lillian said.

A quick shrug. "Can I go down to the beach?" he asked, looking from Lillian to Alexander.

"Lead on, Master Ryan," said Alexander, pointing the way to the path, "but I think we'll drive," he added to Lillian and Miranda, as Ryan took off, oblivious to the rain.

Through the raindrops on the car window, Lillian saw the lane was bordered by a fence, roughhewn and slightly crooked, covered nearly the entire length of the drive with wild roses. The small cottage had been well tended over the years, grass along the flagstone path recently trimmed, and the weathered gray siding and roof slates were sound. Down at the beach, Ryan was already throwing rocks into the water

As she stood at the open door, even at her first glance, Lillian's heart beat faster.

The cottage had indeed been turned into a storage unit, but now dust covers were pulled back revealing an assortment of desks, trunks, and chests, a small mountain of boxes, even a few old and crumpled brown paper bags rested on the top of the stack reaching almost to the ceiling.

"I didn't realize when you said belongings …"

Two small bedrooms downstairs were also filled with boxes and furniture. Only the larger bedroom upstairs, kitchen and the tiny old-fashioned bathroom were free from use as storage space. Alexander explained 'new' thirties era kitchen fixtures had been installed when Ernest II had decided to rent the cottage early in the Great Depression. The old linoleum was crisp and bright, the fixtures clean and sound.

"Without disturbing whatever order there may be, I wanted to give you a bit of an idea of what you have here," Alexander said, gesturing towards the living room. A large double pedestal desk and cedar chest had been uncovered.

"Oh!" whispered both Miranda and Lillian, as Miranda lifted the lid of the chest. Lillian held up an embroidered tablecloth and Miranda sorted through several crocheted doilies and delicate handkerchiefs edged in lace.

"Your great-grandmother Claire was well known for her needlework."

"Look at this! Can you imagine creating anything so beautiful?" cried Lillian, holding the heavy linen to her face, inhaling the sweet scent of the cedar in the folds of the cloth. She examined the intricate stitching in the tiny blue flowers and green leaves and vines.

She gently folded the cloth and tucked it back into the chest. Lowering the lid, she said, "I just never dreamed there would be so much...."

"As I mentioned," Alexander said, smiling at her bemused expression, "my grandfather wouldn't hear of disposing of anything, stubborn as a mule about it, actually, whenever anyone asked about the beach house. But, in the interest of full disclosure, I must confess I stayed here quite frequently during law school. The place was a real haven with my parents, sister and her husband and four kids in our place and I…"

"I should hope so, with this wonderful, quiet space nearby," she said, glancing into the tiny kitchen. "You know, Alexander, you keep saying this is ours, but it should be yours."

"We've been more than repaid anything which may have been due from the past. My grandfather felt very certain your father would change his mind one day, and he made the rest of us sure of it, too."

"WELL, WHAT DO YOU think of that old mausoleum?" Tom asked with a wink when Lillian walked into his hospital room.

She leaned over for a kiss. "You know exactly what I think."

"So, Lilién Bonneau Cherrington—a Southern belle from a South Carolina plantation. Who would have thought there was truth to that old talk?"

"I have brought you a diary and two letters of hers confirming as much, found in the old jewelry box. The letters," she added dramatically, *"were hidden beneath the velvet lining!"*

Tom watched with amused tolerance as she took the book from a protective wrapping.

"And what does she have to say?" he asked, taking it from her.

"We don't know. None of us have read it yet."

Brows drawn together, he said, "And why not?"

"Well, mostly it was the kids. We've all had a chance to discover something first. All on her own, Miranda asked if we could give you first shot at reading these letters and the diary."

She was dismayed at, not fear exactly, but vulnerability cloud his face.

"All of them were written around the time of the Civil

War. I do know the diary begins in 1857. It will all be new for you, too, Dad, not the same time or place…"

Looking down, he contemplated the diary and was quiet for a long moment.

"I know this has been difficult for you, even the kids understand," she said, watching him, "but I think they want to share some of this joy of discovery you've given us."

The lines of his face softened. "They're good kids, Lily," he said, gruffly and then scowled, "You're not going to make me wear those damn gloves, are you?"

"For you, I will make an exception," she said, pushing the white cotton gloves she had brought deep into her pocket.

"Well, girlie, what are your plans now?" he asked, setting the diary on the bedside table.

"Plans?"

"You're not working right now. Or did you decide to go back to Scott's lab?"

She shook her head and tried to smile. "You were right. I lost my bearings."

He held his arms out and she lay down next to him, her head resting on his shoulder.

"Your bearings are fine, Lily, you hit a patch of heavy weather. Come about and head out to clearer skies for a while."

"I know you think I should sail away," she whispered.

"Now Lily, have I ever told you to change your destination just to steer away from a squall?" he said, giving her a one-armed hug. "Sometimes you have to adjust your course and wait for better conditions."

She glanced up. What exactly was her father trying to tell her?"

"The kids are out of school and you're not working right now. Why don't you all go to Easton for a few days? Take your time and look through that old junk to your heart's content."

She sat up and turned to face him.

"Are you trying to get rid of me?"

"Absolutely. I want all of you to really see the place."

"Why?"

He started to answer but stopped, looking away from her to the gray sky beyond the window. She put her hand on his and waited.

"Lily, I've spent my entire life hating that place, from my earliest memory to my last, and running from every connection to it." The heartiness and teasing now gone from his voice, he turned to look at her, taking her hand in both of his. "Now, I find that I want to see the place through the kids' eyes, and yours. I'm a pretty sensible fellow, you know, honey, and I know it took me long enough, but I also know it's time to let go of those old memories. Hearing your stories will help me replace those old, worn out, hurtful thoughts I've carried around far too long.

"Take the *LilyRose*. It's just a short reach to the other side of the Bay. Blow the mildew out of her sails. I'll be stuck in here for a few days and it'll be good for you to get out again, and you know how much the kids love it."

"Not without you! It wouldn't be the same."

"Now, Lily…" he paused, long enough for the unfinished sentence to hang between them like cold winter fog.

"Daddy, please don't say …"

"You've had a lot to deal with, I know, but the kids will need you to be strong if I can't weather this. Oh, I'll fight my hardest; don't add that to your list of worries. If I was meaning to keel over, I wouldn't be in here rigged up like some damn Baltimore clipper."

He reached out and cupped her face gently in his hand. "You *will* be sailing the *LilyRose* without me one day. Do it now, when you know I'm still here. It will make the first time when I'm not that much easier."

WELL, NOW HE'D PLAYED the dying old man trump card, Tom reflected later, wondering if he could sink any lower. Yes, he admitted quickly to himself, absolutely, if it kept his family out of harm's way and it was the only card he had to play.

As the nurse straightened the bed and checked monitors and fluids, he broke open the last of the fortune cookies left over from his culinary escape from the hospital kitchen, absently unfolding and glancing at the little yellow slip.

"Oh, for crying out loud!"

"What is it, Mr. Cherrington?" Laura asked, with a smile and without concern, already recognizing the tone at the end of her first shift with him.

"When the hell did the Chinese run out of Confucius says and move on to Cicero?"

"Well?" she prompted.

Tom made another one of those exasperated sounds and read: "*He who knows only his own generation remains forever a child.*"

"Sounds like more of a judgment than a fortune to me— I'd say you were cheated!"

She bustled around the room a bit more before leaving, and for once Tom didn't have any light-hearted nautical rejoinders.

It *was* a damn judgment, he thought, taking off his glasses and rubbing his eyes. An absolute indictment rolled up inside a little factory-processed cracker. Allowing his past to dictate his future was his grandfather steering his course, only under false colors.

Suddenly impatient with himself, he shoved his glasses back on and picked up the diary. In the ray of sunlight finally breaking through the clouds, the tiny, chipped fleur-de-lys on the cover sparkled. Tom opened it and began to read.

"I'D ALWAYS HEARD STORIES about her being a hateful old woman."

"Oh?" Lillian was shocked to find out her father had consumed the contents of the letters and diary in a single day.

"She died, well, I'm not sure, I think it was maybe ten or fifteen years before I was born. Grandma Claire told me about her, and how she would have liked me because I so closely resembled her grandson, my great-uncle Emil. She would watch him with a softness in her eyes and say things like 'you make me think of my brother, with all your dark hair and talk of boats and sailing.' She was into her eighties by then, but," he added with a good-humored growl, "in all those family stories, I swear I never heard anyone call her Lillian!"

"What about your great-great-grandfather?"

"He'd died long before my father was even born, I believe, well before the turn of the century. All I ever remember hearing about him was that this Lilién Bonneau blamed him for everything bad that ever happened, just as my Grandfather apparently blamed Lilién's brother. After reading this, I can understand her a bit better."

"Was your grandfather always a controlling person?" Lillian asked.

"Any memory I have of him, he was. But after learning all of this maybe we can understand more about him as well. Which," he added, pausing to listen, and then smiled, "brings me to something important I want to ask."

"What's that?" Lillian asked, as Grace and the kids came in with ice cream.

"Now that you're all here, I have a request," he paused, looking at each one of them. "We've been talking about why I've never been one to talk much about family history."

"Hilariously understated, but true," Lillian said wryly, scooting further down on the bed so Ryan could sit next to his grandpa.

"I know I've hurt you, Lily, by keeping my secrets. I want you to find out about this many times great-uncle of mine."

"What?"

"Find out what *really* happened to this fellow Bonneau," he said, gesturing towards the diary on the table in front of them. "Knowing you, it'll just take a bit of research."

"*You* want me to research an ancestor? 'They're dead, they don't matter' was your answer to my question for a school assignment, remember?"

"I remember, and I was wrong, Lily, because they mattered to you."

"Why this particular fellow?" Grace asked, looking at him with a cross between amusement and suspicion.

"I did a little snooping of my own and found something you didn't," he said smugly.

Opening Lilién's diary, he took out an early tintype of a blond young man with a kind and sensitive face. Wearing a white suit and high white cravat, he stood with his hand on a short column. He had a thoughtful expression and was facing slightly away from the camera.

"Who...?"

"Wilson Hall, Lilién's young suitor," Tom said, indicating the name on the back of the picture, as well as the date of 1860. "A young man who features heavily in her early diary entries and the one who wrote the letters, very impassioned letters I might add, about the demise of their engagement. And now, look at this one!"

"Oh, is this her brother?" she cried, taking the other tintype. With unruly dark hair at odds with the crisp naval uniform he wore, the young man was clean-shaven but for a rakish set of sideburns. His stance erect and formal, but unlike so many photographs of the time, there was a hint of a smile on the lips and merriment in eyes that were bold and direct.

"This character was a sailor in the United States Navy who left his Southern family at the start of the War Between the States and, allegedly, made off with the family wealth. But, in this account," he said, holding up the diary, "he is an honorable young man, torn between duty to family and duty to his country, which was determined in his mind by his oath as a naval officer. Clearly, Lilién loved her brother and believed in him.

"Now, take a look at this, which Grace had a devil of a time finding on the boat for me this morning." He handed over another photo of another man in the more modern military uniform of the United States Merchant Marine. Taken nearly a century later, an unmistakable swagger to his smile but the resemblance was distinct, from the thick dark hair and set of their eyes to the strong jawline and cleft in the square chin.

"I know that doesn't preclude him from being a scoundrel in other areas, and I also know there are bad seeds in every bunch. Ever since I heard about him, it's always bothered me he was tried and convicted without proof. Because I looked like him, which we now know is true, and because my passion was to go to sea, I was convicted along with him. In a way, this Brendan Bonneau is the reason I ran away from home.

"My grandfather referenced him an awful lot when I was growing up, not by name but with epithets like 'that Rebel uncle of yours' and so on, and every calamity that befell our family was somehow his fault. Whatever this man might have done, his actions have mattered to a great many people long after he died. Hell," Tom added, "it's possible he didn't even survive the war!

"But, no matter what happened, it seems like people in this family have overreacted to it in each generation—my grandfather with his penny-pinching and fierce demand for loyalty and obedience, me with my flight away from him and anything to do with family, and you, Lily."

"Me?"

"Well, you have to admit the way you were raised has had an effect on you, from your choice of career getting all of those old things into your life, maybe even to choosing a husband, drawn to Aaron and his old established family. Maybe we need to come about, face the truth, and make sure this next generation sets off on an even keel!

"Will you do this for me, Lily? Find out about Brendan Bonneau, help prove that this ancestor of ours, who looked like me and was a fellow sailor at that, wouldn't have done something so dishonorable?"

PART II

BRENDAN

Wilmington, North Carolina
&
Camden, South Carolina

December 22, 1864

"A bullet, gentlemen, has a path called a 'line of trajectory.'
All you have to do to insure safety
is to stand to the left or right of this line."

Petty Officer James F. Taylor of the
blockade runner Advance while under fire

Chapter Nine

A Complex Case of Conflicting Loyalties

"ALL STOP!" CAPTAIN SHAW commanded in a hoarse whisper.

For the third time since crossing the inner cordon of blockaders, First Officer Brendan Bonneau repeated the order through the engine room tube, and the steamer slowed gradually and stopped. Seconds later the gray shadow of a Federal ship crossed the starboard bow less than fifty yards away.

Loaded down as she was with food and medical supplies, the steamer *Kendal* still maneuvered easily through the Atlantic. The high tide and darkness were favorable, the thin sliver of a waxing moon obscured by the fog shrouding the North Carolina coast.

The men on deck crouched behind the ship's bulwarks and stacks of deck cargo for protection against a sudden attack. Not a sound was made. No one moved or spoke.

A hint of cigar smoke and the sound of hushed laughter was carried in the gusts of wind crossing *Kendal's* port bow. Finally, the blockader moved beyond them.

From the bridge located between the two paddle wheels, Captain Shaw ordered the engines and once again they made their way toward the mouth of the Cape Fear River and the port of Wilmington.

"By God, that's the closest one yet!" laughed Lieutenant Carolton softly.

"I swear I could have bloody well reached out and grabbed myself a Yankee," said Lieutenant Nance, new to the crew, coming out from behind the shield of deck cargo.

Captain Shaw stopped him with a quick jerk of his hand.

"Don't relax too much, boys, we've still got a long way to go," whispered the coast pilot Ross Sanderlin, who guided the *Kendal* around Bald Head Island towards the mouth of the river. Sanderlin knew every reef, shallow and landmark along the Carolina coastlines and up the Cape Fear River, all the way to Wilmington.

The fog thickened. Other points along the way were just as dangerous, but there was spirit in a chase, there was action in facing an enemy. Here, though, creeping along the coast, wending their way through the Union's last line of defense before Fort Fisher...well, no matter how many times he made this run, this was always the place that spooked him.

And the place he most missed having his Colt revolver at his side, the difference between honorable service as a lieutenant in the United States Navy and first officer aboard a blockade runner flying the flag of another country. Unlike some foolhardy captains, Shaw would permit no weapons on board, from deck canon to personal sidearms. To be caught armed was to risk charges for piracy, and they all knew the penalty for piracy.

Sucking on a lemon drop to keep his mouth from drying, Brendan strained his eyes searching through the fog into the darkness. Cape Fear was a crucial point in their voyage, and new blockaders were joining the squadron all the time, making the triple cordons much more challenging to breach.

"Captain, port side!" Brendan whispered as he saw the dark shape of a second Federal blockader bearing down.

"All stop!" Captain Shaw and Brendan hissed the command almost simultaneously.

The wake of the larger vessel pushed them towards the shoals, and there was no sign they had been detected.

"Keep clear of the shallows," said Sanderlin, crouching down close to the Captain, yet keeping his eyes focused starboard towards the shoreline. "We should be just about in sight of the Big Hill now."

The Big Hill was not much of a hill, more of a mound, Brendan thought, about the height and width of one of the tall, broad old oak trees near his home in South Carolina. At least it served as a discernible landmark along the coastline and told them the distance to the protective guns of Fort Fisher.

"Go ahead easy now," Shaw ordered, "port two points."

As the helmsman turned the wheel slowly to port, a whistle shrilled and commands were shouted on the blockader looming off their port beam, "All hands! All hands! Runner in sight!"

"Swarming like bloody sharks tonight!" the captain swore under his breath before commanding the course change.

Brendan prepared for the inevitable attack, but on the blockader, sailors were scrambling in the opposite direction, shouting "Runner off the starboard bow!"

"Starboard bow…? What the hell?" whispered Shaw and Sanderlin together, as the distance grew between the two ships.

"Shepard in *Advantage* was behind us all the way," Shaw said as shots rang out. "Poor devil."

"Well, he's certainly given us an advantage," chuckled Sanderlin.

"He'll go without a fight. He and his crew will be on another ship by our next run, and *Advantage* will have a new name and be flying the stars and stripes in a week." Shaw nodded to Brendan. "Let's get on past Fort Fisher before this fog lifts."

BRENDAN BONNEAU WAS MORE anxious than ever to reach Wilmington safely.

Four long years had passed since being abruptly banished from his family home in South Carolina and it was his intention to go back, no matter what his reception. General Sherman had wreaked havoc through Georgia, and the capture of Savannah was imminent. Speculation in Bermuda's busy port at St. George's was that Sherman was now planning to march north, turning his attention to the Carolina's.

Brendan knew it was inevitable that Federal troops would soon close up Wilmington, just as most all other Confederate ports were now closed to blockade runners.

Captain Shaw and the Edinburgh-based company that owned the *Kendal,* placed the utmost importance on shipping out cotton, tobacco, and turpentine and bringing in much-needed medical supplies, clothing, and food. While freely admitting they were in the business to make money, the owners refused to carry either munitions or luxury items, choosing to do their part by providing for the basic needs of the serving men and the civilian population. Shaw and the owners made some allowances for the officers to use their own cabin space to carry their own cargo. Inbound it was usually lightweight necessities such as safety matches, needles, thread, and tea, but outbound, more than one of them routinely carried one or more cotton bales, which they could sell or barter on their own terms.

Although it had been a profitable way for Brendan to serve, he could not think of the Confederacy as his country, frankly, he couldn't think of the collection of rebel states as a country at all. Just as extraordinary was the fact that the United States Navy, in which he once proudly served, was now considered his enemy.

THE *KENDAL* WAS MILES up the Cape Fear River when the sun rose to reveal a clear and cold December day.

Trent Tilford, company supercargo, was in his element now and gearing up for the auction that would empty their hold and help fill Buchanan and MacGregor's coffers, and to purchase cotton and turpentine for the return to St. George's. Brendan left the deck to pack up his few belongings and pulled the straps on his saddlebags as the whistle signaled their arrival.

Morning was the best time to be in rowdy Wilmington. Even the wharves were quiet, but that would soon change as the auction of all imports would begin later in the morning. Tilford hosted evening entertainments while in port. Serving the best food and spirits, it was the way to court and placate the local businessmen, politicians, and local commanders, and had become fondly known as 'Trent's Affairs."

"Merry Christmas, lad. Good luck with the reunion,"

said Shaw as he saw Brendan step off the gangway.

"Thank you, sir. I will return as quickly as I can…"

"Listen here," Shaw said, looking at Brendan with his piercing blue eyes, "you take all the time you need to get this business done. If you don't make the return, I'll promote Hudson and you can get the next run back. If there is a next run back, that is!"

The Captain put his hand on Brendan's shoulder. "You haven't missed a day with me since I signed you on and you deserve a leave. But," he added, a glint of humor lighting his eyes, "I hope you've not been my good luck charm!"

The captain turned and walked across the dock towards Sanderlin, calling out orders to the crew already scrubbing down the ship.

HE HAD PLANNED TO STOP first to visit his Aunt Sarah Bonneau, thinking it prudent to hear the latest news of home before showing up on the front step. Over a year had passed since he had last seen his aunt, the business on board during their brief unloading and loading always kept him fully occupied. He had never considered the possibility his aunt and her small household might have left Wilmington, but he found hers, as well as the neighboring houses, boarded up.

Even more troubling, old Glen McRae was gone. His tiny house near the waterfront was locked up tight and the neighbors had not seen him in over a week. Leaving a note was not an option; he had to hope McRae was home when he returned to Wilmington.

"Crawlin' with trash, it is." The old man at the livery stable shook his head, pocketing the money Brendan paid him. "Crooks from every part of the country've hit town, makin' the old folks 'fraid to stay."

Brendan had been warned by Sanderlin against waiting to hire a horse. Given the current condition of the rails, the Wilmington pilot had advised he may need to continue on horseback far earlier than planned, and horses for hire were scarce.

"Now sir," said the old liveryman, hobbling into a stable, "she's seen her younger days, but Jumper is a fine old girl," he added, leading out a rather pathetic animal.

Brendan stroked the mare's russet coat. Although her dark brown eyes were alert, with her sway back and protruding hipbones, Jumper looked as though she couldn't jump the lowest rail of a fence. He was relieved much of her journey would be spent riding the train to Camden.

The cold, bright day turned gray on the interminable journey home. Between the pitiful condition of engine and rails and the many stops along the way to ferry troops and supplies, the once enjoyable trip felt endless. Over the noise of the train and smell of soot, Brendan asked other passengers what they knew about the impending invasion.

The speculation about Sherman's planned march north was grim, some even said the worst was saved for South Carolina, "that hell-hole of secession," leaving his home right in the path of the same destructive force that had brought down Georgia.

An infantry captain, returning home to Columbia on furlough for the first time in a year, also thought Sherman would cut the Carolinas in two.

"There are those that have it in for us, as we fired the first shot, n' all." He gave a short laugh, deepening the lines of fatigue etched in his face, leaned back in the hard seat, and pulled the brim of a sweat and grime-stained slouch hat over his eyes. In a voice that was beyond weary, he added, "Real proud of that first shot, weren't we?"

In the stained, torn, and threadbare gray coat, its gold braid long since gone and the leather of his boots cracked and pulling away from thin soles, Brendan knew the captain was relatively well dressed. Many men in his command would be without coats and shoes at all. All blockade-runners were now bringing in more food and clothing, but never enough to meet the urgent demands of the army and he felt self-conscious of his own uniform, while far from new being modified from one of his old ones, the wool was thick and warm and his boots whole. Serving on a blockade-runner, fraught with danger as it could be at times, had its benefits.

Florence, once just a small railroad town, was now the location of a new prisoner of war camp. Stockade, they called it, although it stretched out over several acres, with little shelters the men made for themselves out of tree branches scattered about, a pitiful effort to fend off the weather. The Union prisoners would be the last to benefit from any supplies brought in, he knew, but what angered Brendan was the wanton cruelty and neglect. Food was scarce, but there were still lumber and mills enough to provide makeshift roofs and walls to keep rain off men and any kind of floor to keep men off mud.

The callousness of small men finding power where they could, taking out their own inadequacies on those who could not fight back, and so shortsighted and shallow-minded they could not see how this maltreatment could affect their own sons, brothers, and friends in Northern prison camps. Was it, Brendan wondered, a side effect of the slave society these men sprang from, to be able to look at a person and not see a living, breathing, *feeling*, human being?

Light rain turned to a deluge as they pulled out of Florence and continued on the sixty-mile leg to Camden. He tried to rest, but the hard bench and jarring, stop-and-start progress made sleep impossible. Glancing at his pocket watch, he saw it would be at least another hour until they reached Camden.

The watch had been a gift from his father on the occasion of his graduation from the United States Naval Academy in 1858. Six years ago. Six years that felt like a lifetime. The last time he had ridden this route was when he and Jems Barkley returned home after graduation, both eager to begin their first assignment aboard the brig *USS Dolphin*.

He closed his eyes, remembering...

ALL NEW TO ONE ANOTHER, the crew regarded them with

suspicion and knew little about them other than the fact that they were two Southern boys on their way to stop slave traders in the West Indies. Certainly, none of the crew knew about the plantations they called home. The Barkley's Cardinal Heights and Fleur-de-Lys combined consisted of over two thousand acres producing cotton and tobacco with the labor of hundreds of slaves.

On which subject, the Bonneau household was mixed and often volatile. Heated arguments filled the air regularly since Brendan and his little sister Lilién were old enough to voice their own opinions. Their mother and older brother, Louis Charles, were adamantly opposed to emancipation. His mother, he knew, could not recognize the humanity of the slave, from the field hand she would never see to the house servant she spoke to daily. Louis, on the other hand, could but simply did not care. Sure of his place in the future of Fleur-de-Lys, he wanted nothing to change and would not be drawn into any discussion.

His father recognized, welcomed, the time for emancipation was rapidly approaching. He and Josiah Barkley, and Edgar Hall, their neighbor to the west at Laurelton, joined together to present transition schemes to the local planter's council, gradually replacing slavery with a payment and barter system while preparing all citizens, black and white, for the inevitable.

Rejection would be a mild euphemism for the way the men were treated at that first meeting and subsequent meetings in the year leading up to the war.

His father had not been content to bide his time but made the decision to prepare those under his care. Using the catechism, Charles educated several slaves who could be trusted to learn quickly and discreetly, though Brendan believed the discretion had more to do with his wife's disapproval than the current law of the land.

His first students were his own servant Old George, and Mayah, their mammy. Brendan was to instruct his servant, Gabe, and Lilién, her maid Jenny. Charles believed this basic knowledge would be their best preparation for the freedom to come and optimistically believed it would not take war to settle the matter once and for all.

Charles cautioned his children on the serious consequences if caught. Their students would at the least receive severe beatings and Brendan knew the penalty to owners was a steep financial fine for each infraction. Charles was willing to risk his money, but Brendan had overheard Josiah cautioning Charles, suggesting some of their neighbors might not be satisfied with a simple pecuniary retribution against him.

Brendan smiled at the memory of "teaching" Gabe. By the time Charles had made his decision, Brendan and his best friend Wilson Hall had long since taught Gabe to read and write, using a much broader field of study than the approved catechism of the Roman Catholic Church. Gabe was not only an eager student and fast learner but a natural mimic. Whether it was Charles's low, slow drawl, the visiting Englishman that toured the plantation on a mission to purchase their cotton, or Edward Cherrington's cold, clipped Yankee speech, his precise imitations kept the boys highly entertained.

Brendan caught himself before being flung into the aisle as the train once again lurched to a stop. Other passengers on board the small, crowded car did not even move from their positions or glance up from their reading. He stood up and stretched, envious of the snoring captain next to him. Sanderlin was right; he would ask how long this delay could last. Close enough to Camden now, it might be faster to take Jumper and ride the rest of the way.

Assured that the cause was a minor obstruction on the line, he returned to his seat.

A year into the Paraguay Expedition, while still aboard the *Dolphin* in Montevideo, Uruguay, he received a letter from his mother with news about his brother. Louis Charles was dead, and Brendan expected to return home to work with his father and take on the responsibilities of Fleur-de-Lys. No explanation, no expression of grief or condolence, only demands. Several days later his father's letter arrived.

Louis had died after being thrown while riding home from visiting Camden, the horse must have shied during the thunderstorm, his father wrote. Despite their differing temperaments and opinions, Charles had no such reticence in expressing his love or grief for his oldest son, sharing memories and offering his sympathy to Brendan, no demands, only that he return as soon as his obligation would permit.

A riding accident, thunderstorm or no, was, Brendan believed, a very unlikely cause of Louis's premature death, excellent horseman that he was. A duel or a backend full of buckshot from a cuckolded husband would be more in line with his brother's character, given Louis's penchant for pursuing anything in a skirt that took his fancy.

Louis had been found the day after the storm, on the trail cutting through the old Robinson plantation. Neither Ames, his body servant, or either horse had been seen. His father wrote that he feared Ames had been injured and stumbled off into the woods in a delirium, but searchers had found no sign of him. Brendan had read the letter aloud to Jems.

When he paused, Jems had filled the silence with Brendan's own thought, "A search party, with hounds? What the hell could've happened to him?"

There had never been a satisfactory answer to that question.

Far beyond their personal tragedy, much had changed in his absence. Finally arriving home in late December 1860, Brendan immediately boarded the train in Norfolk for home. While en route, South Carolina had voted to secede from the United States.

Disembarking in Camden, he had stepped down onto the soil of a different country.

A chance encounter with Wilson Hall in Wilmington the

previous April was the last direct news he had of home. Serving with the Quartermaster's Office and on his way to Richmond, Wilson told him his mother was well with a small group of servants at Fleur-de-Lys. His own father, Edgar, older than Charles by many years, had been quickly discharged home with a case of pneumonia, much to his family's relief.

Since he had first learned of Lilién and Wilson's broken engagement, Brendan felt more grief for the loss of their happiness and future together than he had when learning about his brother's death. Perfectly matched and very much in love, he remembered Lilién's heartbreaking sobs when she told him why she had eloped so abruptly with Edward Cherrington.

Brendan attempted to speak of Lilién, but something in his friend's demeanor silenced him. Wilson quickly changed the subject, but the wariness remained.

Another loss. Another death, Brendan had thought, watching his best friend walk away.

Brendan had not received responses from several letters home, whether because of the deplorably inconsistent mail service or the fact he was still far from his mother's good graces he did not know. He prepared himself for anything from icy politeness to being thrashed with a buggy whip. Mother should have been somewhat mollified, learning she had gotten what she wanted, after all, his service to the Confederacy.

She would hold onto her anger and use it against him until it suited her to bestow her forgiveness, he thought with a sudden surge of impatience. Perhaps if his father was home, he thought, smiling, now that he had experience in commanding a company of men, he would allow himself to have command authority over his wife.

BRENDAN SHARED JUMPER'S RELUCTANCE to leave the car when, finally, they arrived in Camden. Turning up the collar of his greatcoat, he mounted and gently urged her forward into the pouring rain.

Lambert's, the local general store, was the place to find

out the latest news of the county, he knew, steering Jumper towards the main street where wagon wheels cut deep furrows of mud into the narrow, familiar lane. As he neared, he looked up and saw one of the Fleur-de-Lys' house servants, Lilién's young maid, Jenny, standing outside under a sagging, dripping awning.

"Jenny!" he called out, waving to her as he waited for a wagon to pass.

"Mister Brendan! Oh, my Lord, it is so good to see you!"

Dismounting, he caught her up in a hug. "Why are you standing in the rain? And crying? Let's go inside…"

Jenny stepped back and shook her head. "Gabe's in there, arguin' with Mister Lambert!"

"Arguing with Mister Lambert? Imagine that," he said, smiling, most of the town had argued with the cantankerous old storekeeper. "Good to know some things never change."

"Last week he offered to trade with us for our last shoat. Now he says he can't take it, cause he's leavin' and we have to pay cash money for our supplies. Well," she paused, and Brendan could see Jenny had not changed either, feisty as ever, rolling her eyes with hands on her hips, "no one's had cash money for years and I don't know where he expects us to get it now! It ain't growin' on our trees!"

Jenny cautiously stepped inside as Brendan held the door for her, and he paused before closing the door, taking in the scene.

Gabe was leaning on the counter, "But *you* asked us to butcher and deliver it!" Intentionally mimicking her or not, his deep voice conveyed something of Leah Bonneau's aristocratic hauteur which was as intimidating to Lambert as Gabe's size. "*You* should at least pay for it!"

Brendan did his best to hide his amusement as he saw Lambert step back.

"Can I help?" Brendan asked, smiling at Lambert's visible relief when he looked over as the bells on the shop door jangled. Gabe turned, his eyebrows drawn together over the dark eyes and seconds passed before his scowl disappeared.

"Br….Mister Brendan!" He reached out to grip Brendan's hand.

"What's the problem here, Gabe?"

"Well, sir," he said, glancing over at Lambert, slipping easily into the façade of formality they had in front of others, "last week Mister Lambert promised Mrs. Hall to trade …"

"Mrs. Hall?" Brendan asked, surprised.

"Yes, sir," he said, lowering his voice, "we work for Mrs. Hall now—"

"I can't do any trading," Lambert interrupted, crossing his arms, "with *anyone*. I heard Sherman's coming through and I'm leaving. It's cash or nothing."

"Mister Lambert." Brendan reached into his pocket and took out a double eagle, jingling others loudly as he did so, assuring Lambert's undivided attention. "I am very well aware of the fact General Sherman's troops will soon journey north, but it is unlikely he will arrive in Camden this afternoon."

He turned to Gabe, "Have a wagon with you today, Gabe?"

When Gabe nodded, Brendan dropped the gold coin into the shopkeeper's hand. "I would like you to load up the Hall's wagon with as much in the way of quality provisions as it will carry—anything you have."

"Yes, Mister Bonneau, very good," he said, closing his hand around the coin.

Brendan began to draw three of the wicker chairs closer to the old stove. "Gabe and Jenny will wait with me by your fire. I am sure you understand I am anxious for news of home?"

He saw Lambert hesitate, a flush creep across his face. Lambert, Brendan knew, was as in favor of emancipation as his father had been, but also knew his tolerance did not extend to the idea of Negroes lounging around his storefront. Brendan shook his head at the inconsistency, and while he had no wish to antagonize the old man, he had no intention of allowing Gabe and Jenny to wait for the transaction to be completed outside in the freezing rain.

Brendan saw him glance at the gold in his hand before

turning toward the storeroom. "You will be certain to cover that with a tarpaulin won't you, Mister Lambert?" Brendan called, hearing only the backdoor slam in response.

While Lambert and his assistant loaded the wagon, Brendan filled three mugs with the strong chicory brewing in the back room and helped himself to a loaf of heavy, dark bread, the first food he'd had since leaving the *Kendal*.

"Now tell me," he said, setting the cups on the table between the chairs, and tearing off pieces of the bread, "why are you working for the Hall's now?"

Gabe said nothing but looked pointedly at Jenny, who was wearing the defiant expression he remembered well.

"Mister Brendan," she said, holding out her hands towards the stove, "you know I have always tried to be good about doin' whatever your mama wants, but I couldn't see doin' some of the things she was askin'. They were just livin' in a couple of the rooms of the house and she wanted me to dust *and scrub the carpets* upstairs! With all the gardening and hauling wood and water we had to do," she paused, folding her arms tight across her chest. "I said no."

Brendan winced. Gabe rolled his eyes at the memory.

"'Well, then' said Miz Leah, 'you want to be free? Get out.' So Miz Sarah sent us to the Hall's and Miz Hannah was real good about takin' us in. 'Cept for Delphine, she didn't have any help at all at Laurelton."

"Your Aunt Sarah's been here since early summer," said Gabe, quickly, "so Miz Leah is not all alone."

Brendan drained his cup. "No one else?"

Gabe shook his head and told him about the gradual loss of servants, "Lainy went to work for your uncle over in Spartanburg and the last of the hands left with impressment teams. Delphine and I, and sometimes Mr. Edgar, go over every day and see to things."

"How has Father taken to losing both of you." Brendan stood up, refilling his cup behind Lambert's counter. "I haven't heard from him in months. Has he been home since?"

At the long pause, Brendan looked up. Jenny put a hand

to her cheek. "Oh, Mister Brendan....", she whispered.

"I'm sorry," Gabe said quietly, "I wrote...."

"When?"

"Late summer. He was with Kershaw up in Virginia and wounded on the first day of the Wilderness campaign. The doc didn't give him much of a chance, 'specially if he stayed in the field hospital. Before the battle started up again, Old George brought him back home. Got him out of there before the forest fires on the second day, thank God."

"We all kept hopin' he'd perk up and get better," Jenny added, softly, "some days he'd seem his old self. But he lived long enough to spend time with Miz Leah and see his sister, and summer on the place again."

Brendan stood at the windows. The rain had ceased but water still dripped from the storefront awnings. Gabe added more wood to the fire.

"What happened to Old George?" Brendan asked, turning back to them.

"Mister Charles told him if he wanted to keep fightin'," Jenny said with a sad smile, "that he should get up north and fight with the Yankees. Said he had done his own duty to his state and his wife, and Old George had done his duty to Charles. But he said it was time for Old George to put hisself first. And he did. Waited until the end, though, built the box and dug the grave hisself, then he went—"

"Grave?" Brendan asked, startled. "Not the family crypt? What did mother say?"

"Weak and hurtin' as he was, Mister Charles made sure all of us heard his last wishes on that score. He was wantin' to be in the ground—"

"'*His* ground,' he said," Gabe corrected her gently. "Once he passed it was as though the spirit left Miz Leah. She didn't fuss about it."

They sat quietly until Lambert appeared at the counter, list in hand and ready to settle accounts.

Traveling together for the first mile towards Fleur-de-Lys and Laurelton, he listened to other news of the county, of neighbors and friends who had perished in the fighting, those that had refugeed to other areas and the few who remained. Watching them ride away, Jenny turning every little while to wave and smile at him, he realized for the first time how lonesome for home he had been. Would Fleur-de-Lys even seem like home without his father, without Lilién and now without Gabe and Jenny?

And Mayah.

Before parting at the crossroads, Gabe told him about Mayah.

"She knew, Mister Brendan. She told us that after Mister Charles was laid to rest she was goin' home." Tears were streaming down Jenny's cheeks.

"None of us saw her after the service," Gabe added, his usually mellow voice gruff. "Your Aunt Sarah found her, still in the chapel, not long after sunset."

MORE NECESSARY THAN EVER, yet the idea of going home now was as bleak as the day.

Along the two-mile ride to his home, he saw that although the land was untouched by the ravages of battle, fields were overgrown and gone to seed. He scanned the rain-soaked fields, remembering his father. He had known, somehow, that his father was dead. Learning the truth today wasn't as much of a shock as it was a realization of grief he had known for some time, compounding the loss he felt when they parted that day in Virginia nearly three years before.

After the disaster at Hampton Roads, Brendan had accepted counsel and a new assignment from his mentor and former instructor Captain Everleigh, an assignment that they all hoped would help end the war faster and keep him from having to bear arms against north or south. Everleigh set up the prisoner exchange that took him to Aiken's Landing, and on to Richmond to meet with Captain Shaw of the new blockade runner *Kendal*.

His father was attached to Kershaw's Brigade, part of the

Peninsula Campaign. Before leaving for his new assignment, they met in Williamsburg and spent a day together. Strangely, Charles seemed less careworn and anxious than he had the January night when Brendan left Fleur-de-Lys. Thinner but dapper in his uniform, he was almost jovial as he walked with Brendan along Duke of Gloucester Street, telling tales of the past year.

"And now promoted to Captain," he said, finishing his tale with a self-deprecating smile and a nod towards his insignia, "Which simply means I am one of the oldest, mind you."

And then he asked Brendan why he resigned his commission; until then only Captain Everleigh knew Brendan's true reason for his abrupt change of allegiance.

On Saturday, March 8, 1862, aboard his ship the *USS Congress*, for Brendan the battle at Hampton Roads started with a playful skirmish. Washday for the Federal crews, Lieutenants Anderson and Kearsey spent a cheerful few minutes cleaning out their sea chests, pelting him with well-worn and ripe-smelling socks, early gifts for his birthday two days later.

From the first alert when they witnessed their old *Merrimack*, now ironclad and renamed the *CSS Virginia*, emerging from the Elizabeth River towards the Roads until the last, when he was fished out of the James River by men from Camp Butler, the day was a series of vague, surreal images.

Only the few moments when Jems Barkley boarded the surrendered *Congress* from the Confederate ship *Beaufort* remained vivid in his mind.

Face to face and shocked into inaction at seeing one another, Jems recovered first, and smiled with his usual swagger, "You, sir, are my prisoner!" he said, formally, no doubt thinking it all a great joke. Neither of them heard the whistle of the shell before it hit, ripping out a hole in the side of the *Congress*, blasting fragments of iron and splintered wood across the ship, and Jems, his friend since childhood and former shipmate, was dead on the deck beneath him.

Stunned by the concussion, the screams of pain, pounding of guns and shattering of the ship around him became dreamlike and distant, acrid smoke and the smell of blood surrounding him in a haze.

Roused by the screams of one of the young seamen pinned beneath the fallen rigging, Brendan knew he had only been saved by falling against the cushion of his friend's body. Jems had taken the blow and lay dead, his eyes still wide with surprise, his cocky smile erased forever by the jagged shard of oaken rail protruding from his chest, only inches from where Brendan's head had come to rest.

The *Beaufort* was pulling away to escape the barrage from the Federal shore batteries at Camp Butler and the *Congress*, not allowed to surrender by friend or foe, was again being pelted with shell and hot shot from the *Virginia*.

Brendan, stunned to find all of his limbs still present and intact, crawled to where a young seaman whimpered in pain but was still fighting. With his one free hand, Dennis was brushing away the smoldering embers from his shirt and pushing at the heavy spar pinning him to the deck.

"Thought I was a goner, sir—" Dennis said.

Another shell whistled overhead. Brendan threw himself over the boy, shrapnel from the deck hitting along his legs and back like buckshot. Not pausing to check his injuries or conditions around them, Brendan worked at freeing the frantic boy from the tangle of rope and shattered wood. Dennis screamed when Brendan finally hoisted it away. Bone protruded through a ragged gash in his forearm and the blood-soaked and dirty white duck fabric of his shirt.

He ripped off the shredded sleeve and quickly bound the boy's arm, Dennis blanching even more beneath the soot and blood as Brendan tied it off close to the elbow in a clumsy tourniquet.

"If I help you, can you swim?"

"I'd rather try it than stay here if you don't mind, sir," Dennis grimaced as he tried to move, but Brendan stopped him and crawled back to where Jems lay to say goodbye, for himself and for Jem's little sister Arabella, now all alone in the world. His cap lay beside him, and without thinking, Brendan caught it up and tucked it inside his shirt.

Before helping Dennis to his feet, Brendan surveyed the *Congress*, seeing the carnage shells and hot shot at close range had wrought. He had to help Dennis, and there was nothing to do but abandon ship and swim to shore only a few hundred yards away. The guns of Camp Butler were still smoking and aimed towards the Beaufort.

"What about the others, sir?" the boy asked, as they stood at what remained of the portside rail, bravely poised to jump despite his pain.

Before Brendan could answer, another shell from Virginia blew the deck out from under them, sending them into the James River along with their shipmates, some alive and struggling towards the shore, others beyond all torment.

As darkness neared, with the *Congress* now a burning shield between the beach and the *Virginia*, Brendan and several others who were still able-bodied, spent hours rescuing survivors and recovering the dead from both the *Cumberland* and the *Congress*. Including Jems, whom he found and carried himself.

Finally, beyond exhaustion, he was led to a cot by one of the 5th Indiana. Not even the explosion of his own ship sometime after midnight woke him.

One month later, April 10th, while other survivors of the two ships were being honored at a banquet in New York City, Brendan sat before Captain Everleigh, ready to resign his commission in the United States Navy.

BRENDAN RODE DOWN THE back lane, a shortcut to Fleur-de-Lys and the route to the family cemetery. Along the way, he dismounted to collect blooms from a clump of Christmas roses and sprigs from a holly bush, tying them together with a long strand of the ivy growing along the rail.

Rain fell again, gently now, not the downpours of earlier in the afternoon. Hitching Jumper to the fence under the shelter of a large magnolia, he walked beneath the wrought iron arch of the cemetery gate, found the marker he was searching for and set the simple offering on Mayah's grave.

The news had hit him like a blow to the gut. Both Gabe and Jenny knew it would, and why they did not let him hear about it from anyone else and waited until he could be alone and recover from his grief with some dignity. Until that moment, he had not realized just how much he had counted on seeing Mayah, to be taken care of once again.

He laughed at the thought, but the laugh caught in his throat, knowing what he wanted most was not dignity but to feel the solace and warmth of her arms around him, hear her murmured comforts while he lay his head on her bosom and cried like a child.

Charles's gravesite was located beneath the spreading branches of the old oak, a temporary roughhewn placard in place. He thought of his father working on the plantation he loved, rolled up sleeves, muddied boots, his good-natured grin. Brendan knew he would appreciate the simple, homely marker, just as he preferred being buried in "his" ground.

Mindless of the mud, he sank to his knees beside his father's grave, removed his hat, crossed himself and bowed his head. No prayer came to his mind or lips, only more warm tears to mingle with the cold rain dripping from the oak leaves high above him, for the aching emptiness he felt at the thought of never having his father's wise, kind counsel again, and for the senselessness of the waste and destruction the last four years had brought to all of them. All of which might have been averted if the warnings of wise men like his father had been heeded.

He crossed himself again.

He still carried the double eagle his father had given him that long-ago spring day at the camp near Williamsburg. Brendan had tried to refuse, knowing his pay as an officer on a privately-owned blockade runner would be substantial, but accepted when he saw how much it meant to him. Remembering its warmth when he took it from his father's hand, he gripped the gold coin tightly.

Darkening now as dusk neared, he started up the tree-lined lane and saw Fleur-de-Lys in the distance. Massive white columns stood like sentries on either side of the entrance.

Brendan paused beneath the shelter of the huge, gnarled oak nearest the house, the one he and Gabe used to climb, skin their knees on, and hide from Mayah after raiding the kitchen.

At dusk, on a rainy winter day such as this, the air should be scented with the smoke of burning pine from the house, kitchen, and cabins, over the sound of rain there would be talking, laughter and songs from the quarters and probably, the rhythmic clanging of Jake the blacksmith. Jake had lived in the shop near the barn; a constant presence as dependable as his father.

Now, the stillness was broken only by the softly falling rain.

Before he could dismount, a woman stepped from behind the door, the heavy, old pistol in her hands aimed at his chest.

PART III

LILLIAN

Annapolis & Easton, Maryland

*If you cannot get rid of the family skeleton,
you may as well make it dance.*

*George Bernard Shaw
Immaturity, 1930*

Chapter Ten

Gold Among the Dross

EVEN FOR THE SHORT sail across the Bay, Lillian took care to follow the usual pre-sail checklist she learned at the same time as her ABC's. Charts, fuel, water, rations, PFDs, life raft, radios, flares, etcetera, etcetera, etcetera. She had rolled her eyes and said it flippantly to her father once after watching *The King and I* on the VCR during a very long voyage to Hawaii. Without hesitation, he had responded, "One of those etceteras could save your life, girlie."

Confident sailor though she was, Lillian was relieved to see the Chesapeake was tranquil on the morning of their departure. She stepped into her father's shoes and routines shifted to give each of them new duties. Even if the Captain wasn't on board, everyone still heard his voice when they closed hatches, started the engine, and released the lines.

Busy as they were, none of them noticed the man watching from the boardwalk above, his green eyes hidden behind dark glasses.

Once out of the harbor and facing into the wind, she cut the engine and the kids raised the mainsail and jib. Since returning from the wedding, it was another wonderful example of sibling camaraderie, each helping the other, calling out their signals without the least trace of the sarcasm and meanness they often had at the least provocation.

Luffing smoothed with a few turns of the winch, an effortless tack, a successful jibe, and they were heading south on a broad reach at a steady ten knots. She kept the kids involved and learning about charts and weather and wind, and what to be vigilant of even on the shortest trips.

Alone in the cockpit, she found herself wondering about how her mother would have felt to find such a secret had been kept from her. And then laughed aloud, comparing her own recent experience of finding out her husband had had three affairs in as many years, to the fact her father owned a million-dollar estate. As secrets and surprises went, she would take the latter.

Stepping up through the hatch with lunch, Miranda looked at her curiously.

She shook her head. "Just a funny thought. What's Ryan up to?"

"Reading the radio manual," she said, tossing her windblown hair out of her face and sitting down, setting the tray between them.

"Good." Grandpa had given both of the kids "sailing" assignments. Miranda's was to read up on her rules of the road, and Ryan, radio operation. "Got your sea legs yet?"

The only one of them susceptible to seasickness, Miranda pooched out her cheeks and picked up a soda cracker in answer.

"We'll go over rules of the road, it'll keep your mind off your stomach."

Miranda steered while Lillian ate lunch and watched, experiencing another of those remarkable moments as a mother when she had to remind herself that the young woman in front of her was once her little baby. Not as unconsciously smooth as the adults, still, Miranda steered with confidence, keeping an eye on the wind indicator, sails, and the Bay around her.

"Mom..."

One of Grandpa's rules was that an adult take the wheel when there was a course change involving traffic and Miranda had spotted a barge up ahead.

Lillian took her place at the wheel. "Ready about."

Miranda took her place at the mainsheet. "Ready!"

"Helm's alee!" Lillian said, and steered through to a starboard tack and Miranda turned the mainsheet winch until the sail filled and they were back on a close reach, well away from the container-laden barge on its way north to Baltimore.

WHEN THEY REACHED THE eastern side of the Chesapeake, motored into the little cove, and secured the *LilyRose* to the pier near the beach house, bright afternoon sun lit up the green grass in front of the cottage and the bright pink roses climbing along the old fence.

The cottage was folk Victorian in style, with decorative touches in the trim around the windows and the wide, covered porch overlooking the cove. Seeing it from a different vantage almost made it appear larger than it was, propped on its little hill above the beach.

Alexander had stopped by, opening windows to air out the house for them, leaving a plate of home-baked cookies, a huge vase of cheerful white daisies and a dinner invitation from the tenants of Cherrington House for the following evening.

When Lillian had assured him she had no intention of selling the estate, he had the delightful old Wedgewood gas stove serviced, and a pale blue retro style refrigerator had replaced the old icebox, now the first antique stored in the new storage shed erected behind the cottage. A large refuse bin, although she couldn't imagine needing it, was also set up nearby.

Miranda surveyed the mountain of furniture and boxes in front of them while she ate a cookie, seasickness gone as soon as her feet hit solid ground. "Where do we start?"

She laughed at Miranda's expression.

"Remember—and help me to remember— not to hurry. In fact, let's take off the covers and I want you to video everything, just the way it is right now, don't move anything. Do that slowly, in all the rooms, in all directions. We'll call it our pre-disturbance survey."

"Why?" Ryan asked from the doorway.

While Miranda got busy she tried to explain, "Because once we move things, we'll never know how it was when we first started."

"But why would we ever care where it was when we started?" he persisted, obviously confused. She stifled a sigh, knowing it probably would never matter, but wanted to approach the task ahead of them methodically.

"Well, it might not matter but if it did, we'd be sorry we hadn't, wouldn't we?"

Before he could ask anything else she sent him back to the boat for work gloves.

Their little cove was very quiet, gentle swells rocked them all into an early bedtime after a quick, late dinner. Ryan was in his berth in the bow, while Miranda slept in the big berth at the stern. Claustrophobic after too many years of having a bedroom ceiling just a few feet overhead, Lillian preferred to sleep in the relatively open space of the main cabin.

She stretched out, eyes closed, listening to the usual tinkling of halyards against the aluminum mast, bumpers rubbing against the dock and boat and the trills of crickets on shore.

She began to open Lilién's diary for the third time and hesitated. Again. Why was she so wary about delving into this personal history she had craved for so long?

I am her namesake, she thought, feeling the familiar tingle that happened whenever she made a significant connection to the past from the present, again, like the stream of bubbles from a well-connected electrolysis clip, she thought, the current working its way through the sediment masking the truth of the past from living eyes. She opened the diary.

Fleur-de-Lys April 25, 1857. I am too exhilarated to sleep, knowing at this time tomorrow my mind will be as full of memories as it is now of anticipation. As I lay in bed, I could see my exquisite new silk glowing in the moonlight which floods the room tonight. Precisely the color of the pale yellow primroses which bloom in spring, the double skirt festooned with bows of the same silk and is so voluminous, I feel as though I am clothed in a cloud!

On the eve of her fourteenth birthday and first formal ball to be held in her honor at the family plantation *Fleur-de-Lys,* Lilién Bonneau wrote in a heavy, adolescent script, many vivacious flourishes and scrolls throughout.

Mother thinks it plain but has promised that I may wear Grandmère Louisa's topaz and diamond necklace for the occasion.

Another tingle swept through her, remembering the beautiful jewelry that she had held in her hands just yesterday before all of the jewelry, coins, and documents they had discovered went into a safety deposit box at the bank. Would there be other entries to give provenance to pieces they had already discovered?

In her next entry, Lilién wrote about the first dance with her father; of her big brother Brendan and how dashing he was in his dark blue frock coat, white silk shirt, and black silk cravat patterned with silver Fleur-de-Lys, and how he stepped in the few times she did not have a partner, how he and Wilson Hall had honored little Amelia Hall and a few of her friends who were too young to attend the ball with a dance in the long hallway outside the ballroom, with Jems Barkley keeping a lookout for Leah and other disapproving matrons.

Brendan is by far the best dancer, holding me tightly and lifting me higher than anyone else. No doubt, it is both because of his strength as a sailor, and as my brother, he is allowed more familiarity, freedom from the timidity we feel when dancing with others. Exhilarated, and safe, his strong hands upon my waist as he lifts me high above the dance floor.

Fewer entries about her oldest brother, Louis Charles, and those were written with a hint of tolerant disapproval.

After Gracie Moore and I found Louis in the far alcove with my friend Leticia Taylor, I teased him during the next dance. "She must love your deep blue eyes, dear brother!" to which he replied, batting his eyelashes, "Little sister, Miss Leticia would love my eyes if they were pink like your pet rabbit's if it meant she would be mistress of Fleur-de-Lys one day!" "But Louis," I gasped at him, "if you believe that, why were you hidden away in the alcove with her?" to which he gave the most wicked smile, twirled me round and round but refused to answer!

Many paragraphs were dedicated to Wilson Hall from the neighboring plantation, *Laurelton*. She wrote of his kindness, humor, even the way he seemed to take no notice of her mother's forceful temperament.

I was disappointed Wilson reserved his first dance with me late in the evening but happy he chose the Strauss waltz, assuredly the longest dance of the program. Mother refused to allow many waltzes, as she still does not consider them as proper as cotillions or minuets, she is terribly old-fashioned. My one concern was he might be as clumsy as Jems Barkley, who spent most of the first quadrille of the evening stepping on my toes whenever he was near.

Wilson was strong and sure, smiled at me so sweetly and asked me how I was enjoying my birthday. He appeared so different to me, not only because his newly tailored frock coat and stiff white cravat made him appear so serious, so handsome, not the farmer or funny friend I was accustomed to. No, something else, something in the way his lovely blue eyes held on to mine until I felt a strange tingle in my chest, the effect making me quite out of breath and my heart beat faster. The laughter and chatter around us gradually subsided until the only sounds were the whispers of silks and rustles of tarlatans as they swept across the gleaming parquet floor, even the beautiful music seemed muted and distant. A languor seemed to have descended over us all, whether from the music and the warmth of the evening, the late hour, or the punch, I cannot say.

Wilson's tall, blond good looks were apparent in the photograph, although his serious countenance made him appear diffident, almost timid, not the teasing, confident presence Lilién described. Lilién filled several pages with her vivid memories of friends and neighbors in attendance, the glorious food, the music played by the orchestra brought all the way from Charleston.

The diary continued, filled with Lilién's reminiscences of other parties and picnics at plantations throughout the county as well as concerts and balls in Charleston and Savannah, Columbia and Wilmington, more of her vivid descriptions of silk gowns, satin gloves, and sandalwood, silk and ivory fans new for every occasion, as well as Lilién's conquests of the beaus of the county, although her narrative invariably returned to Wilson Hall.

Exhaustion from the early morning and activity of the day finally closed Lillian's eyes. She reluctantly set the diary aside, turned off the light and, imagining the antebellum scenes, fell asleep to the melody of the Southern Belle Waltz playing somewhere in her own memory.

"WHY DO WE HAVE to empty all the drawers?" asked Ryan, master of the whys and why nots of everything.

"We need to search through the letters, pictures, and diaries for Grandpa. Remember?" asked Lillian, adding, "Don't you think a few boxes will be easier to take home with us on the boat than a bunch of clunky furniture?"

"What's the difference which desk it comes from?" Ryan asked, holding down the flaps of a new carton while she put on a strip of tape. All paperwork, photographs, diaries, and calendars were packed into boxes, each numbered and a brief summary of contents recorded.

Each item, from walnut desks to an embroidered tablecloth would eventually be recorded on an inventory form, which would help Lillian decide what would be kept, insured, sold or, as much as she tried to deny it, tossed.

"Well, even though I can't see what room it used to be in, it will be interesting to know which family members used the furniture and help give us a better understanding of our family."

"But wh—"

"Because I said so," she smiled, ruffling his hair.

Added to the large furniture and paperwork she had expected were the chests, boxes, and cabinets filled with things like the crocheted and painted linens they had seen on their first visit. Handmade quilts, silver, glassware, crockery—etcetera, etcetera, etcetera, Lillian thought more than once. Boxes of textiles and housewares were glanced into and set aside for another time; this trip was to search for information about Brendan.

Obviously, it wasn't everything from the big house, Lillian thought when she and Miranda took a break on the shaded front porch and Ryan was investigating tide pools further along the cove. Not all the furniture, anyway, it couldn't possibly have fit. Everything they had seen so far was very good quality and seemed to have some significant financial or sentimental value, and all packed and stored with care.

"It's weird, isn't it, that the Reynolds family saved all this stuff for Grandpa?"

"After they had been swindled so badly?" Lillian asked, glancing up from the bundle of letters she was sorting, her brow wrinkled from the pain of another headache. "I suppose… but from what Alexander said, it was Ernest who was the problem and the Reynolds family didn't hold a grudge across generations. But you're right, it is a strange reaction."

"Um, speaking of strange reactions, Mom… sometimes you're like, well, listening to or seeing something, well, something else. Is that what Vera was talking about?"

Lillian had chosen not to wear gloves while working that morning, eager to feel anything, any kind of energy from these artifacts from her ancestors, but a few times, she had noticed her daughter looking at her oddly. She shrugged, "I wouldn't mind understanding it better, but I don't think it's anything to worry about, you know how dramatic Vera is," she smiled, but Miranda didn't seem reassured. "It only happens when I touch metal, and the oddest thing is, I can handle several things in a desk drawer with no reaction at all, but the next will give me a strange, winded feeling. It's just a bit disorienting, that's all. Not painful, unlike this damn headache."

Of course, Lillian thought, when Miranda went back inside, she didn't plan on telling anyone about the perceptions that often accompanied the breathlessness. Along with the occasional visions, most often feelings of subtle happiness or a bleak sort of sadness, very rarely, a not so subtle surge of desire. Fear and pain only once, that afternoon in the lab when she had touched a gold brooch and collapsed in blinding agony, conscious of what she could only think of as … well, of evil.

In the shade of the tall cedar tree, the cool breeze against her face, she tried willing the early symptoms of the migraine away, there was so much furniture to move and so many boxes, drawers, and trunks they hadn't yet glanced into.

Making up for lost time with her family history put her in a constant state of sensory overload. Still, far from drudgery, this minutia of everyday life was fascinating to her, and she was grateful to old Mr. Reynolds. The diaries and calendars would provide structure, letters, photographs, bills, notes and even scribbles on matchbook covers would help fill in the blanks. *How* she was going to organize it all once they returned home was another matter.

"Mom," Miranda called, "does this big trunk have a secret key do you think?"

Miranda was kneeling next to an old wooden steamer trunk, its clasp firmly latched, and beneath the beautifully etched brass escutcheon plate were the initials L. C. B. After examining it closely, she turned to ask Ryan to get her toolbox, which he was already holding.

She smiled. "When I have a job again, I'm signing you on full time."

With the magnifying glasses, she saw exactly what she wanted to see and found the tool she needed. The heavy, old flathead screwdriver was occasionally used as a screwdriver, but, with the marks and stains to prove it, more often as a substitute hammer or a convenient paint stirrer. She thrust it in and turned, and by the look of the scratches and wear on the lock, the same way her family members had done for generations. The latch opened with a satisfying *clunk*.

Miranda lifted the lid. Everything inside was individually wrapped in thin, tissue-like muslin and each bundle tied with a silk ribbon.

"I have a *very* good feeling about this," Lillian said, gooseflesh rising on her arms.

They leaned in as Miranda picked up the first bundle and untied the white ribbon.

"Ooh!" she and Miranda said together, as they unwrapped a lightweight silk dress in an old-fashioned ashes-of-roses hue, with cream colored lace trimming the collar and sleeves, the long skirt falling in soft pleats.

Lillian reached out and caressed the material gently. "I think I remember seeing this in one of the framed photographs in the first box …several women and young children…"

"Do you think it belonged to Lilién?" Miranda held the dress up and twirled.

"I don't think so, honey. The style is turn of the century and for a young girl. Lilién would have been around sixty or so by then. A granddaughter, maybe?" She helped Miranda fold it back into the protective cloth.

In the next bundle, there was a simple white linen and lace tea dress, gray knit bed jacket, and a beautiful but well-worn Thirties-era, quilted floral robe. The trunk's built-in drawers held beaded headbands, decorative hair combs and fans, several pairs of gloves, beaded coin purses and a very tarnished silver hairbrush, comb and mirror set. Ryan, bored by all the feminine accoutrément, started to make fun, exaggerating their oohs and aahs with each new discovery.

"It's…heavy," Miranda said uncertainly as she untied the thick red ribbon around a larger bundle. A waterfall of sparkling fabric poured from the wrappings. Of deep, wine red velvet, the low bodice starred with crystal beads, the skirt falling from the empire waist was covered in beaded black tulle. Even Ryan stopped his teasing and said, "Whoa!"

Miranda immediately held it up and admired herself in a dusty bureau mirror.

"Prom. Next year. *Can I?*"

At the very idea of the delicate Edwardian masterpiece in the midst of frenzied, raucous high schoolers, she replied in an equally breathless voice, "School dance? Never. *Ever.*"

Nestled on top of the last ribbon-tied bundle was a blue velvet box, inside a necklace and earrings, delicate daisy chains of diamonds with bright yellow topaz at each center.

"*Oh!* Lilién wrote about these in her diary," Lillian told the kids, "She wore them the night of her ball…" The ribbon crumbled at Miranda's first tug and the cloth slipped away from the shimmering, festooned flounces of Lilién's yellow silk ball gown.

"Oh, Mom, look! Can that be fixed?" Miranda brushed her hand lightly over one of the cracked folds in the fabric. "Mom?"

But, Lillian's throat had closed, and tears stood in her eyes. Caressing a fold of the fabric glowing in a shaft of the late afternoon sunlight, her thoughts were with her great-great-great grandmother as she danced with her father, teased Brendan, and smiled up at Wilson while the orchestra played and couples waltzed across gleaming parquet floors.

"Mom, are you crying?"

Ryan's iPod, not to mention their work, lay neglected that afternoon after they uncovered an early Victrola and a cabinet full of old record albums of popular jazz from the Roaring Twenties, through Big Band swing of the Forties, to crooners of the early Fifties.

Lillian showed Ryan how to wind up the player and tighten the needle. Accustomed to the clarity of digital and sophisticated themes of modern music, the kids laughed at the scratchy, tinny sounds and the sometimes silly, sometimes sappy lyrics of the dated music. Miranda videoed as Lillian taught Ryan to dance the Charleston.

Ryan served as disc jockey and they worked to the scratchy sounds of old songs like *Shine on Harvest Moon*, *Ain't She Sweet* and *You Belong to Me* until Miranda finally threatened violence if he played *You Tell Her I Stutter* even one more time.

"SO, WHAT DO YOU think?" Alexander asked, once everyone had been introduced and drinks served.

"Beautiful," Lillian said, smiling, "Pictures, old or new, or even our rainy-day visit, hardly did it justice."

She looked around the torch-lit patio garden where the Schrader's were hosting the Cherrington family for their first meal at Cherrington House. Sparks flashed from a huge rock barbeque as Louis Schrader flipped hamburgers and hot dogs and juices hit the hot coals beneath, at one corner a large steaming pot waiting for the fresh hard-shell clams. Loretta delivered a large bowl of green salad, and a kiss to the cook, and hurried back to the kitchen. Lillian was glad to see there was happiness in the house, now.

She turned to Alexander's mother. "Margery, Miranda and I were talking today about the care that was taken in selecting the items to save. Do you know anything about that?"

"Grandma Reynolds was *not at all* understanding of Albert's decision at the time, and I was a very young wife with small children, so I wasn't very involved in the process, I'm afraid," she said, with an apologetic smile, also glancing at Alexander. "Neither of us thought it was practical, to be honest. But he would not be swayed."

"Well, I'm very grateful to him, to all of you."

Laughter and cheering erupted from the far end of the garden that opened to a long, torch-lit expanse of lawn, where the kids were playing volleyball.

Between the three families and a few overnight friends, there were enough for small teams and Lillian could see that Miranda was already coaching her team of the youngest and smallest, including ten-year-old Liam Reynolds and nine-year-old Misty Schrader. Little five-year-old Cherry Reynolds was cheering loudly from the sidelines. All older boys on the other team, including Ryan, they were now the ones laughing but Lillian suspected Miranda would have the last laugh before dinner was served.

"… you know, I believe it all started with Thomas Crawford, my husband's," Margery said, counting on her fingers and then waved her hand, giving up, "well, several time great-grandfather, a Southerner who moved north after the Civil War. He either knew the Southern wife before he moved or made friends with her later, but he ended up settling here and marrying a Reynolds." Margery's brow was wrinkled, her eyes looking off into the distance, recalling long dormant details. "The Cherrington men, starting with Edward, had never liked him and made no secret of it. None of those factors made friendship between the Cherrington, Reynolds and Crawford families very easy, and the last straw, of course, was when your great-grandfather took the property."

"What did Ernest II have against Thomas Crawford?"

Margery shook her head. "Who knows? But, of course, that's all ancient history. Can't really matter now, can it?"

Lillian smiled, but thought of her father, and his need to find out about Brendan.

"Alexander, I was wondering, do you know where the Cherringtons are buried?"

He nodded. "Spring Hill, a public cemetery in Easton."

"I could take you sometime if you like," said Gina, Alexander's wife as she joined them, holding out a plate of Chesapeake crab canapés, "but now, I really want to know what wonderful discoveries you've made!"

After dinner, sparklers helped to light their way home to the *LilyRose*.

"Did you see those guys when we won?" Miranda was still laughing as she skipped and twirled her sparklers.

Walking backwards ahead of them, Ryan held his sparklers aloft. "Beating them didn't stop Clayton from asking you out!"

"Oh? That's nice," Lillian said. Miranda glared at her brother in the dim, staccato light.

"Isn't it?"

"I guess, but you said I couldn't date until I was sixteen."

She bit her tongue, not mentioning how futile *that* particular rule had been."

AFTER ONLY ONE NIGHT of reading her words, Lillian could almost hear Lilién's voice; warm, softly Southern. All of her entries about Brendan were affectionate, about his teasing and brotherly advice, his protectiveness and how much she missed him when he was away at the naval academy and later when he was assigned to the *USS Dolphin*.

Lillian gasped and sat up as she read the next entry.

Fleur-de-Lys. September 10, 1858.
Father has invited a Mister Edward Cherrington
from somewhere up north, Maryland, I believe,
to stay through the week. Mister Cherrington is
a dealer of rare weapons and heard of Father's
collection through Mister Lambert of Camden. I
am not certain at all that I like him. Father teased
I am suspicious of all Northerners. He, Mother,
and even Wilson tolerate Mister Cherrington's
company well enough.

Always go with your first instincts, Lillian thought. Of course, Lilién had eventually married Edward Cherrington, but she had not grown fond of him in the first few entries of the diary. From the words and tone of Wilson's letters found in the keepsake box, Lilién had jilted Wilson. What had caused such a shift in affection and what had eventually happened to poor Wilson? Between the autumn of 1858 and early 1860, there was a long gap in entries. In early 1860, she resumed her journaling and the girlish loops and flourishes were gone when she wrote about the death of her eldest brother, Louis Charles, killed in a riding accident one stormy night

Columbia. February 14, 1860. I know Mother would never have allowed my visit to the Robinson's had Father not intervened and escorted me himself. He insisted it was not healthy for me to be enclosed in an atmosphere of gloom and grief. No harm could come of our attending a small gathering with friends. Father's final word on the subject was to speculate how long Louis Charles would remain cloistered and draped in black if it had been another member of our family to perish.

I must admit I am pleased to be relieved of my mourning for the evening. Father declared we should not dispirit the assembly with black and I could honor Louis Charles by wearing a token of remembrance. At Christmas, he presented both Mother and me with identical brooches, brilliantly colored opal hearts, surrounded by sapphires and diamonds. Seeing it displayed on the bodice of my midnight blue velvet brought my last day with him vividly to mind.

Fleur de-Lys. March 10, 1860. Brendan's birthday today and we all miss him so and are anxious to hear more about his mission to Paraguay. He will not be home for many more months.

Father asked me into his study after Wilson and little Amelia Hall had left for

Laurelton. Father told me Wilson has asked his permission to call on me! I felt myself grow suddenly lightheaded, and with such a sensation of joy in my heart!

Smiling at my expression, Father pinched my cheek softly. 'Mother and I have spoken at length with Edgar and Hannah about the future of Laurelton and Fleur-de-Lys.' Father must have seen my impatience, for he smiled and began to speak about Wilson, 'That you are prettier than any girl in the county and sharp as a pin has not escaped the young man's notice. He also said he has been crazy for you since he was fifteen, with a dark flush to his face quite like your own,' father added with a wink.

'Now, my dear, what are your feelings in this matter?' he asked me, 'do you care for young Wilson, Lily?' I did endeavor to stop myself from smiling, to be demure and answer as a lady should. As father talked on about how Wilson will call upon me and accompany us to Columbia for the annual Governor's ball, I could not keep the lightness of heart I felt from my face. Father saw this and gave my cheek another pinch.

Laurelton. April 29, 1860. Wilson has begun to call quite often now, along with little sister Amelia, whose greatest joy is to tease the entire span of their visit! Today is Wilson's birthday and Father and I attended a small party in his honor at Laurelton. I am so at home at Laurelton, even Father is more relaxed in the company of Edgar and Hannah, while little Amelia has pursuits of her own and is not in constant verbal attendance. Wilson and I can be alone with our own conversations, while still gently chaperoned by the others.

Her feelings for Wilson were sincere, and it was obviously both romantic attraction and a true friendship existed between them. She wrote as often about their shared views on the issues of the day and things that made them laugh as she did about his tenderness, affection, and chivalrous concern for her comfort.

Chapter Eleven

The Calm Before the Storm

THE KIDS WERE IN Easton with the Reynolds's for an action-packed escape from the afternoon heat in an air-conditioned theater. Lillian was enjoying time alone at the cottage.

> Fleur-de-Lys. October 20, 1860. I have, at long last, completed a painting of Fleur-de-Lys which is suitable as a gift for Father's birthday. I took it at once to the kitchen to show Lainy and Jenny. Jenny's hands and apron, even her face was covered with flour, but her look of pleasure told me how much she admired it, and how much she loves me. Mother has informed me that I will own Jenny when I am eighteen. Had *I* any freedom in the matter I would set her free the very next day, regretfully, as we discovered when Brendan attempted to free Gabe four years ago, our state does not give its own citizens the freedom to manumit slaves. *Il est ridicule!*

Though born to a world of wealth and entitlement, Lilién did not see herself as entitled to use the free labor of others. Being comfortably trapped by the forceful opinions of Leah Bonneau, the laws of the age and the state in which they lived had not prevented Lilién, Brendan, and Charles from making changes and preparations where they could.

Drowsy from the close warmth of the house, Lillian poured herself a glass of iced tea and moved out to the cool breeze from the Bay and the wicker chaise on the now shaded front porch.

Fleur-de-Lys. October 22, 1860. Father returned home from his week in Charleston this afternoon appearing so dispirited I presented his gift before guests arrived for his birthday party. Pausing at the door to his study, I watched as he worked, his forehead creased in worry and his lips pressed tightly as he urgently wrote some missive. He appeared to have aged even in his short time away. I knew he and the others of like mind on the Planter's Council had been urging caution in the discussion about states' rights and slavery.

Still in his traveling clothes, shirtsleeves rolled up to his elbows as he preferred, at least when Mother was not present to scold him, he ran a restless hand through his thick black hair to keep it off his brow, silver strands glinting in the lamplight. His face had slackened recently, making him a bit...well... jowly, creating a not-so-dignified resemblance to our lazy old bloodhound, an observation which I certainly will never share with anyone.

I thought I should not disturb him and began to leave but the rustle of my skirts caught his attention and he looked up.

"Hello, Lily darlin'!" The worry lines faded as a smile lit his eyes.

"Hello, Papa. Welcome home." I tiptoed to kiss him when he stood to greet me. "I wanted you to have my gift before the party tonight."

I could see by the expression crossing his face he had forgotten, but his frown disappeared when he glanced at the linen-wrapped package I held.

He set it gently on his desk and untied the silk ribbon. "Why, Lily, you've painted her portrait!" he said, as the fabric slipped to the floor. "What a beautiful lady she is, too, by God!"

I was so pleased to see the joy lighten his expression and looked at his face as he studied the painting. He gestured, made approving noises at the colors, lines, and shadow, even pointing out the detail in the tall pines and the rows of yellow and orange lilies bordering the house. Fleur-de-Lys on a bright summer morning.

> *He grew quiet and tears clouded his dark blue eyes. He set the painting on the small table in front of his desk so that he would be able to see it while he worked.*
>
> *"Thank you, my dear. You have made this a much happier birthday for me," he said, gathering me up in his arms for one of his generous hugs. He released me and, pinching my cheek lightly, added, "Now, I had better prepare for our guests or your mother will certainly make it a very unhappy birthday!"*

Lillian caught herself nodding off again. She looked at her phone for the time and saw nearly an hour had passed. She got up and stretched and added more ice to the warm tea.

> Fleur-de-Lys. November 7, 1860. Mister Abraham Lincoln has been elected president. Apparently, the Planter's Council is to assemble immediately, though Father has not explained why.

Reading Lilién's thoughts written over a hundred and fifty years before, Lillian had a sense of watching chess pieces being moved into place by duty, loyalty, and greed, sometimes simply by fear of change and, mostly, moved by the omniscient decisions of faraway politicians. History buff that she was, in Lillian's mind, the War Between the States began in April of 1861, but fears of war were reaching Fleur-de-Lys much earlier, and she was pleased Lilién was informed and curious about the politics of the day, not a sheltered belle, ignorant and uninterested in the world around her. The entries became more serious as the day neared. Finally, there were new entries about Brendan.

> Fleur-de-Lys. December 25, 1860. Dear Brendan has made this the happiest of Christmases! He has finally returned from his travels to South America and service aboard the *Dolphin*, and he is to have a prolonged leave through the holidays! However, he has returned to a very different country, as we received the word with his arrival that South Carolina has seceded from the United

States. What that means for all of us, I cannot know.

Fleur-de-Lys. January 20, 1861. Poor Brendan! Mother has been on a mission since he has been home, determined he should resign his commission in the United States Navy as so many other military officers from our state have done. In response to her heckling at the dinner table this evening, father raised an eyebrow and said he sincerely hopes the husbands of South Carolina do not take their oaths of loyalty as lightly, or there will certainly be a widespread rebellion amongst the wives of our State. That quieted Mother on the subject for the duration of the meal.

After Mother left the room, I asked about the oath he had taken, and he repeated it for me with a solemnity that brought tears to my eyes.

He explained to me and Father that he understands well enough that he is free to resign his commission and swear an oath to the new government. But he feels it would be a gross betrayal of his loyalties, and the oath would be made to a new government that seeks to preserve the institution of slavery, which we have all been fighting, in our own way, for years. When his furlough ends, he travels back to Annapolis next week to meet with his mentor, Captain Everleigh. Neither his opinions nor his oath are ambiguous. I understand why he feels so torn.

Lillian yawned, set the diary aside and picked up her phone, a quick Google search led to several variations of the oath of a nineteenth-century United States naval officer, but eventually, she found the oath attributed to the time period of Brendan's service.

I solemnly swear or affirm to bear true faith

and allegiance to the United States of America, and to serve them honestly and faithfully against all their enemies or opposers whomsoever, and to observe and obey the orders of the President of the United States of America, and the orders of the officers appointed over me, according to the articles of war.

Lilién was quite right. The oath was unambiguous, and Lillian was surprised so many Southern officers of their day changed their allegiance. Yawning again, she knew she should put the diary away and get busy. She turned the page.

Fleur-de-Lys. January 22, 1861. Mother was in a frenzy over the news we received from Charleston, by way of George Denison of Angel Oaks Plantation. Wilson and Amelia are staying these few days before Brendan is due to leave for Annapolis. We were shocked when, as the fiercest storm of the winter raged outside, Georgie arrived. A Lieutenant Hamilton, who recently allied his loyalty to the new South Carolina Navy, (as Georgie has himself, though I do not believe he has ever sailed anything larger than a raft.) and has issued a call to other United States naval officers sympathetic to the Southern Cause to pledge their loyalty by commandeering their ships to Southern ports. When Georgie finished his speech, he presented orders for Brendan to report to Charleston, and he departed almost immediately, leaving the rest of us waiting for Brendan's response...

The howling wind and rain lashing at the window outside and the blazing fire snapping on the hearth inside were the only sounds...

A shrill whistle from a ship out in the Bay jolted her awake. The diary was open, lying face down where it had fallen on the floor. Disoriented, she looked around, certain she had heard thunder, but the sky was hot pale blue all the way to the horizon.

After a long time, Brendan took the orders to the fireplace and dropped them onto the fire. He watched them burn while Mother ranted and screamed at him in the most vitriolic manner. I wanted to remove Amelia from this frightening scene, however, could not force myself to move from my place. Both Brendan and Father tried to reason with her, but in the end, Mother had her way and Brendan was banished. He left not an hour later, dressed in his uniform, to report to his superiors. Gabe and Wilson rode with him as far as Camden. I am not certain when I shall see him again.

Fleur-de-Lys. March 2, 1861. Mister Cherrington arrived last week for an extended stay, rather inconveniently. Indeed, it is difficult to remember how it is he became such a close acquaintance of our family.

Wilson is behaving so strangely lately. He has taken to showing up unexpectedly and unannounced, and most surprisingly, without his little sister. As bothersome as I find her sometimes, Father was very insistent that we are chaperoned on all outings. Even Mister Cherrington, Edward – he has repeatedly requested I call him by his Christian name, has been making subtle comments about Wilson's behavior away from my presence. He has made several kind overtures and one day even brought me a bouquet of hothouse flowers from Columbia.

Fleur-de-Lys March 15, 1861. I understand Wilson is anxious about the war and what it will mean for all of us. Like Brendan, Wilson is torn about how best to serve. He is not of violent temperament, and believes, as both of our fathers do, these issues should be resolved by diplomacy and common sense. Mother, however, demands to know when he intends to enlist as many of the other men in the county have done.

This afternoon, he stopped abruptly during our walk and kissed me! While I did not find the gentle touch of his lips to mine at all objectionable, I pulled myself away, chiding him severely. I expected the teasing smile or some Wilson-like remark, but he only seemed confused, as though he believed I was expecting and desiring such behavior from him.

Poor Wilson, Lillian thought. His behavior was normal enough, even given the restrictive Victorian society. After all, he and Lilién had been betrothed for over a year and he was facing a long, difficult, possibly permanent separation soon after their wedding.

March 28, 1861. Fleur-de-Lys. At dinner, at Mother's prompting, Mister Cherrington answered that he will return to Maryland soon to serve in his father's regiment, his father being some grand Colonel in a cavalry unit. It does seem odd, and I caught a wry glance exchanged between Father and Wilson, that Mister Cherrington does not ride, but always takes the trap when traveling between here and Camden. If Louis Charles had been present, he would have delighted in revealing the great flaw in this plan. Indeed, I seem to remember him telling me some time ago that his father was a banker in Baltimore.

Wilson has chosen to serve with the Quartermaster's Office in the ambulance corps if the worst should happen. Mother chided him, saying it was a lazy man's way to serve since there will be but few Southerners in need of such aid, only Yankees. About to protest that no one was braver or more industrious than Wilson, I saw the sadness in my father's expression and knew he was imagining the horrors of war and the reality of men against rifle and cannon, sword and bayonet. To my mind, Wilson's decision shows not only the greater bravery but reflects his strength of character and compassionate heart.

Only ragged fragments remained of one page, and another brief entry was illegible, heavily blotted and followed by several blank pages. The next entry after this transition was in sharp contrast to the graceful handwriting and descriptive passages throughout the diary.

> April 13, 1861. The war has started. We received word this afternoon. Shots were fired upon Fort Sumpter early yesterday morning…
> Cherrington House, Easton, Maryland. April 18, 1861. Edward and I arrived last night.

About to close the diary and her tired eyes, Lillian was jarred fully awake. Edward! What happened to Wilson? The letters from Wilson found in the diary were dated the third and fourth of April 1861. Within weeks, dreams of love and happiness with Wilson had died. Soon after arriving in Maryland, Lilién was treated with indifference by Edward and as an enemy by his family, their hatred increasing with every Confederate victory, their mockery with every defeat.

> Edward turned his considerable charm to convincing me that I could not endure the humiliation once Wilson's actions became widely known. He urgently told me of his heretofore unexpressed love and promised to take me away from all memory of the pain. Still in shock, Brendan and Father both away from home, I turned to him, trusted in him and we eloped, married in a small chapel at a small town just north of the border in Virginia.

Dear Jenny helped me, how deep her
disappointment will be that I cannot send for
her, God only knows when that time will come.
I so wish I could have her loving presence in my
life among these strangers.

Eastern Maryland was strongly pro-South at the start of
the war, and there was no mention of Edward's service to the
Confederacy, or to the Union, for that matter.

Lilién wrote about the Confederate victory at Manassas
and Union defeat at Bull Run, without triumph, only concern
about her father and Brendan and the many friends left behind.
From the tone of the few short entries, Lillian could tell that,
apart from a few friendly neighbors, Lilién lived very much
alone. Apart from brief notes about local happenings, Lilién
wrote nothing of the personal thoughts and opinions and hopes
that enlivened her earlier entries.

Cherrington House. April 28, 1862. How long
ago I wrote my last entry in this diary. The early
entries from the days of my childhood are like
the tales about one of Jane Austen's delightful
characters that Jenny and I talked and laughed
over in secrecy, anticipating the happy ending to
their stories.

After so long a time of misery and
hopelessness, I received as delightful a surprise
as I could have hoped for, a letter from Brendan
announcing that he was on his way to Easton, to
arrive in time for my birthday!

Edward is away for the entire span of
Brendan's visit and I revived enough to care
about the state of the household, though until
now I had been content to leave the details to my
mother-in-law   and   her   condescending
housekeeper.

How strange we appeared to one
another. I know I was wan and pale compared to
the vivacious girl I had been, could it only have

been just a year ago when I had seen him last? Brendan was gaunt and pale, his handsome face still battle-scarred from his near escape from the *USS Congress* at Hampton Roads only weeks before. His eyes, though, had changed most and lost the spark of humor with which he once beheld the world, even our mother, most of the time.

His arms squeezed me tight and the gloriously familiar scent of him had not changed at all and took me at once back to the comforting memories of home. I held him for some minutes, happy and yet crying. He had tears in his own eyes when I finally released my hold upon him.

Although still in the uniform of a lieutenant of the United States Navy, he confessed he has already resigned his commission, which would be effective upon returning to Annapolis. He will join the crew of a blockade runner to bring supplies from neutral British ports to either Wilmington or Charleston, a way, he said, he could serve but not fight against either side.

I was stunned at this news, knowing Brendan's dedication to both his oath and the values his oath represented. At my expression, he reluctantly told me about Jems Barkley. I could tell he did not wish to linger on the topic and sensed there was something he was not confessing about the sudden alteration of his allegiance.

As we parted that first night, he presented me with a letter from Father. When I took it with a degree of trepidation, a bit of the old smile returned to his eyes, and he pinched my cheek gently, "The letter is not from Mother, little sister, you have nothing to fear."

I had tried to write to father many times since my departure, each time envisioning his bitter disappointment and his loneliness without Brendan and me at home. To learn now that he himself was far from home and serving as an army officer and leading men into battle, was too extraordinary to contemplate.

His letter was kind. He expressed his regret at my belief that leaving home was the solution to whatever dreadful event had occurred, and that he was not present when I needed him so urgently. He expressed his love and concern for me and promised as soon as the war was over he would come to me, even before going home to Fleur-de-Lys. If I was happy and content in my new life, he would be pleased for me. However, if I was not, he would see me home safely with no questions or recriminations.

I cried throughout the night and wished I was still a little girl and could climb into bed with my big brother who had always kept me safe from thunderstorms and ghosts and other fearful things. Still, knowing he was near was immensely comforting.

The next day was spent visiting near neighbors who had become friends, and the Reynolds held a small dinner in his honor. Little Sylvia said to me later that she had never seen me so happy, that I seemed like a different person from the woman she had known for the past year.

Far too quickly the time came for Brendan to return to Annapolis. Before leaving he asked about Wilson.

Incredulous, he shouted at me. "I do not believe it! Wilson would never ... he is not the sort of man who would abuse anyone in such a manner! A child, as young and helpless as Sally? My God, Lilién! How could you ever believe such a thing?" He stood abruptly, turned his back to me and looked out the window towards the cove until he regained his temper. When he turned back, he spoke more calmly. "To risk all that meant most to him, which was you, *little sister, not to mention my friendship and both families high regard? No," he insisted, shaking his head. "No, I will* never *believe it!"*

"Please, Brendan," I begged him, "do not be angry with me! I wish with all my heart I had not seen what I had seen nor listened to Edward's encouragement to run away!"

He knelt beside me, comforted me, and soothed my crying.

"Lilién, if you want to go home to Fleur-de-Lys, I will take you. Today, as soon as you can ready yourself."

I so wanted to say yes, but all I could do was resume crying when I told him I could not leave Edward because I am now expecting his child.

The next morning dawned gray and miserable, clouds heavy on the tall pines along the drive as Brendan left to his new duties. He gave me a sad, final salute, turned, and rode down the lane towards Easton.

Lillian caught herself nodding off again, a remnant of a dream of the broad expanse of windows that looked from the Cherrington House living room still in her mind. She set the diary aside and turned off the light, empathizing with Brendan's reaction at Wilson's transgressions. Lillian was as puzzled at Wilson's behavior.

But, how could she know anything with such certainty about a man who lived and died in another time and place? She did know there was much more to the story about the end of Lilién and Wilson's engagement than anyone would ever know.

After the lengthy entry about Brendan's visit, there was one brief notation about the death of Edward's mother, Ermaleen Cherrington, in June of 1862. As an indication of their closeness, she wrote, she hadn't even known the dour old woman's Christian name until the day of the funeral.

Lilién again stopped writing regular entries. Either life

was too mundane or too depressing to write about.

Cherrington House. December 25, 1862. If not for little Amelia, born as the autumn leaves fell in early October, I would go back in time, back to the night before I eloped with Edward. In the short span of her existence, she has brought meaning and a degree of contentment to my life. I have refused to have the sour-faced-nurse, appointed by my mother-in-law, mind and tend Amelia, preferring to take care of her myself. No doubt they believe me to be from lower social order, but Edward has not forced the issue and allowed me to have my way. Not, however, about the christening, insisting no child of his would be baptized a "papist".

One very brief entry without her usual place and date was heavily blotched and obviously written with a shaking hand. Lillian's throat ached in sympathy as she read.

My chest feels like a hollow drum, my arms are aching, empty, my eyes have no more tears to shed, no prayers in my heart. My little Amelia, the one light in my world, is gone. She failed to thrive after the fever which gripped her in summer. Frail, her lips tinged with blue, I knew she could not live. I took the vial of holy water and baptized my child as the sun rose this morning. She died in my arms only a short while later. I have nothing. I ask myself why God has stripped me of all love and affection, of all of my joys. What is there to continue living for? My prayers bring no answers, only emptiness, and silence.

Lillian held the diary to her chest, crying for the heartbroken and lonely young woman. She wiped her tears and read on, not wanting to leave Lilién and go to sleep, almost as though she would be abandoning her to bear her loss alone all over again.

LILLIAN WALKED BACK TO the cottage alone. She had enjoyed the trip to Easton and the visit with Gina and Margery but felt anxious and irritable after visiting Lilién's gravesite.

The gravestone was sound, the grave and surrounding cemetery well cared for, but Lilién was alone, isolated, no other family members nearby, not even baby Amelia who had died in her arms. Not her son Ernest, who was born in August of 1865, the only surviving child of her marriage to Edward. Still, it was not Lilién's isolation that had troubled her as much as a strange attack of vertigo as she knelt next to the grave. No pain, nor the breathlessness that often preceded her headaches, just the dizziness that was momentarily overwhelming and left her feeling out of sorts.

Cherrington House. January 22, 1865. I was standing at the cove, looking south as I was wont to do when feeling homesick, although tonight that was not what compelled me to the farthest point of land from the house. My head ached, I felt so tired and hopeless and was wishing with all my heart Brendan would show up in that blockade runner of his to carry me away to safety as he had once offered. Imagine that, running the Federal blockade for the Confederacy safer than life in my own home. I knew Edward had gone but could not bear to go back inside the house, warm and dry though it was.

From the water to the sky, the day was every shade of gray. Pebbles on the beach, mists curling through the topmost boughs of the tall pines, old, weathered wood of the pier and the bark of the bare, wet maples lining the path from the house. Even the tears I wiped from my cheek were opaque in the dull winter light.

Thinking myself completely alone, I was startled by a step behind me.

"Excuse me, ma'am. Are you Lilién Bonneau?" a hesitant Southern voice said behind me. Mississippi, I thought immediately.

"I am," I said, turning to the young man, his crumpled old slouch hat in hand.

The tall, rawboned lad stared at me, at the bruise I knew was darkening on my cheek.

My hand flew to my face. "I fell."

He tossed his dirty blond hair out of his eyes and said, "My mama used to fall a lot too, ma'am."

No one, not the servants or even my mother-in-law had ever challenged my excuses, by word or look, about the bruises that had routinely appeared on my face since the second year of my marriage. Even this morning when Martha was kneeling over me when I revived, not a word was exchanged between us about what had happened

Until this young stranger stood before me.

"Who are you?" I blurted out rudely.

"Thomas Crawford, at your service, ma'am." He gave me a bit of a salute and a swaggering smile, tossing hair out of his eyes again. Gray eyes, like the day, I noticed as he continued, beautiful quartz crystal gray eyes. "I was sent, ordered by your brother, Lieutenant Commander Bonneau, who has commissioned a delivery for you."

My heart jumped as he handed me a letter with Brendan's bold handwriting. "Brendan! How is he? Where is he? When did you last see him?"

"Well, ma'am, the last time I saw him, he was raisin' a funny gold flag and deliverin' me into enemy hands. A gold flag just like that ring you're wearin'," he nodded towards the fleur-de-lys ring I wore on my right hand. "I do know for certain our ship got through the blockade before Fort Fisher fell."

Also, on Brendan's orders, he was to speak with me alone and my husband was not to know about the trunk he delivered, which, young Thomas explained, was now hidden in a thick stand of cedar trees near the gate.

"Do you know what it is?" I asked Thomas

He shook his head vehemently. "No, ma'am."

If Brendan did not want Edward to know about the delivery, he would have good reason, and I never for one moment considered taking my young visitor into Cherrington House. It would never do to have our busybody of a housekeeper tell Edward that a young Southern sailor had come to call.

"The neighbors," I said, gesturing to the east, towards the Reynolds' estate. Jane and young Sylvia had been true friends and would help me, first by excusing my rudeness in showing up unannounced and allowing me to hear about Brendan in the warm comfort of their home.

Lillian started as the diary dropped to the floor. Disoriented, she reached up to shield her eyes from the bright morning sunlight.

She had fallen asleep in the lumpy Victorian chair again, one of the cedar-scented antique quilts pulled over her. But when, she wondered, had she come into the cottage? She remembered being restless and edgy on the LilyRose, even the open cabin too confining, but didn't remember walking up to the cottage.

She didn't want to wake the kids so early, so she poured a cup of lukewarm tea from the carafe on the counter and continued reading until she reached the final entry.

Cherrington House. May 1, 1865. In answer to my first letter home last month, Aunt Sarah has kindly responded, but with the most tragic of news.

My father died months after he was injured in the Battle of the Wilderness. Mother succumbed to grief and shock in February when Fleur-de-Lys and everything it contained was burned the night Sherman's troops moved through Camden. Even reading this, it does not seem possible, cannot be true...

Aunt Sarah, who had moved from Wilmington during the last years of the war, is in good health and has returned to her home now that War activity in the town has eased. Gabe and Jenny remain at Laurelton with the Halls, residing in the overseer's house and continuing to help Edgar reestablish some semblance of order to the place. She writes that Brendan, when he visited briefly at Christmas, deeded Fleur-de-Lys to Gabe, certain the end of the war would bring both their freedom and an urgent need for money and provisions. Of Brendan, they have had no word, and not since he returned home when he persuaded Mother and Aunt Sarah to move to Laurelton for safety.

Although Aunt Sarah does not believe this, Mother seems to have convinced herself he has stolen our most precious family possessions. I know that Brendan could never behave so dishonorably. Indeed, of this I have proof, as some of those treasures are hidden safely in my neighbor's attic. How I wish I could hear from Brendan again.

Wilson, she mentions, is also in Wilmington, working in a local firm as an attorney. At her insistence, he is staying with her while he establishes himself, in return for the Halls' hospitality during the final months of the war.

I dreamt the end of the War would mean I would go home to Fleur-de-Lys to be with my family once again. Now my parents and my home are gone and with no word from Brendan, I fear he is gone as well.

I would love to see dear Jenny, but I am once again expecting a child in summer, and so must remain.

After reading Aunt Sarah's letter, a shroud of desolation settled over me and I lay down on a soft carpet of grass and cried, knowing how I must have hurt Father and disappointed Mother. At least now they will never know the truth about my life. Safe enough, warm enough, yes, but I would rather have endured the greatest physical hardships with my family than this forlorn exile.

EXTRA FURNITURE HAD BEEN moved to the shed or arranged in the small bedrooms, making the living room now, almost, a living room. Thrilled to find bookshelves filled with books when the last shrouds were pulled away, they remained in place, a perfect way to make the cottage feel like a home. The eclectic assortment of furniture included a magnificent early-nineteenth-century maple highboy, two floral Victorian wing chairs, "Miranda's" nearly threadbare blue velvet fainting couch and what was a well-used but still handsome brown tweed sofa, along with a walnut secretary desk, a few small mismatched tables and one Depression-era electric lamp that was safe to use.

"What did you find?" Coming back into the cottage after a break, she laughed as Miranda jumped and squealed in surprise.

"Diaries!" she held up the stack. "Edward Cherrington's…," she paused, before adding, "Mom, I don't think Lilién was exaggerating. He doesn't sound very nice."

"Where—" she asked, startled when she sank deep into the wing chair's springy ottoman.

"From…" holding diaries in one hand, a bundle of letters in the other, Miranda glanced at the empty box beside the chair, "the double pedestal walnut desk. Which do you want?"

"People are usually more honest in their diaries; I guess I'll start with one of those."

Struggling out of the ottoman to her daughter's amusement, she settled into one of the wing chairs and glanced inside each diary to find the earliest dated January of 1857. Primarily ledger columns full of figures, most of them about the value of his gun collection and the state of his inheritance from his father, broken up by short paragraphs of narrative.

In February of the next year, he wrote about initiating a courtship with Miss Georgeson of the neighboring property, not reticent at all about writing down the fact she was her ailing father's only heir and the valuable land would soon be hers. Lillian was immediately struck by his calculating nature. Even notations about his own mother's poor health were written about in a tone of impatience rather than concern. The first reference to Lilién was towards the middle of the second book when he wrote during his September 1858 stay at a Camden, South Carolina boarding house.

Edward wrote about the extensive collection of weapons at Fleur-de-Lys and the obvious wealth of the family. Very interesting, especially after reading Lilién's first impression of him.

> February 1860, Camden, South Carolina…Now that the prince is dead, some sort of riding accident befell the poor fellow, it seems the inheritance of this immense plantation will fall directly to the second son, who has chosen a naval career.
>
> The girl has several suitors, of course, being reasonably pretty and very rich. The most serious threat being her infatuation with young Hall from the neighboring plantation, a match all seem in favor of. However, there is always a way to disengage a young lady's attention from someone, the trouble being how best to go about it.

Lillian continued to scan the journal, a foreboding in her chest as though she was reading a mystery with one of her favorite characters in jeopardy.

Another brief entry about the neighboring property. "Miss Georgeson dead of scarlet fever, and father sold off and moved away before I could act, worst luck." He returned to South Carolina again in late February of 1861, entering callous predictions about the chances of the war and the value of South Carolina cotton if war was to come, and a brief paragraph, "Disengagement effort commences. There are ways to shake the faith of even the most infatuated belle, and now is the time to develop a strategy. One I have in mind will render the engagement defunct with the same impact as a Yankee cannonball.

In April of 1861 he followed with a notation about the purchase of laudanum, under the column of neat figures the words 'a worthy investment.'

Lillian closed the journal with a sick feeling.

LILLIAN SAT IN THE cockpit, sipping tea and watching the last light of the evening dissolve into midnight blue, very soothing to weary, weak eyes irritated by dust and sometimes tears. Sorting through these personal belongings, reading letters, diaries, with her ancestor's faces looking out of countless photographs, brought their world so vibrantly to life, sometimes Lillian would have said they were her very own memories.

Stars were appearing now, and the night sounds of frogs and crickets, a distant owl and water lapping against the boat were all equally soothing. She closed her eyes and rested her head against the lines, breathing deeply of the fresh salt air gusting in from the bay.

Through the open hatches, she could hear the kids, still talking and laughing in the galley.

As much as she had enjoyed the journey back in time, Lillian was ready to be home. She was worried about her father, who hadn't been his usual self when they had talked earlier in the day.

"SOMEONE SHOULD HAVE CUT off *her* head!" Miranda had read Lilién's diary most of the night. Lillian wondered if she should allow her daughter to steer the *LilyRose* in her current state.

"Miranda!"

"Sorry. But," she continued, not sounding at all sorry, "you read how hateful and mean she was—to everyone! She didn't just *own* slaves, she was cruel to them and to her whole family, especially Brendan!"

"Leah Bonneau was a woman of her time and place. In those days, the law of the land allowed slavery."

"But a lot of people, the rest of the family even— "

"Yes," Lillian said, holding up her hand, "attitudes were changing, but gradually. People with a lot of power and wealth like Leah were dependent upon slavery to keep their position and were unwilling to risk their way of life. And security. They were afraid of the idea of a population of freed slaves, even afraid of being killed by them."

Ryan had been listening quietly at the bow and walked cautiously back to the cockpit.

"If they were so afraid of dying," he asked, "why did they start the war? I bet a lot more of them died in the war than if they had just freed the slaves. Most of them would have been happy to be free, wouldn't they, not try to kill the people who freed them?"

"But there were probably many, those who had been severely mistreated, who may have taken their revenge—"

"Like Randi?" Ryan made a hand across the throat gesture.

"Okay, looks like we have traffic," Lillian said, glad to be able to change the subject. She stood up and took the wheel from Miranda, now glowering at her brother. "Ready about!"

Back on course, Ryan took a turn at the wheel.

Lillian's cell phone rang. She saw the hospital number displayed and smiled.

"You're not monitoring our progress, are – oh, hello, doctor. Yes, of course, I understand. We're on our way now."

Chapter Twelve

Sailing Too Close to the Wind

SHE NOW KNEW WHY her father hadn't sounded himself on
the phone the night before. He chose to begin a new course of
treatment during their absence and kept it to himself, not
wanting her to 'fuss'. The reaction to his first dose was slight; the
second had nearly killed him.

DEAR DUNCAN,

Lillian paused again, pen poised over the paper.

The hospital waiting room was quiet, with just one other
occupant watching home and garden programming on a small
flat screen in the far corner. Both kids were staying over with
friends now they knew their grandpa would be fine.

Sun shone through tinted windows where she sat,
waiting, tapping the old Federal Government ballpoint on the
tablet, both found in a desk drawer in the cottage, not knowing
how to begin a letter that had to say so very much and so very
little. Surely, she thought, reading Lilién's delicately worded
Victorian diaries for several days should help.

*After all that happened as a result of our three
minutes of indiscretion, I felt as though there must be
something I should say now that all is, or at least appears
to be, settled. Congratulations on and thank you for the
creative diversionary tactics, or what my father called "le
ruse de guerre." Hope the battle was not too hard won in
the last wonderful picture, and I anticipate one day being
vastly entertained by hearing the tactics and strategies of*

both sides.

My first instinct, of course, is to, ironically, say I am sorry. But, at least about those three minutes, I am truly not at all sorry. We have skirted politely past our attraction to one another, perhaps this was inevitable. That it was a night where circumstances converged like weather systems for a perfect storm, well, maybe that is what happens when honesty is suppressed for too long.

The time for coyness being officially over, yes, I love you, Duncan.

And you weren't going to say too much, she thought, wryly, reading the words that had flowed so smoothly, so unconsciously from the sharp tip of the old pen, a faint furrow in thick, viscous black ink, little daubs at the end of each word and punctuation mark.

I was attracted to you from the day we met, and since then my instincts about you have proven to be reassuringly sound. From your overtures these past weeks, I let myself hope … but our timing, well, I won't use the current crude phrase, but our timing certainly has been <u>most</u> *unfortunate.*

What I can say I am sorry about, without the least hesitation or trace of irony, is that I gave no thought to your child. Whatever problems in a marriage, a child is a blessing from which you will receive the unconditional love that is otherwise indescribable – and free of the complications which exist in every other relationship. And you, I have no doubt, will be a blessing of a father for any child.

She paused again, blinking back the tears in her eyes and swallowing against the hard knot in her throat, imagining Duncan holding his child, the intensity of those blue eyes only for the little one in his arms. She rubbed her eyes impatiently.

I am also sure I cannot afford to abdicate my senses or my sense of responsibility as the mother of teenagers. This is a critical time for me to, as the captain would say, stay on an even keel.

Of course, I need to be strong for him as well. Not only because of his illness but because he has given me a special assignment which has thrown the door wide open to my family tree, a line going back to the American Revolution on one side and to France before theirs, unfortunately, on the other.

Researching my own history has led to a stockpile of letters and diaries which is why pen and ink have special appeal for me today – as well as some reluctance to trust any further 'indiscretion' to a digital medium…

Given everything, I think it best if this letter includes a resignation from my brief employment at Voyagers. I know there will be a time when we can meet as friends and colleagues once again, but proximity, for now, I think, is best avoided.

I have paused several times while writing, Duncan, still trying to not let you go, I suppose, but there is no more to say, except…

May God bless you and keep you safe, always.

Love,

Lillian

THE DEBRIS TRAIL OF the *SS Rhiannon* was short and began with the shattered remains of the portside sidewheel and pieces of the hull, the smaller bits of wreckage and cargo were only indeterminate lumps under layers of sand and sediment. Much of it was scattered along the top of a slight ridge, above where the ship rested on her keel relatively intact, stern to bow along a gentle slope, like a submarine heading for deep water. Duncan looked at his watch again. At this depth, he had only a short time to investigate and left the others to set up the grid.

The water cooled noticeably but visibility was still good. Four crewmembers worked at laying out the white plastic PVC pipe, placing the frame of meter-square grids over the debris field, Gail and Zach worked at the closer end of the unit, Josh and George he could barely see at the farthest point.

Moving away from the grid, he descended along the ridge towards the ship, passing an empty, partially collapsed frame of the thickly encrusted starboard side wheels, pausing to watch a young loggerhead turtle, gliding along the ridge, no doubt searching for lunch. When it reappeared, Duncan saw a large, ethereal moon jelly trailing from its jaws. Strange choice, he thought, seeing several more likely specimens near the wreck, from spiny lobsters and the small, brightly striped sergeant majors to the meatier, dull, brownish-green tautogs, some skirting between thick fronds of sea rods and others above anemones with white filigree-like tendrils. In the distance beneath a ledge in the ridge, a sand tiger shark waited benignly for nightfall.

A large, odd-shaped clump beyond the wheel might be one of the boilers, he thought, trying the look past the large mass of spiny brown sea urchins to make the evidence before him agree with the images of the side scan sonar he reviewed before diving. Continuing his descent towards the bow, a sudden, disorienting wave of dizziness swamped him.

With nothing nearby he could take hold of, he stopped and tried to breathe normally and remain still until the vertigo eased. At least he hoped it was vertigo, he thought, grimly amused by the thought of the sea spinning around him as though he had once again wandered off from the classroom tour to be left standing alone in the undulating water tunnel aquarium.

Still disoriented, he looked back up the length of the ship to the ridge, but visibility had changed and he could no longer see the others beyond the wheel through the greenish haze. Trying to calm his heart rate and take regular, measured breaths, he realized he could not. The tank gauge read three-quarters full, he saw that much clearly even through his blurring vision as he grappled for the valve.

Before he could move towards the others or make a distress signal, Gail was next to him passing over her regulator. He breathed deeply, panic subsiding and nodded to indicate he was ready to ascend.

On the slow progress to the surface, they buddied-up. If

she had not been a professional diver and trusted colleague, he might have suspected her of tampering with his equipment.

The evening before, she waited until all the others had left the galley and once again offered her no strings attached or for old-time's sake companionship, whatever he wanted to call it.

Sex. He wanted to call it sex and the kiss they shared was a great start.

He knew unfaithfulness to *Lily* should not be his first thought but was pretty much the only one that troubled him. He was not taking another woman into his stateroom, no matter who it was, and knowing Vera had the room directly across the hall from Gail's made him pause. While these unromantic thoughts crossed his mind, she broke the kiss and a wry, wary look crossed her face.

"Saving it up for someone special, are you?" she had said, the cynical tone deceptively softened by her Irish lilt, giving up on him but still holding him close. "Well, I'll wager it's not Victoria, so it must mean that photo of you and Lillian was the real thing."

She had been annoyed, he could tell, but her eyes had been sympathetic. Now, her warm brown eyes held on to his during their slow, deliberate ascent to the platform at the fifteen-foot decompression level, reminding him of the time years before when they had practiced the procedure together. They had been lovers then, "friends with benefits" had been her own description of their relationship, and he had to agree it was apt; very friendly, very beneficial.

They reached the platform and surface-supplied oxygen and she took back her regulator for the last time with a wink

"A BIT OVERWHELMED," SAID Lillian the next afternoon when her father was stronger. "So many beautiful and interesting things, clothing and books, furniture and quilts, it's hard to believe they stored it all in the beach house for you for all those years."

Tom shook his head in tolerant exasperation and smiled, "I'm sure that was as good as finding a treasure chest for you."

"For all of us, the kids…" she started and then paused and handed him her tablet, "Watch this."

The tinny sounds of an old Victrola and the Moonlight Serenade filled the room and Tom watched Lily teach Ryan the foxtrot, "he's quite a good little dancer!" she said, switching to another video of Miranda and Ryan, laughing and stumbling as they both tried to do the Charleston in the narrow corridor cleared out between the furniture and stacks of boxes.

Tom watched the series of short videos of their fun and adventures at the old place, feeling the weight of that secret burden lift from his shoulders, from his soul. She had accepted his reasons for waiting so long without judging, removing, not adding to the shame and fear each memory of the place evoked. He recognized his grandmother's treasured Victrola, some of the tunes were familiar. He recognized other furniture, and the cottage itself, which he had been inside only a few times but nothing, he decided, could stir up the old hurt and fear, not with all of those most precious to him happy, and safe.

"I must have forgotten to shut off the camera," she said, as the last video went on for some minutes. After the dance, Miranda and Lillian were emptying the drawers of his grandfather's huge old walnut desk, and Ryan continued on as deejay.

"Ryan has a decidedly eclectic taste in music," he chuckled, as the theme changed from a romantic fifties crooner back to Roaring Twenties silliness.

"*Uninformed*, I think, would be the correct–

"What's happening here?" Tom asked, indicating the left side of the room.

She looked closer at the screen and at the odd, greenish glow along the edge. "I'm not sure, reflection from the sunlight, I suppose, or the battery getting ready to go."

As if in confirmation, the video ended abruptly.

NO MATTER HOW HE shrugged it off to the others, Duncan knew his 'vertigo' had been caused by a lack of oxygen.

He made sure no one touched his gear when he came back on board, and had watched for reactions, but failed to note any gasps of surprise or frowns of disappointment at his return from the deep.

He spent the rest of the day 'recovering' and checking every inch of his dive gear for answers. He did not have far to look.

He had been the odd man out on the team but had gone through the five-step pre-dive check with the others as well as a few steps he had developed on his own. Before diving, he clearly remembered testing his regulator and air flow with the tank closed and fully open. Somehow, between checking the valve himself and diving, the valve had been turned back more than halfway towards the closed position. Some divers followed a protocol insisting on a quarter turn back to relieve stress on the valve, but Duncan did not. At the surface and in the shallower depths, adequate air passed through the valve, as he descended farther both the pressure and his position served to cut the air flow gradually until he was starved for oxygen.

He tried to remember exactly who had been near while he prepared to dive. An Atlantic Energy geologist was the only one completely new to the ship, on board to do some independent study of the area before the contractor signed off on the proposed mineral exploration. Other than that, only Hugh, a maintenance tech, and Vera had been on deck.

In the seldom-used third deck conference room, leaning back in one of the comfortable high-backed chairs, Duncan was enjoying the view of a silvery blue ocean, and the pale coral-colored sky edged with periwinkle blue clouds on the far horizon.

He read Lily's letter again. Goodbye, as far as she was concerned. He felt an impulse to turn his back on everything and go to her again. And laughed at himself, remembering how well acting on impulse had worked for him before. Someone had tried to kill him, now, it was more than intuition or chivalrous instinct; her safety demanded he keep his distance.

A sound from the door distracted him from the letter.

"And what has you hiding away here in the gloaming?" He heard Gail's husky voice before he saw her and bit back the answer he might have given to anyone else at that moment.

She slid up onto the table near him and rested one sandaled foot on the arm of his chair.

Gail didn't deserve rudeness from him, especially after today. She was his friend and had been his lover years before he met Lily and became involved with Victoria. She seemed to know when he needed her. In fact, he felt guilty. Their intimacy occurred only according to the ebb and flow of his needs but he also knew her well enough to know she wouldn't put up with being used.

He surprised himself by handing her the letter, which she took with a little quirk of her eyebrow, lay back on the table and held it up to the fading light.

He watched her eyes move over the page, a bit of a smile a time or two, a frown. He caught himself appreciating the view she presented in front of him, her long hair fanned out on the table, down her silhouette to the toes on his chair rest. Not showy, not overtly seductive, but sexy as hell.

She finished the letter, folding and slipping it back into its envelope.

"I don't know what to say, Duncan." Tucking her foot under his chair's armrest, she pulled herself up gracefully and set the letter aside, "except she's right, your timing sucks."

He laughed. "You have no idea."

Whatever she saw in his expression made her eyes soften. "Don't tell me you're the one man in America who doesn't hold with divorce."

"Baby—"

"That baby, if there is one, is *never* yours, Duncan."

"And how would you know such a thing?"

"One," she held up her index finger and he was glad he had confided in her, glad to finally be able to talk with someone he could trust, "Most of your crew know you haven't lived together for over a year—which is why I even bothered to check in with you last night. Two," she added her middle finger to the count and nodded towards the letter, "Lillian writes 'these several weeks'—if you were still sleeping with your wife, you'd *never* be hounding the help—"

"Since when have I ever *hounded* the help?" he asked, both affronted and amused.

"And three," ignoring him, she paused before adding the last of her arguments, narrowing her eyes and examining his face, "you do have a somewhat sexually deprived look about you."

"*What?*"

"But I might be the only one to see that."

"Thank God." He leaned back in the chair and closed his eyes. "What is it? A facial tick, uncontrolled drooling I've been unaware of—"

He opened his eyes when he felt her slide onto his lap, her legs through the arms of the chair had him effectively entrapped. She leaned forward and moved her hips, her smile now thoroughly seductive when she felt his answering erection against her.

"No," she answered as though there had been no pause or change of position. "Just something in your eyes."

"You think teasing me will help?"

"I *never* tease."

"I'm married to one woman and in love with another, and you want to make love to me?" He had meant to tell her he couldn't, had meant to lift her off him somewhere before or after that rhetorical question, but had been distracted by her subtle flexing of certain muscles.

"What are friends for? Besides, Duncan," she said, adding in a whisper, "you owe me."

Warm and familiar, intimate and passionate, but safe, he thought, languidly savoring the feel of his body responding to her, wanting to lose himself in this sensory full-immersion.

He had no idea how much time had passed when he was brought back to consciousness by her low moan when she finally broke their kiss.

"Touch me, Duncan," she panted against his neck, trembling because he had been touching her and far more intimately than he had intended. Clearly, while he had been merely sightseeing and enjoying the view, Gail was determined to reach their destination.

Running lights now softly illuminated the room and he could see the need in her eyes as they met his. With more deliberation and tenderness, and his own need growing, he touched her.

LILLIAN WAITED IN HER father's room while he was in X-ray, reading an article about Duncan, this time an actual news article in the science section of the Baltimore Sun about the new ship and expedition. Despite her deliberate attempt to harden her heart, she could not help being interested and distracted by the photo where he smiled down from the bridge of the *Fleur-de-la-Mer*.

"Maritime archaeology is always treasure hunting; but now it is — or should be—a respectful, methodical and holistic way of salvaging treasure from the site of a shipwreck. To everyone on this team, our company, as well as any entity we might contract with, the entire wreck is the treasure. Fragments of wooden timbers or a plain pewter plate are documented and conserved, respected, in the same precise manner as a silver tankard or a pile of gold coins. Don't get me wrong, we love a nice pile of gold coins as much as anyone, but that is not our main goal."

I reminded Captain Scott there are many who believe every wreck site, particularly those of military ships, should be considered sacred ground and not be disturbed at all.

"I respect those who hold that view but firmly disagree. Truly, I believe it honors the dead to find out why and how they died and recover and restore what they left behind. And it is in no way comparable to the scenario of digging up a graveyard; it is a shipwreck — like a car crash or a building damaged by a storm, as Keswick Mansion in Baltimore was last year. If we felt that way about the houses we live in, poor "Lady" Keswick would have had to remain unburied in the ruined old Victorian turret where she died, and Keswick Mansion, built just after the Civil War, would be

left to time, weather, and looters—and not fought over by land developers and historic preservationists.

"For myself, once a Coast Guard officer and now a maritime archeologist, I would personally prefer to have my remains and belongings recovered respectfully. The soul is gone. I don't believe it is a mark of respect to allow the corporeal remains of an individual or civilization to fade away to the elements. Far better to retrieve the tangibles, to remember those who are lost, instead of leaving them to disappear forever or left to salvagers with less honorable intent."

I asked about the incident the day before that involved his emergency ascent during one of their initial dives to the site. Scott shrugged it off.

"A brief spell of vertigo, in itself not dangerous, unless you happen to be standing on a high ledge or scuba diving. It was very disorienting, and if my team hadn't been close by I might have been in serious trouble."

The diving team is Zach Wilkinson from the Annapolis Nautical History Museum, Josh Taylor and George Hobart, both regular Voyagers crewmembers and freelance diver Gail O'Brien. This tall, willowy brunette had effectively "buddied-up", sharing her oxygen supply with Scott on the slow ascent to the surface.

Gail! Lillian fought back a surge of jealousy at the idea, knowing Gail and Duncan had once been involved. She *was* beautiful, with a self-confidence Lillian had envied and a charming Irish lilt that lifted the offensiveness right out of the profanity routinely flavoring her speech.

When I asked why the lovely young lady instead of one of the others, Scott's eyes twinkled, but he answered seriously, "Gail and I have dived many times together, we've practiced the technique and she's the smallest – meaning she had the most air supply available to get us to the surface-supplied air platform at fifteen feet. I'm fine now and have since been checked out by our medic—and he's not nearly so pretty.

"Now," he went on to explain, "some shipwreck sites are ideally suited to leave 'in-situ', reasonably protected from the elements, and possible to safeguard from looting. A diver's museum and a way for archeologists to monitor stages of deterioration and other factors." The SS Rhiannon, traveling between Annapolis and Charleston when she was forced off course and sank in a hurricane in September of 1865, was once

considered such a site but the area is now targeted for exploration by Atlantic Energy. Recovery of the Rhiannon was arranged by the Institute of Nautical Archaeology (INA), contracting with Voyagers for support in terms of equipment and manpower.

We toured Voyagers new research vessel, Fleur de la Mar, while Dr. Scott described the long, tedious process of searching for and identifying a wreck, permit procedures and regulations involved, and finally preparing a pre-recovery site plan and photo mosaic—

"So, what's our next course of action, my girl?" Tom asked, wheeling into the room.

Startled, she dropped the paper. "Course of action?" she asked, confused, straightening up his sheets and pillows before the orderly helped him to bed. He gave Tom a salute before sitting in the chair and wheeling himself out of the room.

"What's next? From the diary and letters, we know about the family, we know where the plantation was, but we still haven't learned much about Brendan. His sister only has good things to say in her diary, but old Edward believed the worst of him and passed that down the generations. We need to find out why, and I would sure like to see what that place looks like."

"Cherrington House?"

"Oh, hell no! That plantation, Lily of the Valley...what was it? In South Carolina?!"

"Fleur-de-Lys. Lilién writes in her diary that it was burned."

"She was *told* it was burned, and maybe Sherman did torch the big house. Be interesting to know if there was anything left, and what family survived after the war."

"Now you're interested in the other family members, and their houses? I thought you just wanted to know about the sailor."

"Well, all I know, girlie, is that your job has only begun."

"We still have a lot of boxes to go through, Dad, we've barely scratched the surface—"

"Going to the source might be faster, you know."

"If I didn't know you loved me so much I'd think you were trying to get rid of me, *again*. Besides, which one of us is more experienced in digging into history in this room?" Seeing his determined expression, she added, "I have a friend, Janet, curator at a Civil War museum in South Carolina. I've already e-mailed. She'll be able to put me on the right path."

"It's less than a day's journey."

"You *are* trying to get rid of me!" Her eyes narrowed. "Why? What did the doctor say?"

"Not bad news, actually," said the doctor, who walked into the room, smiling. "I believe the saying goes "we have fair winds and following seas!""

"God Almighty," Tom grumbled. Lillian giggled, knowing her father's prejudice about the modern usage of the old mariner's funeral blessing.

"I suspect you should take that as the doctor intended, Dad. Give the landlubber a break."

TOM CONSIDERED TELLING LILY *why* he had suddenly unveiled his past. He'd been coming to it, it was true, but Scott's revelations about the international smuggling network and potential danger to Lily was enough for Tom to find any way to not only make her financially secure but keep her safely busy and changing routines as much as possible.

Impatient to be at Lily's house with his family, when the doctor told him the new treatment might curb some of the effects of the chemo, make him stronger and able to leave the hospital sooner, it was all he needed to hear. Allergic to some damn additive in the mix, the cure had nearly killed him. Slow and steady wins the race, he reminded himself.

He glanced at the newspaper Lily had dropped when he came in. And as for Duncan Scott, he would bet the *LilyRose* that whatever the man had suffered, it was no simple attack of vertigo.

GOD, BUT THESE HAD been three of the longest days of his life.

The first starting with an early dive when he'd nearly died and ended with an unexpected but admittedly welcome episode of heavy petting, far more sophisticated and satisfying than any he had experienced during his teenage years.

But, not exactly how the night had ended. Afterwards, he and Gail had gone to the galley, raided the pantry and had cookies and milk while watching an episode of The Walking Dead. They said goodnight with a friendly smooch outside her cabin, still friends, and all debts real or imagined paid in full. He fell into bed rather zombie-like himself.

Waking late the next morning, he felt terrific until remembering someone still unknown and aboard the ship had tried to murder him the day before. Far worse, a call from Trey informing him the reporter from the Sun was just arriving aboard.

The annoying woman had stayed a fair portion of the day and by the time she left, his usually endless store of courtesy and tolerance for company was again at a very low ebb.

Retreating to his quarters, he read the report he had received from his security man. Cal had dredged up some interesting information, but nothing linking anyone on board to George and Nick or hinted at a reason to kill him. And now, the third day was the charm, heavy weather had moved in, preventing any progress for another day.

HER FATHER'S SUGGESTION SHE go to South Carolina to research the history of the Bonneau family and discover what remained of Fleur-de-Lys was another of many so unlike him, Lillian again wondered what had prompted him to want to know the truth about his past. She wasn't buying the impact on the generations bit. Even though she knew he was right, she also knew there was more to his suggestion than he was letting on.

She had finally received a reply from Janet, a friend since college, who was now head curator at the Columbia Civil War Museum. She was perpetually flummoxed when people expressed surprise that a young African American woman would choose to be head of a museum about the Civil War, particularly in the state that was first to secede and started the war in order to maintain slavery as a right.

"Like I shouldn't have a personal interest in the Civil War?" she had vented to Lillian once, "like curators of all Civil War museums are supposed to be fat old white guys whistling Dixie and waving the Stars and Bars?"

"I had no idea you were Southern aristocracy, not to mention descended from French blue-bloods! Sorry I didn't respond right away, but you know how I am about a treasure hunt—I had to start looking! I'll have a copy of the deed made for you. Attached is a newspaper write up from the Columbia Banner in the summer of 1860 about the plantation in its glory days before the war. The plantation house named "Fleur-de-Lys" was completely burned during Sherman's campaign north in February 1865.

A tingle of anticipation worked its way down her spine as the grainy image slowly opened on her screen.

Glory days, indeed, Lillian thought, examining the details of the house in the pencil sketch illustration, brick with white verandas along both stories and four large windows on each floor on either side of the columned entry. The article noted the extensive formal and kitchen gardens, and the classic architecture of the house including French Renaissance-era stained glass windows in their small private chapel. The Bonneau plantation was three thousand acres, with over a thousand cultivated acres of cotton and tobacco…worked by one hundred and twenty slaves.

"Come on down and I'll take you on a field trip up to the site of the old place. It'll be like old times!"

PART IV

BRENDAN

Fleur-de-Lys & Laurelton Plantations
Camden, South Carolina

December 1864

"We are not only fighting hostile armies but a hostile
people, and must make old and young, rich and poor,
feel the hard hand of war."

General William Tecumseh Sherman
Letter to General Henry Halleck,
December 24, 1864

Chapter Thirteen

Traitor, Roué, and Thief?

"WHO ARE YOU, SIR, and what do you want?"

Brendan recognized his father's old Kentucky flintlock before he realized the woman holding it was his mother.

Barring the door against him, perhaps even a slap or two he had expected, but to be met by his mother on the front step of their home with a gun in her hand was well beyond her usual display of temper. It did not help him to know she was an excellent shot. It did, however, help to know that in her current state, she may not have considered the ineffectiveness of damp powder. The dim light exaggerated her tired eyes, the pallor of her skin and the silver streaks in her once dark hair.

"Hello, Mother," he said, easing himself off Jumper and taking off his hat, "I've come home to help you."

Her eyes flashed recognition and narrowed but continued to regard him with no lessening of suspicion, the heavy pistol still poised to fire.

"I've come home to help you," he repeated, more gently, keeping his eyes on her while tying Jumper tight to the hitching post in the unlikely event the gun went off. He stepped once towards her, slowly raising his hands. "Please, Mother, put down the gun."

He wondered how long this standoff could go on as the rain ran in rivulets down his back. If he had to physically disarm her or leave the premises, which would he choose?

"Leah? Where are you, honey?" Brendan heard a weary voice from inside the house and saw a figure pass by the window of his father's study. When his Aunt Sarah saw the tableau in the front yard, he saw her move quickly towards the door.

"Brendan! God in heaven, what a Christmas present!" Sarah cried out even before rushing from the doorway to fold him in her arms. "Oh, Leah! Look who's come home!"

When he saw that his mother had not moved, Brendan withdrew from his aunt's embrace and moved her gently out of range. How long could his mother hold up that heavy pistol?

"Leah! It's Brendan! Can't you see it's your son?" Sarah scolded, hands on her hips, reminding him more of Mayah than the dignified, soft-spoken woman he remembered. "Oh, for goodness sakes! Put down that gun right now!"

Leah slowly lowered the gun, keeping her pale blue eyes fixed on him. "A son gone to forfeit," she said, "and lost to me." Leah turned and walked into the house, shoulders slumped, now holding the gun loosely at her side.

Once the door had closed between them, Sarah turned back to him. "I am so sorry, my dear. What a welcome!" She reached out and hugged him again. "You poor thing, you're soaked through! Come inside—"

"I'll take Jumper to the barn," he said, putting on his hat once again, and turning to unhitch the horse, but looking back, "Aunt Sarah? Is Mother...?"

"She is much as she has always been, my dear, intractable and insensible to any but her own opinions or feelings. I'm afraid she's just gotten worse since, well... since ..." Sarah paused, searching Brendan's face.

"I know," he said, turning to lead the horse away. "I saw Gabe and Jenny in town."

Sarah watched him from the shelter of the doorway. "Come into the kitchen when you've done, honey, it's warm and dry."

In the kitchen? One of his favorite places while growing up, but Brendan could not remember a time when he had seen Leah near the old brick structure behind the house.

As he slogged his way through the muddy path towards the barn, it heightened his sense of desolation not to have two or three young boys laughing and running out to stable his horse, wanting desperately to see one part of his old life that remained unchanged.

STEPPING INTO THE DETACHED kitchen, he remembered Mayah's beaming smile, spoiling both he and Gabe with thick slices of freshly baked bread slathered with butter or an afternoon sample of the evening dessert. Now all but one of the large plank tables were gone, replaced by two cots and furniture from the main house.

But it was warm and dry as Aunt Sarah promised, and Brendan brewed a pot of coffee on one burner of the big cast iron range as Sarah set out two of their fleur-de-lys emblazoned teacups and saucers and told him about leaving Wilmington. The streets were unsafe at all hours, and any goods to be had were priced so only the suspiciously wealthy or *blockade runners* she added with a wink, could afford them.

"Well," he added, pulling open his saddlebags with a smile, "one of the advantages of being a *blockade runner* is that I have at least brought a few rather scarce necessities."

"Oh, honey, I was happy with just the idea of real coffee! Gabe brought over a nice striped bass last week, but other than that it has been so long since we've had much of anything besides dried pork, cornmeal, and old carrots. Anything new will surely be welcome."

As they talked, Sarah chopped up the vegetables and ham and soon had it simmering in a large stewpot on the cast iron stove.

"Old Lambert was selling out and leaving town, so I had him load up the Hall's wagon with supplies; Gabe will bring some over tomorrow."

"I do miss those two," she said, shaking her head, "but the more I tried to reason with Leah, the more resolute she was about sending poor Jenny away. So, I spend most of my time here now," said Sarah, nodding towards the two chairs drawn up to the fire, a book lying open on the table between them. "No sense in lighting fires all over the house, with only the two of us."

"Mother...?"

"Yes, I *did* have some trouble convincing your mother," she admitted.

The kitchen was more familiar now, filled with comforting aromas while his coat steamed dry on a hook near the fire. His aunt's newfound abilities in the kitchen were at odds with his memories, though she appeared the same, with her long gray hair braided and pinned high on her head like a crown, an ivory cameo embellishing her old, wool dress.

After stirring in some dried sage, Sarah glanced up at him and laughed at his expression, seeming to read his mind. "If anyone had told me a few years ago I would be making decisions, not to mention supper, for your mother...but I simply agree with all she says and then do as I think best. She passes the time in her room or your father's study," she added, "even on cold, damp days like this, I'm afraid."

"I saw Wilson Hall in Wilmington last spring," said Brendan, as they sat down in the two parlor chairs drawn close to the fire. "He said Lainey, Sid and Ben were all here, as well as some of the hands, and there was still plenty of food. What happened?"

Before answering Sarah paused to sip the steaming coffee. "Oh, honey, you don't know how good that tastes!" she said, breathing in the aroma and holding her feet towards the fire. "Just after I moved down, early in the summer soon after Charles was brought home, the army sent requisition teams for supplies. After that, well, there wasn't much left, but we've managed.

"During the summer, we helped Lainey move over to Spartanburg. Your father finally found where her three children had been sold off to before she came here. Before he passed, he encouraged her to go to them. She works for your Uncle Kendrick now. But the hissy fit your mother had, let me tell you! I said, 'Leah, Lainey is a free woman now, she can do as she pleases', and... well, I don't mean to repeat what she said! Sid and Ben and the others had to leave with the impressment teams—"

"All of them? I understood there were always some hands left behind to help."

"All. It certainly brought any productive work on the place to a standstill and…" Sarah's voice faltered, and she stood up, went to the stove and stirred the stew, "…and they were all so sad to go. It was wrenching.

"Still, I'm not sure how long the men will stay, no matter what the penalty."

"Why do you say that, Aunt Sarah?" Brendan asked absently, holding a candle higher, looking into the depths of his bags for the other items he had brought, and jumped when Sarah stamped her foot on the floor.

"Well, why in God's name should they keep slaving for the Confederacy? It was their loyalty to Charles—and his to them—that kept them on Fleur-de-Lys. There were still about thirty here when the impressment team came. Came back, I should say. A Captain Lyles was in charge and had been in the area once before, Gabe said, and taken over a hundred of the men."

"Lyles? Of all the …. With the impressment team?"

"Edgar and Hannah said the Lyles were one of the families most set against your father's reformation schemes." Sarah covered the stewpot, moved it from the highest heat and sat down with him again. "All I know is that he sure seemed to take pleasure in his task. It doesn't make any sense since we could have kept Fleur-de-lys working hard to supply food and cotton."

"But the children…little Ruby, and Ezra…and—"

"Taken with their mothers, most of them to work in mills, or so the good captain said. Turns out most of them are at some of the other local plantations now.

"Did he try to take Gabe?" he asked sharply.

She raised her eyebrows at his tone. In the old days, she might have scolded but now only shook her head. "No, but he did ask, and I was surprised to hear him ask for Gabe by name. That arrogant little whelp laughed when I questioned his authority!"

"Sounds like him. Where was Gabe?"

"Gabe and Jenny were still living here at the time, of course, but Jenny was over helping Hannah and Delphine put up a batch of peaches. Gabe saw them coming and went up the old oak tree, the one right near the house. And I have to tell you, I was mightily impressed with how fast such a big man could move! Grateful, as well. I do *not* know what we would do without him."

"The Lyles have had it in for Father, Edgar Hall, and Josiah Barkley because they argued for emancipation. I'm sure it gave him no end of pleasure to take anyone he could."

"If the laws of this state had allowed planters to free slaves, Fleur-de-Lys might still be a working plantation and survive, no matter what the end result of this war."

"That still wouldn't have stopped men like Lyles and the impressment teams. It was the lawmakers, for the most part, most of them big plantation owners with the most to lose. They didn't want change and didn't want anyone to have a chance for success. Father was too polite in his arguments. He should have berated them for the cruel, conscienceless bastards they truly were."

She gave him another sharp glance but had a twinkle in her eye. Brendan was silent, thinking about the arguments ensuing in the household in the years before the war, Father arguing about the merits of emancipation, mother adamantly opposed and always having the final word in any discussion. Brendan remembered his father's good humor, shrugging off Mother's venom with the words, "And that brings this meeting of the Fleur-de-Lys planter's council to a close."

"What exactly did happen with Gabe and Jenny?" Brendan asked.

"Let us just say your mother 'emancipated' Jenny rather abruptly one day. Jenny said no to some outlandish housekeeping chore and in front of Gabe and me, no less! It didn't matter that Lilién and the United States government had already freed her, mind you. I didn't blame Jenny for talking back and I tried smoothing things over. But, your mother would not relent, and so I wrote a letter and sent them over to the Hall's."

"Why did Gabe leave with her? How have you managed?"

Sarah looked dumbfounded.

"Honey, I thought you knew—Gabe and Jenny are married! Both Gabe and Delphine, and even Edgar come over to help us. Gabe brings whatever he can when he goes hunting and fishing, but it seems even the wild things have gone into hiding lately. He is doing the work of two men, well, more like four or five, bless him, looking after all of us.

"I do hope we can reintroduce them here in the springtime, though, let them have the overseer's place. Your mother's displeasure will fade by then, I should think."

"Like it did with me?" he asked, meaning to smile but one did not rise to his lips.

She reached over to pat his arm. "Honey, your mother lives in the past, mostly, which is probably for the best. The times she is truly aware of our circumstances she can only mourn what she has lost."

Lost, Brendan thought, staring into the fire. What has not been lost? Louis Charles and Father dead, Lilién might as well be, and she will always look on me as a traitor.

Their home, too, would be lost. He knew with certainty the house would at the very least be badly damaged and looted. Far more likely, it would be burned to the ground.

"I want to move you and Mother to a safe place."

"I know our situation is a bit uncomfortable, but we're safe enough, aren't we?"

Brendan stood up and added more wood to the fire. "Sherman's troops are marching north from Savannah soon. Some say very soon and right through Columbia on their way to Richmond."

"Oh," said Sarah quietly. "I see. Isolated as we are, we have not heard much of Sherman since just after he left Atlanta."

"Well, he's had a busy six weeks and the residents of Georgia will always remember his visit. Would she consider going to Uncle Armand?"

"Honey, I never know if she'll consider coming down for supper, but I always try!" laughed Sarah, starting for the kitchen door.

"No," said Brendan. "I'll go."

Sarah hesitated before nodding. "You will likely find her in your father's study."

The heat from the fire dissolved as soon as he walked out of the kitchen.

He shivered in the cold dampness of the dark hallway recalling a dismal autumn afternoon when he was ten, and he and Gabe, Wilson and Jems had crept inside the family mausoleum on the old Robinson plantation. The sight of cobweb-draped coffins, the deep chill and a rank smell permeating the air had sent them all running for home.

He paused at the door to the study and then walked in slowly, thick carpet silencing his footsteps. Leah leaned against the window as she sat on the cushioned bench beneath, staring absently at a handful of letters in the gray light. Sensing his presence, she looked up, all of the anger and coldness she had greeted him with earlier still in her eyes.

WHEN HE HAD FINISHED explaining the threat to her, he paused, waiting for a response but his mother continued to look at him as though waiting for him to finish an amusing story.

"Mother, do you understand?" he asked gently

"Leah," Sarah interjected when Leah's eyes flashed, a warning most of them had learned not to ignore. "It would be wise to move before Sherman's army marches north."

"Sherman's army is not on his way north, Sarah." Leah ignored Brendan as though he had not spoken. "That gentleman, Mister Sparks, said Sherman is in Georgia and we had nothing to fear."

"That was many weeks ago, Leah, and Mister Sparks may not have been privileged to the same information as Brendan. More likely," Sarah added in a whisper to Brendan, "he wanted to return and help himself to more of the family silver."

"I'd like to help you both move over to Uncle Armand's for the duration of the war, Mother. It can't be long now—'

"Ungrateful wretch!" Distracted from her anger at Brendan by her anger at her brother, Leah finally addressed Brendan directly. "Do you know he has never once apologized for—"

"Mother!" he snapped at her, unwilling to listen again to her skewed recollection of 'the insult' which they heard about whenever her brother's name was mentioned. A misunderstanding which his uncle had indeed repeatedly apologized for, to no avail. "This is war and Spartanburg is out of the line of fire. You would both be much safer!"

She did not respond, only glared at him and he knew if she lived through the war, his would be the next oft-repeated story of umbrage and indignation.

"What about Wilmington—"

"Wilmington?" Sarah shook her head emphatically. "No, thank you! I would rather take my chances here than on the sorry streets of Wilmington."

"Just to stay at your place until *Kendal* is ready to sail—"

"You are *not* going back!"

Aunt Sarah had obviously spent too much time with his mother, but Brendan knew that hidden behind the command was fear. Despite her bravado of cooking stews and tending fires, she was frightened.

"War's not over yet," he said, with a shrug, "the *Kendal* might belong to a private owner, but a crew can't just abandon ship whenever they might like."

Sarah did not respond but gave him a look before standing up to tend to the fire.

"No, I don't mean for you to live in Wilmington but to come back with me to St. George's on our next voyage. We often take passengers and you could stay with friends of mine and be comfortable and safe until the end of the war."

"Oh, honey, you must be teasing!" Sarah laughed at the notion but had the old twinkle in her eye. "Listen to that, Leah! You and me on a blockade runner!"

"Bermuda?" Leah said. In the bright light from one of the new candles Brendan had brought, she looked at him as though he suggested she fly to the moon. The argument wore on through the evening. Leah adamantly refusing to leave, no matter what the threat, no matter what options were suggested.

"Mother, you do not understand!" Brendan finally shouted, slamming down his fist, causing Sarah to jump and making the dishes rattle on the old oak worktable. "You have heard what happened in Georgia. The same, possibly worse, will happen here!"

"You will not raise your voice to me, young man, no matter what tone you may take with your shipboard white trash." Leah gazed at him impassively. "Expect me to take passage to some tiny island and be subjected to all manner of indignity? You must be crazy to believe I would even consider it, or think *I* am crazy."

"Indignity…?" His mother's face appeared mildly perturbed, as it had been when she scolded him when he was a child. How could he tell her of the indignity he feared for her and for his maiden aunt? Brendan could only look back at her, unable to voice his worst fears.

Details in her face blurred, and colors faded to black and white before his eyes finally closed. A comforting warmth radiated through the thin fabric of his shirt and warmed his shoulder. He opened his eyes to see Sarah standing over him, her hand gentle on his back.

"Come upstairs now, honey. You are tired out and there's nothing more you can do tonight," she said quietly, holding out his now warm, dry coat to him as Leah continued to sip tea from the delicate china cup.

"Don't you worry," said Sarah, leading the way with a candle in a silver holder, raising it high and making the shadows dance on their way up the long staircase. "We'll make her see the sense of leaving. Right now, honey, you need to sleep."

Brendan expected a cold, dark night huddled under a pile of quilts, but opening the door to his old room, golden light and warmth from a fire burning on the grate welcomed him.

"When you and Leah were having supper," Sarah explained at his look of surprise as she lit a candle on the nightstand.

"You didn't need to go to all the troub —"

She actually pushed him, though gently, into the wing chair nearest the fire. Gesturing for him to hold up a foot she pulled off his boots and peeled off the wet socks, setting them along the hearthstone to dry, clucking and fussing at him, "Oh my dear, your poor feet! I should have made you take off these boots when you first arrived!"

He began to tell her that dry feet were much more common to ducks than sailors, but the teasing caught in his throat, remembering the last time someone fussed over him was dear old Mayah, right here in this room almost four years ago.

"I'll stay," he said finally, yawning and rubbing his aching eyes. "If she won't listen to reason and leave, I'll stay until the danger is past."

"I *am* sorry I spoke to you so crossly," she paused in her business, resting her warm hands on his cold, clammy feet. "I know you have your duties to attend to, and as much as I would love to have you home, Brendan, you cannot expect to protect Fleur-de-Lys from Sherman's legions. Your life is more important than any house, even Fleur-de-Lys.

"And we both know if they want to burn it, it will burn!" Finished with his feet, and now filling a warming pan, the copper pan rattled and sparks flew as she dropped in coal after coal. "As distressing as that is, it is no more than so many other Southerners have had to live through."

He watched her in silence as she slipped the pan between the sheets, swiping it vigorously across the length and width of his bed.

Again, he wanted to tell her not to go to such trouble for him.

"Thank you," he said, instead, as she set the warming pan beside the hearth.

"You are entirely welcome, my dear. Now, I shall leave you to get some sleep and talk with your mother again. About the hard, cold facts you could not bring yourself to say."

"But... Aunt Sarah..." Brendan paused, wanting to spare her any embarrassment.

"Goodnight, Brendan."

THE ROOM WAS FROZEN in time, unchanged since the night he had left so hurriedly.

In the painting over the mantle, the black hull of the clipper ship was invisible and only the highlighted crests of the waves, wind-filled sails and white stripes in the United States flag were visible in the gloom. He was surprised his mother hadn't destroyed the painting and had his room emptied as soon as he had left the house.

Feathery cobwebs draped from high on the dark chandelier above him to the masts of his models of the *USS Constitution* and *Stag Hound* still on the mantle. Gold lettering along the spines of Melville, Scott, and Cooper glinted from the far corner bookshelf. He wondered whether the miniature sea chest was under the bed where he had left it, with its hidden bits of nautical memorabilia collected by the boy who dreamed of being a sailor since he could remember. Now silent, the comfortingly familiar tick of the old carriage clock had been the background to studying, working on his ship models, or whispered nonsense when Wilson, Jems or both would spend the night, which was often in those years before they left for school.

Numb with fatigue though he was, pulling on the thick flannel nightshirt Aunt Sarah had hung near the fire warmed his body and his heart, comforting, though still a poor substitute for one of Mayah's hugs.

Brendan had been frequently banished to his room without supper by his mother, often without a clear understanding of his infraction. Just as the pendulum had swung from angry rebellion to hungry repentance, Mayah would appear with a plate of thick toasted and buttered bread and a frothy glass of milk. Whether these respites were approved by either parent he never knew, but she understood the lesson had been learned and only resentment would be fueled by a night of hunger and neglect.

As sustaining as his aunt's stew had been, he would have given a year's wages in gold to see Mayah with her beaming smile and a tray in her hands.

EARLY THE NEXT MORNING, Edgar Hall sat in the kitchen while Brendan ate a breakfast of ham and cornbread and invited Leah and Sarah to live at Laurelton for the duration of the war.

"We're smaller and well off the road," said Edgar, sitting on the rough bench near the fire, his cold hands wrapped around the warm porcelain cup. "If we tear up the road and pull over some of the dead trees, hell, they might not even know we're there at all!"

As he talked, Brendan looked out of the long windows of the kitchen at the wispy feathers of low clouds entwined through the tops of the pines beyond the northern edge of the kitchen gardens. It was true, Brendan thought, conscious of his mothers' eyes on him, Laurelton Plantation was perhaps remote enough and small enough to avoid attention. With rich bounty like Fleur-de-Lys, Mulberry, and Cardinal Heights closer to hand, raiding parties might not strike out far from the main roads on their way north.

"And we'll be together, Leah," Edgar continued. "Hannah and Amelia would love to have you visit. I'm just sorry we didn't think of it sooner."

"Thank you, Edgar," said Sarah, not waiting for Leah to answer. "I do admit it has been a bit lonely here by ourselves. What do you think, Leah, wouldn't it be just like old times?"

"I believe I made myself quite clear last night," she said, nodding politely, as though acknowledging the remark of a stranger, and stood up. "If you will excuse me, I must leave you to write some letters…"

"Well now that's a shame, Leah," said Edgar, stopping her from leaving the kitchen with a gentle hand to her arm, adding, "Before you came into the kitchen, I was telling Sarah how much we hoped you would consider joining the rest of our company at Laurelton for a short Christmas visit."

Leah paused at the open door, the silence broken only by the softly falling rain and the cheerful call of a chickadee from the holly bush beside the kitchen.

"I do beg your pardon for our late invitation…"

Brendan and Sarah's eyes met, both recognizing Edgar's new strategy at once.

Before the war, socializing with other planters and notable citizens throughout the state had been a duty she performed with such zeal Brendan had once been wrested from his sickbed prematurely, so he would not miss the chance to meet several distinguished guests at a gathering in Columbia.

"Edgar," said Sarah, casually reaching for the teapot to refill their cups, "did you mention the Chesnuts from Mulberry have been invited as well? In all my visits I have never made their acquaintance and I should so like to."

Leah's stern features immediately relaxed into a smile. "Why Edgar, that would be lovely. It has been some time since we have socialized with anyone in the county, hasn't it, Sarah?"

"Indeed, it has, Leah. Thank you, Edgar, we accept."

BORED TO TEARS WITH the isolation, young Amelia Hall, now a tall, pretty sixteen-year-old, was thrilled with the arrival of guests for the holidays. She was also as infatuated with Brendan as she ever was, and followed him through the house, eagerly asking questions about life on a blockade runner. She tied boughs of pine and holly to stair rails and banisters, strategically placed sprigs of mistletoe, and sighed enviously at Delphine's little Muriel, the six-year-old giggling delightedly when Brendan picked her up and twirled her around or pretended to gobble up her plump little cheeks.

Even Leah, who appeared to have forgotten about other guests that never arrived, relaxed and enjoyed herself. She visited with Edgar and Hannah in the parlor while Delphine and Jenny cooked, and Gabe and Brendan moved furniture around to accommodate the guests. Aunt Sarah, visibly relieved to be removed from the lonely isolation of Fleur-de-Lys, was content to sit and watch the activity.

At dinner, Leah only raised an eyebrow at Gabe and Jenny seated at a small separate table just inside the dining room, near Brendan's place at the main table. With Hannah's blessing, Brendan had moved in the table from the parlor.

Delphine, laughing, had waved her hand at him when he asked her and little Muriel to join them. "Bless you, Mister Brendan, but I haven't cooked this much in an age. Baby's goin' to bed and this ole body's jes goin' to the kitchen to give her feet a hot mustard soak!"

"But Mister Brendan! Miz Leah will surely have a fit and leave the room!" Jenny had stopped in her tracks with a large, steaming bowl of gravy.

"Well then, she will miss our very special dinner, won't she?" He took dishes from the cupboard and set their places himself.

Jenny sputtered her refusals on her way back into the kitchen until Brendan took her hands in his. "You do know you are family now, don't you?"

She nodded shyly, glancing at Gabe.

"The president has not only freed you, our hostess has invited you and Gabe to join us for Christmas dinner. I am not having my family, any of my family, eating in the kitchen the one day I am home. Understood?"

An air of festivity prevailed as they feasted on the pork roast and onions, freshly baked bread and Jenny's sweet potato pie, food none of them save Brendan had enjoyed in any quantity in months. Talk of old times dominated, the war and what would happen after, ignored.

"How is Miss Arabella?" Brendan asked as Jenny served Hannah's homemade raspberry cordial after supper. "If she is over at the Heights, I'd like to call on her tomorrow if—"

He stopped as the room went quiet.

"And who is Miss Arabella?" Sarah asked, not

understanding the hush any more than Brendan.

"The little sister of an old friend and I have something of his I'd like to give her," he said.

Hannah was now visibly troubled but silent.

"What is it?"

The silence deepened. When Brendan saw Hannah blink back tears, the evening's warmth seemed to drain from him, his fingers gripping the stem of the delicate crystal glass cold.

"She's not—"

Hannah shook her head "No, but …"

Edgar cleared his throat. "You know, son, it's been a while since I've had the chance to have a cigar with someone. While Gabe brings in the tree, let's leave the ladies to their cordial and step into my study."

"*WHAT?*"

Brendan felt as though the old gentleman had delivered a swift punch to his gut.

"Wilson heard it from Miles Barber. Miles said he saw her himself—he did *not* admit to anything else," Edgar smiled grimly and went on, "only that it was some brothel in Wilmington."

"How did she get from living with a maiden aunt up in Richmond…to …that?" Brendan asked, still winded, thinking of how she had looked up at him as they danced the waltz at Cardinal Height's annual harvest ball soon after he and Jems had returned from their first voyage on the *Dolphin*. Her shimmery blue dress was the exact sapphire shade of her eyes, candlelight from the chandeliers above highlighting her long auburn curls. Laughing and teasing but not allowing him to steal a kiss out on the veranda after the dance.

Their only kiss was a week later, in the warm autumn twilight on the porch of Cardinal Heights, the night before he and Jems left on their yearlong assignment on the *Dolphin*. Being a good friend, Jems had stepped away, though not far since he was also a good brother.

Demure in a white cotton dress sprigged with tiny blue flowers, she stood two steps above him, so they were close and at eye level with one another. Brendan gave Arabella a gift he had been carrying around for some weeks.

"Reminded me of your eyes, Bella," he whispered.

Delighted, she slipped the little star sapphire ring onto her right hand without hesitation and smiled up at him with ... love. He did not remember how it had happened, but the next thing he knew her lips were on his and his arms were around her and altogether too soon Jems was whistling a tune in the front hallway in warning.

Edgar's next words finally penetrated.

"Well, there are some who believe that she went up there to await the birth of a child."

"My God." Brendan sat down suddenly. "She had a child?"

Edgar shrugged. "Not really sure if there was ever anything to it but mean-spirited gossip by some of the jealous old cats around here—you know how some of them talked about the little minx. But after Josiah died, with Jems in the Navy, there was no one else but the manager over at the Heights. She couldn't stay there alone, after all."

"Poor girl," he whispered, draining the brandy Edgar had offered him. The cigar smoke and heat from the fire now oppressive, Edgar nodded kindly as he excused himself to step outside.

SOUNDS OF LAUGHTER AND Christmas carols brought him back in from the cold. He knew his time with these people was precious. Time enough to worry about Arabella on his way back to Wilmington; he just hoped he would have time enough to find her, to help her, somehow.

Gabe brought in a small pine tree to decorate. As he was leaving the room, they were all surprised to hear Leah's voice.

"Gabriel?"

"Ma'am?"

"Bless us with Silent Night," she asked, somewhere between her usual command and a plaintive request. "Charles so loved to hear you sing Silent Night."

"Yes, ma'am," Gabe's deep voice softened.

Not imitating anyone now and with no need for accompaniment, Gabe sang the hymn in his rich baritone. Even Delphine got back on her tired feet and ventured in to listen.

As he finished the last verse and the word peace lingered in their minds, everyone in the house was reaching for handkerchiefs. Gabe smiled and bowed shyly at the applause before escaping.

GRATEFUL AT HANNAH'S INSISTENCE he stay the night, Brendan was stretched out on the comfortable old sofa in the parlor. Candles were out, and the room dark except for the firelight that set the crystal and silver ornaments on the tree to sparkling.

Laurelton, already significantly smaller than Fleur-de-Lys, had a leaky roof that put their two guest rooms out of commission until Edgar and Gabe could make repairs, and left Wilson's bedroom to Aunt Sarah and his mother. He glanced around the parlor, remembering chess matches most often lost to Wilson, and the wrestling matches he most often won… and most often resulting in broken trinkets and vigorous scoldings from Hannah.

Little Amelia had always been somewhere near, too, like tonight. His eyes rested on the shadow of mistletoe in the doorframe, his heart still touched by the evidence of her enduring infatuation. An infatuation only intensified by his absence, not to mention the denial of friends and social interaction for far too long. Trying to steer him towards the mistletoe, each time, to the amusement of the others, he would be led almost near enough, only to turn around, step aside or back away, while pretending never to notice the bundle of greenery above them.

Until she maneuvered him towards the doorway once

more after Hannah announced the last carol, and he finally feigned surprise and chivalrous delight at finding himself so placed. So sweet, he thought, smiling, remembering her tightly puckered lips in a face that was much too similar to Wilson's, although he would never admit that thought crossing his mind at such a moment, especially not to Wilson.

Tomorrow he would find the Fleur-de-Lys documents and prepare his will. Impossible to know what might happen in the coming months, setting his own affairs in order before going back to the ship was now of prime importance. While he wanted to provide for Lilién, he could not risk leaving their home and his mother's livelihood in the hands of Edward Cherrington.

He knew also, any discussion about safeguarding some of the more precious possessions and documents would need to be broached cautiously with his mother, not wanting to risk upsetting her into moving back home prematurely. This social visit had to extend at least until the danger from the approaching Union forces had passed.

Comfortable as he was, it pained him to know that Fleur-de-Lys was completely empty and alone for the first time in its existence, left vulnerable.

Pretty Arabella, too, was also alone and even more vulnerable. Mistreatment at the hands of her conquerors would be without the justification of being spoils of war but she was every bit as much a victim of the war as her brother.

It was Jems who had called him a prude when he had declined to go into a Kingston brothel when the Dolphin had put in for supplies a month into their first mission. For days afterwards, he suffered through his crewmember's descriptive tales of all he had missed, mentally wavering between regretting his decision and gratitude for his prudishness.

Not prudish, he thought. Prudent. And influenced by two early experiences that had determined his moral code much more effectively than a lengthy, dogmatic catechism.

He had been on his own with Louis Charles in Charleston, who promised his sixteen-year-old brother a night on the town full of surprises. As they walked down a narrow lane, Brendan remembered how curious it was that the windows in one of the houses were covered in crimson draperies, the light behind them casting a soft red glow into the darkness of Beresford Street. Louis had walked into a big, brick building as though he owned it, and within moments and without a backward glance to his little brother, walked up a wide, thickly carpeted stairway, laughing with a bold, voluptuous woman in a revealing dress of emerald green satin.

Brendan, trembling near the door and slowly waking to the nature of the surprise, was appraised by four other women still seated in the parlor, who whispered and giggled as he politely drew off his hat. The hostess nodded to a girl who sat quietly to one side, brown hair drawn up into a knot, wearing a floaty, pale gown that reminded him of the wispy pink clouds at dawn. Before he knew what to think, she had his arm and was guiding him towards the same stairway where he had last seen Louis, looking up and smiling sweetly, saying words he was not quite able to comprehend.

The small room to which she led him was just big enough for the large bed and a table that held a crystal decanter and two glasses. Phoebe was young and demure enough not to frighten him, experienced enough to reassure and instruct. After two, rapidly consumed glasses of wine and several deep kisses, he was a willing student.

Never sure how many hours later, he followed a servant downstairs, slightly dizzy, weak-kneed and in love. As he followed Louis out of the establishment, he glanced around in the hopes of seeing Phoebe, who had disappeared from the tiny bedroom during his prolonged state of oblivion. She was now the only girl in the parlor, lips rouged and every hair in place, and wearing a lavender gown every bit as enticing as the pink. Brendan saw the madam nod towards her, and not acknowledging his presence, Phoebe went and took the arm of a beefy old fellow with a hearty laugh and big hands.

The next instant Brendan was outside puking in the gutter and Louis had laughed at him all the way back to their hotel.

Not long after returning home, Charles realized his younger son was laboring under the weight of a very guilty conscience. During a long walk on the plantation, his father adroitly approached the topics of human nature and a young man's natural urges, following deftly with an admonition about his obligations to control those urges and honor the weaker sex.

"What if they do not honor themselves, sir?" he had asked, echoing Louis's justification the one time he had tried to talk to his brother about the experience, immediately cringing inside at the disappointment which had crossed his father's face.

Charles had frowned and shaken his head. "Son, your conscience is troubling you because you *know* your obligation is to care for and protect those who are weak and helpless, not to take advantage of that vulnerability in any way."

Charles ended the talk as they neared the house with practical counsel about the risks involved in engaging in such behavior and frequenting such establishments, which Brendan swore fervently never to do again.

After a big one-armed hug, Charles walked away, reminding Brendan over his shoulder that Father Fortiér was visiting and would be available for confession before Mass the next morning. Brendan groaned, certain he heard his father chuckle as he walked up the path towards the house.

"BRENDAN?"

The soft whisper did not belong to the shimmery pink vision or the searing, intense memory of Phoebe's whispered encouragements, her body beneath his, her legs around him, slowly taking him in…

"Brendan?" the whisper repeated with some urgency, a small, warm hand shaking him. "Kiss me again. Please?"

As her lips touched his, his arms went around her, pulling her on top of him, crushing her to him. While his tongue explored her sweet mouth, his hands explored her body and tugged at the delicate drapery of her dress.

The sound of tearing fabric, followed by a small shriek

and thump on the floor beside him had the effect of a pitcher of ice-cold water, banishing both the dream and his physical reaction to it. He opened his eyes to see the firelit parlor of Laurelton, and little Amelia sobbing against his shoulder.

"What...? *Amelia*? What are you doing?"

"I just wanted another kiss. A *real* kiss! What were *you* doing?"

"*Oh, God!*" He sat up abruptly, pulling away from her. "I'm sorry, so sorry. I didn't realize it was you... I was dreaming... I think..."

The more he apologized, the more she sobbed and given the circumstances, it seemed the height of boorishness to tell her not to cry.

"Miss Amelia, *please* do not rouse the house," he beseeched, peering through the long veil of her light blonde hair she endeavored to hide behind. "It would be most distressing for all concerned to end my visit with your father switching me all the way back to Fleur-de-Lys."

She peeped back, meeting his mischievous eyes, and a hiccup that might have been a giggle slowed and quieted her crying.

"I am so sorry, *please* forgive me!"

"I *do* forgive you," she insisted, lifting her head and looking at him with a timid sort of defiance, "but ...I ...just..."

During the long pause where he feared more sobs were in the offing, he watched her delicate profile in the firelight. He reached out and gently touched her cheek.

"Just what, dear?"

She gave a deep, shaking sigh. "...I *really* liked it."

Laughing, he resisted the urge to kiss her again, fearing it might very well seal their betrothal.

He gently tousled her curls instead. "Amelia?"

"Hmm?"

"Go back to bed."

Brendan waited until the golden circle of light from her candle faded away and the top step creaked, as it always had as long as he could remember. Once he heard the door to her room close softly, he fell back on the pillow, covered his face with his hands and swore.

IN WILMINGTON, A YOUNG WOMAN sat on a dais at the center of a large room in the glow of several lamps, reading to a large assembly. Men sat or reclined on an assortment of chairs, rough wooden benches, camp cots and steel beds, even one rather battered velveteen-covered chaise lounge, a throne of sorts commandeered for the young Shelby King. The few women were dressed in their best for Christmas Eve and listened to the story but remained vigilant and ready to cater to the unpredictable needs of the men.

Even while reading, Arabella wondered about the men gathered around. The audience was an odd mix that, before the war, would never have shared an evening's entertainment together. Tonight, she looked up from the page and her glance took in the weary faces of old warriors, baby-faced boys, war-hardened men of every age in between, all gazing at her with rapt attention waiting for the next sentence of the story.

For each character, she used a different tone or accent, but for the narrative, she relaxed into her own voice, which, she was told, was a pleasure to hear because she could be sassy, sultry, or soothing.

"And which was it tonight, Captain?" she had asked the handsome Virginian cavalry officer who had made the observation early one evening.

"Just depends on who you were talkin' to and what you were sayin', ma'am," he had said with a wink, before putting on his hat and striding out into the night.

Lucas Kershaw had told her outright that he liked to watch and listen to her read so he could imagine ... other things. She answered him as boldly, that if he *must* she would rather not know about it, thank you very much. But now, Lucas, when she glanced towards the back of the room, was leaning against one of the support columns, and smiled that slow smile of his that let her know exactly what he was thinking.

Let him think whatever he wanted, she thought, trying not to blush and give him even that satisfaction. She had not been able to be there for what he needed most. He was too close, had been her brother's friend and used to pull her braids when she was little. There were other women here who could tend to him.

Others she could help, and would, because somewhere Brendan may need kindness and tenderness. If it could not be her, let it be another.

She turned to the last page.

> *Scrooge was better than his word. He did it all, and infinitely more; and to Tiny Tim, who did not die, he was a second father. He became as good a friend, as good a master, and as good a man, as the good old city knew, or any other good old city, town, or borough, in the good old world. ...*

The good old world for most of these men was gone. Arabella glanced up from the page at the general, who had lost his wife to illness at the end of the first year of the war, his son in the battle of Chancellorsville one year later, and finally, his home in Atlanta only weeks before. He listened with his head back on the padded wing of the old chair, his eyes closed and the lantern light revealing tears streaming down his face. Was he remembering Christmases past, or anticipating the bleakness and emptiness of those yet to come.

She looked down at the book once again, willing the knot of pain in her throat to ease as she continued on through the final few lines, until finishing the story in her most soothing voice,

> *May that be truly said of us, and all of us! And so, as Tiny Tim observed, God Bless Us, Every One!*

Before standing to accept the cheers and applause from her audience, Arabella kissed the sapphire on her ring and whispered, "May God bless and keep you, Brendan."

ALTHOUGH HANNAH INVITED HIM to stay again at Laurelton, he politely declined, truthfully explaining he wanted to spend his last night at Fleur-de-Lys and not mentioning his desire to avoid another nocturnal visit. He had spent the remainder of the night on guard, more alert than when crossing all three cordons of the blockading squadron into Wilmington during a full moon.

Miss Amelia did not venture downstairs in the morning.

Before leaving for Camden he asked to talk with Edgar privately. Better to tell her father the whole truth to his face and take whatever ire the old man wanted to throw at him, than have Amelia tell anyone half-truths where he would certainly seem, at the very least, like an opportunistic *roué*.

No sooner had the door closed and Brendan standing in front of Edgar Hall trying to formulate the speech to protect Miss Amelia's honor and his own hide, when Edgar succumbed to a fit of laughter so long and so hard it threw him into a prolonged paroxysm of coughing. Brendan stood by helplessly, about to call Hannah when Edgar regained his voice.

"'*Oh God!*'" Edgar emitted a fairly precise imitation of Brendan's panicked exclamation of the night before, despite the laughter still burbling out of him. "God Almighty, son! I meant to make you confess the whole damn story but couldn't hold it back any longer! I been wantin' to let go of that since last night!"

Unable to sleep, he had ventured downstairs to read in his small study near the parlor, Edgar explained between sporadic bouts of laughter. When he heard Brendan moan in his sleep he listened closely, at first with concern followed by alarm, hearing Amelia's urgent whispering, which had soon changed to the squeal and thump to the floor.

Brendan's high color and facial expressions seemed to add to his amusement.

"I never thought to be so pleased to be eavesdropped upon, sir," he said, as they shook hands, relieved beyond measure at the old man's insomnia and sense of humor.

"And I haven't been so entertained since comin' home

from the war!" Edgar continued to chuckle as Brendan walked from the room.

BRENDAN FOUND OLD SEBASTIAN Hiatt, the lawyer his father had always used for legal matters still living in Camden. After completing business, Brendan returned to Fleur-de-Lys.

His mother still clung to the notion she would be returning home after the Christmas holiday and could not be convinced of the prudence of hiding and safeguarding valuables from the deserters and looters from either army. To be fair, he thought, lighting the fire in his bedroom, his mother had not seen the evidence of war many of the others had. She had not left the plantation for almost four years and would not listen to realistic accounts of nor try to imagine what was happening beyond its boundaries. Still, what made it possible, he wondered, to watch your husband die, servants taken, land and house go to seed and disrepair, and yet cling to the notion that war would not touch her?

Like his own bedroom, his father's study was frozen in time, the memories crowding in as he looked at each wall, tabletop and shelf and the reading nook near the fireplace where Charles could often be found. The small tapestry inherited from Grandmère Desjardins still hung on the far wall and the deer browsing in the shaded glen seemed as real to him as always. The sword used by his great-grandfather in the Revolutionary War hung above the mantle.

During his last visit home before the war, his father had shown him where to find the key to the safe and talked about the importance of preserving the deeds in the event their home was threatened. Inside the lower drawer of his father's desk, he found and pulled a lever, which opened a hidden drawer. Inside the narrow space was a small silver key.

Lilién's small painting of Fleur-de-Lys now hung in a special place on the left side of the mantelpiece, the portrait of his mother a dominating presence over the center. He took down the smaller picture, revealing the safe built into the brick wall.

Brendan opened the safe and drew out a handful of documents, some in scrolls and others in soft leather folders, as well as two velvet covered boxes. He searched through the documents, found what he had been searching for and returned the rest to the safe, locking it again.

Putting the picture back into place, he remembered the early spring morning when Lilién had sat on the southern knoll, gazing towards the house, watercolors in hand. He and Wilson had just ridden home from an all-night card game at Cardinal Heights and Lilién couldn't be bothered with either of them, her brow furrowed in concentration, working to capture the house in the soft light. Sitting on the grass in her simple yellow dress, she had resembled one of the nearby daffodils nodding in the breeze.

Even now, in the candlelight, Brendan could see the delicate colors and the fine detail. He felt his chest begin to ache at the memory of those carefree days, warm breezes carrying the rich scent of the freshly plowed and planted fields.

The crystal brandy decanter on his father's desk was nearly full, reminding him to write and tell Gabe to hide anything else remaining in the cellar. He poured himself a glass before leaving the study and held the candle high, the flame guttering in the drafts on his ascent of the long, winding staircase.

He set the brandy and candle on the hall table near Lilién's bedroom. He was not surprised to find the door locked and having no notion as to where to find the household keys, he set his shoulder to the door and pushed.

White sheets shrouded the furniture and as he pulled them away, Brendan could see her room must have been left as it was the night she eloped. Candlelight reflected in the silver-backed mirror where it sat on the dressing table, and on the mother-of-pearl inlays in the old rosewood jewelry box inherited from their Desjardins ancestors. The box stood open, a long gold chain spilling over the side. Had Jenny been too upset to tidy the room these many years? Far more likely, she had been forbidden to touch anything and the door locked forever.

Three steamer trunks were half packed with her newly

purchased trousseau. Lilién had been preparing for her wedding trip with Wilson when their plans had gone so terribly awry. He heard the wind buffeting the house before feeling the draft from the windows and catching a shimmery movement out of the corner of his eye. Holding the candle high, he nearly dropped it when he saw a shadowy figure hovering in the corner.

"Who...?" His voice sounded odd in the cold, empty house, his body broke out in icy sweat. Still, he stepped closer and yanked away the white shroud.

Lilién's wedding dress, the dress she should have worn to marry Wilson, was fitted to a wire dress form and stood next to the tall Cheval mirror.

He remembered the January morning not long before his banishment when he had looked in to say good morning to Lilién as he prepared to ride into Columbia with Wilson. Returning upstairs to retrieve a forgotten item, he had seen that Lilién's door was ajar and peered in to say another goodbye.

The dark red cherry wood around the oval mirror was the perfect frame for the portrait in its reflection. Lilién stood quietly, contemplating the woman she saw, long, dark hair tumbled down her back in a cascade of natural curls, trying on her new pale pink ball gown. The low-cut satin bodice and sleeves edged in lace ruffles gave her a new air of sophistication.

About to turn and leave silently, he had seen her frown slightly and could not contain his laughter when she reached up to tug the bodice higher. "Oh, you!" she had yelled at him, her cheeks red. He moved quickly out of range before her hairbrush flew across the hall and clattered across the shining oak floor.

HIS ROOM, NOW NOTICEABLY warm compared with the damp cold of the house, felt even more like a tiny island in a vast ocean tonight, he thought, adding wood to the fire. He sat in the blue velvet chair drawn close to the hearth, slowly savoring the brandy, watching the flames as his eyes grew heavy and his thoughts wandered, trying to form a plan for the following day.

Even with train delays, he knew he could make it to

Wilmington, but there was no way of knowing if *Kendal* was still in port. Would he have time to find Arabella?

Arabella…He closed his eyes against the heat and brightness, immediately drifting backwards, drawn deep into the comfort and warmth of the chair.

Lilién was smiling up at him as they danced the night of her birthday ball. His father in Virginia, tired, sad, and dignified in his uniform. He and Wilson racing their stallions along the back trails between the two plantations. Darkness aboard the Kendal, the taste of fear in his mouth and salt spray on his lips, the sound of shots fired. His mother's angry eyes above his father's pistol. Jems dead on the deck of the Congress, amidst cannon fire and the smells of blood and smoke. Louis laughing at him on a lamp-lit Charleston street. Amelia's first nervous kiss, her mouth opening under his. The girlish giggle now a moan as his hands moved over the silken length of Phoebe's back. Arabella leaning over him, tears streaming down her face, clutching his hand to her cheek. Soldiers, some in gray, others in blue, holding torches, setting fire to Fleur-de-Lys, destroying his home in fits of savage pleasure. He tried to run from the fire, but he could not escape from the light or shield himself from the searing heat.

He woke with his head throbbing and heart racing when logs shifting on the grate sent out a shower of sparks and the crystal glass slipped from his fingers and shattered on the marble hearthstone. Gasping for air as though he had been running for his life, his mouth was tinder dry and his body drenched in sweat. Several seconds passed before he recognized his surroundings.

Walking unsteadily to the washstand, he poured water into the basin. The pitcher slipped from his hands and hit the table, the delicate china shattering against the gold-veined marble top.

Mother will have my hide for that, he thought, *first a glass and now her pitcher.*

Pushing aside the glass with his sleeve, he splashed his face, hoping the cold water would soothe the searing pain behind his eyes. How stupid, to worry about breaking a pitcher, he thought in wry amusement, a short laugh escaping him at the thought of his mother's angry face, her haughty voice scolding him at the sight of the broken pitcher in the smoldering remains of Fleur-de-Lys. And then he was laughing, soundlessly, uncontrollably until the laughter changed abruptly to body wrenching sobs. Brendan leaned on the washstand, hands holding his head, gasping from the pain and the waves of nausea washing over him.

"God damn it!" he shouted, slamming his fist on the cold marble. Fleur-de-Lys would be the burned-out shell the war had made of their family and there was nothing he could do to prevent it. Grabbing hold with a fierce growl, he hurled the washstand across the room, the porcelain basin shattering, the marble top and oak frame cracking against the far wall.

BY MORNING, HIS DESPAIR of the night before had given way to resignation and determination to protect and preserve something of their family heritage. The memory of his outburst had faded as well, recalled like one of the images from his night of restless dreams.

He paused to say a final goodbye to Fleur-de-Lys.

In the bleak winter sun, the house had a dignified appearance, like a stately old woman with her shoulders squared and head held high. He checked the tarpaulins covering the load on the old wagon once again and turned to Jumper.

"All right, girl, time to go."

PART V

LILLIAN

Annapolis & Easton, Maryland

Knowledge is Power

Lord Francis Bacon
Meditationes Sacrae', 1597

Chapter Fourteen

The Black Diary

"GENEALOGY CENTRAL" IN LILLIAN'S living room consisted of two long folding tables displaying the collection of Bonneau and Cherrington historical documents, which grew more extensive with each box they opened. Tom, now out of the hospital, had chosen to stay with them instead of living aboard *LilyRose*. He wanted to take an active interest, or as he put it, "Now that the damn cat is finally out of the bag, I'm determined to stay at the control end of it!"

The photographs of her father and Brendan hung high on the wall behind the tables to illustrate the reason they were on this mission, like sentries monitoring their progress.

Three large studio portraits of Lilién, one of her alone, seated with the requisite palms and Doric columns, one with her son, young Ernest, and another much later portrait with a man who resembled Wilson Hall, but clearly was not. These also went up on the wall. Lilién Bonneau Cherrington had been a beautiful woman, petite and slender with thick, dark hair most often done up in a mass of ringlets in the fashion of the day.

Lillian made her plans to travel to Columbia and stay with Janet the week following the kids' scheduled sports camps, while Aaron had Miranda and Ryan for a long weekend.

When she told them, both kids immediately whined at not being included.

"I want to go with you," Miranda said matter-of-factly, "I want to help Grandpa, too."

"And I'd love to have you along, but Miranda…"

From her expression, Lillian could see Miranda trying to

mentally work out another justification to go along, to spend time with...her mother. *What the hell am I doing?*

Feigning defeat, she raised her hands and gave a quick nod, "If you really want to—."

"Yes!" yelled Miranda.

Lillian started counting. One thousand one, one thousand two…

"No fair!" protested Ryan, the automatic, inevitable response of all siblings.

"This won't be fun for you, like artifact conservation, and if you want to come along, you'll miss going with your Dad to see the Orioles."

"Never mind!" he said, grinning as she pulled his baseball cap over his eyes.

WITH MIRANDA AT SOCCER camp and Ryan at baseball camp for the week, her father encouraged her to drive to Easton and spend time at the cottage.

The narrow lane, the house, cottage, and cove were all now so familiar, it was difficult to believe her first sight of the place was only a few short weeks ago. Open doors and windows soon had a cool cross-breeze blowing through the cottage and she was pleasantly reminded of how much work they had accomplished, welcomed by open spaces and the arrangement of comfortable old furniture.

At the end of her first afternoon, the kitchen cupboards and shelves were washed and lined, and several empty boxes littered the front yard.

Time capsules, she thought of each box opened during the afternoon. Less revealing of personalities than the diaries and letters, still, the yellow and blue Pyrex mixing bowls and bright, solid color Fiestaware baking dishes were wrapped up in an assortment of hand-painted linens and terrycloth towels, every flower imaginable represented on the old textiles. Which grandmother loved flowers so much? Who was the best baker, she wondered, setting a slightly dented and tarnished tin flour sifter on the window sill.

She had worn gloves for most of the morning work, not wanting to risk another headache. She removed them to sort through the two boxes tucked inside a large cherry wood wardrobe. Only the single notation, in a plainly shaking hand, was written on the top of each box. 'Claire.' These had been packed much earlier than the others, the yellowed tape dry and brittle She propped a photograph of her great-grandmother nearby while she took out each item, held it up and inhaled the fragrance, faint but the essence still clung to the folds of fabric. Chanel, or Joy, perhaps?

Linen and silk scarves, sweaters and several dresses, most simple cotton frocks, printed with flowers or geometric patterns. A cotton flour sack was filled with underthings, stockings, and socks, gloves, and handkerchiefs. Familiar, everyday items, well-worn and some nearly threadbare, as though whoever packed them away couldn't bear to discard any of her possessions.

The last, still inside its own department store box was a dressing gown of rich chocolate brown silk, with slightly padded shoulders and a wide collar embroidered with a filigree of gold and white peacock feathers, the long sleeves and belt in sheer voile of a slightly lighter shade.

Not resisting the impulse, she held it up to herself and looked in the mirror while, she imagined, her great-grandmother smiled indulgently.

THE NEXT MORNING, IN her oldest work jeans, a tank top and her hair tied back with one of Claire's scarves, she walked to the long bramble hedge of blackberries at the edge of the meadow, determined to pick enough for a pie and a few jars of jam.

As much as she loved the cottage and discovering history in every box, being outside was glorious, she thought, climbing up the bank leading to the meadow. Still early, there was a cool breeze from the Bay and the sky was a bright cloudless blue, the long walk a good way to loosen the kinks brought on by sleeping on the springy old bed in the tiny back bedroom.

The ornate wrought iron bed, made up with recently discovered lace-edged linens and antique quilts, was comfortable enough at first, but the linked metal spring looked and felt like it was made from barbed wire. Afternoon plans included driving to Easton for a foam pad, or two.

Her last experience with the joys of berry picking had been at a 'pick your own' berry farm with one busy Miranda, running amok in the strawberry patch and a tethered Ryan, who ate two berries for every three she put in the pail. That night she ended up with one crying from sunburn and bug bites and another with a tummy ache. Lesson learned: Wait till kids are older to take them to a pick your own berry farm.

That was the trouble, she thought, the briefest window of opportunity between the age when kids were old enough to do and enjoy those things with parents, and the age when they didn't want to and then wouldn't. But now, she thought gratefully, Miranda and Ryan were excited and eager to be part of the effort to find out about Brendan Bonneau, so much so she had to promise Miranda she wouldn't make any important discoveries without her.

OPENING THE ROLL-TOP SECRETARY desk late in the evening, she found paperwork still in its many slots and small drawers. An assortment of coins, stamps, rubber bands brittle and falling to pieces at the slightest touch, oxidized or rusted paper clips and fasteners, bills and notices, and several light, newsy letters, all completely bereft of information about Brendan.

At the bottom of the last drawer, she found a large brown envelope with two books. Lillian glanced inside the first, black leather-bound journal and recognized Lilién's handwriting. Only partially used, the first date was nearly fifteen years after the final entry in the white satin diary and the few entries were written not long before Edward's death. The other was wrapped in a gentleman's white silk scarf, another diary, covered with pale blue satin. Well used, every page from beginning to end filled with Lilién's writing, the entries also beginning in 1879. Both treasures, but neither likely to have information about Brendan.

The old bed was much more comfortable with the new, thick foam pad she had bought earlier. She felt her muscles relaxing at once, the comforting drift into oblivion as soon as she closed her eyes.

Thunder woke her only an hour later, the bedside lamp was still on and rain was beating against the windows and drumming on the slate roof. She opened the black diary to the first entry dated was late February 1879 and was as dramatically different in the tone it began with as it was in appearance from Lilién's first fleur-de-lys diary.

> I woke late this morning feeling ill and desperately sad, though I should be happy knowing that I shall finally have another child, due early in summer. Instead of the living presence so nurturing to me during my last confinement, a dull ache throbbed in my lower back, an emptiness of spirit settled in my heart. My tears began falling the moment I woke.
>
> Ernest's bright eyes and wonderful stories would have cheered me, but he was spending the day with Rory Leverette in Easton. He would not be home until the next day when our friends were invited to a long-planned and now much-dreaded dinner party.
>
> Martha looked in repeatedly, clucking worriedly that she would summon the doctor. We both knew Edward would not allow it, begrudging the small amount the doctor charged for his fee. Thinking to distract me from my misery, she brought a letter. Dear Jenny's handwriting lifted my spirits, though only for a moment.
>
> Wilson Hall is dead.
>
> Even after eighteen years, the pain of his

betrayal is still as fresh as my irrational and silent certainty of his innocence, despite witnessing with my own eyes, him lying with one of the Fleur-de-Lys house servants in the straw in our very own barn.

What—God Almighty!

She had been close to nodding off to sleep, but now, sitting straight up in bed, she gripped the diary.

No, it just can't be, not Wilson!

Lillian thought of the angelic-looking young man in the tintype…but, of course, it *could* be possible, remembering numerous slave narratives and biographies setting more than enough precedent for such behavior among plantation owners, and their sons. But…*Wilson?* She lay back down and focused once again on the page.

> I so desperately wanted to remember him as he was before, before everything changed, and so sent Martha to fetch something from my steamer trunk, which had been secreted away in the attic for fifteen years.
>
> I blessed Brendan's name once again as I held my lovely yellow silk, in my memory still as pristine and beautiful as when I looked at it in the moonlight the night before the ball. I lay down and hugged it to me, remembering Wilson, our first dance together, the long rides around the plantations with the interminable chatter of his sister, of the last time we were alone, the look of confusion on his face after the one kiss we shared.
>
> If only I had shown him how I truly felt about that kiss! And that dreadful, dreadful morning only days later and the letter he sent, imploring me to believe he did not do what was so plainly evident to all our eyes, begging me to see him, begging me to trust him…

The certainty of his innocence returned as Lillian read

Lilién's earlier memories, earlier than even before her fourteenth birthday and the beginning of her white diary. His many displays of kindness and gentleness to her, to her family, their servants.

Lilién wrote about her memory of the winter day in 1859 when Wilson and his father had returned home from a long trip down to Charleston. She was with Hannah and Amelia when the men rode in. Wilson had called to his mother but shook his head at Lilién as she also started to approach the wagon. Hannah asked Lillian to take Amelia into the house and wait for her. It was only after their engagement Wilson had finally admitted they had found an escaped slave somewhere south of Columbia, a woman who had been badly beaten and very near both death and confinement. They had secreted her away, and Hannah had nursed Delphine back to health, and the baby, little Muriel, was born healthy.

He doctored the animals, even Lilién's sick rabbit. Many of the entries were blotted and streaked as though she cried onto and wiped tears from the pages as she wrote. Lillian put her hand over the last smudged entry, …. *Poor Lilién*, Lillian thought, closing her eyes, *poor Wilson…*

Edward walked into my room without even the perfunctory courtesy of a knock on the door. He stood by the bed looking at me with contempt. If my prayers had any power at all, he would disappear from the face of the Earth; simply dissolve into a vapor right before me.

I closed my eyes, mutely hugging the yellow silk as though it forged some link to the past, and to Wilson. My Wilson, I thought, trying to ignore the increasingly intense pain radiating through my body

"I see Martha was not exaggerating this time. You are in quite a state."

I opened my eyes when he pulled the letter roughly from my hand and watched his eyes grow even colder as he scanned the few lines. A derisive laugh escaped him.

"Wilson Hall! My God, you don't mean to say you still have feelings for that…that… scoundrel! After what he did to you, my dear?"

His tone changed and there was a warmth in the last words I could not trust.

"My feelings are for the Wilson I remember." I meant to speak

quietly, but a sob rose into my voice as I added, burying my face into the silk, "not the Wilson I saw that morning."

He was silent for so long that I wondered if he had left the room. Please, God, just let him leave me to my pain and grief.

"That morning?" he finally said, all traces of false warmth gone. "Shall I tell you about that morning, *my dear wife?"*

When I lifted my head, he raised one hand to rip the dress from me, the other to slap my face fiercely. He was on top of me, pulling my dressing gown away and forcing my legs apart with his own before I could recover.

"I told good ole Wilson, as a trusted friend, you had confided in me, confided that you were feeling neglected, that you felt as though he did not care enough for you to show you affection. I watched as he tried to show you the depth of his ardor, only to be rebuffed. Did you enjoy your kiss in the garden, my dear? You needed to believe that he was a man with animal appetites, you see, to believe that he might go hunting for ways to relieve those appetites."

"Edward, no!"

His weight and my struggles only exacerbated the agony now radiating down my legs. He held himself over me, not showing he heard or felt me at all, only the threatening promise of more pain as he waited, hard and ready.

"I was to be the master of Fleur-de-Lys. With your over-protective menfolk gone, and sweet little Sally, assured it was all in fun, and taken with the idea of having a bit of gold, was quite willing to help me by posing with the dear oblivious boy. The carriage ride back from Camden the night before was so cold, I shared my flask with him. Young Wilson, not being much of a drinker, was unfamiliar with the cordial. I explained that it was a unique blend of spirits, as indeed it was. A very special blend-- heavy with laudanum."

Rage such as I had never felt before coursed through me. I screamed and tried to escape from beneath him. When I could not, I pummeled at his face with my fists. I heard his exhilarated laughter at the same moment he forced himself inside me. The pain of his brutal entering was insignificant to the pain in my heart, the pain of truth exploding through my mind.

I clawed at his eyes. "How could you!" I screamed over and over, biting at his neck, shoulders, arms until I could taste blood, remembering

Wilson's confusion at seeing me standing above him, panic at Sally crying beneath him, recoiling from her as though she were a viper poised to strike, looking down at her and at his own state of dishevelment, shock on his pale, handsome face.

Edward grabbed my hands, held them over my head, forcing them back into the bed until it felt as though my arms would break. His increased control over me only seemed to heighten his passion, and he spoke slowly, emphasis in his voice at each savage thrust.

"So there would be no doubt as to the nature and degree of his attentions, I, of course, had to ensure there was evidence she was thoroughly bedded. What do you think of that, my dear, it was not your darling Wilson who lay with her, it was ...me."

Revealing this cruel exploitation enhanced his pleasure. "When the opium fog lifted, his second called demanding satisfaction, which I accepted, of course! Your pathetic champion was left standing with his pistols at dawn on the old Wateree Trail—" He crushed my fingers in his tightening grip, and I felt a sharp, pain in my shoulder as he forced my arms further back, "while we crossed the border into North Carolina."

Searing, pulsating pain shot through my belly. So mindless, so cruel, even the hot gush through our legs as I lost our child did not dissuade him from his ascent to climax. The strength left my arms, the rage left my mind and I lay beneath him, weeping silently.

A whimper escaped me when I woke to weight shifting on the bed. I braced myself, but only felt a cool, gentle hand on my forehead.

I opened my eyes to see Thomas, his gray eyes meeting mine in the same direct, compassionate manner as on the first day we met. Martha was fussing with the bedclothes, tucking hot, flannel wrapped bricks around my body and whispering urgently to him about the impropriety of being in my bedroom.

Thomas Crawford, the young sailor with the long, dirty blond hair and Mississippi drawl who arrived at the cove one winter day with a message from my brother. He returned with the news of Brendan's death four months later and had never left.

"The doctor is on the way," he said, softly stroking my hair and ignoring Martha. "What happened, Lilién?"

"*Mister Crawford!*" *Martha admonished again.*

He did not stop stroking my hair or look away from me, but finally spoke to her.

"I will remain with Mrs. Cherrington until the doctor arrives. Please bring her strong, sweet tea. The doctor will want hot water, as well."

The stiff tarlatan of her skirts rustled indignantly as she left the room.

Thomas's hands were strong but very gentle as he supported me and held a glass of brandy to my lips. Even the small sips helped warm me, from my throat to my stomach, flowing into my limbs.

Thomas's eyes held mine while I spoke, haltingly, but without the horror I should feel at the idea of discussing such private affairs with a man. He showed no shock or embarrassment, only held my hand gently and, although anger hardened his gray eyes and tears softened them a time or two, he did not interrupt.

We were quiet when Martha returned, bustling around with the tea tray, obviously stalling to avoid leaving me again. Thomas finally dismissed her rather brusquely, and when the door closed nodded for me to continue.

"Before he left me... he ...said 'All you have cost me, and... and not even a good breeder.' Blaming me for what he brought on himself when he destroyed my life. Poor Wilson..." I closed my eyes, a shaking sob escaped me when I once again remembered the anguish in his eyes that terrible morning.

"How did you know to come?" I asked sometime later.

The hint of a smile crossed his face. "Your littlest of servants, Lilién. It seems Mrs. Youngs forbade any of them to interfere, but Barry disobeyed and ran across the meadow for help. I saw him running and knew something was wrong. I gave him Samson to ride to fetch the doctor. I hope he manages, his feet didn't touch the stirrups."

"Sweet Barry," I whispered. The boy, not exactly a servant, was the eight-year-old orphaned nephew of one of the maids. I had overruled Mrs. Youngs and allowed the boy to stay. He attended the local day school, did little jobs to earn his keep and looked at me adoringly whenever we met. "My hero. I would knight him if I could."

DULL GRAY LIGHT SEEPED through lace-covered windows

when Lillian woke, rain was pounding on the slate roof and thunder still rumbled in the distance.

Stretching, she felt every lump in the old mattress even with the thick new pad. Household chores catching up with her, she thought, every muscle in her body hurt.

She opened the black diary again. In between the two lengthy entries, there was a brief, undated notation about a miscarriage.

> Cherrington House. February 27, 1879. I await the last possible moment to join our guests. Edward would not permit cancelation although I know our guests, *my* friends, would understand. I was weak, still shaken by the experiences of the previous day, nevertheless, I felt it would be good to have them here for the evening. Far better than being alone with Edward, certainly. Pouring a second glass of brandy, I endeavor to prepare myself for an evening of lighthearted chatter.
>
> Martha made disapproving faces when I had her ready my black velvet. I am determined to wear mourning for Wilson and my child and am surprisingly unconcerned about the opinions of others. I have spent the day remaking the style to resemble an evening dress which recently appeared in Harper's.
>
> The modest lace fichu and jabot I removed entirely, exposing the plunging v-shaped neckline. No one in our circle wears anything so daring and never black except for the layers of dull crepe and bombazine used to entrap relieved widows for years. Martha, not content to criticize only my dress, scolded me for the jet combs I have used to hold my hair in a simple chignon. Perhaps she is afraid for me, knowing Edward prefers the tight, unnatural ringlets.

My eyes moved to Grandmére Bonneau's diamond and topaz necklace resting against my skin, the bright sparkles in the candlelight igniting a treasured memory of my mother's loving expression when opening the blue velvet box and revealing them to me for the first time.

Being only fourteen Jenny had to shorten the chain so that the heavy pendant did not hide within the bodice of my yellow silk. Now, on its full length of chain tonight, the pendant certainly drew attention to my décolletage.

After clipping on the drop earrings, I surveyed myself only to find the mirror reflects a somber-eyed stranger, not the happy young girl who lives within those memories. If only I could stare into their bright prisms and exist within that world once more.

I wondered at my témérité the instant I entered the drawing room. I could see that Mary Prescott, Janice Leverette, and young Sylvia Crawford all admired the overall effect of my dress and jewels, while the eyes of Franklin Leverette and Sloan Prescott were momentarily riveted to my bosom.

Thomas's eyes, however, met mine, a sad smile hiding in their depths.

I smiled at Franklin, who kissed my hand in his usual Continental manner. Edward appeared to have bitten into something exceedingly sour.

The conversation revolved around the prolonged cold threatening to linger into March and the recent efforts to provide relief to the Irish as they suffered through yet another famine. When President Hayes's temperance and post-Reconstruction policies were discussed, Edward's voice grew louder, his responses more antagonistic. I was relieved when dinner was announced.

Incredibly tired as I was from the ordeal of the previous day, I tried to ignore the politics being discussed among the men and listened to the softer conversations of the women. I wanted to be a good hostess and join in on their topics of interest.

"I believe, sir, we shall have to agree to disagree!" Sloan, usually soft-spoken and very polite, raised his voice.

An awkward silence followed, all eyes on Edward until he shrugged and poured himself another glass of wine.

At that quiet moment, dear Sylvia chose to lean towards me, "My dear Lilién, your dress is lovely. I know black is becoming fashionable in New York and Paris, but I hope there is no other reason..."

The others had turned their attention to me as well, and seeing this, Sylvia blushed vividly. I quickly put my hand on hers and smiled, "Oh no, my dear. I recently saw a drawing of a black dinner dress in Harper's. I thought I would try my hand at creating something new."

The sound of clapping hands diverted our attention back to Edward.

"I applaud your little fiction to justify the morbid display, my dear, but do not be shy. Tell our friends why you are so pale and wan, mourning for your long, lost lover." He paused long enough to drain his glass. "And pray tell, is he the one who gave you those jewels? Or perhaps some other...?" He looked pointedly from me to Thomas.

Mary and Janice gasped audibly, Franklin and Sloan exchanged glances and Sylvia's hand began to slip from mine.

"Yes, in a way, Thomas did give them to me, dear," I said, looking only at Sylvia, still holding her hand. "They were sent to me many years ago by my brother Brendan, who was once Thomas's commander. These are heirlooms from our Desjardins family," Our guests relaxed visibly at the innocent explanation of Edward's intimation, "which once belonged to my great-grandmother Louisa, who was murdered during the Reign of Terror."

"Oh, how terrible!" exclaimed Sylvia in sympathy while Edward glared at me suspiciously, likely wondering if I possessed other jewels from my highborn relations.

"A Papist whore like their queen, no doubt," Edward sneered. He appeared to have forgotten we were in polite company and stared at me with observable disgust. "Did they carry her head around Paris on a pike as well?"

"Sir!" Outraged, Franklin stood abruptly, his chair scraping against the floor.

"Now, see here, Cherrington..." Sloan's voice rose again, now in appalled sympathy.

The warmth drained from my body as the sick imagery of his words struck me. Relating the story of her grandmother's fate and the family's *narrow escape from France was one of the few times I had ever seen my proud, outwardly cold-hearted mother in tears.*

"At least she was not a traitor," ignoring everyone else, Edward concentrated his attack on me, "like that brother of yours, switching his sworn allegiance to make it rich instead of fighting the ignorant Southern scoundrels who started the war."

"That is not true!"

"No, it is not true."

Everyone turned to him in surprise when Thomas spoke for the first time.

Edward scoffed. "You were one of them!"

Thomas nodded agreeably. "I was a fifteen-year-old mess boy on the blockade runner Kendal, until very late on one dark night in late December 1864." As Thomas began speaking, Franklin resumed his seat and Sloan's posture relaxed. "Aboard a tiny skiff in the middle of Cape Fear, under the guns of Fort Fisher and surrounded by the Federal Fleet, US Navy Lieutenant Commander Brendan Bonneau changed my own allegiance and advanced me to Seaman in the United States Navy."

Thomas smiled at my expression. "Enough time has passed, and I don't rightly think he would object to the truth being known. He gathered information about the weaknesses in the defenses of the blockading squadron along the Carolina coastlines and any other strategic information to relay to his superiors in Annapolis."

Edward countered Thomas's revelation with mockery, inferring it was Brendan's fault our blockade was not more successful.

Thomas shrugged, the slight gesture further illustrating just how little weight he gave to Edward's opinion. "Each year the blockade was more effective, with more runners turned away, sunk or destroyed. The important thing to know is that Brendan Bonneau was no traitor, and he fought the War in an honorable way."

"And how is it his own ship escaped capture through the course of the war?"

"A fast ship, a good captain…and, sometimes, a signal flag," Thomas said, glancing at my ring.

I held my hand up to display the gold ring on my right hand. "A fleur-de-lys! Thomas told me about the flag the first day we met…" my throat tightened, remembering the last day I had seen Brendan, riding towards his new assignment. "He found a way to serve both sides with honor."

"Honor?" Edward laughed outright.

"Yes, honor!" I retorted, now behaving as rudely as Edward in front of our astounded guests. "He worked to bring supplies to starving people and information to his government to help win the war! How is that not honorable?"

"Nothing honorable about a traitor, spy, or a thief. Isn't that what your dear Mother called him with her dying words?"

"Brendan Bonneau was no thief." Thomas interceded again, politely but firmly, maintaining the same relaxed bearing. Only his narrowed eyes, glinting like crystal in the candlelight, revealed the contempt he felt. "And I do believe it is time you stopped insulting your wife and her family in my presence, Cherrington."

"What are you going to do, Crawford? Call me out? You would be the second Southern idiot to challenge me to a duel."

Thomas paused thoughtfully, before answering with his native Mississippi drawl which had faded during his years in Maryland, "Well now, Cherrington, that sounds a mite too upper crust for me. I was thinkin' of a good old-fashioned thrashin' behind the woodshed."

Franklin and Sloan laughed outright but the women looked even more fearful of Edward's menacing expression.

I might have once feared Edward after such an exchange, or at the very least felt embarrassed for him. No longer. I had no more fears for myself, only a sudden, angry impulse to stop this escalation of tempers. I faced my husband across the long expanse of the table.

"Êtes-vous ivres ou simplement …un crétin complet? Peu importe " I waved my hand dismissively and leaned forward, the topaz and diamond pendants moving against my skin. I looked into his strange dun-colored eyes and spoke in a language he did not understand and in the same aristocratic manner as my mother.

I had not planned to disguise my message in another language, but indeed, it was a remarkably effective way to stun the assemblage. Franklin whistled a low, slow whistle, and delight danced in Janice's eyes, clearly the only two persons in the room to know I had called my husband a cretin and damned him to Hell for all eternity.

Edward's expression gave away nothing; in front of guests or alone with me, he would never reveal his ignorance though he could in no way mistake my message. I held his eyes, issuing a challenge for him to respond as the clock on the mantel chimed the hour.

Chapter Fifteen

Coming in from the Cold

THE GRANDFATHER CLOCK IN the living room was chiming as she woke. Chiming for a long time, she thought, groggily reaching for her phone.

Noon?

The gloom had lightened only slightly, and rain still drummed on the roof above, no doubt responsible for lulling her back into such a deep sleep. Disoriented, she sat up, and Lilién's diary slipped from the bed onto the floor.

Listening to a favorite movie on her computer, she spent the afternoon baking almond blackberry scones and decorating the living room. Movement stretched aching muscles, and star-trekking and blasting aliens were not only a reviving jolt out of the past, helping to shake off the heavy sense of melancholy she had woken with, but also an antidote to the finely written and delicately worded Victorian letters and journals.

Brightly patterned chintz draperies that matched the two overstuffed chairs went up on the wide front windows, bringing color and uniformity to the room. From one of the cedar chests, she draped a blue and white touching star quilt over the back of the sofa.

WHEN THE RAIN FINALLY abated, she left the cottage and treated herself to a walk along the rocky cove and long, mid-week talks with both Miranda and Ryan. Once in for the evening, she showered and put on Claire's brown silk dressing gown.

She filled the kettle and lit the old Wedgewood, deciding how to spend the evening. Each time she reached for it throughout the day, she felt an aversion, no, it was stronger, she thought, looking thoughtfully at Lilién's black diary.

Instead, she took out the small blue diary. Even less likely to contain useful information about Brendan, it would still give insights into Lilién's life, and, she hoped, inspire better dreams and a more restful night.

When she opened the front door to secure the loose latch on the screen for the night, she heard footsteps on the gravel drive and saw someone walking towards her only by the bobbing beam of a flashlight.

"Lillian?" It was a familiar voice, but she couldn't see his face.

"Alexander?" she asked, stepping out onto the porch.

"No."

"*Mark?*"

At the sound of her indrawn breath, he turned off the flashlight and said quickly, "I need to talk to you."

"I've wanted to talk with you, too. I've called…"

"I know."

"How did you know I was here," she asked, as he drew closer.

"Sarah passed on what Vera told her about the inheritance, with a little coaxing. I knew you weren't home, so I took a chance and drove out …"

"Sarah …?"

"Only because you never told her…or anyone else, it seems," his voice was gentle, "I'm sorry...so very sorry." He stood at the edge of light spilling from the window and paused before adding, "I'm not asking for your forgiveness, Lillian. I know the things I said, what I did, were … unforgivable."

"You've told me, and I *know* you're sorry about what happened. What's going on?"

"It's a long story, but—"

As the kettle came to a boil, it let out a sudden shrill blast and he startled as though he was ready to hit the ground.

"Come in," she said, stepping towards the open door. When he hesitated, she added, "It's all right, Mark. Please come in."

She went inside and turned off the stove. The high-pitched shriek gradually subsided to a steady whistle, a low hum and then silence.

Mark hesitated at the door. "Before your sodding knight in shining armor made his reappearance, you don't know I wouldn't have pressed my advantage as far as it would have taken me. You're far too trusting, Lillian."

"I know you enough to still trust you. I don't know what was going on with you that night, but if you *ever* do anything like that to me again, I won't need Duncan's help to let you know just how I feel about it!"

He closed and locked the door behind him. She didn't object, seeing very clearly now he had darkened and straightened his hair, giving it a heavy, coarse appearance, and when his eyes met hers, contacts had subdued the vivid green to a nondescript hazel.

This was a very different man from the one who had both kissed and threatened her. Tonight, he was scared to death, and not only for himself. She could smell it on him, the unusual pungency of his sweat and something else she couldn't identify, made her own hackles rise.

"What's going on, Mark?" she repeated, gesturing towards the small kitchen table.

"I went out to meet with Vic on Monday," he said, sitting with his back against the wall, in the shadows just beyond the soft ring of light. "When Nina said he would be late for the appointment I walked around the place, checking things out while I waited."

She listened as she set the tea to brewing in the blue-flowered porcelain teapot she had discovered the day before, and set out cups, milk, and sugar and some of the scones. He took his time, describing the extensive Andrastus Shipping complex that she had been curious about but had never seen before. He paused long enough to help himself to a second scone.

"I have something…significant… to tell you, but I want to have another scone before you throw me out."

She raised her eyebrows. "Please tell me you're not married?"

He laughed, those smile lines making his face more familiar, the tension suddenly gone. "No, I'm not married," he said, shaking his head, "though that might be easier…

"I have a friend in what's now known as the NCA, the National Crime Agency, fairly equivalent to your FBI. They've been close to connecting Andrastus Shipping to drug smuggling into the UK several times but have been unable to get the proof needed to get to the top. What has *always* been known about Andrastus Shipping is that there's enough legitimate business and money to shield almost anything.

"Knowing of the connection between Andrastus Shipping, Voyagers and the museum, but not knowing what a *stellar* individual he was," Mark smiled wryly at the emphasis, "NCA felt Scott, with his former Coast Guard knowledge and connections, might be the way they were alluding authorities looking into their activities."

Lillian scoffed, still wondering what bomb he was about to drop.

"At the suggestion of my friend, I was approached by the agency to accept an assignment. They contacted Josiah Prentice and offered the funding to create a new position—"

"*What?*"

He reached over and put a hand on hers, gently but firmly. "To be there to glean what information I could through the museum's work with Scott, and…"

"And…?"

"You."

"Me?"

"I was told you and Scott were involved—actually," he said, annoyed, "I was originally told it was Vera and Scott who were involved. Imagine the confidence that bit of *intelligence* inspired when I realized the truth. Not to mention their complete misinterpretation of the word 'museum' in this case, assuming, no doubt, the Prentice House Museum of the Nautical History of the Chesapeake Bay was something akin to Greenwich, imagining I would just slip in unobtrusively.

"Working with and being close to *you* was thought to be one way to discover Scott's connections to the Andrastus smuggling network and the museum as a possible transfer point. Of course, it took me all of a *week* to realize that, while someone may have revealed your attraction to one another, I knew you weren't involved in anything I was there to discover, Lillian, eavesdropping on you and Vera was all the scrutiny that angle deserved."

He had the nerve to smile then, relaxed his grip on her hand and went on. "Mainly, I was to be involved in any expeditions and field work involving Voyagers."

Which was the primary reason Vera had taken such an immediate dislike to him, Lillian remembered. Duncan's expeditions during Mark's first year were in far-flung locations for extended lengths of time, and Vera had been shut out of most of them.

Unlike the high security of the main terminal of Andrastus Shipping, the *Jupiter* was practically security free to those on board. Mark could talk with any of the crew from Duncan to the galley crew, come and go, and have access to all areas of the ship without difficulty.

"And it all worked brilliantly, though it didn't take me long to realize I wouldn't learn anything through Scott, because he wasn't involved, or even aware.

"On our second date, when you said you were glad I wasn't going for the job?" he said, and she remembered their conversation about the lead conservator's retirement, and their assumption Vera would get the job, "that's when I realized I *had* to have the job—"

"Had to? Why?" She slipped her hand away to reach for the teapot and poured more tea into both cups.

"Do you remember Scott's expedition to the Gulf? I reported back and told them Voyagers and Scott were dead ends, but they wanted me to stay on for a while longer. They had become aware of a new link between Andrastus and a smuggling network working in the West Indies that included drugs and the usual contraband, but also antiquities. And it also involved Scott —but not Voyagers."

"How involved?"

"Again, something NCA *should* have been aware of much sooner. He was, essentially, playing for the same team, contract work for British Customs contacts in Nassau, Kingston, and Hamilton."

Not completely convinced, NCA wanted Mark to remain undercover.

"Frustrating, spending time looking for something that wasn't there, and knowing someone else is getting away with murder." She used the cliché without thinking, but he tensed again.

"Moulton retiring so suddenly when I thought my time was nearly up, meant I *had* to get the job. The old man was utterly malleable to Prentice's recommendation I be the one to go on Voyagers expeditions when it only required one conservator. Vera would *never* have been, and there was no way I could have trusted her to keep my secret. But staying longer also increased the likelihood of your being hurt by whatever might happen with me, and yet we still had to work together. Becoming the lead gave me the control I needed and ended our relationship.

"I know I should apologize for rushing you into spending that weekend with me," he added, his eyes meeting hers, "but I'm not at all remorseful. Only very sorry if you felt used."

"I accepted your invitation, Mark, and made the decision to stay," she said, as he reached for her again. Warmer now, she noticed his hands no longer shook. Returning his gentle grip, added, "I admit I felt…a bit scammed when the announcement was made so soon afterwards."

"A bit scammed? When we talked my first day back, you were hurt, confused and angry."

"I wasn't in any way unprofessional in my demeanor

towards you."

"After the weekend we shared? That's how I knew you were hurt, confused and angry, and I don't blame you."

"Did you go to London?"

"I did, but not to attend Crossrail meetings," he said. "I am sorry, Lillian. I would have told you the truth about this if I could have."

"Isn't it just too bad you didn't? I would have known you weren't *really* my boss," she said, accepting his apology with a seductive smile, amused by his expression.

"By this spring, Voyagers was in the clear and as soon as Prentice had his stroke I knew the museum would be closing. I started pushing to get released to go home. Two things got in the way.

"Something happened on *Jupiter*'s last trip down to Jamaica, when they went to Kingston to transport recently recovered artifacts for an INA project. George Andrastus had commandeered space for a company shipment down to the Caymans and another back to Baltimore. According to the DEA, the incoming shipment was confiscated, and the word behind the scenes was that Scott was somehow involved in the bust, which was used to generate some agitation within the organization, to get to the top.

"For me, it eventually meant a new lead they wanted me to investigate, which I was in no way trained or prepared for. Earlier on that night at the lab, I found myself in the middle of a minor-league drug deal I couldn't get myself out of without trying what they were selling. Something like Ecstasy, they said. I figured if kids take it at raves and rock concerts, how bad could it be?

"All the while I'm thinking, '*I'm an archeologist, for Christ's sake, what the fuck am I doing here?*' Getting in way over my head was where, and whatever was in that capsule hit fast and was not Ecstasy. Once I sealed the deal, I got the hell out of there. I didn't want to go home, I was too restless but too paranoid to be in public. I went to the Museum, hoping something would distract me while I came down."

At the sympathetic sound that escaped her, he gave a rueful smile.

"When I saw you... unexpectedly, I've honestly never felt love as deep or desire as overwhelming, and...well, it took whatever control I had left to walk away."

She remembered the joyous look he had greeted her with, the trembling urgency in his caress, and the uncharacteristic coldness that had so quickly chilled his eyes at her rejection.

"When I saw Scott, I was hit with a violent combination of fury and jealousy, even before I saw you together." His grip tightened when he saw her tears, "I'm sorry, Lillian, *very* sorry. My baser instincts let loose and once I got started... well, the control was gone."

Mark had needed a safe haven that night. She withdrew her hands and reached for a napkin and blotted away her tears. "I've come to think of that night as some kind of perfect storm we were caught up in, Mark, and you bore the brunt of it."

"Have you talked to Scott lately?" he asked, pausing to drink the tea that had grown cold in his cup, "or talked with him on your cell phone while you've been out here?"

"No, and not since the night before the second picture hit the paper. Why?"

"Do me a favor? Turn it off and take out the battery?"

"What? Why?" she asked, going to the fridge for wine, suddenly needing something stronger than tea. She held up the bottle and he nodded.

"Could you text your family, say your battery is going dead or something? Use email or turn it on only if you need to?" At her look, he added. "I'll explain, I promise."

She picked up her phone and texted her father and the kids, and did as he asked, hoping her instinct to trust him was correct. When she suggested they move to the living room, he hesitated, scanning the room and its broad expanse of windows before flipping on the outside floodlights and turning off the lamp so the only light shone in from the porch. He glanced outside and then sat on the far end of the old tweed couch giving him a view in all directions.

"Even with Prentice knowing what I was here for, I could only get out to Andrastus Shipping a few times, and only to the public areas or Vic's office. I tried to get Prentice to set up meetings, a chance for a tour, anything. Of course, he was pleased about having a full-time subsidized position, but he also didn't want me risking the relationship with his friend *and* the museum's largest benefactor.

"I know Vic isn't in the office much these days, but I managed to get an appointment with him on Monday to discuss some of the museum's transition issues. I went out early and while I waited I snooped around, quite openly at first."

"In the distance I heard a woman, crying," Increasingly nervous as he talked, he paused, lowering his voice, "Sobbing. I followed the sound, but before I could find where she was, I heard two men talking about her, George told the other to either stop—" Mark looked away for a moment before continuing, "*tormenting* her, or find a way to shut her up. It was Nick who answered him, something I couldn't hear. Then they talked about Scott—"

"Mark, you will never, ever convince me Duncan knows anything about this. He *is* former Coast Guard, for God's sake!"

"I think Scott's discovered something. I heard George say, 'it hasn't worked. We need to get rid of him.'"

"That could mean end his partnership—"

"No." Mark shook his head vehemently. Recounting the memory, she could see he was on high alert again, ready to jump and run at the slightest noise. "George was talking about how they're being investigated big time and they blame Scott because of the shipment brought in on the *Jupiter*."

"My God, Mark," she whispered, leaning forward, "not Vic?"

"No, Vic wasn't there, I'm sure. I got the impression they're very proud Vic doesn't know the big picture in his own organization."

Poor Vic, she thought, and a poor reward for his generosity and trust, to be so abused by his own family. Victoria's antics, annoying and extravagant as they were, were harmless, those of a spoiled child. This, as her father would say, this was the big league.

"He said something about both of them needing to go to Kingston the next day. I heard Nick again but couldn't make out the words. George was angry at him, very angry. He told Nick he was an idiot for having tried to set up a diving accident because it would never work. And even if it did work, there would be media attention, government intervention, and investigation into his death. That's when I backtracked and got the hell out of there."

"My God," she repeated, her own hands growing cold. "It wasn't an accident?"

"I don't want you caught up in this. It's *my* fault if they link the two of you… from the picture," he added, reaching for his wine. "The others were a nice touch, but I'm not sure everyone bought it. That's why I wanted you to turn off your phone, Lillian, if they are monitoring him, they more than likely know about you. They could track you and you would never know."

"They didn't see you or know you heard them?"

"Hell, no!" He paused, quaffing the rest of his wine as though it were water, and went to the kitchen for a second glass. "The few people I did meet weren't anywhere near George and Nick. But Nina knew I'd come in to see Vic. Official spy training or no, I'm not good enough to go in and meet with Vic after hearing his family members plotting murder." He looked across the living room towards her, it was still hard to reconcile the new look to the voice. "I called Nina and apologized, told her I had another appointment I'd forgotten about and rescheduled."

"Have you told Duncan?"

"I tried. I went to his lab first. He wasn't there, only Mariah and a few techs. I told her I need to talk with him. I was hoping you knew where he was."

"On the ship, I think, but Vera emailed he was on his way back to Annapolis soon." She reached for her laptop to read Vera's last email again.

"Part of what I heard is that someone in Scott's side of

the organization is watching him—no," he shook his head, "I didn't hear who."

"But why come out here…?"

"I thought he might be here."

The umbrage she started to express died unspoken. Why wouldn't Mark think that after what he had witnessed in the lab? "We *really* haven't —"

"You don't owe me an explanation. I *did* think he might be here, but I also wanted to see you and didn't want to risk being together in town. Or worse, at your place," he ran his fingers through his hair. "With the resources of Andrastus Shipping and the stakes this high? Everything he does is probably being watched, his cell phone, computers, his car, are probably being tracked. And, if they do know I was at the compound, and that I may have heard something? I don't want to give them any other reason to suspect you know anything.

"But," he added with an exhausted shrug, "at least I finally have something to report."

He excused himself to the bathroom while Lillian checked her email.

Vera's last message was sent Lillian's first night at the cottage, so Duncan may already be in Annapolis. Lillian replied in such a way to invite the latest news. Vera would do the rest, probably within the hour, she thought, glancing at the time, surprised it was still well before midnight.

Mark's fear was contagious, and she shivered when she saw how brightly the light from her laptop illuminated the dark room. Going to the window, she looked beyond the light towards the cove. Not even a light breeze ruffled the tall Spartina grass covering the embankment between the lawn and rocky beach.

"Lillian?"

Camouflaged in Claire's dark dressing gown, Mark couldn't see her in the shadows.

"I'm here."

He took her hand and drew her towards him and she felt no sense of fear. She returned the embrace until finally he leaned down and kissed her gently.

"I should go," he said. "It's a bit of a trek to the car."

"Where is your car?"

"St. Michael's. A visit to another maritime museum seemed a plausible enough reason for me to be out on this side of the Bay, if I were to need one."

"That's over two miles away! Let me at least drive you over—"

"No," he said, tensing again.

"Well, why don't you stay? There's nothing more you can do tonight."

"I hardly expected to receive such an invitation when I ventured out here …"

"You're exhausted, Mark, and if they *are* looking for either or both of us, isn't it better we're not alone? I'll have heard from Vera before you leave, too.

"Come," she said, leading the way back to the little bedroom, almost relieved to have an excuse not to use the old bed after the troubling dreams and broken sleep of the past two nights. She doubted Mark would have difficulty sleeping anywhere, the way he groaned with relief as he sprawled diagonally across the bed. By the time she pulled an extra quilt from the blanket rack and spread it over him, he was asleep.

TO KEEP FROM PACING the floor while waiting for Vera to respond, she poured herself another glass of wine and settled on the sofa with Lilién's blue diary. From the date, she knew the first entry would be about the death of Edward Cherrington in April of 1879. Only weeks after the dinner party Lilién wrote about in the black diary, Edward had "some mishap" while traveling away to Baltimore one morning. His horse had shied, the local constable had told her. The doctor's report said he had died of injuries after being thrown from the carriage.

Lilién expressed no false grief and admitted only to weeping with relief that her long sentence was over. She wore black, she wrote, only in public as a formality for a month and moved on to mauves and lavenders far sooner than the usual conventions dictated. Her friends and neighbors all knew the truth of his character and did not judge her. *"I would wear red silk ruffles and dance the cancan were it not for the impact my behavior may have upon my son."*

Far different in tone from the black diary, this was once again the real Lilién writing detailed descriptions of people and places and her opinions on the news of the day.

At thirty-seven, for the first time in her life, she had freedom. Soaking it up, as neglected flowers drink water, Lilién was now allowed to bloom.

Entries were lighthearted, about outings with Janice Leverette, Mary Prescott, and Sylvia Crawford, and travels with her friend Lydia Chase to Washington and New York for plays, concerts, and shopping excursions. She also wrote about plans for visiting South Carolina for the first time since leaving. Besides the few affectionate comments about Thomas, there was no mention of any other men in her life.

> Cherrington House Cottage, June 1, 1882: I am blessed to have such friends. Lydia Chase, Mary Prescott, Janice Leverette, Sylvia Crawford, and Thomas, of course. I must admit, to my shame, I feel sometimes almost angry at Sylvia. Even before Edward's death, my affections for Thomas had begun to change. Of course, I had always been aware he was attractive, even as a young man with his forthright speech and rough manners.
>
> This increasing physical awareness of Thomas, and of other men of my acquaintance, make me feel quite guilt-ridden. I spoke with Lydia and she was very practical, as though it is the most natural thing in the world for me to be emerging from the shell within which I enclosed myself during the long years of a loveless and violent marriage. I did indeed feel better after our talk. Lydia is someone I trust to not only keep

my worries to herself, but not judge like Mary might, or be shocked as dear Sylvia, or worse, insist on introducing me to someone as Janice no doubt would.

Janice does not demure to praise the physical characteristics of men, those she can see and also speculates about particular attributes hidden from view. No one is safe, from the grandest gentlemen we might pass on a city street, to the tradesman who worked in the sandy mud installing the slate path to the cottage. Franklin seems amused and I wonder that their marriage survives such behavior.

Interesting, Lilién has her own 'Vera' in her life, Lillian thought, glancing over at her computer.

Janice does not shy away from shocking us. She shares her thoughts about men in general and her private experiences with her husband in particular. When we returned home from a weekend in New York, Mary whispered to me she would have difficulty meeting Franklin's eye when he met us at the depot. At the very instant Mary reminded me of Janice's tipsy revelations of the night before about his prowess in their marriage bed, Franklin arrived, looked our way and smiled. Mary giggled, and I turned away so quickly I very nearly fell from the platform.

I have not slept well these past nights, my last in the old house for a long while, I hope. Tomorrow my clothing and personal accoutrements will be moved from Cherrington House, and I will spend the first night in my little cottage. Alone. Finally, alone, where everything is new, light, bright and clean.

The kitchen is tucked into one end of the main gathering room, with a cooking stove, cupboards, and even a small icebox. The walls are shell white, the painter called it, tiles of muted aquamarine and cream-colored chrysanthemums cover the wall behind the sink and countertop. New dining and cookware fill the cupboards and shelves. Enameled measuring cups and silver spoons, and the new pressed-tin flour sifter waited patiently on the corner shelf for me to bake a blackberry pie.

A tiny room in the back contains a water closet, with a wash basin and a cast iron bathtub, propped up upon four clawed feet. One tall window opposite the tub's backrest looks out to the eastern end of the cove. Crisp white tiles are interspersed with French botanicals. A tiny rabbit behind a patch of blue irises, a ladybug perched on the petal of a bright sunflower, a bee humming among the spikes of lavender and larkspur, a red-breasted robin on an evergreen bough. Each time I look closely, I seem to find something new.

Lillian's computer chimed out the arrival of two emails in rapid succession. She yawned, set the diary aside, and reached for the computer. Nothing from Vera.

Lilién's delight with her new cottage bubbled off the page, whether describing details of lowly building materials or the décor she planned for the parlor. Chills started up her arms when she read about the "sweet wrought iron bed, painted white, with a pattern of a fleur-de-lys within its custom scrollwork." "The parlor, shelter from the heat of the sun or an afternoon shower, has bright, chintz-covered chairs, and draperies framing the lace covered windows that could be opened wide to let in the fresh breeze."

Drawn inside Lilién's heart and mind once again, Lillian unconsciously stroked the floral chintz of the chair near her as she read until her eyes grew heavy.

Lillian sat up and stretched, glancing at the computer screen and the clock, wondering why tonight of all nights it was taking Vera so long to respond. Each noise sent her to the window to look in all directions. The wind had picked up after midnight, and the recently mown lawn, still damp from the day's rain, shimmered in the floodlights.

Could Mark be exaggerating? He had never been one for hyperbole, the opposite in fact, and even though the strain of living for over a year with a secret identity must dig into the psyche somewhat, there was no misunderstanding what he had heard, or the attempt made on Duncan's life. Shivering, she dropped the curtain back into place.

> June 20, 1882, Cherrington Cove Cottage. I quite enjoy the peace and solitude of the cottage, once I convinced Martha I would be quite safe, I was finally on my own. Only three days until the Prescotts, Leverettes, and Crawfords visit for the first time. The Chases, regretfully, were called away unexpectedly to Lydia's ill father, but they have asked that I please include John's nephew who is currently visiting from England. I will miss Lydia, my first friend after my arrival in Easton as a young bride, and I will certainly be hospitable to their nephew. A doctor, she mentioned, here for his own rest-cure, but from what is a mystery. Adam Stuart and I have not yet been introduced, but Lydia assures me he is a gentleman and I will enjoy his company. If the subtle lift of her eyebrows is any clue, he must be handsome. Of course, I would have no doubt about his appearance if it were Janice extolling his virtues.

> June 28, 1882, Cherrington Cove Cottage. To say my little party was a success would be understating the truth in the extreme. More accurately, my life was transformed on that Midsummer's Eve.

> My guests arrived in a group, welcomed

by bright sunlight and a cooling breeze from the Bay. I was as light of heart and peaceful of spirit than I believe I have ever been, standing on the small veranda watching them walk down the lane. A pleasant picture they made, the ladies in soft pastel dresses twirling their parasols, while the gentlemen wore crisp linen suits and straw boaters. As I smoothed the skirt of my new pale blue and linen-striped Holland lawn, I caught sight of a fair-haired man in their midst and felt my legs grow so weak I was forced to grip the rail.

I knew, of course, it could not possibly be Wilson Hall, but something about Adam Stuart recalled him to my mind so forcefully I found it suddenly difficult to breathe.

As the group approached and I could determine his features more closely, I saw he did indeed share Wilson's height and patrician, refined features. The initial impression was muted by his unique traits, green eyes not Wilson's blue, and his deep, English-accented voice offering me a polite greeting. When our eyes met, however, some spark within me flared to life and sent tendrils of warmth throughout my body. That I knew something so outrageous I cannot say how, but in an instant, I knew we were destined to be lovers. Something in the way his own gaze held mine for a long moment… did he also experienced some similar reaction, or indeed, know our destiny as surely as I?

Oh dear, Lillian thought, *sounds like trouble,* rather like the green-eyed blond Englishman with the deep melodious voice currently in Lilién's bed just a few feet away. She glanced at the computer. Finally, an email from Vera. So engrossed in Lilién's diary, she hadn't heard the chime when it hit her inbox.

Not lengthy by Vera standards, but thorough enough

that Lillian knew Duncan was on board and safe and returning to Annapolis the next day. She was sure if there had been gossip about any part of the Andrastus Empire, another incident or a new person on board, Vera would have written in great detail.

She went into the bedroom to see if Mark could possibly be awake, but he had not moved, not even to take off his shoes. As she slipped them off and drew the quilt further over his shoulders, he didn't stir at all. Three days since his visit to the shipyards, days of gut-wrenching anxiety, this was probably the first time he felt safe enough to sleep.

She felt her own body relax for the first time since he arrived. Actually, she had been tense, edgy and achy most of the day, she realized, pouring herself another glass of wine before delving back into the journal.

> My duties as hostess kept me quite occupied, thankfully, and I endeavored to divide my time amongst my guests. I did steal glances now and then and caught him looking back at me more than once. While Sloan and Franklin's amusing tales of their recent train journey to the wild west of Wyoming kept us all laughing, I watched as Dr. Stuart played with little Christina Crawford, dangling his pocket watch temptingly within her reach and swinging it away, causing giggles of delight until baby tired of the game and cried. He gallantly relinquished the timepiece and did not flinch in the slightest when the little one put it immediately into her mouth.

> Our afternoon was all sunlight and laughter, and too soon I was saying goodbye. I wondered when I might see him again and from the way his eyes met mine when we parted, I knew he wondered as well.

> I retired early but could not sleep. My mind was in turmoil and despite all of the windows open to catch the breeze, my room was still over-warm from the evening heat. I donned

my dressing gown and slippers and ventured outside.

The bright light of the full moon beckoned me forward. I could not contain myself but walked down the path until I reached the far end of the pier. I stood marveling at the depth of the sky above, rippling light on the water around me, and the black silhouettes of the tall pines bordering the lane. My white muslin glowed like a lantern and a slight breeze ruffled the bow, as though urging me to untie the sash, let the gown fall from my shoulders and dive into the cool water of the cove. Modesty and caution prevailed, though I admit I wanted to very much. I did allow myself to loosen the sash and held the dressing gown open to catch the wind like a sail.

I admit to feeling rather brazen, but knowing I was quite alone, enjoyed the sensation of the air billowing through and around my nightclothes. Even as a child I had not known such a glorious sense of freedom. Finally, cool and refreshed, I turned back to the cottage.

I saw him standing on the little knoll where the path leads to the pier.

"Dr. Stuart."

I tied the sash of my robe securely, wondering how long he had been watching. From his expression and demeanor, quite long enough, and I was swiftly gratified to have obeyed the vigilant little whisper of my conscience.

"Mrs. Cherrington." He gave me a somewhat formal bow, and his voice was even more resonant in the moonlit darkness.

"What brings you back to my cove tonight, sir?" I could not keep the amusement I felt from my own voice. What must he think of me?

"A most fortuitous bit of…well," he smiled himself at the pun as he held up his watch, "timing."

"Ah." I smiled as well, but disappointment was evident in my voice. "Yes, I saw your little games today, and hoped your timepiece robust enough to withstand baby's attentions."

I made to walk past him and continue to the cottage.

"I had thought the cottage to be a day retreat only. I did not dare

hope to see you again so soon," he said, slipping the watch into his pocket, and although he stepped no nearer, his eyes met mine, "It does not surprise me, however, to find the beautiful woman of the day is now an ethereal goddess of the night."

"Sir, you flatter me—"

"Yes."

Now he did step closer and we were within arm's reach of each other so that I had to look up to meet his gaze, wondering at the grave tone that answered my teasing remark.

"Most sincerely, and quite inadequately, I am afraid," he said, "Earlier today, as introductions were made, Mrs. Cherrington, I sensed some…some spark of …recognition…?"

His face was fully illuminated so that I could see every feature, those that reminded me so much of Wilson and his own, which I had studied surreptitiously but comprehensively throughout the day. The tears that filled my eyes remained hidden in the shadows, but I could not keep the tremor from my voice as I answered.

"Resemblance, not precisely, certainly, but you bear a distinct resemblance to a man…a man I have always loved and should have married."

When he made no move or comment, I continued. Darkness and his kindness, and in some way, his appearance suddenly allowed me the freedom to beseech Wilson's understanding and forgiveness. I told him the entire story of what happened. Even to my champion and friend, Thomas, I had not allowed myself to admit the worst of Edward's vile actions, but I inexplicably felt safe with this stranger and told him everything.

"He chose his opportunity well. Without my father or brother to turn to, Edward was present to declare his love and offer an escape from the terrible humiliation and betrayal. And I, the naïve innocent I was raised to be, believed him."

He reached into his pocket for a handkerchief, bereft as I so obviously was of such accoutrement. I held the soft linen to my eyes, perceiving the faint scent of vetiver, and…and of him. I crumpled it in my hand and continued my story, telling him shamelessly of my loveless marriage and isolated existence, and of the violence that escalated until the terrible day when I finally learned the truth about Wilson. Dr. Stuart made no interruption, but for a few sympathetic murmurs or an outraged tightening *of his features.*

"A day does not pass when I do not berate myself for the misery I caused and the terrible, terrible hurt I inflicted upon a most precious friend."

Finally, I finished my sordid tale and wiped the tears once again from my face. "What must you think of me, Dr. Stuart?" I drew my arms close around me against a sudden chill.

"But, my dear Mrs. Cherrington! Hardly more than a child, to be manipulated in such a way—" He paused, his green eyes glittering very much like emeralds in the moonlight. "Do not continue with this self-condemnation, for surely now the spirit of this kind man knows the truth and grieves for what you have endured."

He offered his arm and we walked slowly up the path to the cottage. As we walked, he told me his own story, of the death of his beloved wife three years before.

"Our marriage was a happy one and Mary a nurturing wife and charming companion. I believed she suffered more for me than for herself through her illness. I was powerless as her husband and physician and could only watch her very gradual and painful decline," his voice faltered, and he paused a moment before continuing. "After her death, my anger turned inward, and it was some time before I could bring myself to rejoin society. Until my own physician, a friend and mentor, declared my grief to be not only selfish but soul-damaging.

"I must admit to only reluctantly accepting the invitation from Uncle John, whom I had not seen in many years, hoping the company, sea air, and new vistas would help me escape the lethargy of spirit that gripped me."

We reached the cottage and I squeezed his arm lightly before releasing his gentle support. Stepping up onto the porch, I turned back to him, and I looked at him instead of up, my face now illuminated, his in shadow.

"I did not understand a conversation I overheard between Uncle John and Aunt Lydia soon after I arrived, she expressing her concern that meeting you might prove difficult."

"Difficult?"

"You share a resemblance to my wife, as you say I remind you of your fiancé. At first glance, I am afraid my reaction may have seemed quite discourteous. If that was the case, I do apologize, Mrs. Cherrington."

"Lilién…please call me Lilién."

"Lilién." He reached out and placed his hand upon my own. *"Throughout the day, however, hearing your lovely voice, observing your grace of movement and…the glorious abundance of your dark hair sparkling with reds and gold in the sunlight…"* he paused, reaching to touch a strand which had become loose from the tangled bundle, *"although I am grateful for the impressions which were initially quite astonishing, and have allowed for such a candid exchange between us."*

We stood quietly. I knew he, like I, did not want this private moment to end. At once there seemed nothing more to say and yet I knew I stood upon the threshold of some new and unexpected chapter. Did he feel the same?

"Dr. Stuart…"

"Adam."

"Adam," I began again, knowing what I was about to ask and yet not at all sure of how to phrase such a question. His hand rested once again on mine, reassuring and warm. *"When we were introduced, our eyes met …"*

"Yes."

"There was something else… something beyond the resemblance to Wilson, a certainty of some … some future…" I foundered awkwardly, my voice trembling, unable to continue in the same forthright manner and ask the question, once formed in my mind sent red into my cheeks that he must surely see even in the moonlight.

"Intimacy?"

"Yes," I whispered.

"Yes," he answered, with a smile in his voice, *"and I am most grateful to hear you acknowledge our mutual attraction so honestly. I presumed my … my response to your beauty was simply a boorishly masculine one."*

My only response to his admission was another wave of embarrassment, and I looked away.

"For tonight, however, I should leave you," he said, gently caressing my hand. *"May I call tomorrow?"*

The idea of his leaving, that we might risk losing this delicate link to daylight and the rules of conventional society, brought tears to my eyes once again.

"Please... Adam... do not leave..."

He hesitated only a moment before stepping up onto the porch and drawing me gently into his arms. "Lilién," he whispered my name tenderly.

"Lillian?"

When she opened her eyes, Mark was sitting on the floor beside the sofa. His green eyes were familiar, she thought, and then shook herself awake. Of course, they were familiar, it was Mark. He had merely taken out those dark contact lenses and was more himself again. He had taken off his shirt and freshened up, his hair damp and beginning to curl again.

As he read the email from Vera, she saw him visibly relax as his eyes moved over the screen.

"Vera would have said if there was anything of interest."

"No doubt," she smiled and closed her eyes against the light. "I'll go see Duncan tomorrow and find a way to talk to him away from the lab. Why are you awake already?"

"I thought I heard someone in the room. What were you reading about?"

"My great-great-great grandmother Lilién having sex."

"Brilliant," he said, yawning. "Where?"

"Right here in this house, with a tall, handsome, green-eyed Englishman. How's that for a coincidence?"

"Not *thoroughly* coincidental enough for me," he said. Lillian opened her eyes. The wicked smile in his voice was in those eyes as well.

"Sorry. It may have been a dream. Lots of strange dreams this week."

"Your subconscious at work, Lillian, maybe that's what woke me," he said, sleepily, leaning over to kiss her, "and I'm sorry, too."

Very sorry indeed, she added to herself, her lips tingling from the fleeting kiss, trying not to feel disappointed as she watched him walk back to the bedroom. If anything more was ever going to happen between them, it would be up to her. After his behavior at the lab, she knew he would never make the first move.

His body was as lithe and tanned as she remembered,

until the demarcation showing what he called his 'English rose' complexion at the loose waistband of his jeans. Also gone was the smell of fear he had carried with him when he arrived. He was back to smelling like Mark, God help her; something in the man's scent worked on her like a drug.

Picking up the diary, she searched unsuccessfully for Lilién's midnight confessions with the handsome doctor. Maybe it *was* her subconscious at work, she thought, her eyes heavy. Yawning, she scanned several pages. The last entry she remembered was Lilién's timid Victorian revelation about venturing out into the cool evening air.

> …I admit to feeling rather brazen, but knowing
> I was quite alone, enjoyed the sensation of the air
> billowing through and around my nightclothes.
> …

The scene Lilién described was so tranquil and the pull of sleep too strong, Lillian's eyes closed, and she felt her body drift. She heard the diary fall to the floor as she fumbled for the quilt on the back of the old sofa.

I took his hand and led him into the cottage.

Any courage I may have felt in the warm moonlight ebbed when we stood in the close confines of the little parlor.

My body responded to his warmth and strength, the ardor in his voice and quickening heartbeat. My mind, however, could not forget the pain that from our first time together had accompanied such physical relations with Edward. My arms slowly, tentatively, rose until my hands rested lightly against his chest. I was unable to keep the tremor from my voice.

"I am… a bit frightened."

He drew away and looked into my eyes. "I do not mean to be in any way indelicate, Lilién, … but have you never once known pleasure during…intimate relations?"

Tears started in my eyes at the tenderness in his voice and I could only shake my head.

He reached out to rest his hand on my cheek and his lips were gentle against mine, caressing, and unlike any kiss I had ever known. Edward had used his mouth with the same violence with which he used his fists and manhood. Remembering dear Wilson's embrace in the garden, and my own insincere response to something that might have been as special as this kiss brought more tears to my eyes.

I felt the heightening of Adam's desire as his body tightened. His kiss grew more insistent and yet I knew he held his passion in check for my sake.

"Lilién," he whispered drawing away from me quite suddenly, resting his lips against my temple, "are you quite certain?"

Certain? I asked myself, uncertain now if the fear fluttering through me was at the idea of his staying or the thought of his leaving. In answer, I took his hand and led him back to the bedroom, conscious of the jumbled mess I had made of my bedclothes in the restlessness that had taken me out into the night.

Adam looked only at me, stroked my hair gently but with an intensity that told me he was seeing ephemeral glimpses of his Mary. In this muted light, his resemblance to Wilson was striking.

His hands began to move over my body, each new touch sending those same tendrils of sensation spiraling through me. Quickly, deftly, he untied the sash of my peignoir, slipped the soft muslin from my shoulders and let it fall to the floor. He pulled the few pins from my hair allowing it to fall free while his kiss grew more intimate, his tongue fleetingly touching mine, causing me to gasp and my knees to weaken.

He took my hands and moved them to his shirt.

Until quite recently, I had no notion that most men performed these intimate functions sans clothing. While Edward would sometimes insist I remove my own garments, he loosened his own only enough to perform the act quickly and forcefully before leaving me.

My fingers trembling, I unfastened the buttons as he slid the straps of the gown from my shoulders and it too dropped to our feet. When I had clumsily undone the last, his shirt fell open and he pulled me close.

Our first skin to skin touch, his chest and belly against mine made me gasp, astonished by this warm intimacy I had never known. His whispered endearments halted with a sobbing moan, vibrating through me, as though he was a man who had not known he was dying of thirst and had unexpectedly been presented with a silver goblet of fresh, cool water.

I whispered my own breathless encouragements and French endearments as Adam's hands moved down my back and he pulled me even closer against him. I knew he was ready, had felt his hardness against me at our first kiss, but was I? Even with the animal instincts overtaking him, Adam understood my fear and was not forceful in his passion. His body grew taut as my hands caressed his back and I moved against him, telling myself and endeavoring to show him I was not afraid.

He stepped away and looked at me, now completely unclothed in the bright, lace-dappled moonlight. I felt no embarrassment, due, I think, to the expressions crossing his face as he turned me slightly toward the light.

Awed, almost worshipful, his eyes moved over my body. I myself seemed to be made of lace, paisleys spiraling around my breasts, flowers blossoming across my belly, and when Adam reached out to trace the tendrils of a vine along my arm, his hand was absorbed, too, chameleon-like into the pattern.

His touch, his gaze, the moonlight, kindled a long quiescent ember within me, and the shadowy camouflage offered a shield, granting a power I had never before known. Adam, hair tousled into his eyes, leaned down to take my hardened nipple into his warm mouth. He suckled gently. A…sensation, too intense to be pleasure, though certainly not pain, spiraled through my body, robbing me of breath, causing my womb to clench and my inner thighs to ache. Impulsively, I reached to touch myself, moaning again at the swollen, tender wetness my fingers encountered. Adam drew away, watching me, pulling off his shirt and at the laces and buttons of his trousers until, soon, we were each clothed only in the same exotic patterns.

My hands roamed across his skin, my fingers threading through the silken strands of his hair, glowing pale gold in the moonlight. He sat on the bed, guiding me to stand in front of him, as he alternately suckled and fondled my breasts, sending the same streaks of joyful agony through me until I was compelled to touch him.

At his sharp intake of breath, I began to draw away, believing I had caused him pain but his hand covered mine. I felt the velvety flesh harden even more under our combined touch.

He lay back, pulling me with him. "Take me, Lilién," he whispered, "take me inside."

FOR A TIME, LILLIAN simply sat on the edge of the old bed and watched him sleep.

His jeans now draped over the footboard, he lay on his

back, one arm up over his head and Lilién's lace-edged sheet drawn up to his waist.

Listening to Mark's deep, steady breathing, she fell almost trancelike into the same rhythm and took pleasure in the surreptitious contemplation of his features.

Smooth brow, wide straight eyebrows, and long dark lashes, but no hint now of the lines that fanned out from his eyes when he smiled. Light and shadow accentuated his long, straight nose, strong jawline and wide mouth.

She stood up and closed the door quietly.

When she turned back to the bed, the clouds finally cleared, allowing intense moonlight to shine in through the curtains. Mark, the bed, and when she opened the ties of the robe and let it slip from her shoulders, her own body, were now patterned with paisleys, roses, and vines.

She sensed Mark was awake by a subtle change in his breathing. In fact, she noticed with amusement, that he didn't appear to *be* breathing. She sat beside him again, reached for his hand and placed it on her breast, where it disappeared, chameleon-like, into the lace.

MOANING FROM A RESIDUAL TINGLE of pleasure from the night of vivid dreams about Lilién and Adam, she fought against full consciousness. Rain fell heavily again, and gray light filtered in through the lace that moonlight had made so magical for their first time.

Lillian was first aware of the unusual weight, and second of her fingers playing with, entwined in, someone's hair.

Her eyes flew open.

In the bedroom, in Lilién's white bed where Mark still slept, his long form curled on and around her. *Okay, maybe not sleeping.* He laughed at the gasp his touch elicited and looked up at her, bright-eyed, lines of fatigue and anxiety now gone.

"Bonjour, Madame!" he said, adding a lovely stream of what she presumed was fluent and perfectly pronounced French, which she did not understand at all.

"*What?*"

"I said, Good morning, Madam. I did not know you spoke French!"

Chapter Sixteen

Storm Warnings

HER FATHER LOOKED AT her strangely, his gaze lingering on the scarf she had tied in her hair, at what she was holding out to him and back up at her face.

"They're just blackberries," she said, watching as a memory passed through her father's eyes, sympathetic with those who looked at her strangely and asked what was wrong when she had her déjà vu moments. "I thought you loved blackberries."

He raised his hand and touched the blue, gold and green floral and paisley silk scarf. "This was your great-grandmother Claire's," he said, before giving a short laugh, "but then I bet you already knew that!

"She went with me," he said, "the first time I was taking out a little skiff I had bought from the neighbors. Grandfather had gone to Baltimore on business, so that made it a good day at the start, knowing he'd be gone for an entire week.

"She had a big, white metal bucket with her, I remember, and said she was off to pick blueberries for the day. Well, Jake and I had found this fantastic patch on the little island just a short way up the cove." He laughed, his expression clearing. "My grandmother was a brave woman. I had painted and polished my little boat to a shine but hadn't spent much time testing her seaworthiness. We spent that whole day picking berries. We both got sunburned, I got stung a few times, but I have to say it was probably the best memory I have of my childhood," he took a blackberry from the bowl and popped it in his mouth. "The blueberry pies and muffins weren't bad either!"

Tom's expression clouded again, and he examined her face feature by feature, from her stubborn chin to her brown hair.

"Dad?"

"Maybe it was because I was so set against anything of my past, but I never saw until today that you share a resemblance to her."

"Oh? I haven't noticed that in the pictures we've found."

He examined each feature again, lingering on her eyes. At first uncomfortable with the scrutiny, she realized that he wasn't looking at his daughter, but through her to see the elements of the woman who had helped him survive his childhood.

"Not the infamous square chin? That looks to come down through the Bonneau family."

"No, not that distinct inheritance stamped on Brendan and me. No, it's your eyes" he said, shaking his head and smiling at her expression. "Not the color, honey, the deep, dark brown is definitely your mother's. It's the way you see things and mirror back what you're thinking or feeling. Sometimes I've caught that look and felt a jolt of memory. Now I know why."

"HEY, STRANGER," MARIAH SAID, glancing up from her computer in surprise when Lillian walked into Voyagers.

After trying so diligently to avoid Duncan, there was nothing else to do but to see him in person.

"Hey yourself," she said, smiling and trying to keep her voice natural, noticing how Mariah minimized her screen. But was she Googling tips on workplace espionage or the secrets of Sappho? "How's everything?"

"Quiet. Too quiet with everyone gone. His Majesty's back and that's livened things up," Mariah said, giving her a slow up and down look. "I've missed having you around"

"I've missed being here. I thought I would see if there were any projects I could help with, now my Dad is better and I have some extra time. Is Duncan in?"

Mariah appraised her, taking in everything from her painted toenails and tight white Capri's to the navy and white striped sailor tee that was a bit too scoop-necked for regulation.

"He's talking to Trey, but go on in. He won't mind," Mariah said, nodding towards his office with a slight smirk, "he definitely won't mind."

Lillian stepped inside, closing the door softly behind her. On the phone, he stood looking out the window as he finished a discussion about the wreck, how they were finally ready to resume diving after a recent summer squall.

"…at least for a few days," she heard him say. He lowered his voice, adding, "after that, I'll have to go to Kingston… no, I'm not sure, but let's wait until I'm back on board."

Over a month since she had seen him, and her body responded as always with a startling awareness of her beating heart and an instinct to touch him, as though he was a part of her own self she had been without for far too long.

Never far from my deepest thoughts was a line from a beloved old book and very romantic when she first read it as a teenager, but she hadn't truly understood what it meant or how it felt. She knew, now, it was being apart from someone you are somehow bound to in heart, mind, and spirit and the smallest trigger, a scent, a song, or the gray-blue depths of the ocean, brings them instantly to mind.

After ending the call, he stood looking out towards the harbor until she tapped lightly on the door. She couldn't help smiling at his expression when he turned and saw her.

"Lily…"

"Mariah said to come in…I hope it's a good time," she said lightly, reaching out as she walked towards him.

"Lily…" he repeated, taking her hand, frowning as she gave a slight shake of her head. "Always a good time for such a pleasant surprise...what can I do for you?"

She knew he had seen the warning in her eyes at the same time he felt the paper hit his palm. His gaze sharpened, and he met her eyes with a question.

"Vera told me the good news about the wreck," she said, sliding up to perch on the edge of his desk, smiling up at him. "Now that Dad's so much better and I have some time, I'd like to get back to work."

"I'm glad to hear both. Of course you can come in, anytime. Still have your key?"

She nodded. "I read the article in the Sun. How are things on the…Fleur?"

MY GOD, SHE WAS GORGEOUS, Duncan thought, looking down at her, taking in the beguiling smile, healthy glow of her skin, and the faint scent of lavender. He didn't need to read whatever was on the note she had slipped him to know she wanted his attention.

What *was* she doing here in her make-up and perfume and uncharacteristically tight pants? And the shirt, my god, he thought, when she leaned forward slightly. He hoped he was responding properly, feeling as though he'd just been clobbered by a boom after a faulty jibe.

"Here, Lily," he pulled out his chair, gesturing for her to sit, "take a look at the latest …"

She hopped down from the desk, the flirtatious façade dropping immediately as she looked through the images. He leaned against the desk and opened her note.

ONLY MINUTES HAD PASSED since Duncan last looked at his watch. Time was crawling, and nothing could distract his mind from thinking about Lily. He glanced again at her note.

LilyRose 2300.

He paced, difficult as that was in the cabin of a thirty-foot sailboat, sat again at the console, looking at the most recent images of the side-wheeler from Trey.

Despite his delight at seeing Lily again, she might as well have been trailing a string of red warning pennants in her wake. At the office on a rare day he was in town, dressed more, well, more deliberately alluring than he had ever seen her, the note and look of caution in her deep brown eyes. He was glad to be in a port with a nearby water supply because he had run the tanks dry from shaving twice followed by a long cold shower... her motives not quite clear.

It certainly wasn't about the job, and it wasn't personal—well, not personal enough to justify shaving twice, he was sure. No, the cryptic note and the warning in her eyes could only mean she knew something she shouldn't and was worried about him. But how? Her father would never have told her.

He looked at his watch again. She didn't know his real home was a sailboat only two piers away from the *LilyRose*. Done with waiting, he left the boat to walk around the marina to honor the discretion of her invitation and make sure he wasn't followed.

"SEATON? HE DIDN'T TRY anything—?"

Lillian had started to tell him why she'd needed to see him, her demeanor much more subdued than when she had visited his office earlier in the day.

"Do you know anything about this?"

He sat across the short span of the galley table from her. No flirtatious looks or low-cut anything now, her gaze serious and direct.

LILLIAN WAITED, WATCHING DUNCAN weigh how much to tell her.

"Yes," he finally admitted. "I found out about the smuggling on *Jupiter*'s last run."

"Not about your business partner's and wife's family planning to 'get rid' of you?"

"I suspected it would be inevitable if the stakes were high enough, but I admit I did not expect it to happen on board my own ship," he said, reaching his hands across the table for hers but she sat back and crossed her arms.

"I've been working on ways to get to those who *are* involved, without getting anyone killed or destroying Vic. I'm sure Vic doesn't know—at least I'm sure he doesn't *want* to know."

"That's what Mark got from what he overheard. What will you do now?"

"I have ideas and people I trust," he said. "I'm not sure that includes Seaton. Particularly after recent events."

"Before coming to Voyagers this afternoon, I searched Josiah's office. It's not spelled out in black and white, of course, but there was enough in the paperwork to convince me it's true. Mark is on assignment with the NCA."

"That doesn't negate what happened between the three of us. He may have his own agenda now."

"No, I don't think so." She shook her head. "I trust him, and you need to talk to him. He's wanted to work *with* you for the last year, but his higher-ups didn't want you brought into the investigation. The only reason he came to me is because he couldn't get to you."

"He tried?"

"Right after leaving the shipyard. Didn't Mariah tell you?"

He paused before answering. "No, and that would be unlike her."

"Does Mariah know the real reason you wanted those photographs? If she knows and isn't to be trusted, the Andrastus family knows the first one was real, even Victoria."

Confusion in his eyes was quickly replaced by another expression she knew too well.

"Lily," he said, again reaching out his hands, this time gesturing with his fingers to hand hers over. "That was for *you*. News about me upset you, I came looking for you, upset you even more *and* gave Seaton the opportunity to take advantage of you…" he met her eyes, adding, "I know your values and I know my obligations, no matter what feelings we have for each other. I accept the responsibility and deeply regret what happened that night. Coming up with a plausible story to mitigate the damage was just an answer to a prayer."

"Vera's?"

"I'll tell you my side of that story one day," he said, smiling, "but now I'd better go." Gripping her hands tighter, he made no move to stand. "I'm grateful you've told me what you heard, and all Seaton told you could be true. Forewarned is forearmed, and I will talk with him, tonight. But, please don't get further into this, or come back to Voyagers, either. I'll give Mariah some excuse.

"And Lily," he paused, "it *is* my fault you don't have a job anymore. Do you need money? Call it an advance, a loan, a gift, I don't care…"

She shook her head, tears in her eyes again.

He released her hands, stood up and waited by the ladder, waiting for her to join him.

When she didn't, he leaned across the table and kissed her.

"Please be careful," she whispered as he turned and stepped up through the hatch.

She waited until she heard his footsteps fade, put her face in her hands that were still warm from his, and cried.

AS WHEN SHE WAS seventeen and home much too late, her father demanded to know where she had been. Now, unaccustomed to higher command authority, she responded with an almost Miranda-like reaction.

"And don't raise your eyebrows to me, missy!"

"I'm a bit old to have a curfew, *Daddy*."

She dropped her purse and keys on the hall table, kicked off her shoes and went to the kitchen. He followed and sat at the table and watched as she poured herself a glass of wine, waiting to say more until she was sitting next to him.

"Driven to tears *and* drink," he observed dryly. "Your uncharacteristic nocturnal wanderings must have something to do with Duncan Scott."

"The only person who's ever driven me to both. At once,

anyway," she added, trying to smile at him, seeing through his stern expression. Wiping tears away with the sleeve of her sweater, she added, "I'm sorry."

"After what you've both said to me, I thought you meant to avoid one another."

"And we have, but I …I had to see him tonight."

He was waiting for her to elaborate but she believed Mark's warning, believed Duncan was in danger and anyone who was important to him was at risk as well, the true reason he had taken such prompt action to deflect attention from her, she knew now. To tell anyone else the truth, even her father, meant she would be involving him, and her children.

Before she could fabricate an excuse that did not involve attempted murder or adultery, her father interrupted her thoughts.

"A blind man could see you're more frightened than lovesick, honey. Is this about the smuggling?"

PART VI

BRENDAN

Wilmington, North Carolina
December 26, 1864

In the midst of suffering and death ... a woman must
soar beyond the conventional modesty considered correct under
different circumstances.

Phoebe Yates Pember
A Southern Woman's Story, 1879

Chapter Seventeen

Arabella

THE RAMSHACKLE RAILROAD'S MANY delays worked in Brendan's favor and the train was just pulling into the Camden station when he arrived. He stowed his cargo on the train, saw to Jumper and boarded the rickety car for the dismal trip back to Wilmington.

A unit of Georgia infantry was aboard, being transferred to Fort Fisher as well as several officers on their way to Richmond, the line from Wilmington through Greensborough and Danville now the only way to reach the capital of the Confederacy. There, they said, lines were in even worse condition, running with cars that were windowless and in serious disrepair, traveling at a snail's pace over rails that were nearly worn out.

Arrival in Wilmington was announced before the whistle blew and the train lurched to a relieved stop by the sharp scent of turpentine and the low tide smell of rotting fish wafting in the salty air. Despite the discomforts, Brendan had slept, deeply, folded awkwardly in the narrow seat.

Heavy clouds darkened the sky, only a vague band of light on the western horizon indicated it was not yet night.

After commandeering the services of a Wagoner, he loaded his trunks onto the rickety old buckboard, tied Jumper to the back and they started for the wharf. The driver reminded him repeatedly, when the wagon threatened to rattle apart along the rutted or cobbled roads, he was lucky to find any kind of a wagon with Wilmington in its current state.

"Some calls it Yankee fireworks woke us Christmas

Eve," the old man said, with a hoarse guffaw, "all I know is there was no fire and whatever the hell they were plannin' didn't work. Damn noisy, though."

From the early hours of Christmas Eve, through Christmas Day, Otis described the bombardment that had Wilmington in an uproar, as though Yankees would be sailing up the Cape Fear at any minute. When the bombing quieted, so did the panic.

Still, he said, the Yankees would be back and sooner than later. Otis reported that two other runners had slipped through after the *Kendal*, and not long before the first explosion, and the three vessels were now loaded. The *Wild Rover,* just returned from the steam presses, was now set to sail before midnight, one of the fastest turnarounds ever, he said, adding, "Cotton's piled so high on deck, won't be a lack of hidin' places from Yankee bullets!"

A way to shield volatile barrels of turpentine from Yankee bullets, as well, Brendan knew, smelling the heavy evergreen tang on the air. Not only valuable exports, cotton, and turpentine were excellent combustibles when in need of a quick escape.

The Wagoner said *Kendal* would have already been at the steam presses across the river to have her own hold loaded with hundreds of bales of cotton, but for engine troubles.

"Thomas!" Jumping from the wagon, he called to the young mess boy idling by the stern.

"Aye, sir!" Thomas answered readily. "We didn't expect you back in time," he added, looking anxiously toward the bridge, where Jack Hudson was calling out orders to the crew.

Brendan had forgotten about Hudson; no doubt Shaw had already promoted him for the run to St. George's. He wouldn't be happy about the demotion; the man had barely concealed hostility towards Brendan as it was.

"Don't worry about Hudson, Thomas. He can do my job this run, at least until it's time to collect the pay!" he laughed, paying the driver for his services and giving Jumper a final pat. Charging the driver with her return to the livery, he headed towards the ship.

Brendan stowed his belongings in his cabin where he would have normally carried his own bales of cotton to sell in St. George's. An hour later he headed towards the docks with a feeling of grateful reprieve; Thomas had confirmed the news *Kendal* would not be ready to leave until the next evening at the earliest. And when he had given the boy a merry Christmas by appointing him to stand guard duty for extra pay, the youngster's face lit up at the thought of having the first officer's cabin all to himself for the night.

KNOWING WHAT HE DID about Miles Barber, he would not be drawn to the lowest of the dockside establishments nor could he afford the highest. He was counting on old McRae to be home tonight so along with other intelligence, he could suggest a strategy for Brendan's search of the Wilmington brothels.

Stiff and uncomfortable, he almost regretted his choice of attire. He was so rarely out of uniform these days, his old fawn colored breeches, and white linen shirt with the high cravat, his cape swirling around his legs as he walked all felt strange to him. He made his way to McRae's small house near the old Crenshaw warehouse and saw a warm glow in the parlor window.

"Brendan!" Old McRae looked through a crack in the door and then swung it wide. "I wouldn't have thought you'd have time to visit your aunt's old friend tonight. You must be heading back to St. George's soon!"

He waggled his wiry eyebrows, but Brendan didn't need the warning to know not to speak openly. One of Everleigh's cautions came to mind: The truth, whenever possible, is best.

"Engine problems, sir, keep us in port longer than anticipated—," he broke off, nodding to the other gentleman, who was none other than John Dawson, the mayor of Wilmington.

Brendan removed his hat as McRae made the introductions and wondered if McRae had drawn the careworn and gray-faced man into his network. Against secession from the beginning, Dawson had had to ease his views to preserve his position once North Carolina left the Union.

Whether or not their visit had concluded, once Dawson realized Brendan was an officer on a private blockade runner, his pleasant expression soured, and he excused himself brusquely.

"You can't really blame him," the old man said, pouring the brandy and gesturing towards the recently vacated chair near the fire. "Between the army, the crews, and the high prices, his town's imploding all around him and there's not one damn thing he can do about it." He waggled his eyebrows again, adding, "not much anyway."

He sat down heavily in the frayed old chair and lifted his own glass, raised it to Brendan in salute and drank.

"Now, sir, what news from Bermuda?"

While relaying information about the frantic state of affairs in St. George's and what he had just learned from the Wagoner about the runners ready to leave Wilmington, Brendan placed the letters from Charles Allen on a tray next to his usual seat by the fire. He glanced around casually. On the bookshelf near the door, he saw the correspondence, tucked safely between Hawthorn's *The Scarlet Letter* and Cooper's *The Pathfinder,* for him to carry back to the U.S. Consul in Bermuda.

"YOU SAY SHE WAS seen near the docks?" When Brendan nodded, McRae added, "Talk to Rick at Merry Times. Tell him I sent you, he might remember a girl of her description. You don't have an image, I suppose?"

Brendan paused briefly before reaching for his watch. The little picture was cut and shaped perfectly within the gold cover.

McRae studied the picture thoughtfully and then cleared his throat gruffly, handing the watch back to him. "Damn shame...something is familiar," he paused, then shook his head sadly, "No, I'm sorry, lad. I do hope you can find her, but ..." the old man stopped as though he had misgivings about what he had been about to say. "A bit of advice. First of all, I think I have known you long enough to know you'll see things you're going to object to, and if you want to find this girl you're going to have to ignore them and not play white knight to the damsels. Most of them either have someone else to fight their battles or can fight their own.

"You won't need to bother with the transients in their covered wagons and tents along the edge of town, and … well, be prepared if you go to River's Run," he said, adding at Brendan's look of surprise, "let me just say, dear boy, if she has been at River's, what did you say, since August? Well then …." At Brendan's expression, McRae added gently, "I suppose I shouldn't presume, but you *have* been in a brothel?"

Brendan hesitated, but nodded and answered, "In Charleston. A place called Grace's."

"*Oh, well then,*" McRae was impressed, his eyebrows waggling again.

Brendan clarified the impression quickly. "Once. A very long time ago."

"Grace's is at one end of a very broad spectrum. Expensive, with clean, pretty girls, private rooms and time to indulge. At some of these other places like River's, it's a wide-open warehouse kind of affair, where the customer goes to a bed where a candle is lit to let them know a girl is unoccupied, with a dozen others, friend or foe, going at it around them like beasts."

McRae poured more brandy into each of their glasses. "She won't be the same girl you left behind, son. I hate to say this, but if you have any feelings for this girl and she has lived such a life for so long, it, well, it might be best you never find her."

BRENDAN SAT IN THE back booth at the Blue Star Tavern, bolting his second whiskey and trying to decide if he should tell Shaw he wouldn't be making the trip back to St. George's, trying to shake the lingering abhorrence he felt. Maybe Jems was right, maybe he was a prude, or prig, or whatever label anyone wanted to put on him, but the only reaction he could muster was shame at his own gender and pity for the other.

And dread, having not found one clue as to Arabella's whereabouts in his first attempts.

Once the ship was ready, there would be no other reprieve. Understanding as the captain had been about Brendan's need to look to family matters, he was not so sure his understanding would extend to a girl to whom he had no formal obligation.

He still had a job to do for Everleigh, and he needed to take the information he would collect from McRae back to Charles Allen. As the US Consul in Bermuda, Allen was on an island in more ways than one, as most of the people were distinctly pro-South. In Allen, he had found not only a reliable way to transfer intelligence to Washington but a friend with whom he could share his true identity. The Confederacy was holding on tenaciously to thin strands of hope and as it did, thousands continued to die needlessly. If he could play one small part to bring it to a close, he had to try, but the obligation to duty never felt as burdensome as it did tonight.

He owed old McRae for the vivid descriptions that prepared him for what he had found at the Cape, a wide-open room at the top of a bare plank stairway, in addition to being cold and drafty with open rafters high above.

Rain pattering on the tin roof helped mute the chorus of guttural moaning, whispers and whimpering, and the thumping squeaks and rattles of bed springs echoing around the cavernous space. The only attempts here towards discretion were bed sheets draped around each cubicle, apparently making this a higher-class establishment than River's.

A candle was lit in the little, curtained cubicle nearest the stairs.

He had peered in cautiously to see a broad-faced woman reading a book. Twirling a strand of straw-colored hair with one hand and holding the book up close to the light with the other, Brendan was envious of her oblivion to what was going on around them and had to clear his throat for her to acknowledge him.

She sighed, slapped the book shut and looked up, winsomeness softening her expression immediately as she took in his appearance.

He stepped behind the curtain and crouched beside the bed, explaining his mission before any natural misunderstanding could occur. The girl gazed thoughtfully at Arabella's picture in the candlelight, and handed Brendan's watch back, shaking her head sadly.

"Good book?" he asked, standing and handing her a coin for her help.

"Nah," she'd said with a shrug, "but readin' seems to scare off the worst of 'em."

HE *HAD* TO FIND Arabella and though McRae had warned him against going to River's Run, he did not agree with the old man. He thought of his father, and the words he had spoken about his duty to protect those who were weak and vulnerable.

River's was the last den of iniquity to search. He tossed back the rest of his drink, pulled his still dripping cloak and hat from the peg and once again headed out into the rain.

"Brendan Bonneau?"

He looked away from the entrance to River's at the man who had just brushed past him.

"If *you* are contemplating going into that establishment," a deep voice drawled, "I fear the South is truly lost." Lucas Kershaw reached out his left hand. "How are you, Brendan?"

"Major Kershaw."

Shocked at the appearance of his brother's best friend, his presence in this unlikely place and the worn empty-sleeved uniform the haggard man wore, it took him time to respond.

"I was indeed contemplating such a feat, but not for the

reasons you might imagine."

Brendan explained himself as they moved away from the entrance when two men staggered out, laughing as they stumbled down the stairs. Kershaw looked incredulous and then laughed outright.

"Arabella Barkley? Good God! If she were in a brothel, she'd be running the place, not at the mercy of any man!"

"Thank God." Brendan's voice shook, he leaned against the roughhewn timber of the building and had to pause before asking, "Do you know where she is?"

Kershaw's amusement softened as he watched Brendan's reaction. "I remember Louis saying you were sweet on her. You had better brace yourself. She may not be a whore, little brother, but she is not the sweet young thing you remember."

"BRENDAN BONNEAU, HOW *COULD* you believe that?"

"I did *not* believe, I did not *want* to believe it, but Miles Barb—" Brendan protested quickly trying to reconcile his last memory of Arabella with this sharp-eyed woman, now standing in front of him, hands on her hips as though ready for a fight.

The girl was there, though, he saw clearly enough when she first caught sight of he and Lucas starting up the steps to the hospital, where Lucas said she had been working for months. The relief and joy on her face told him everything he needed to know and mirrored his own.

Lucas told her where Brendan had been searching, gave him a pat on the back and Arabella a one-armed hug and walked away as she hissed like an angry cat. Brendan could hear Lucas laughing as he walked down Water Street.

"Miles!" A sharp laugh escaped her. "Isn't that a fine way to thank me for nursin' him back to health? Not to mention pluckin' lice and combin' nits out of his hair! He said he loved me and I told him that wasn't love that was gratitude!"

Her blue eyes blazed in the half-light of the streetlamps. Brendan was glad to be in shadow, certain of the landed-fish look he must surely have on his face.

"Well, he took *that* all wrong. I like Miles well enough or did anyways, but I don't think I could love anyone I'd plucked lice off for three days. My God Brendan, he was *covered*!" She paused for breath and looked up at him, no longer angry, no trace of the former coquet about her, either. "Would you mind buyin' me dinner? I'm more than half starved from workin' all day!"

Seated at the tavern he'd left only minutes earlier, they sat in a back booth away from the rowdiest clientele, and he watched as she devoured a plate of catfish and fried potatoes unabashedly, so unlike the days when the girls only picked daintily at their food, as though lack of a healthy appetite was some kind of enticement.

Rather like the Old South, Arabella was beyond that kind of guile now. She talked about the three years she had worked as a nurse, first in Richmond, then Atlanta, until she had moved to Wilmington the previous autumn to escape the unwanted attentions of a most grateful patient

At first, she told him between bites, it was just sitting nearby, bathing feverish brows, writing letters home, or reading innumerable chapters of Dickens or Thackeray.

Under the strict eye of her aunt and other chaperones she could do no more until one night as she was leaving for home and the first casualties from Mechanicsville arrived, she was commandeered into service by a frantic surgeon. She learned to handle chloroform in a hurry, she told Brendan, and found a way to be truly useful despite the indignation of her aunt.

"God Almighty, Brendan! I do not understand what all the fuss is about! We are all just mortal bodies and it does *not* take long to stop being shy when you have to help a poor armless gentleman scratch an itch, poor thing, layin' there cryin' in an agony of body and spirit. We both cried and laughed, but he was more comfortable and I was less bashful when that was done with." She paused long enough to drink most of the beer from her cup, still ladylike enough to dab her mouth with a crumpled handkerchief that served as a napkin.

"You're shocked," she said, smiling. "Is it my nursin'

stories or my bad manners?"

"How could we have ever known what was to come the last time we saw one another?" He remembered Jems's teasing as Arabella stood on the porch, waving to him as they rode away that night. "I was still in the United States Navy and swore to keep my oath even though it made me a traitor to my family, and my friends. Now I am an officer on a blockade runner, which is truly not much better in the eyes of some. Are *you* shocked?"

"Doctor Berton said if it wasn't for the medicine and supplies you all bring in, there would be a lot more sufferin' and dyin'."

"Word is that the squadron will be ready to launch a new attack soon. Before long Fort Fisher will be taken and Wilmington lost to us."

He reached into his pocket and drew out Jems's crumpled and stained kepi. "I've kept this for you since Hampton Roads."

He watched as she held it gently, subdued to silence, the candlelight reflecting on her tears. Before he could reach out to comfort her she threw back her shoulders, pulled the cap on over her tangled mass of auburn curls.

"Jems saved my life that day. I only wish I could have saved him, too, Bella."

"He would have been happy just knowin' he saved you. Did he know?" she looked up at him, the tears now flowing freely down her cheeks.

He remembered waking to find Jems dead on the deck beneath him. "When he thought he had me captured, he laughed at me. Seemed to think it a mighty good joke."

He reached over and took her hands in his, warm and rough and a bit slippery from the greasy fish. When she returned the embrace, he felt his ring brush against her own and turned her hand to look at it. The gold band with its shining star sapphire was now on the third finger of her left hand.

His eyes met hers.

"When I moved from Richmond to Atlanta, the doctor said it would save us both from a lot of interferin' busy-bodies if

I wore a wedding' ring and said I was … um…married."

He was surprised when rose flushed her cheeks at such an innocent admission, after her graphic nursing testimonials of the past hour. She pulled her hands away and used the old handkerchief to wipe her eyes and blow her nose.

"Wouldn't Jems think it an even better joke that you tried to save me," her eyes widened in mock horror, "from a fate worse than death."

He raised his glass. "To Jems."

She echoed the words softly and drank again. The gusto she had exhibited earlier had vanished, and signs of fatigue shadowed her young face when she pulled off the kepi and slipped it into her satchel. About to suggest he escort her home, she caught his eye.

"So, tell me, sailor, just where were you goin' to look for me tonight?"

"*Looked*," he corrected wryly, turning on the wooden bench to stretch out his long legs. He reached across the table for her hand again. "After Merry Times, I went on to the Cape, where, after pocketing my silver, the keeper invited me to 'go on up and have a look see'," he mimicked in a flat mid-western twang, "an experience I will not forget anytime soon."

Arabella giggled, color again flooding her cheeks.

He studied her in the flickering candlelight and held her small work-worn hand, feeling both the calluses on her palm and the strength of her grip. Paradoxical, from the determined bearing of her petite frame, eyes that reflected both vulnerability and strength, the no-nonsense heroics of her three years of nursing and the innocence now casting a rosy glow in her cheeks.

Just as openly, those blue eyes moved over him, resting on his hair, his mouth until their eyes met. Shattering glass and a barrage of swearing and laughter shook them from their reverie.

"Tomorrow—"

Her eyes widened in alarm, "Oh, God damn! What time is it?"

He pulled out his watch at the barked order.

"Almost midnight," he answered, watching her bravado

fade.

"I'm locked out. Matron is hell on girls who miss curfew. The one time it happened I had to go back to the hospital and sleep in the storeroom."

"I have a room at the hotel—".

The old demure batting of eyelashes quickly replaced the panic, "Mister Bonneau, now *you* have succeeded in shocking *me*."

Covering his embarrassment at the improperly phrased announcement, he jumped up from the bench and held her cloak for her, "For you, Bella, for when I found you," he stammered as she laughed at his discomfiture, "I'm going back to the ship tonight."

Her weariness was even more apparent when she stood, but as he slipped the cloak over her shoulders he heard her whisper, "We'll just see about that!"

They walked through the noisy tavern and into the street, the glow faded into the heavy Cape Fear fog that muted the streetlamps along Water Street.

Laughing as they slipped and tripped on the wet, uneven cobblestones, memories of old times kept them warm. The spirits of those they had lost did not intrude but hovered just beyond the outer bands of light they passed along the way.

PART VII

LILLIAN

Annapolis, Maryland

"Truth is the beginning of every good thing..."

Plato
Laws, 360 BCE

Chapter Eighteen

Ouzo Makes a Window for The Truth

AFTER THE LATE-NIGHT warning from Lillian, followed immediately by a meeting with Seaton at his apartment, Duncan knew it was time to talk to Vic.

Guarded though it was at first, after hearing Seaton's entire story he believed the guy and sometime in the middle of the night, he told Seaton some things as well and hoped he did not find himself regretting it anytime soon.

Vic often attended an afternoon social at the Greek Orthodox Church each Saturday before returning to his estate for dinner. Victoria, customarily, if she was in town, was always out late.

The housekeeper's expression brightened immediately when she answered the bell.

"Dr. Scott!" Sophie beamed up at him and, as usual, beckoned him down to her level so she could kiss each cheek, and giggled, as usual, when he returned them with gusto.

"Mr. Andrastus will be so happy to see you! And I'm cooking one of your favorites tonight! How did you know? You must stay for dinner!"

As he approached the study door, Vic walked out, his expression both worried and sad until he caught sight of Duncan.

"My son!" he cried, with not only true pleasure in his greeting but relief in his eyes. Vic grasped his face, and like Sophie, planted the traditional kisses on both cheeks.

"What brings you all the way out to our side of the village, my boy?" Vic asked, worry settling behind his eyes again;

a natural question, people always wanted something from Vic.

"I was in the neighborhood and the aroma of …" he paused, turning his nose towards the kitchen and sniffing the aroma of roasting lamb and garlic, "PAIDAKIA... was too much to resist."

Sophie, eavesdropping from the kitchen, called out, "I've already set another plate!"

"Yes, yes! Stay for dinner! Tell me all about the new site, and the new ship! Such a *beauty*!"

When he'd moved from the mansion, there were very few things he truly missed. Good conversation with Vic and Sophie, not to mention Sophie's cooking, ranked at the top of the list.

Tonight was like old times, Duncan thought, and knew Vic was remembering so many evenings shared in just the same way. Back in Vic's study after dinner, Vic was pouring the ouzo again. Vic was as generous with his ouzo as he was with his money.

"The ouzo makes your eyes sparkle, my boy! Like the night so long ago in Agios Nikolaos, Pelegia's, eh? Remember little Clio?" Vic chuckled at Duncan's expression.

"Not so little Clio, as I recall."

"Drawn to you like a honeybee to a rock rose and after a few drinks you were her willing captive!" Vic chuckled indulgently. "The ouzo worked even on our Saint Duncan."

Sadly, Duncan had only hazy memories of that night and Clio. More vivid were those of her breasts, the largest he had ever found himself in bed with, truly memorable, even if he never remembered exactly how he got in her bed, or away from it, for that matter.

"Very …unforgettable," he replied, smiling, and allowing Vic to enjoy his memories, "but probably not something I should be reminiscing about with my father-in-law."

"Nonsense! You were a healthy young man! But fortunate for you that a photograph did not find its way into a newspaper!" Vic chuckled again, but Duncan could hear the sadness in his voice as he added, "I have met her if I am not mistaken…"

"Which…?" he stopped when he saw Vic had not been one of those duped by the three photos. "That obvious, was it?"

"I am sure only to those who know you best."

"Yes. Lily worked at Prentice House."

"Ah yes, Lillian. Josiah was very fond of her. Lily, you have called her?" he asked, his eyes lighting up as though guessing the answer to a riddle. "So that will be *la Fleur*! And you have loved her for a long time?"

The bottle was empty when Duncan had finished telling an abbreviated version of the story. He ended with an apology, which Vic waved away.

"I must admit I ignored my misgivings, pleased as I was to have you truly be my son, and Victoria displaying such good sense at last..." Vic shook his head sadly. "An old fool. Did you come tonight to tell me this marriage is soon to be dissolved?"

"I was hoping Victoria would make the decision herself, but for reasons she hasn't shared with me, she doesn't want to be with me or to let me go. Tonight," Duncan raised his glass, "I'm here for the good company, Sophie's cooking, and the ouzo. But, you're right, if Victoria doesn't, it won't be long before I file for divorce."

"Perhaps then, we might get back to our old ways once again…" Vic raised his own glass to Duncan and downed the last of his ouzo. "Now, too much ouzo for an old man means I must go to sleep. Goodnight, my son, do not wait so long to come again."

Vic clapped him on the back and walked unsteadily towards his room. Duncan watched him, now sure that Vic, while more than likely suspecting something, did not know the full truth about the smuggling activities

Too much ouzo for him meant he wasn't driving anywhere for a while, and although he had a few times since he had moved out, didn't relish spending the night in the house, even if Victoria was not home. He followed his nose back to the friendly old kitchen and took his favorite seat across the counter from Sophie.

She dished him up some combination of cookie and cake, still warm from the oven. In one bite, coconut, chocolate, and a wonderful zesty orange flavor had him nodding and giving her an enthusiastic thumbs up. A large cup of strong coffee appeared a moment later.

"Mr. Andrastus tells me you have an exciting new project, Dr. Scott. What kind of treasures do you expect to find?" Sophie was old-fashioned in her approach to shipwreck excavation, take the gold, leave the keel.

"There are treasures, and then there are treasures," he said, holding the plate out for more. "I think these are the best cookies I've ever had."

About to tell her the latest news of the recovery efforts, they were interrupted by rapid, staccato steps echoing across the expanse of tile in the foyer. Duncan knew who was standing in the kitchen doorway by Sophie's sour expression.

Sophie set the cookie jar on the counter near him and left the kitchen.

"Hi honey. I'm home."

"Come upstairs. I want to talk to you," Victoria said.

He looked over at her, dunked the cookie in his coffee and ate while Victoria grew more impatient. The short pink dress hugged the curves of her body, he saw that she was as svelte as ever.

"You're looking a bit haggard, Victoria. Your activities lately… how did someone recently express it, screwing your way up the eastern seaboard, must not agree with you."

Her mouth dropped open as she gasped.

"Cookie?" he asked politely, gesturing towards the jar on the counter.

"You, and whoever said that, can go to Hell!"

"I came here tonight to see your father. And I don't relish going "home" to relive old memories. Last time I walked into our apartment, you were a little busy."

He reached across the counter for one of the cookies still cooling on the rack.

"You told me you weren't the jealous type, so what did

it matter to you?"

"*Jealous?* I wasn't jealous, I was outraged. We'd only been married nine months and I was away for six." If he had told her he wasn't the jealous type, it was because he only at that moment discovered he was the jealous type. "You knew I'd gotten back that day, but for some reason, I had to co—arrive home to find you rehearsing for the lead in a remake of Deep Throat."

Her finely shaped eyebrows were drawn threateningly over narrowed almond-shaped eyes.

"That will teach you to leave your wife alone for so long—"

"You were in Greece most of the time I was diving near Alexandria. I wanted to fly over to see you, and invited you over to the *Jupiter* – hell, you could have done the backstroke over from Crete in an afternoon," he remembered the confusion he had felt about her unwillingness to see him. "Or lived aboard, as I wanted you to."

"Maybe I thought you didn't truly want to…" she paused, an uncertainty had crept into her voice he had never heard before. "That you didn't really want me …"

"*What?*" He choked on the last of his coffee, finally making her smile. "We barely came up for air our entire honeymoon. I had to beg for mercy! Why would you think that?"

She shrugged, trying to be nonchalant. "I suppose because I …I bullied you into it."

"Did you? Well, then I let myself be bullied, Victoria."

He walked around the counter to put the dishes in the sink and gestured to Victoria to come with him to the foyer, where he stopped at the stairs. She took two steps up to be on a level with him just as she always had.

"After all the years you've known me—as your friend, as your father's partner—is that the kind of man you think I am? Is that the kind of man you want? One that can be bullied? Or one who would forgive such blatant infidelity?"

"You weren't in love with me."

He hadn't been totally off the mark in his teasing. On edge about something, her body was taut, shadows accentuated her golden cat's eyes, glowing in the light of the large chandelier above them. He doubted too much sex was the reason; she thrived on it, an admirable if exhausting quality. He remembered their honeymoon in Europe quite fondly, nostalgically, in fact. Only weeks after returning and settling into their new apartment upstairs was the last time he'd had sex.

"No. I wasn't *in* love with you."

Should he tell her why he allowed himself to be bullied, as she put it, allowed himself to be carried into marriage on the current of her willpower?

"But I did love you, married you quite willingly *and* intended to honor our vows." He watched her expressions change as he spoke, and for the first time, he saw tears sparkle in her eyes. "Since you did come back from Greece the year before so hell-bent on marrying me, I assumed you would, too. You weren't *in* love with me, either, Victoria, and never lacked companionship. Why were you so determined?"

She didn't answer, only glanced around the foyer nervously.

"I need to talk with you, Duncan," she finally said, lowering her voice to nearly a whisper. "Please?" Surprised by the beseeching tone which was echoed in her eyes when they met his, he nodded and followed his wife up the stairs.

WATCHING HER LOCK THE door behind them, taking note of the new, heavy-duty security latches, he wished again he hadn't helped Vic finish off the ouzo.

"What is it, Torrie?" he asked, trying to clear his head and keep his voice casual, even slipping in the pet name she usually didn't put up with.

She paused in their small kitchen long enough to pour herself a glass of wine, reading him well enough to know he'd had enough, no matter what her intentions were.

"You really shouldn't be drinking while you're pregnant."

She didn't answer, except to look him in the eye while

she drank down the first glass and poured a second.

"Were you pregnant?" When she didn't answer, he added, "Torrie...you didn't—?"

"I would have, but I miscarried."

"I'm sorry."

In the living room, he sank down onto the big, comfortable couch.

"Why?" she snapped, following him. "Would you have claimed it as yours?"

Hearing the pain and loss behind her anger as she paced the room, he bit back a sarcastic remark, "I would have accepted the child as yours, as would your father. He'd be heartbroken to think you would ever consider abortion, under any circumstances."

"Come here, Torrie," he said softly, and after taking the glass from her hand and setting it aside, pulled her gently onto his lap. When she had nestled in, he put his arms around her and was more comfortable than he expected to be in her company. "Now, what did you need to tell me?"

"I'm worried about you."

"Thank you...?" he said, a bland, confused and hopefully beguiling expression on his face when she looked up at him. "Why the wifely concern all of a sudden?"

"When Papa put George in charge in Athens when he was so sick? He knew why Papa sent me back to Greece. Papa didn't approve of Theo because he was so much younger than me—a child, he called him, and because of some old history with his family. He said he would cut my allowance if I didn't start behaving myself." Duncan knew all of this, but now that the words were flowing, he didn't interrupt. "I was angry... and George said if I went back home and married you, it would make Papa happy, and keep you on our side—no matter what."

"What? Being Vic's friend and partner wasn't 'on your side' enough for him?"

He felt her shake her head against his chest.

"And I knew you were teasing, but you did say, once, we should get married. Remember?"

He did, clearly. Not long after he had given up on his infatuation with Lillian, Torrie came out to the *Jupiter* on some administrative errand for her father. Plenty of flirting and teasing over the years, but nothing had happened until that night. One of the rare times she had come out to the ship on her own, and had shown a real interest in the work, and in him.

Her visit followed a period of increasing and uncharacteristic truculence on his part. For months after meeting Lillian, he couldn't stop thinking about her, no matter how occupied with work, she was always at the back of his mind, or front and center when he was looking at their picture. Trey had even risked insubordination and told him straight out he needed to get laid.

"You were wearing pink that night, as well, pale pink, at least for a while…"

She responded with the same cross between purr and growl he remembered, too.

Working after dinner in the small alcove office off his stateroom, she had been both businesslike and beautiful in some scoop necked tee shirt dress and high heels, all totally unfit for shipboard life. Her long, dark hair, usually falling past her shoulders in unruly waves had been clipped up, giving an unobstructed view of her sun-bronzed skin against that soft, coral pink and her golden eyes had been artfully accentuated by brown and gold shadow.

Noticing and fully appreciating the effort, he was still immune to the effect and hadn't let himself respond to the light touches or long looks she cast his way. Until he had stood up to do something, he never did remember what it was afterwards, and she had reached out to him, hooked a finger through his belt loop and tugged gently.

Obligingly, he had stepped towards her, expecting her to stand and lift her face for a kiss. He could have done that, happily, but he could have walked away.

Instead, she had leaned forward and put her lips on him.

She had made that throaty little growl as she felt him respond to the heat and pressure of her mouth through his clothes in exactly the right place. Immunity crumbled like an old brick wall in an earthquake.

"And…" she said, bringing him back to the present, "George said he would pay me..."

"*Pay* you?"

She continued with her disjointed, vague attempts at explaining until, not sure if it was her or too much ouzo, he finally cut her off.

"Wait a minute, Torrie—stop!" He held up his hand to stop her rambling. "You gave the interview about the baby to *help* me?" he repeated, closing his eyes, remembering...

She nodded, using the chenille throw from the back of the sofa to wipe her tears.

"Then you, of all the *fucking* times, had to get your own picture in the paper!"

"You must have read why I did that." Would she believe him any more than her father?

"Give me a break, Duncan! You were covering your own ass, or hers! We've all seen the picture of you and her on that sailboat, and those other two weren't your type at all!"

At least Lillian's ex had fallen for the ruse, Duncan thought wryly.

"Does *type* matter to most men, Torrie? Especially after two years?"

Her eyes widened. "Two years?"

"I'm married, remember?" he said softly.

Her mouth quivered, tears filled her eyes again and she dropped her head on his chest. "No, you're not…" she sobbed, "but…but…I am!"

His hand, moving to comfort her, froze in mid-air.

"What did you just say?"

"To Theo!"

"You were already married, *are* married, to…to little Theo?" The diminutive description had been Vic's and described more than just the kid's stature.

Her crying gradually eased, and she nodded, overlooking the slight, obviously relieved by his remarkably calm, rational tone.

"When? Where?"

"The week before I came back from Crete, up in Papigo, a tiny little village up in the mountains where no one would know me, or my father, or you. It was a game at first. I was angry at Papa and *hated* George, even then, and loved the idea of getting more money out of him."

"So, what happened to the game? Theo got jealous when we had a real honeymoon and I expected a real marriage?"

She nodded, mopping her eyes again. "We thought if you found me cheating in our bed, you would move away and find someone else. I didn't think you'd want to upset Papa with a divorce!"

"And you think all this isn't going to upset him? Cut your finances even more—you do know, Torrie, most thirty-five-year-old women don't get an allowance from their father?"

Her expression was bleak when she looked into his eyes. He knew she was no longer worried about money.

"Why tell me now? What's changed?"

She moved from his lap and reached for her wine. When she shivered, he put the blue throw over her shoulders.

"George just told me he would help me, Duncan. I didn't know the bad stuff at first—"

"Bad stuff?"

BAD STUFF, HE THOUGHT, appreciating Victoria's understated assessment of her cousins' threats against her and everyone she held dear, as she confessed the entire scam. The manner in which George had infiltrated Vic's company was far beyond what he considered possible when he and Trey first looked down at that pallet of currency.

Big league was right.

Bad stuff. Big league. Duncan thought of the euphemisms for the evil being spread around the world by these people, and for what, money? Victoria had sobbed out the entire story of worldwide drug smuggling, death threats, torture, and blackmail.

George, her own cousin, blackmailing her for cooperation and silence by holding her young step-sister Helena, holding her in the same foreign brothel they threatened to imprison Victoria in if she did not cooperate.

Having so recently heard Seaton's report that included the sounds of a woman crying in the "inner sanctum", he knew that it was Helena, only miles away, more than likely under almost constant sedation and locked up somewhere inside the shipping company compound.

George had accused Victoria of losing control of Duncan and had threatened Theo after he was recognized in two of the pictures. The week before, when Nick had supplied some of their own photographs of Helena to reinforce their threats, Victoria had sent Theo away.

She had clung to Duncan until he promised to stay through the night. When she fell asleep in his arms almost instantly, he tucked her in their bed, envious of her oblivion, the effects of the ouzo long since sobered out of him.

With trepidation, he went to the desk where she had hidden the photos. Sobbing, Victoria had described how Nick had dealt them out to her like playing cards.

He'd felt anger plenty of times, so angry he had literally seen red, but he had never been compelled to kill. This was a new kind of emotion for him …this was a slow, cold burn, fluid and agonizing, his blood draining from his heart and pooling in his gut like iced quicksilver before flowing throughout his body. The room itself seemed to chill as he viewed the series of photos, his fingers numb, his mind unable to reconcile his memory of that sweet, innocent young girl to the use she was being put to in order to control her sister.

Victoria had once teased about Helena having a crush on him, and after the overt appraisals or outright propositions he was hit with routinely, he found her bashful smile and furtive glances sweet. In the short time it took to scan the half-dozen photos, he was trembling with fury, tears streaming down his face and so cold every window in the room should have been opaque with frost.

Duncan slipped them into the envelope, hid them again in Victoria's desk and left the apartment long enough to go to the car to retrieve his Beretta. He checked Victoria's computer, phone, and apartment thoroughly for bugs and tracking software and found nothing. Relief washed over him and with it, a physical fatigue so profound all he wanted was to lie down on the couch and sleep while he waited for Cal to assemble his team. Now was the time to go in, low activity and minimal security at the compound and both George and Nick on a ship traveling back from Kingston and not due until sometime early Monday morning.

Vic must have some notion of what was happening in his company. Is that why the relief crossed his face when he saw Duncan? In the morning, he would find out just how much Vic knew, and fill him in on the rest.

Rubbing his face, he could not help comparing the beginning of the evening with the end. In Vic's study, talking about Lily—

His eyes flew open. Vic's study. Talking about Lily, who she was, what she meant to him—

"*GOD ALMIGHTY!*"

He threw back the latches on the door and if there were stairs beneath his feet on his way down to Vic's study, he never felt them.

He searched fixtures, shelves, and electronics. He wasn't an expert in hidden surveillance devices and programs but was reasonably sure there was nothing to be found. To be sure, Cal would give everything the once over again when they returned with Helena.

Unwittingly, his own actions had increased the pressure on Victoria and already caused irrevocable harm to a sweet, young girl and placed her life in serious jeopardy. None of them could afford that kind of mistake again.

Seaton was correct, it was time for them to work together. Before going back undercover, the man could prove his mettle by leading the way in tonight and Duncan had an excellent idea for his next assignment.

Remembering the girl's frightened eyes and Mark's description of the pitiful cries he'd heard, his jaw tightened, in both anger, and at the cruel paradox of finding out he was a free man and the next part of his plan would have to be distancing himself so effectively from Lily she would probably never speak to him again.

His phone vibrated. Cal and his team, and Seaton, were all at the rendezvous point.

Chapter Nineteen

Battening Down the Hatches

SUNDAY AFTERNOON, WITHOUT A hug hello or complaint following a week at camp and weekend with her father, Miranda ran into the kitchen and skidded to a stop beside her.

"Mom, that hot guy you work with is here!"

Reaching into the refrigerator, Lillian nearly smacked her head bringing out the potato salad. After hugging her excited daughter hello, she handed the bowl to Miranda and sent her, disappointed, to the backyard.

Mark had agreed to let Lillian make the first contact with Duncan but insisted she stay away from anything else to do with the Andrastus family. Sure his time in Annapolis was over when they had parted ways two days before, they had said good-bye.

She paused, glancing outside first, gratified to have taken the time to shower and change clothes after cleaning house all weekend in fits of nervous energy. Mark's hair, the natural deep gold again, shone against the royal blue of his shirt. He had a workout bag slung over one shoulder and was on the front path talking with Aaron, who was posturing like some ridiculous rooster. Good grief, she thought, Mark couldn't help being tall.

Ryan's hair was bleached nearly blond from his week at camp, Lillian noticed, stepping onto the porch. She held her arms out, putting her son on the spot in front of Mark, but it didn't take Ryan long to run over to her.

"I've missed you, kiddo," she said, hugging him tightly. "Why don't you go say hi to Grandpa and Grace and wash up for dinner? Mark and I will be back in a minute."

The screen door had barely closed behind Ryan when Aaron gave her an overt up and down appraisal. "Geez, Lil, you're looking great."

"The tone of surprise is very flattering," she said, further annoyed when he moved close and put his hand on her shoulder.

"New workout routine or something?"

"As a matter of fact," she said, brushing his hand away, "and so much better than the last."

Mark had turned away to examine the roses climbing along the porch railing. The light finally dawned, and Aaron gave her another slow up and down.

"Behave yourself around the children," he said, with a knowing glance toward Mark. "By the way, something's come up. I can't have Ryan next weekend."

"Aaron—" she started, knowing how disappointed Ryan would be. Was it true or was he simply retaliating for the affront to his manhood? *Try behaving yourself* for *your children for a change.*

"Sorry for the bad timing of my arrival," Mark said, as she turned back to him when Aaron drove away.

"Couldn't have been better," she said, giving him a hug and a quick kiss, "but I thought we said our goodbyes the other day."

"Developments," he said, still holding her when Miranda's friend Brianna rode up their driveway on her bike.

"Whoa!"

The precocious Bri had good taste, Lillian thought, gesturing for the girl to go inside. As soon as the door closed behind her, an immediate explosion of poorly hushed giggles filtered out from behind the open windows.

"Now you're in trouble, Mom," Mark said, as Lillian rolled her eyes.

"Did you and Duncan talk?"

He nodded. "Late Friday, and again this morning. He's found out a lot since your visit, some you need to know, and he wants to bring your father into the discussion."

THE NIGHT HER FATHER admitted to knowing about the smuggling, she had told him the truth about Mark finding her at the cottage, and her meeting with Duncan. At Tom's reaction to hearing Mark's name mentioned, she explained enough of the mitigating circumstances of the night at the lab to allow Tom to be civil to Mark after his surprise arrival.

Once the three of them were in her office, Mark approached the subject directly with another apology. Her father relaxed enough to sit and ask Mark about his mission.

"At ten tomorrow morning, Vic will be going to Andrastus Shipping to officially relieve George. Scott believes there could possibly be fallout as Vic takes control."

"Why not just have George arrested for the *Jupiter* shipment?" Lillian asked, relieved to be past the subject of 'the night at the lab' for the last time.

"No real proof, I imagine, and," said Tom, eyebrows raised at Mark, "I suspect your agency, and others, *want* dominoes to start falling now."

Mark nodded. "Agents are in place at several locations here, as well as in the UK, throughout the West Indies and Europe. If successful, this promises to make a significant impact on drug and antiquities trafficking, at least for a while."

"And your role here, now the museum is closed?" Tom asked.

"Having finally convinced my contact with NCA that Scott is on our side, they have reassigned me to another location—"

"Where?" Lillian asked, realizing, even before seeing his expression, that he couldn't tell her where he would be assigned next. He gave her a bit of a smile before continuing.

"Scott has arranged for new security for Vic while he manages the transition, and Victoria and her step-sister are on their way out to the *Fleur-de-la-Mer* as we speak. From all indications, I wasn't seen that day, and no one suspects me of anything.

"I leave for my new assignment late in the week. In the meantime, we both thought it best if I were to stay here when…well, as you say, when the dominoes begin to fall."

"Stay here? But I thought you said I wasn't in danger…"

Mark looked at her for a long moment. "After some of the things we've discovered about these people—if either of us truly believed you were in danger, Lillian, we wouldn't give you a choice. You and your entire family would already be in some faraway place by now—"

"What do you mean—things you've discovered?"

Again, he paused before answering. "Bad enough, that although we don't think you are in any way compromised, it would be irresponsible to leave you vulnerable. I know I proved dangerously inept as an undercover drug agent, but I promise, I won't let you down again. You mentioned the other day some family trip planned soon…?"

She nodded. "The kids and I. We go to South Carolina on Thursday, Ryan, too, Dad. Aaron's canceled again."

Tom made a disgusted sound.

"We're back on Sunday. But what about you? You're not up for a long trip yet, but I don't think you should be on your own here, either."

"We'll go over to Easton on Thursday morning and stay a few days. I'll ask Grace if she wants to come along, and let Ryan show us around. It's about time, don't you think?"

"Perfect. Ryan will be honored," she said, and turning to Mark, added, "That's all of us away from home for a while."

"Good. We'll have a better idea where things stand in a few days, and I'll stay until Cal gives the all clear."

Tom stood up. "I'll leave you two to iron out the details, but if you agree, Lily, I see no harm in taking precautions."

THE COVER STORY WAS true enough, although instead of a new job, it was back home to England and with the lease up on his apartment, Mark would stay with them a few days while he finished at the museum.

From the time dinner was over, Mark was in high demand. He and Ryan teamed against the girls for volleyball.

Soon after the girls' one-point victory, he was hauled inside to play a video game with Ryan.

Ryan followed closer to Mark than his own shadow, while the girls hovered like infatuated fireflies. Lillian wasn't so sure she liked the look in Brianna's eyes.

"Baptism by fire," Tom observed dryly after she had mentioned how isolated Mark had been in the past year. When Miranda and Brianna sat on either side of him the second Ryan vacated his place on the couch, he added, "Better intervene, Lily."

THE HOUSE WAS FINALLY quiet and Mark was decompressing in the living room while she made up the bed in the guestroom. She was surprised to hear Ryan's voice in a whisper, followed by Mark.

"Hey, mate. Aren't you risking a dozen lashes being up after lights out?" The Captain's nautical jargon was contagious even to non-sailors.

"I wanted to warn you."

"Warn me?"

"Randi and Bri, they're planning to sneak into your room."

"Blimey...when?"

"Not sure."

Lillian smiled at the hint of amusement in Mark's voice when he asked, "Why?"

In the pause that followed she knew Ryan had his usual contemplative look and answered with his usual shrug.

"What...hmm... what do you think I should do?"

Again, a pause, another shrug, and Lillian had to bury her face in the pillow when Ryan answered. "Don't let Mom catch you."

"I am in your debt, sir." She peered around the corner in time to see Mark hold out his hand. Ryan must be looking puzzled again. "Means I owe you, dude. Big time."

"Tomorrow will be easier," she said, once Ryan had gone

back to his room.

"If I get through the night. I know you heard that bit of intelligence."

"What's your strategy, Mr. Bond? Any tips about this kind of scenario in the secret agent's handbook?"

"Treated like a sex-object and mocked all of an evening. What do you think, Lillian? Big brother, big bad wolf, or gay?"

"I think I would like to be awake when my father catches them in the act, *if* they have the nerve to even get close to your door."

"I have sisters. Girls can be deviously determined."

"*If* they breach the outer defenses, I am sure you will be both creative and chivalrous. Or scream for help – I'll be right across the hall."

They discussed watches so that there were always two adults awake at all times. She and Mark would have the evening and midwatch, her father and Grace, who was staying for the week, would relieve them at sunrise.

"Quite a surprising welcome from your family today, but then I've been surprised by you before." He held out his hand, adding, when she put her hand in his, "Better stay away from that diary, Lillian, it wouldn't do to distract the security guard."

"Your caution makes me realize just how serious this situation is. Another Mark I know would have encouraged me to keep reading. Seems a bit surreal, your being here after everything. I'm surprised Duncan would even suggest it."

"You know what they say, 'better the devil you know'."

She laughed.

"That was somewhat of a rude, scoffing noise," he said with mild umbrage, but squeezing her hand gently. "I hope the transition goes well tomorrow," he said, changing the subject.

"Sorry you'll be stuck here with us and not part of the action."

"I was a part of the action briefly, and that will suffice," he said, his grip tightening again while he told her about their early morning raid on the Andrastus compound to rescue Helena.

"I didn't know Cal and his team were all former Marines. It explains a lot about Cal, I suppose, but they were far more than just your ordinary security detail this morning."

Mark described the small but thorough commando-style raid on the compound. Cal, his three agents, as well as he and Duncan all wore full protective gear, he told her, complete with night vision. "We'd used an enhanced sort of Google Earth to show them where I had heard the crying, but Cal was also using thermal imaging, in case they had moved her elsewhere within the compound. They hadn't, and we went straight for the unit she was being held.

"They had to be very sure no one was on to them. There was only one guard posted outside in that section. One of Cal's agents was first in and shot him before he could even react and with barely a whisper of sound. Another was inside with Helena who was sobbing again. It looked like he was in the act of drugging her when he was, shall we say, interrupted. One of the agents was a woman, but the girl went right to Scott. Held on and wouldn't let him go. He carried her out of the compound and held her while we drove back to the Andrastus estate."

"Poor thing," Lillian whispered, her voice shaking, "and poor Victoria. Thank God she finally broke down and told Duncan and thank God you heard what you did. I wonder what will happen when George discovers she's missing."

"I'm sure we'll hear at some point, as Cal also left behind a few well-hidden devices to capture their movements between their return and Vic's announcement.

"Now you know why we weren't willing to leave you on your own. As your co-worker and friend, it makes sense I'm here. Being seen anywhere near Andrastus Shipping tomorrow would also compromise my next assignment."

"Some similarly under-funded museum in another god-forsaken colonial outpost?"

"Wherever I go, the scenery will never begin to compare."

LETTING THE KIDS SLEEP late the next morning, she made arrangements for Brianna to be picked up earlier than planned. Divide and conquer for Mark's sake, who made it through the night unmolested. More importantly, there was no way to know what might happen as those dominoes started to fall.

The potential danger was underscored by discussing what they would do if there was any sign of trouble, and by her father retrieving his weapon from the boat and hers from the bedroom safe. He had taught her the proper handling of firearms by the time she was nine-years-old when her mother was ill and they were sailing the world. Pirates and sharks and other dangers were a part of that world and learning how to shoot was as important as sailing a figure eight or knowing basic first aid. Still, much time had passed since she had handled a gun, and she made her father and Mark reintroduce her to the particulars of all three weapons. All three would be put out of sight, but within their reach, just in case.

After their week at camp and a weekend with their Dad and Meg, as well as the heavy rain that had settled in overnight, neither of the kids complained there were no practices, games, or any other reason to leave the house. Her father even told her to use his frail health as an excuse to keep them all close to home for a while.

She opened the boxes so recently brought from the cottage and forgotten, hoping they would contain some useful information about Brendan and help keep her distracted and the kids busy. None of the adults had slept well or much, and by mid-afternoon were all anxious about what was happening at Andrastus Shipping.

Ryan and Miranda came into the kitchen at one point after lunch where conversation among the adults had lulled.

"What are you waiting for?" Ryan asked, sidling up to his new best friend.

"Waiting?" Mark asked.

"Yeah, it's like you're all waiting for bad news or something," Miranda chimed in, heading to the fridge.

Shortly after dinner, the rain eased enough to give Mark

an excuse to get out for a run. Even with a new and secured cell phone, Lillian knew he was going to the other side of town to put several cell towers between them to check in with Cal. Thankfully, the kids retreated to their rooms and did not see their grandfather and mother pacing and looking out the windows.

"Cal said it was like cockroaches scattering in a bright light. After Vic formally announced his return, George claimed to have work back in Kingston needing follow-through on his way back to Crete and said that Nick and several others could transfer back with him. It all fits the intelligence we've been receiving."

Everyone else in bed, she and Mark were once again in the dark living room.

Earlier in the evening, Tom had unearthed two old baby monitors from the garage and rigged them up to provide an early warning system, one on the back porch and one on the front, black electrician's tape covering the indicator lights. They sat quietly together, listening to the occasional passing car through one monitor and silence from the other, at least now that Mark had moved it to a higher place on the window sill after the neighbor's cat had startled them with its low rumbling purr an hour before.

"Your dad is brilliant, Grace an angel, and your children a credit to you. I'm sorry for the reason, but not for the chance to be with you, and get to know your family." He touched the little stork symbol on one of the baby blue plastic units, and whispered to her, "Saving these for some future addition?"

"Not too near in the future, you hope, unless you want to be *part* of the family." She said it lightly, but the little flutter of anxiety nagged at her again. Neither she nor Mark had been prepared, in the contraceptive sense, at the cottage.

"I tried to—"

"I *know*," she interrupted, heating at the memory. Even in his ambushed and sleep-deprived state, he had endeavored to not fully consummate the act, until she had cried out something to the effect of *I need you in me, now!* After the briefest hesitation, he'd obliged. Lillian felt her toes curling, remembering the intensity of sensation. When his body tensed and she knew he was going to pull away before his own climax, she had wrapped her legs around him, pleading, demanding, apparently in two languages, for him …well, not to.

"Worried about adding a bit of Old Blighty to your impressive family tree, are you?"

"Worried, such an insignificant little word for the, *life* dominoes to fall if I am pregnant, to borrow a recently used metaphor." She added more seriously, "For me, and you."

"It will be all right, Lillian. And," he said, softly, taking her hand, "this isn't exactly what I meant, but I do remember offering to share my family tree with you, not all that long ago."

LILLIAN'S HANDS WERE FULL in the kitchen when she heard the doorbell. The first unexpected knock at the door since Monday, there was a pause before Tom unlocked and answered the door and Lillian heard him greet Vera and her husband Tony.

Good God, of all the people, she thought when she looked through the living room arch.

She was sure Vera's expression was equally amusing to Mark when she caught sight of him at the far end of the room, stationed near his weapon stored in the high corner cabinet. Like her father had said, any knock at the door could act as a distraction and had to be suspect.

"Why didn't you say you were coming to town?" she asked, hugging her friend.

Vera pushed her back into the kitchen, hissing like an angry cat, "Are you insane?"

"Possibly. Why?"

"Mark?"

"I've told you, he's not my enemy." She told Vera the cover story, but she did not seem convinced. Typical of Vera, leaping and sticking to her own conclusions.

"But, what about…Duncan?"

"Other than he's married and enjoying a second honeymoon on his new boat?"

Vera's expression softened. "But you love him ,and…"

"And *everyone* seems to know that. Even Mark.".

MARK HAD RECEIVED THE call from Cal, and the tension level had relaxed considerably. Mark would leave in the morning, but for tonight, they lay on the couch together one last time.

She had woken in the afternoon to her period, which relieved them of another kind of tension. But along with relief and severe cramps, had come an irrational disappointment and sadness. And, in her news about the expedition, Vera had brought Duncan up no less than a dozen times during her short visit.

"You know Victoria's on the ship for her and her sister's safety. That's not what has you crying, is it?" he asked, rubbing her back.

"No," she shrugged. "The idea that I may be crying over Duncan doesn't bother you?"

She winced. She didn't want Mark to be bothered, or jealous, or possessive of her… did she?

"Lots of stress lately, a good share of it initiated by yours truly. I'm just grateful you feel safe with me and trust me to be here. And …," he paused before adding, "if you *were* carrying my child and I thought I had a fighting chance, you would know how much *that* bother's me."

"A fighting chance?"

"At you, at your heart, *ma cherie, Lilién*." He leaned down and tipped her chin up for a kiss. The kiss and the unexpected French endearment sent gooseflesh rippling down her arms.

"I had no business getting involved with anyone, especially you. As an amateur on a potentially dangerous assignment, and you, going through a divorce, raising two young kids, emotionally attached to the man I was investigating?

"And from my first day, it was a regular dose of either Vera or Trey badgering you and Scott incessantly about each other, which you both handle with impressive patience and grace, by the way, like you did tonight."

"Thank you," she said, wryly, still annoyed at Vera. "That didn't put you off. It wasn't all that long after your first day on the job that you asked me out."

"I knew from eavesdropping your divorce was final. Scott was married, so… you had to do someone, I mean, something, in the meantime," he corrected himself at her look.

"There's the Mark I'm going to miss…"

He searched her face as he smoothed the hair back from her brow.

"I *am* going to miss you," she repeated, softly.

His hand stilled for a moment. "I'll miss you, too."

Chapter Twenty

Fleur-De-Lys

"KNOW ALL PERSONS BY *these presents, that I, Brendan Aubert Bonneau, of Fleur-de-Lys Plantation, Kershaw County, South Carolina, do hereby Manumit and set Free from Bondage, my Slave known as Gabriel Bonneau, born on the twentieth day of July in the year of one thousand, eight hundred and thirty-seven. I do, for myself, my heirs, my executors and administrators, release unto Gabriel Bonneau, any and all of my Rights whatsoever to him, or to any Estate he may acquire, hereby declaring him absolutely Free, without any interruption from me or any person claiming under me. In Witness whereof I have hereunto set my Hand and Seal this tenth day of the third month, in the year of Our Lord one thousand, eight hundred, and fifty-eight.*"

At the bottom of the document was the clear, bold signature of Brendan Bonneau, an imprint of a fleur-de-lys distinct in the wax seal.

They reached Janet's in Columbia in the late afternoon in the middle of a steady downpour. An hour later, thunder still rattled the windows and the electric lights flickered after each bolt of lightning forked across the black sky.

"I had copies made of some of the Reconstruction-era pictures of the area showing several of the plantations, both intact and destroyed," Janet said, once they had all dried off and settled in at her small apartment. She indicated a small stack of photographs, and then opened a file folder with a flourish. "And I found these!"

"Oh!" both Miranda and Lillian said at once, recognizing names on the photocopied documents.

"From Lilién's diary and what I've recently researched, it

wasn't a simple matter to free a slave in South Carolina before the war. How did they manage it?" Lillian asked, finally looking up from Gabe's certificate of manumission. A second, with nearly identical wording, gave Jenny free status, just as Lilién had written in her diary. Miranda traced her finger over the now familiar handwriting.

Janet indicated the date. "I don't think they did manage it, since they were signed in 1858 and 1861 but not recorded until May 1865.

"Well after the Emancipation Proclamation and the war, but they recorded them?"

"Mom," Miranda said, looking closely at the two documents, "in Lilién's diary she said she *wanted* to free Jenny and Brendan wanted to free Gabe, but they couldn't. Maybe this was a way to show that they would have been freed by their—," she looked at Janet apologetically, "by Brendan and Lilién if they had been able to?"

Janet and Lillian glanced at each other and shrugged acceptance of the theory.

"It's possible, these documents could have served to aid their acceptance by the local community," Janet said, "especially considering … this, signed by a lieutenant colonel in the Fifteenth Corps, one of General Sherman's men. Very interesting."

She set the document, written on plain, faintly lined paper, on t.

'I, Jason William Rossiter, First Michigan Artillery, lieutenant colonel in the Fifteenth Corps 2nd Division under the command of John A. Logan, do hereby witness the validity and authenticity of the enclosed four documents: one land and chattels transfer deed; one certificate of marriage; and, two writs of manumission, all supporting the grantee's rights of ownership."

Under the signature, the document was witnessed by Captains Giles Blair and Lewis White and dated February 25, 1865. Laurelton Plantation, Kershaw County, South Carolina.

"He mentions a deed?" Lillian raised her eyebrows at

Janet, who smiled and drew out a fourth document.

"Know all persons by these presents, that I, Brendan Aubert Bonneau, of and heir to Fleur-de-Lys Plantation, Kershaw County, South Carolina, do hereby deed the entire three thousand acres of Fleur-de-Lys Plantation, bordered by the Wateree River, Camden Road and the plantation's oak lane, together with the aforesaid Fleur-de-Lys plantation house and any and all outbuildings and equipage, furnishings, and personal belongings of the Bonneau family to Gabriel Bonneau, family by name and cousin by blood. In Witness whereof I have set my Hand and Seal this twenty-fifth day of December, in the year of our Lord one thousand, eight hundred and sixty-four."

Witnessed by Edgar Hall and Sarah Kendrick Bonneau, and again, Brendan's strong signature and fleur-de-lys seal. Lillian closed her eyes, imagining how he had tipped the nearest available candle, wax with swirls of black soot dripping onto the paper, his ring pressing into the yellow splotch.

Reading through Brendan's handwritten deed once again, the meaning of the words hit her and she looked up at the others with a gasp.

"What?" Miranda asked.

"Family? By name *and* by blood?"

"That's right, and the Bonneau name survived until a generation ago when the only daughter married," said Janet, softly, watching Lillian's face. "They still live there, in the house built by Gabriel in 1872."

THEY STARTED FOR CAMDEN in the afternoon as they were expected for an early dinner with the Bonneau family. The drive from Columbia took them through the congested heart of the city, the outlying suburbs and out to the smaller county roads.

"I grew up down that way," Janet told Miranda, gesturing towards a narrow lane leading right through a vast field of corn. "We'll have dinner at Mama's before you go home—she made me promise," Janet broke off with an apologetic look at Lillian, who laughed.

"Why would I mind? I love your mother and I've never had better food in my life!"

"Well, you will surely be treated to a healthy dose of Southern hospitality!"

At a small crossroad, a tiny clapboard shack that might have once been white advertised bait and tackle and Pepsi Cola in barely readable '60's era signs. Several old pickup trucks parked out front advertised it as a thriving business, despite a veritable tsunami of kudzu advancing on two sides. Further along the old road, fences, trees and even abandoned structures had been engulfed by the invasive vine.

They passed a road sign giving the miles to Camden, and the butterflies stirred again.

"Speaking of Southern hospitality, do they know?" Lillian asked, remembering the deed and its revelation about the blood relationship between the families.

Janet laughed. "Know what? That you're the white folk in the woodpile?"

"Janet!"

"What?" Miranda said, leaning forward.

"Sorry." Janet didn't look at all sorry. "But, if there wasn't already a Saint Brendan, from what your cousin Neera said about family lore, *they* would have had your Brendan canonized long ago. If they don't know, finding out they are blood-related to him will be good news.

"Anyway, I wouldn't worry about your reception, Lillian, she sounded thoroughly tickled."

Just beyond the small town of Camden, they turned off the main road onto a narrow, graveled lane with a large field of crops, soybeans, Janet said, on one side and an open meadow bordered by gnarly old oak trees on the other. An old painted sign hanging from wrought iron brackets heralded the entrance to "Petit Fleurs," beneath was a newer 'Day Care' sign.

Around one more bend, they saw a large white house with wide shaded verandas around both levels and several children playing in the large, grassy yard. Half of the group ran towards the house while the others swarmed the car.

Lillian took a drink from her water bottle, not remembering the last time she had felt so nervous. Miranda waggled her fingers at a little girl standing on tippy-toes to peer into the car, fingertips, big brown eyes, and squished nose framed by a fountain of brightly beaded braids.

During the long drive in the air-conditioned car, the temperature and humidity had risen. When they stepped out of the car, Lillian felt as though she was walking into a steam bath.

"All right you, clear out and let them through!" A tall young woman, holding a baby on her hip snapped her fingers and sent the kids giggling and screaming back to their games.

Janet introduced herself, Lillian and Miranda to Neera Jackson. Her cousin, Neera Bonneau Jackson. Lillian was surprised to see tears in her eyes before being enveloped in the woman's arms, baby and all.

Inside the old house, the temperature and humidity were both subdued by the cross breeze flowing through the wide, screened veranda.

A man, about her own age, Lillian thought, tall, broad-shouldered and handsome, was James Morgan, Neera's brother. Another cousin, but there were no hugs or even a handshake from him, only a barely perceptible nod of acknowledgement. Chloe was James's pretty and shy fourteen-year-old daughter.

"Grandma Althea," Neera said, her voice raised slightly as the old lady walked slowly towards Lillian, her eyes still sleepy from an afternoon nap. "This is Lillian Cherrington, the descendant of Lilién Bonneau."

The old woman hooked her cane over her arm and stood holding both of Lillian's hands in hers, smiling. "Miss Lilién!" she exclaimed in an equally loud voice, "I remember hearing about her when I was just a little girl. Grandma Jenny surely did love that lady!"

Althea led Lillian to a set of chairs on the long, shaded porch, one of which was plainly reserved for Grandma, with reading glasses, lotions, books, and magazines all within easy reach.

"Set down here by me," she commanded gently, dropping her spare frame into the comfortable upholstered chair and watching as Lillian did the same, while still holding her hand.

"Grandma Althea is the great-granddaughter of Gabriel and Jenny," Janet told Lillian and Miranda.

"Who were given this land in 1864 by your—what did we figure, Grandma, two or three time great uncle? – Brendan," said Neera, handing the baby over to her niece.

"Because they earned it," James's deep, hard-edged voice broke through. He stood at a distance, leaning against the kitchen door frame with his arms crossed, clearly not sharing the women's sentimental view of the family history.

"They *all* earned it," Neera said, rolling her eyes, "but how many other families do you know gave away the plantation to the former slaves, blood relations or not?"

"Your brother doesn't maybe know all of the history, Neera," Althea scolded, gently." Sit down and listen, Jimmy, then you'll understand a bit better."

"Never *wanted* to know," Neera muttered to Lillian.

Although no documentation existed, it had always been known Gabriel was Charles's nephew, the result of a dalliance between his adventurous brother and a free Jamaican woman. He acknowledged paternity, but when the mother died when Gabriel was just two years old, he also acknowledged he couldn't be saddled with raising a child.

While they visited with Althea, Neera and Chloe were in and out as they watched over or gathered up the daycare kids as parents stopped by, until finally only their own four-year-old Taren and one-year-old Drew were left. The little one, immediately smitten with Miranda, plunked himself onto her lap and looked up at her adoringly with his striking gray-green eyes.

They had several photo albums of each generation. Except for one studio picture of Gabe, Jenny, their daughter Brenda Ann and son Charles Wilson, these photographs were informal, and many included the building of Petit Fleurs.

The earliest album included several photographs of Wilson Hall and his family at Laurelton. The bonds formed between the Bonneau and Hall families before the war had clearly only strengthened afterwards.

In the grainy black and white photographs, Wilson was far more handsome than in the tintype hidden in Lilién's diary. His fine-featured good looks were still apparent, but the diffident quality in his expression was gone. His blond hair was longer and sideburns more rakish. In one photograph, with a date 1872 penciled on the back, showed Wilson supporting the first wall to be raised. Relaxed and smiling, his work shirt open at the neck and sleeves rolled up on his forearms.

In each picture, smiling or not, he looked directly into the camera, and it seemed to Lillian that there was a definite message in his eyes. *What is it, Wilson?* Lillian felt her heart beat quicken when she met his eyes, searching for an answer.

Lilién's diary was brought vividly to life by these real-life images of Wilson, of tall, broad-shouldered Gabe, working hard in each picture except for the few where he was looking at Jenny, the love for her obvious in his eyes. Jenny was tall, slender and a bit plain, but with spirit in her eyes and almost always with hands on her hips, reminding Lillian immediately of Neera. As if the paperwork Janet had discovered was not enough to prove a shared bloodline, photographs of Gabriel revealed the square, stubborn Bonneau jawline of which her father was so proud.

AFTER DINNER, JANET LEFT to go back to town on a mysterious errand, saying only that she had more surprises, and would be back the next afternoon. Their overnight accommodation was the Bonneau's guest cabin, 'just beyond', Neera gestured somewhere west and said she would walk them over whenever they were ready.

Lillian helped Neera carry dishes into the kitchen where Althea stood at the sink mashing a tub of steaming sweet potatoes. Even with the exhaust fan running over the stove and a box fan circulating air from the back door, an extra layer of moist heat hovered.

"Grandma, I told you I would do that," Neera scolded.

Neera had several different tones of scold to her, this one nothing like when little Drew had been caught helping himself to spoonfuls of sugar from the sugar bowl.

"Seeing pictures of Grandma Jenny put me in a mind to do it myself," she replied calmly, as though she had been expecting Neera's reaction, mashing away as she added milk from a can and sugar, scooped by handfuls from a tin canister. Lillian noticed there wasn't a measuring spoon or cup in sight.

"Did she teach you how to make sweet potato pie?" Lillian asked.

"I suppose she did teach me," Althea chuckled, sprinkling in another pinch of salt, "by lettin' me be with her in the kitchen, pestering her to let me stir, add spices, crack the eggs!"

"At the risk of pestering…may I?" she asked, hesitantly, gesturing towards the old wire potato masher. "I've never made sweet potato pie before."

Althea smiled and handed over the masher and watched as Lillian started to stir the mixture. As she continued to stir, Althea added a few large dollops of butter and several pinches of ground cinnamon and nutmeg, frowning in concentration as she watched the mixture darken.

"Did your Grandma Jenny ever say what happened to Lilién and Wilson?" Lillian asked, Wilson's expression still haunting her thoughts. Althea paused, nutmeg still in hand, and met her eyes. "We found two letters he wrote, heart-wrenching letters pleading for her to see him and allow him to explain something to her. She wrote briefly about what happened, but seemed to doubt the truth of what she saw…"

Althea lowered her voice, so Lillian had to strain to hear over the sound of the exhaust fan, doing its best to pull the excess heat and humidity from the room.

"Seems like it was more shockin' to everybody at Fleur-de-Lys and Laurelton than the first shots fired at Fort Sumter, that's for sure. Old Jake the blacksmith told Grandpa, said if he hadn't seen it with his own eyes he wouldn't never have believed it. Young Mister Wilson caught with one of the young house girls, in the barn with his clothes all cockeyed, Sally crying—"

"No! Wilson *wouldn't…*" Lillian started to insist, remembering again her reaction to Lilién's entries in the black diary.

"Jake ran in when he heard Miss Lilién cry out. Seems she and Cherrington had walked in and caught them, no one knows why they were there at such an early hour, but Jake said Mister Wilson looked more surprised than anyone, and Cherrington looked all gloaty and self-satisfied-like… Mister Wilson was sick for days afterwards, heartsick, but sick in body, too, Grandma said," Althea finished with one more pinch of nutmeg and set it aside, "Mister Wilson told Grandpa he knew Cherrington had set him up. As soon as he could stand he sent a second to call on him—"

"He challenged Edward to a duel?"

Althea shrugged as though, even now, it was still the expected response of a gentleman to such an outrage, "but by then the man was long gone and Miss Lilién had run away north with him."

"But why? It wasn't love…?"

Althea scoffed. "The older brother dead, Mister Brendan disowned, and Fleur-de-Lys was one of the richest plantations in the state?" Althea tasted the mixture again and reached for the sugar. "Mister Charles was away in Columbia. Old Miz Leah was more likely to have shot young Wilson and beaten Sally rather than help Miss Lilién in her misery. Grandma seemed to think it was planned so that Yankee could be her hero, rescuing her from the shame of a broken engagement, and inherit the lot. And then two days later, war started and spoilt his plans."

She stirred again, watching as Althea continued to eye the mixture until she swiped her finger along the side and tried another taste. She reached for the cinnamon, adding another pinch.

"How many sweet potato pies do you think you've made in your lifetime, Althea?"

"Well, now," she said, chuckling, "that's a mighty big number to calculate, seein' as how it was my husband's favorite, and Jimmy's, too." Althea dipped a finger into the mix again, tasted it, eyes closed, nodding in satisfaction. "Thanksgiving and Christmas, Saint Valentine's and Easter, a few fall harvests, a summer picnic here and there…"

As she reminisced, Althea beckoned her to the center butcher block island, where pie crust ingredients were ready and waiting.

Four handfuls of flour, one large scoop of lard, and a few pinches of salt went into a big, use-worn wooden bowl, and using just her fingers mashed it all into a crumbly mixture ready for the cold water, which she poured directly from her glass of ice water on the counter. Lillian laughed as Althea glanced towards Neera and held a flour coated finger to her lips. Lillian could almost hear her scold, "Grandma, nobody wants your drinking water germs in the sweet potato pie!"

As she watched, she thought about growing up on the sailboat where cooking was, for the most part, strictly a necessity, using as few dishes and making as little mess as possible.

In this one hundred and fifty-year-old kitchen, Lillian was presented with another legacy, not as tangible as some found in the old beach house or the images in the photographs, but every bit as valuable. She listened to Althea's memories and learned how to make sweet potato pie.

Althea rolled out the dough in two perfect circles, lifting them like cloth onto the two ceramic pie dishes waiting nearby, Lillian held the potato pan while Althea scooped and filled, and then finished with a flourish of the wooden spoon, leaving a whirlpool swirl in the filling.

"It never stays," Althea said, with a wink, "but I know it's there!"

When the pies went in the oven Althea went for a rest, with an admonition to Neera to keep an ear on the timer.

"I was going to walk Lillian and Miranda to the cabin!"

"Gilley will be home from work soon and needin' his dinner." The only family member not present was Neera's husband, Gilley, who worked a swing shift. "And it's too late and still too hot to take those little children for a walk," adding, without the least hint of guile on her wrinkled face, "Jimmy will walk them over."

CHLOE WALKED WITH THEM, she and Miranda carrying the overnight bags, laughing and talking nonstop, a sharp contrast to the few syllables Lillian received in response to her conversational attempts towards James.

James had been silent during dinner, Grandma Althea and Neera speaking for him, to which he appeared accustomed. A self-employed landscaping contractor and divorced since Chloe was a baby, they had offered, and he had been in and out of the house through most of the visiting. He was no more talkative on their walk to the guest cabin. She gave up and walked the last bit of the way in silence, enjoying the sounds of the bees among the wildflowers and the variety of birdsong from the high canopy of pine and oak trees.

The path broadened out to a wide, graveled lane, on one side there was a row of gnarly old oaks, their branches sweeping low to the ground and intermingling, very much like the Cherrington estate, she thought, apart from the tufts of Spanish moss draped along their limbs.

The girls had stopped talking and James was waiting nearby.

She looked up and saw Fleur-de-Lys.

While looking at pictures or talking about Gabe and Jenny, she had wondered about the ruins. So, *this* was the surprise, or at least one of them, Janet had been so gleeful about.

No longer the grand palace of the 1860 sketch, nevertheless, the ruins still had an ethereal kind of beauty.

"She'll be crying any second now."

"I'll try to maintain my dignity," she said, not looking away from the ruins.

Only two of the four columns remained standing at its full height, while the others lay broken and crumbling. One ivy-covered chimney stood at one end, fragments of moss covered walls and stairs which reached halfway to the second floor. A long, gently curving balustrade remained, leading towards one of the high walls where three tall, arched openings now framed only the tall pines of the forest behind the house.

Lillian knew, once, three pairs of French doors led to a balcony off the ballroom and thought of Lilién in her yellow silk, waltzing across polished parquet floors with Wilson Hall.

"Mom!" Miranda called out to her from the far side of the ruins, near one of the crumbled walls. She was kneeling and touching something gently. A lily. "Just like in her diary, remember? Lilién wrote about the lilies!"

"It's on the late side for lilies," James commented.

"Late?" Miranda asked, stroking the bright yellow petal softly.

"Lilies are usually done in early June around here," he said, shrugging. "Cabin' round back."

Before following, she reached out and touched the petals herself.

As she stepped out onto the lane again she saw an old hitching post, the rusting iron partially obscured by vines. She saw the faint impression of a fleur-de-lys in the metal. Who was the last person to hitch their mount here? Gabe? One of Sherman's officers, perhaps Brendan himself?

As Chloe and Miranda took the lead once again, Lillian heard Chloe say, "This is the way to the slave cabins." Very matter-of-fact, but Lillian didn't feel at all matter-of-fact, standing between the ruins of the home where her own ancestors had lived and the foundations of what were the slave cabins where James and Chloe's ancestors had lived.

Now she understood the expression on James's face at his grandmother's suggestion, why this young black man did not want to show the descendants of former slave owners around the old plantation. However, to see Fleur-de-Lys for the first time with Gabe and Jenny's family, even if James could not share her familial goodwill, was yet another miracle in this entire search.

Several uneven platforms remained, moss covered, with seedlings and grass growing up between the bricks until they were nearly obscured. Two had chimneys still intact, also thoroughly covered by ivy.

Chloe and Miranda raced back towards the house. Lillian couldn't understand how they could run around and look so perky in the evening's oppressive, humid heat.

As they followed, James volunteered that the original road into Fleur-de-Lys had been closed off many years before, leaving only the walking trail linking the two home sites.

"Relic hunters used to scour all the old, burned or abandoned plantations, looking for coins, silver, and jewelry, for anything they could sell."

An old well stood nearby, its bricks and peaked, shingled roof as moss-covered as everything else, but strands of a frayed old rope still hung from a cracked wooden handle. She leaned over and looked down where a locked grate covered the hole, understandable given the number of busy children growing up nearby. She reached out to touch the handle.

"What's so interesting about this stuff?" James asked, watching her. "An old hitching post, a well, a lily? Why does any of it matter to you? Why touch everything?"

She laughed at his expression.

"We've recently discovered this branch of our family, so unlike you, and I grew up on a sailboat, not knowing about past generations and not in a historic home, surrounded by pictures and mementos. And, well," she added, seeing his sympathies were not kindled, "the lily is because Lilién mentions the lilies in her diary when she writes about painting a picture of Fleur-de-Lys for her father. And, as an artifacts conservator, I'm always interested in old stuff. But these aren't just old, they are things my family, *our* family, used, touched, every day. There's energy from the past here."

Another scoff, no attempt to conceal his skepticism or contempt.

"Energy from the past, in these things? If I felt like that I'd never walk over here again. It's nothing but a danger to the kids, and I've been after Grandma to let me tear it all down, but she won't budge. As long as she lives, at least, it will stand."

The summer kitchen stood behind the ruins. Built of the same brick as the house, it had escaped the fire of 1865. She stepped inside, where Miranda and Chloe were already sitting at the table next to a window with a view out into the shaded woods to the east. A large, open-hearth fireplace dominated the room, a thick cast iron bar and hangers still protruding from the old brick. Lillian was drawn immediately to a wide, narrow window, beneath which a scarred countertop met the brick enclosure of a large cast iron stove.

As she ran her hands over the scratches and gouges in the smooth, work-polished old wood, she felt the familiar tingle almost immediately.

"More energy?" James asked, the cynical edge still in his voice.

"I've been in a few summer kitchens," she said, her hands still touching the counter, "but usually there are just open hearths with brick ovens and long tables."

She tried to keep her voice light, but there *was* energy, a great deal of energy as she touched the wood, the familiar heavy breathlessness in her chest, along with a tingling in her fingers. Felt in her work many times and so often lately at the beach house, as though there was an answer to a question just beyond her reach, threads of the past weaving their way into the present. Still, she couldn't quite grasp hold.

"Great-Grandpa added the basin later and used one of the old slave tables as the counter. Said too many good meals were made on that table to get rid of it. Great-uncle Charlie turned the old washroom in back into a bathroom; he was the plumber in the family."

Above the long counter, low windows looked out to a long stretch of wildflowers and shrubs, bordered by a distant grove of tall evergreens. A sudden vision of spindly young pines enveloped in rainy mist vanished almost as soon as she was aware of it.

James was looking at her warily.

"You're not *really* crying again, are you, Mom?" Lillian could still hear the teasing note in her voice, but Miranda was worried, now that she recognized the look.

"Not yet," she answered, taking a deep, shaking breath.

"Why not?" James's voice was again hard, almost indignant. "Don't you think there was enough to cry about here?"

"*Dad…*" Chloe was embarrassed, but her father had clearly reached his limit.

Lillian closed her eyes, clinging to the sensation, a winter's bone-chilling damp instead of the muggy heat of the summer evening…yes, cold and misty, and a kitchen garden outside the window, empty except for dead leaves and muddy puddles—

"Well?" he demanded again, oblivious to his daughter's hushing.

"Of course, I do!" she snapped, turning to face him abruptly.

She took a deep breath and rubbed her hands together to warm them. The tingle and breathlessness were gone, replaced by a sharp pain behind her eyes. Whatever energy she had been sensing was now thoroughly banished.

"I may have just recently become aware of this branch of my family, but I do know they owned slaves. We know Charles Bonneau worked with other local planters trying to *end* slavery in this state. He and his children wanted to end the practice on Fleur-de-Lys and they did, starting with Gabe and Jenny, there's even proof in the documents Janet discovered. We can't change the past, James, but we can at least be proud to know *our* family tried."

She began to follow the girls into the other room, but paused, smiling at his bemused expression. "Thanks for letting Althea bully you into escorting us. See you tomorrow?"

MOM?"

Drifting, sinking into the mattress as she lay still for the first time all day, Miranda's voice seemed far away. Lillian knew she was just in the cot next to her, in the hot, sticky pitch-blackness of the old summer kitchen.

"Mom!"

"Aren't you tired, sweetheart? It's been a long day." Miranda had been talking nonstop since Chloe left.

"I was supposed to tell you something on the drive down yesterday, but…"

"A message from Grandpa?" she mumbled.

"Mark told me I had to tell you *everything* or he would."

Wide awake now, she turned towards her daughter. "Oh God, Miranda, you and Bri didn't *really* sneak into his room, did you?"

"No…it was just me."

"*What?*"

Lillian was grateful for the darkness. Miranda must be, too, probably the reason she had waited until tonight to relate the story. She knew too well how he looked when Miranda described how he was sleeping, on his back and one arm up over his head. This time, thankfully, he had been wearing more than moonlight and a lace-edged bed sheet.

Just as she was about to take Brianna's outrageous dare and climb aboard, Mark moved aside in time to let her land unceremoniously on the warm spot in the bed.

"I only wanted a kiss!" Miranda assured her.

Appalled, but wishing she could have been a fly on the wall, she said, "Well?"

"He *scolded* me!" she said with an indignant sort of huff, "and said I could get myself in big trouble climbing in bed with a grown man—like I would climb in bed with just *anyone*! But he made me laugh by joking about what Grandpa would do if he caught me, and I made him laugh when I said that's why I waited until he and Grace left to check on the boat! …And …"

"What?"

"He said he …he *loved* you and wouldn't let you down by even teasing me with a kiss."

Lillian heard a somewhat awed tone in her daughter's voice and wasn't sure what she was more moved by. Her voice trembled a bit when she asked, "Not even one little smooch?"

"That's what I said! So, he said okay…but …" she finally giggled, "he said no tongues, and if I stuck my tongue in his mouth he would turn me over his knee and spank my bum!"

Lillian covered her face with her hands and shook her head before asking, "Well? Was it a good kiss?"

During the pause, Lillian wondered if Miranda was pondering the memory or shy about rating the kiss for her mother. With Miranda, it was more likely the former.

"It was pretty cool. Bri's totally jealous."

"Miranda?"

"Am I grounded?"

Surprised she hadn't even considered it, Lillian simply said, "Sweet dreams."

Expecting a sigh of relief, a laugh or at least the squeak of old bedsprings as Miranda settled, she was surprised to hear a repeat of the earlier query.

"Mom?"

"Miranda?" when a long stretch of quiet followed, she added, "you don't have anything else to confess, do you?"

"No…" Lillian could hear Miranda shift and knew by the sound of her voice she was leaning on her elbow looking towards her through the darkness. "Do *you*? I mean, Mark said he loved you but from that picture, I…we…me and Bri…thought you must be in love with Duncan Scott. Bri thought the first picture was more *real*. And Mark's so… *young*…"

Good God, she thought, uncertain how close to approach the truth about her recently very complicated love life. Her almost sweet sixteen-year-old daughter was too old for fairy tales but too young for the facts.

"You *are* grounded, from spending time with Brianna!"

"You can ground me. I still want to know."

"First of all," she sighed, again grateful for the darkness when she turned to face Miranda, "like I told you, the pictures were staged to trick that silly columnist, but I won't pretend I don't like Duncan. I do, very much …or …that I didn't *really* like his kiss."

Miranda made a smirky sort of noise but didn't say

anything, obviously not wanting to disrupt the flow of information.

"And I care a lot for Mark, I won't deny that either. We went out a few times about a year ago, but we both understand a permanent relationship wouldn't work for us. He'll be moving home to England soon, and I mean, *really* Miranda, he is *young* and way too good looking to be a stepfather, don't you think?" She settled back on her pillow, expecting Miranda to laugh and say good night, but another long silence followed the rhetorical question.

"Mom?"

"I refuse to answer any more of your nosey questions."

"Just one?" She could hear the smile in her daughter's voice and prepared herself.

"*What?*"

"Who's the best kisser?"

MUSCLES TENSE AND HEART racing, she woke sometime later to a loud noise beyond the cabin walls and opened her eyes to darkness so complete she might as well not have opened them at all. Must have been a dream, she thought, now hearing only the loud chorus of crickets, distant calls of a hoot owl and Miranda's deep, steady breathing.

Finally.

Lillian had followed her daughter's last impertinent inquiry with an indignant refusal to answer while creeping over to the next bed and tickling her until she promised to stop asking questions. Miranda may have had tears of laughter in her eyes as she went to sleep, but Lillian's were bittersweet. Her little girl was definitely growing up, Lillian thought, rolling her eyes.

The light from her phone was reassuring when she checked the time. Just past three. Sunrise was still hours away. At a strange sound from beyond the cabin, her yawn turned into a gasp, and she sat up straight, her senses once again alert.

A screech owl, she wondered, a panther? Whatever it was, the sound sent chills along her arms and raised the hair on the back of her neck.

She waited, listening carefully, her heart pounding. A loud, mournful wail echoed through the darkness.

Miranda slept soundly, undisturbed.

By the time it faded once again, Lillian had slipped on her shoes and, not having a flashlight to hand, used the light from her phone to guide the way from the tiny bedroom to the front door.

The high empty arches of Fleur-de-Lys's ballroom doors were now foreboding black frames against the starlit sky, reminding her of the book covers of the gothic romances she had read as a teenager on long, lonely sea voyages. Delicate but brave heroines ventured out into the dark unknown in flowing white nightgowns with only a flickering candle to guide their way.

Considering what she was about to do sent a fresh wave of chills over her arms, but even in her somewhat flowing cotton nightgown, she had the modern advantage of sensible footwear and a cell phone, all the better to run away and call for help. As she stepped through the gap in the foundation and into Fleur-de-Lys for the first time, a woman's deeply sorrowful cry echoed through the ruins.

Sorry now not to have navigated the paths through the old plantation house in the light of day, Lillian turned toward the sound, and in between each cautious step, listened for several seconds before stepping around the scattered fragments of brick.

As she walked through the arch of a crumbling doorway, the next wail vibrated through her, sending more adrenaline pulsing through her body. Night sounds went silent and the temperature dropped as if she had stepped into a refrigerator. Whether it was truly a paranormal effect or her own body's response to fear, she did not know.

A figure knelt, head bowed and sobbing, although now no sound emanated from her, only a faint shimmering light. Her hands were not together in prayer but held the beads of a rosary and Lillian recognized the dark shape of the crucifix against the silvery glow of her antebellum gown.

Lillian stepped back into the black corner between the

doorway and wall and watched, entranced, the spirit of what must surely be one of the Bonneau women. She felt no sense of fear for herself or for her daughter sleeping nearby, only sadness and helplessness, witnessing this despair and being unable to offer comfort. She calmed her racing heart with deep, silent breaths, and hugged her arms tight across her chest against the penetrating cold as quiet tears streamed down her face.

Was this the cruel, domineering Leah or perhaps even Lilién? Was the spirit here always or was it certain days, certain times only she appeared? Finally, as dawn lightened the eastern horizon, the wailing ceased, the figure gradually grew fainter until dissolving into the gloaming.

Crickets chirped once again, and the warmth of the South Carolina night wrapped around Lillian like a blanket.

INSIDE, MIRANDA STILL SLEPT soundly.

In the old kitchen, she sat down at the table with her journal to record everything, oblivious to the sunrise suffusing the room until drawn out of her reverie by the strident morning calls of robins and mockingbirds.

The ruins were now bathed in bright, morning light and vibrantly colored songbirds sang from the high branches or hopped along the grassy paths inside and around the ruins, but the sorrow she had witnessed still weighed on her chest and the image of the crying woman seemed to be imprinted behind her eyes.

Cheery songs of goldfinches, cardinals, and wrens and the more sorrowful coos of the mourning doves accompanied her as she walked along a path bordered by weeping willow and flowering magnolia trees. At the row of tall pines she had seen from the summer kitchen and in her vision the night before, she hesitantly touched the trunk of the tallest. Living and breathing at the time her family lived and breathed here, she thought perhaps…but no, no new vision, no sensation of breathlessness, just the rough bark against her palm, already warm from the sun.

The winding trail led towards a steep embankment above

a narrow, rocky creek. Beyond, was a broad meadow of tall grass and wildflowers, kudzu roiling over the distant landscape.

She stumbled on roots as the path narrowed and became little more than a trail, trodden only by wildlife on their way from woods to water. At a sharp turn, she was disappointed to find the way blocked by a thick undergrowth of thorny brambles.

Doubling back, she found a new path and followed it only a short distance when she came to a cemetery in a large gated enclosure. The bright morning sunlight was filtered through the spreading branches of a massive oak tree on the eastern edge of the graveyard. More berry brambles, roses, and ivy grew over the wrought iron fences encircling singular graves as well as the entire burial ground. An imposing mausoleum stood at the center, surrounded by clearly delineated sections.

Along the fence line were dozens of graves with simple wooden markers, gray and weathered from age, most of the writing faded completely but beneath these were stone markers with the names and dates clearly inscribed.

Jenny and Gabe were in their own wrought iron enclosure, almost hidden behind a thicket of climbing roses, soft pink blossoms in every stage of bloom, bursting with fragrance and already busy with honey bees. Their granite memorial stones were pitted and cracked, but the writing was distinct. Further along, newer graves, names she now recognized from meeting her family and seeing photographs the day before. Brenda Ann Bonneau, died in 1947, Charles Wilson Bonneau died in 1938. Neera and James's mother, Rhetta Morgan, who had died when they were very young.

Beneath the sprawling branches of the large oak was the grave of Charles Bonneau, the dates on the ornate headstone verified what his daughter had written in her diary. Her great-great-great-great grandfather fought to defend freedoms he opposed from a sense of duty to his fellow South Carolinians, even though he and his closest friends and fellow planters had advocated a peaceful resolution to the end of slavery. And because of Leah, Lillian thought, remembering Lilién's entries about the matriarch's firm convictions and imposing nature. She knelt and cleared away twigs and leaves from the headstone. Why was Charles buried separately, not within the Bonneau family vault? A wave of sadness washed over her, wanting to know more about these people.

Four Bonneau names were engraved on the front panel of the white marble mausoleum, also dull with age and weather, the most recent being Leah Desjardins Bonneau, who also died during the war. The other names were children, Charles Junior, who died in 1836 at just five years of age, Felicité, born in 1845 and lived only three days, and Louis Charles born in 1833 and died in 1860.

There was a lone grave in the far corner with a black marble headstone jarringly different from the gray granite and white of the other memorials. After taking several steps along the path, Lillian stopped, as though she could not, or should not, continue.

Once when visiting a sixteenth-century English abbey, recently remodeled into an inn, at the proprietor's invitation, she eagerly investigated, admiring medieval artifacts, Elizabethan and Jacobean era paintings and portraits. She looked into secluded alcoves, tiny side chambers and then started to climb a spiral staircase to the top floor. On the fourth, roughly-hewn stone step, she had stopped as though a hand rose in front of her. Without questioning the feeling, she turned and went back down.

Now, walking toward the headstone, her heart seemed to stop.

Please, no! I don't want to see!

She walked forward, tears falling even before she knelt beside Wilson Hall's grave.

Wilson Christopher Hall, 1837 – 1879.

Lillian remembered his eyes, both haunted and haunting, looking out of those old photographs.

A gasping sob escaped her as she stood and backed away from the grave and left through the front gate, stumbling along the narrow, rutted path, until she could jump down to the little rocky bank along the stream. She knelt, cupped the cool water in her hands and brought it to her face.

Doing so seemed to loosen something inside her, something she had held in check for too long and she was crying, sobbing with an abandon allowed by being completely alone. For her failed marriage and hurt children, for her father's violent upbringing and her fears for his health, her fears for both Mark and Duncan, wherever they were. For Brendan, Lilién and Wilson, for Charles buried alone under the huge old oak, and for the spirit of the woman who cried in perpetual sorrow in the ruins of Fleur-de-Lys.

SHE WAS BACK AT the old kitchen just as Miranda was waking. They walked back to Petit Fleurs to join the family for breakfast and spent the morning with Althea and Neera, scanning photographs of generations of the Bonneau family and the building of Petit Fleurs onto a flash drive, while visiting and playing with the little boys. Lillian promised to send a photo of Brendan and Lilién to include in their family archive.

By early afternoon, Janet had not yet returned with her promised surprise, and Lillian's eyes were beginning to close, lack of sleep catching up with her. When Althea went for her nap, Lillian excused herself to go back to the cabin for her own.

The ruins, now benign in the hot afternoon sunshine, gave no hint of the despair she had heard from the spirit the night before or that she had felt during her walk. She lay down on the wicker sofa in the living area of the old kitchen with Lilién's diary and opened it randomly, wanting to hold and re-read it in the place so close to where it was written.

Fleur-de-Lys. January 22, 1861. Mother was in a frenzy over the news from Charleston, by way of George Denison of Angel Oaks Plantation. He arrived during the fiercest storm of the winter to tell of a Lieutenant Hamilton, who recently allied his loyalty to the new South Carolina Navy (as Georgie has himself, though I do not believe he has ever sailed anything larger than a raft.) and has issued a call to other United States naval officers sympathetic to the Southern cause to pledge their loyalty by commandeering their ships to Southern ports. When Georgie finished talking, he presented orders for Brendan to report to Charleston. As he was just passing on his way home, he departed almost immediately, leaving the rest of us waiting for Brendan's response. The wind and rain outside the window and the blazing fire snapping in the hearth were the only sounds...

Mother watched Brendan expectantly, as did Father, Wilson, and I. Even little Amelia was uncharacteristically quiet as we all waited for him to speak. I could see the anger in his eyes. I am sure it was as much from being caught unprepared and in front of everyone to the outrageous suggestion that once honorable officers turn traitor and thief.

He said nothing, nor had he moved, but stood looking down at the document in his hand. Father was watching him with the utmost sympathy, but I was certain he would not give his full support to Brendan in Mother's presence.

"Of course you must go," Mother said.

"No." He walked across the room to the fireplace, knelt and set the summons onto the blazing logs.

"You have received orders to report to Charleston!" Mother persisted.

"Lieutenant Hamilton, whoever he is, has no authority over me," he said, not turning away from the fire until the paper was fully consumed. "My loyalty oath was made, and I will not forsake it, not for –"

"Your family's honor?" Mother's voice was steely.

"I will not forsake my oath to the country I swore to protect. I will not alter my allegiance from a mission I believe in to fight for freedoms I oppose!"

"You owe no allegiance to a country seeking to curtail our rights to maintain our way of life!"

"States' rights!" he spat back at her fiercely. "Anyone who declares that states' rights is not about slavery is a liar; anyone who believes it a fool!"

I gasped at the force of his statement, and his words, Wilson's hand tightened on mine. Mother only drew herself taller as Brendan continued more calmly.

"I love you, Mother, and I love Fleur-de-Lys. I would have happily, proudly, come home after my service as you and father wished." He was trying to appeal to her even as I was sure he could see such an appeal was futile. *"But I will not, I cannot, change my loyalty because short-sighted, arrogant politicians force our state to leave the Union for something which should never have been allowed to exist in this country."*

"Well then, you shall leave this house. Tonight—"

"No!" I ran to Brendan's side and clutched his arm.

"—and never return as long as you choose to serve your other master."

He continued to meet Mother's gaze for a long moment, and then looked down at me with sadness. He slipped gently away from me and left the parlor. Wilson put a gentle hand on my shoulder, whispered his excuses and followed Brendan to his room.

I sat with Amelia, who looked close to tears and tried my best to distract her. Hannah Hall was about as different from our mother as the sun was to the moon. I was confident no such scenes at Laurelton prepared her for this display of temper. I was about to suggest we go to the library and look at mother's timepiece collection when I heard Father speaking softly.

Mother interrupted him angrily.

"Understand him? He has forsaken his true loyalty to all of us. For what? You cannot convince me that… some boatload of smelly men compare in any way to the life of benefit and privilege we have given him!"

"Smelly men?" Father was incredulous, incensed enough to raise his voice in a manner I had never heard before. *"I am sure you will recall numerous occasions where we discussed the issue of Brendan's calling to the Navy to serve what was once our country. Through no fault of his, over this issue of 'states' rights' that all of us in this household but you abhor, he has found himself in the position of being an enemy to his own people, or a traitor to a loyalty oath taken in good conscience."*

Father paused and searched Mother's face. *"For one moment, please endeavor to comprehend how this honorable young man must be feeling before you alienate him irrevocably from your life, from our lives."*

Brendan, now in uniform, stood in the doorway. As I ran to him Mother appeared to have turned to stone.

"Please do not go, Brendan, not like this!"

"Do not worry about me, little sister," he said, hugging me tightly, his long sideburns tickling one cheek, the blue wool of his coat scratchy against the other. "Just as I planned, I will report to Captain Everleigh for his counsel."

He held me away from him, studying my face as though he might never see it again. He gently wiped a tear from my cheek and kissed the same spot. Whispering goodbye, he turned from me and left the house.

"Don't go...please..."

"Mom? *Mom!*"

Lillian woke, startled to see Miranda's worried face above hers.

"What? Are you okay?" Lillian asked, sitting up, trying to clear the fog from her mind and rubbing at a tickling sensation on her face.

"I'm okay. Are you?"

Her mouth was dry and her heart racing. She stumbled over to the old cast iron sink and splashed her face and drank some of the fresh, cold water.

"You were talking in your sleep. What were you dreaming about?"

Pulling the dish towel from a nearby hook, Lillian dried her face and tried to remember. "Whatever it was, it's gone now," she said, shaking her head. "I was talking? What did I say?"

"The only thing I heard was "don't go!" Miranda imitated a plaintive note, and paused before adding with a smirk, "Mom? Were you dreaming about Mark or Duncan Scott?"

Chapter Twenty-One

The Family Tree

BY THE TIME SHE and Miranda walked back to Petit Fleurs, Janet had returned, looking very pleased with herself, but wouldn't give hints until everyone was assembled on the front porch again, including James.

"I wanted to have this for you last night, but now I have even more than I expected, so it's even better," she said, handing out copies of a document before giving Chloe a folder. "Why don't you and Miranda take turns reading this to the rest of us?"

Chloe took the folder with a shy smile. As she started to read, all of them gasped in surprise.

```
FEDERAL WRITER'S PROJECT
SOUTH CAROLINA SLAVE NARRATIVE OF:
          JENNY BONNEAU
      EX-SLAVE 89 YEARS OLD
     Jenny Bonneau was born in
1847 near Camden, South Carolina
on the Fleur-de-Lys Plantation.
A widow for the last twenty-one
years, her late husband was
Gabriel Bonneau, also of Fleur-
de-Lys. One grown son, Charles
and three grandchildren live
nearby, and her spinster
daughter, Brenda Ann, will soon
be moving home from Wilmington.
     We met late on a hot July
```

afternoon on the shaded porch of
her home named Petit Fleurs. A
well-spoken woman, Mrs. Bonneau
reports herself to be in good
health except for some arthritis
in her hands and is neatly
appointed in a flax-flower blue
cotton dress with a silver
brooch fastened on the white
lace collar. When I asked about
the ornament, she was pleased.

"Well, sir, it seems a mite
strange to hear the words now,
but since you have come to hear
all about my past, I will tell
you. This brooch come from my
former owner, Miss Lilién of the
Fleur-de-Lys Plantation, where
we was both born and raised."

I asked if it was given
when she was still a slave. Her
eyes widened in horror and she
shook her head with vehemence.

"Oh no, sir, old Missus
Bonneau, Miz Leah, would never
have allowed for that to happen.
No, Miss Lilién give it to me
when she returned from Maryland
to visit, I think it was
sometime in 1885—no, beg your
pardon, it was 1886..." She
paused, looking wistful. Before
I could speak, she continued,
"…the first time she come home
since she eloped North just as
the war began."

I asked about other family

members, meaning her own family. Her answer, like that of many former slaves, surprised me.

"When the war was nearly over, Mister Brendan returned from his duty on a blockade runner to see how we all fared. In those few short days he found that his father, Mister Charles, had died after the Wilderness, and Gabriel and I married and moved off Fleur-de-Lys to the Hall's at Laurelton," Mrs. Bonneau broke off suddenly, tears starting in her eyes, "and through it all, his mother, Miz Leah, was as mean and stubborn as ever when his only thought was to provide for all of us.

"Gabriel and I were in Camden, tryin' to trade one of the Hall's last shoats he'd butchered for supplies. Old Mister Lambert had ordered it the week before but was tellin' us it was cash or nothin' cause he'd heard Sherman was headin' north and he was movin' out. Nobody had cash, so it was lookin' like we'd be eatin' that shoat and not much else for a while.

Mister Brendan had come in on the train and was makin' his way down the muddy street in a pourin' rain when he saw me waitin' on the porch cryin'. He brought me inside, had me sit down by the fire and dealt with Mister Lambert by slappin' a handful of gold coins on the counter! Had him load up our wagon with half the store, he did, with Mister Lambert lookin' so spiteful at us sittin' by the stove keepin' warm, eatin' his bread and drinkin' his hot chicry. Yes, sir, I remember as plain as if it was yesterday."

"That load of goods helped feed us all through the last months of the war." She paused and shook her head, tears in her eyes once again. "We all surely loved Mister Brendan, such a kind person he was.

"Their Aunt Sarah had refugeed from Wilmington and when we left, she and Miz Leah were livin' in the summer kitchen behind the big plantation house. Aunt Sarah was a sensible woman and said it was a waste of Gabe's time and good firewood to set fires all over the house when it was just the two of them. But Miz Leah still wandered all about the house like she was sleepwalkin' all through the dampness of the cold winter days."

When I asked why she and her husband had left their home plantation, only "mischievous" describes the light in her eyes.

"Miz Leah got her ole habits on and some notion in her head we should fix the guest rooms for company, but the only company we 'spected was foragers or deserters! Me an Gabriel were already workin' ourselves fit to die every day, Miss Sarah, too. So, I says no. She say back to me right quick, 'Well then missy, you want to be free? Get out!'

Her smile quickly faded.

"I was sorry to leave, sorry to leave my home and the ladies to fend alone, but there was no changin' her mind. The Halls over at Laurelton took us in gladly, as Missus Hall and little Miss Amelia had a rough time of it after Mister Edgar came home sick from the war. All of their slaves except their cook Delphine and her little girl Muriel had either run off or been taken by 'pressment teams.

"Gabriel looked in on them, bringin' by somethin' from his huntin' and fishin' and cuttin' their firewood and such. A few weeks later, when Mister Brendan was home, he and Mister Edgar arranged it for Miss Sarah and Miz Leah to live at Laurelton too, where we could help each

other and have just the one
house to keep up."

I asked why Laurelton and
not Fleur-de-Lys since it was
reputed to be the grandest
plantation in Northern South
Carolina, which Mrs. Bonneau
acknowledged with a nod and
proud smile.

"Yes sir, indeed it was.
But Mister Brendan had learnt
that General Sherman was movin'
his troops north out of Savannah
and headin' straight for
Columbia. As our home was so
grand and close to the Camden
road, he wanted all of us far
away but settled for Laurelton
when Miz Leah wouldn't go no
fu'ther. By all accounts, people
figured the rich planters of the
state that had started the war
would get the worst treatment.
Blessed unfair, too, given how
most of our family and the
Hall's too, was tryin' to end
slavery in a peaceable way."

Mrs. Bonneau mentioned she
and her husband were married
during the darkest days of the
war, when most of the other
slaves had been taken by
Confederate impressment teams,
and only days before the death
of Charles Bonneau. When I asked
if many attended when they
jumped the broom, she laughed

heartily.

"Bless you, honey! On Fleur-de-Lys, we were Roman Catholic. Mister Charles 'sisted those wantin' to marry have the Sacrament. It might be 'gainst the laws of the State of South Carolina, he said, but we was blessed to have a much older law to follow."

The kindly lady took umbrage at my comment about her former master forcing his popish religious views upon them.

"Mister Charles maybe couldn't free us, but he did treat us as human bein's with feelin's and rights. Sharin' his religion honored us, young man."

Chloe stopped and traded Miranda the folder for the finally sleeping Drew. Miranda cleared her voice and began to read:

When I asked what she had meant about what the young master had done for them, her countenance saddened again, and she gave me a long, measuring look before answering.

"Before returnin' to his ship, Mister Brendan handed over all his money to care for us, even Mister Edgar and Miz Hannah and young Miss Amelia Hall. But he must a had a forebodin' 'bout what was to come. He scribed a deed to the land for Gabe, most with the understandin' it was to

help care for Miz Leah, and be
held for Miss Lilién, so as to
keep it safe from…" Here there
was a long pause and Mrs.
Bonneau looked quite troubled.
I was about to intercede with a
follow-up question when she
continued.

Miranda looked up and met her mother's eyes. They had
learned enough about Edward Cherrington by now to know
why poor Jenny's memories would be troubled.

"But Miss Lilién never
would claim any part of it, even
after her husband died. After
the war, Gabe and I had land to
build on, land to produce crops,
or to sell when times got real
tough.

"Mister Brendan, he died in
Bermuda, sometime after his
final trip on his blockade
runner and we never saw him
again, Lord bless him. We named
our first child Brenda Ann in
his honor."

Pride in her former owners
was evident in her voice, though
sadness was etched in the lines
of her face. I asked about the
war years.

"Hard work, every day, just
to survive. Harder work even
than durin' slavery days 'cause,
leastways at Fleur-de-Lys,
Laurelton and Cardinal Heights,
there was always plenty of hands
to do the work that needed

doin', food to eat and put up,
and clothes to wear for the
changin' seasons. Durin' the war
our livestock was gone, either
with Confedrut requisition
teams early on or Yankee
foragers later. Gardens and
crops destroyed or gone to seed
for lack of workers. We had to
drive the few animals deep into
the pine forest at each threat
of troops in the area."

I asked how they fared
after the war.

"Very much the same as we
did during the war, young man.
But our beautiful Fleur-de-Lys
was gone…" here Mrs. Bonneau
paused, the memories clearly
still quite painful. I asked if
she would like to resume our
talk on another day. She shook
her head and continued to
reminisce. "But the Halls still
had Laurelton, one of the few
big homes nearby not burned the
night Sherman's men came
through. We lived in the
overseer's house in exchange for
helpin' on the place. We stayed
until this house was built, and
our families always remained
friendly.

"'Bout fifty returned home
lookin' for work and a place to
lay their heads after the war,
former slaves from Fleur-de-

lys, Cardinal Heights, and Laurelton but it was a good number of years before we could afford to pay more than food and shelter and schoolin'—"

I asked Mrs. Bonneau what she meant by schooling.

"Mister Charles set a store by learnin', even before the war he went contrary the law to teach some of his servants readin' and writin' and figurin', and had Miss Lilien teach me, and Mister Brendan teach Gabe…" this she said with a roll of her eyes which she did not pause to explain. "Mister Charles said that learning would be more valuable than cash money after the war for our people and he was sure right 'bout that. But, we all worked hard to make the land fit for crops again. We gardened, hunted and fished, foraged for healin' herbs and dyes and shared everything. Pretty much prepared us for this Great Depression, didn't it, now?"

Seeing Mrs. Bonneau was tiring, I moved on to my final question, one that frequently made many of the interviewees uncomfortable, but she answered without the usual nervous laughter, fluttering of hands or shuffling of feet.

"Ghosts? Well now, a fittin' subject to end with, ain't it? Yes, sir. I do believe in ghosts, I certainly do. Gabriel told me what he saw one night, but I didn't believe him, just thought he was tryin' to scare me."

Enjoying the impatient sounds I made to hear more, she paused for effect, seeming to regain some vitality in the telling of the tale.

"Thirty-odd year ago I was over to the ruins of the old house in the early hours, so as to be there at sunrise, to gather some Robin's plantain that grows wild in the old kitchen garden. I sat on the low wall jes lookin' at the stars, near to the little chapel where Gabriel and I was married and waited for the dawn to come. Then, the crickets went quiet, the coldness of a winter fog settled 'round me and a wailin' sound made me jump to my feet. A deep, low cry of sorrow and I might just've cried myself if I hadn't been so scared! It was old Miz Leah, lookin' just as she had before she died...

Gooseflesh prickled on Lillian's arms as Miranda looked up from her reading. To everyone's amusement, the message in her wide eyes was quite evident: *We're sleeping there again tonight?* Still, she eagerly went back to Jenny's narrative.

"...just kneelin' at the rails of the chapel, prayin' her rosry and cryin'. I did cry then, backed up a ways into the trees so as not to worry her. No, sir, after the first startle, I wasn't afeared of her, only sad. I watched her cry and wail and pray until dawn, then she faded into a hazy sort a light and the air grew warm again. Poor woman, to have had and lost so much in her life, and to be 'countable for an awful lot of it, well, then I guess I can understand why she'll be grievin' for all eternity..."

Unlike other 'hant' stories, this had the ring of truth. I asked if she ever told anyone about the ghost.

She nodded, "Gabriel, seein' as how he'd seen her first and I knew he'd believe me, but no one else. We agreed not to talk it around. Miz Leah was family and we cared for our family when they were alive, and, well, we didn't see why we should behave any different when they was dead. I never went back in the night again, but I do walk over and leave a flower in the chapel for her from time to time."

```
Federal Writer's Project #1699   July
2, 1936
D. B. Smith, Camden, S. C.
```

As soon as Miranda finished, Chloe asked, her voice shaking, "Grandma Althea, have you ever seen the ghost?"

Althea was still looking down at her copy of the narrative, heedless of the tears running in little rivulets along the furrows of her wrinkled cheeks.

"I can hear Grandma Jenny's voice in this for sure. She was my great-grandmother, but we all called her Grandma Jenny. Thank you, dear," Althea said to Lillian for the handful of tissues, and nodded to Chloe, "and yes, honey, I did. She took herself."

"Why didn't you ever tell, Grandma?" asked James.

"I never thought much about it, once I knew there was nothin' to fear. That's why she did it, took me over there just before dawn one April morning. Probably not long after she told her story." She patted the copy on her lap. "I had gotten myself so afeared of ghosts from me and my friends telling silly stories I couldn't never sleep and kept waking up Mama and Daddy in the middle of the night. I was a big girl, too, fourteen—too big for that kind of silliness. One night when I had myself in a real bad state, Grandma Jenny sat up with me, asking what I was so afraid of. I told her the stories I had heard, and she just shook her head at me, told me to get dressed cause we was goin' for a walk. She took me over to the ruins and we sat nearby. Well, I was already scared half outa my mind, but she held my hand and told me to wait quiet.

"Just like she described, the spirit came on gradual with a whimpery sort of crying, a winter fog kind of cold and the faint, hazy light. Grandma whispered to me about who she was and why she was cryin'. We said a prayer for her and I wasn't scared anymore, and never was scared of spirits after that."

"You wouldn't want to spend the night with us tonight, would you?" Miranda asked Chloe, breaking the spell and making them all laugh.

ONLY THE EARLY EVENING hum of insects beyond the
screen and the cooing of baby Drew in his playpen broke the
silence on the porch when they all assembled after dinner for
Janet's next surprise.

Althea reached for Lillian's hand again as they sat down
in her special corner. Lillian felt a rare and special connection
with Althea, as though she had known this woman all of her life
instead of only two short days. Perhaps it was their shared blood
or their bond through Jenny and Lilién. Whatever the reason,
Lillian treasured it.

Janet pointed her tiny remote control at her computer
and the screen changed to a solid black background with bold
white letters. WPA.

The Work Projects Administration.

"There were only a handful of interviews ever recorded
on audio. In 1938, this is *one of only five* for South Carolina that
were filmed for the Federal Writer's Project."

Janet clicked the remote and the soundless black and
white image faded away and the grainy salt and pepper newsreel
countdown began, complete with a radar screen beep and reel-
to-reel rattle.

The documentary opened on the same wide porch where
they were currently seated, although bright afternoon sun shone
beyond the screens instead of the golden light and shadows of a
summer evening. A young man in a light-colored linen suit with
a ballpoint pen poised over a tablet introduced himself in a soft
Virginia drawl and sat across from two women seated on a
cushioned wicker sofa.

"Oh, my," said Althea in a shaking voice, leaning forward
in the old chair, "that's Great-Auntie Brenda, and old Muriel
Anderson!"

While Lillian had been transported back in time with so
many recent discoveries, she realized Althea was reliving her own
childhood memories. She glanced over at Althea, who smiled

through her tears and squeezed Lillian's hand.

'Please state your names and ages, ladies,' the bowtied young man asked politely, putting on a pair of wire-rimmed glasses.

'My name is Brenda Ann Bonneau. I was born on May 19, 1866, over at the Hall's Laurelton Plantation. Our family home was the Fleur-de-Lys Plantation of the Bonneau family, but the house and most of our family were lost during the war.'

Lillian heard the proud note in the old woman's voice. Brenda Ann was tall and slender in her bearing, fine wrinkles fanned out from eyes twinkling with merriment. Brenda Ann was in a light, floral print dress, and wearing a single strand of pearls. The two women could not have been more different. The other wore a lumpy cardigan and dark trousers, her arms were crossed in front of her and she looked on with an annoyed tolerance. Her plump, wrinkled cheeks drooped, creating a sour expression and a perpetual frown.

'I am Muriel Hall Anderson, born in August of 1858 also at Laurelton. So, young man, that makes her old and me nigh on ancient!'

He smiled politely and shook his head. 'Not old enough to talk about the War Between the States, which is what I usually ask first—'

Muriel scoffed, and Brenda Ann tried to hush her.

'Young man, I have a few memories of my own and we have stories from our people! Isn't that what this is all about?'

He nodded, accepting Muriel's reprimand graciously.

'Miss Bonneau, you mentioned losing your family in the war…' He gestured for Brenda Ann to continue while holding his pen at the ready.

As Jenny had in the narrative they had

heard earlier, Brenda Ann recounted what had happened to the members of her family. When the interviewer stopped to clarify that he meant her own family, she looked flummoxed.

'The Bonneau family *were* our family. My father was old Mister Bonneau's blood nephew. Daddy came from Jamaica after his mama died when he was about two. That's why young Mister Brendan deeded the land to him before he went off to his ship again, in case he wasn't able to come home.'

'And what of your family, Mrs. Anderson?

Muriel scoffed, 'Well, young man, I can tell you one thing, we did *not* inherit the family plantation. In fact, my mother was fortunate to escape from the Jerrard Plantation with her life, me in her belly and what little flesh she had left on her back.'

The interviewer glanced up from his notetaking, and though he must have heard many such horrifying tales, sympathy was evident on his young face.

'Some years before the War, Mister Edgar Hall and his son Wilson were driving home with supplies all the way from Charleston and found her struggling out of a picked over cottonfield. She was some months along with child, nearly dead and half out of her mind. They hid her in the wagon and took her home and cared for her till she was well and had her choose herself a new name. She chose the name Delphine and was cook and housekeeper for the Halls until she died.'

When Brenda Ann spoke of the rainy February night Sherman's troops passed through the area, Lillian noticed that Muriel became withdrawn.

At Brenda Ann's change of tone, the interviewer paused at his writing and looked up. "Most of the colored folk I have interviewed seem to think fondly of General Sherman, considering him a liberator.'

'I suppose our recollections are *colored* by the happenings of that night.'

'By Sherman's men?'

Brenda Ann paused, and to the surprise of both the interviewer and those watching, she shook her head.

'No sir. It was late in the afternoon when old Mister Sims, from way across the county, rode in to warn the family the Yankees were marching out of Columbia and headed this way, burning everything in their path.

'Missus Bonneau, who was living over to the Halls, got it into her head to go home. No one knew what she thought to do against the Yankees. The only horse was already hitched to the wagon, ready to load up with supplies to hide in the woods, when old Missus Bonneau ran out of the house, into the wagon and drove home before anyone knew what she was about. Poor Muriel was hiding in the wagon and got the ride of her life that night,' Brenda Ann paused and patted her friend's hand. 'Daddy, he ran the shortcut through the woods, trying to get to Fleur-de-Lys before there was trouble, but he was too late.

'From the stories I heard growing up, Leah Bonneau was a hateful, mean-spirited woman, but she was Daddy's family. Not being able to save her troubled him the rest of his life.' Brenda Ann paused, as though seeing her father's memories in her own mind. She patted Muriel's hand again and continued with the story.

'The old lady started the fire that burned the place to the ground. When she got there, the first Yankee officers were just riding up the road. She came into the house from the back, from the kitchen house, lit herself a lantern and was running up the stairs, crying and screaming and carrying on something terrible. That's when Daddy got there, and before any of them could stop her, she threw the lantern down the stairway at one of the officers. Drapes caught, rugs caught and soon with the high winds drafting through the open doors and shattering windows, the whole thing caught. Daddy tried to go in, but the officers held him back.'

Abruptly breathless and cold, Lillian's chest ached with an almost crushing sort of pressure. Her vision blurred, and her heart pounded. She flexed her free hand, somehow feeling the weight and texture of the leaded, patterned glass of the lantern, seeing how its soft, guttering light illuminated rich indigo-blue walls, and glinted off the gold and silver frames, and the eyes in the portraits, as though the subjects were waking in the cold darkness of the empty house. She heard urgent shouts of unfamiliar voices, Yankee voices. And then, down the long winding stair to the wide-open foyer, a big man burst from the shadows, a handsome man with recognizable Bonneau features, and stood gasping for breath, drenched from the pouring rain, his old work shirt torn, eyes wide with fright in his dark face. A little girl with a head full of rag-tied pigtails and her plump cheeks wet with tears cried hysterically at the foot of the stairs surrounded by officers in blue coats.

Lillian kept still, fighting the vertigo and waves of nausea, and now pain, a memory of pain, searing along her arm and into her chest. She grabbed for the handrail just as an officer with gold buttons and braid shining on his coat whisked the crying child into his arms, the lamp fell from her hand, shattered on the landing, and the room exploded in flame.

Althea didn't speak, but took Lillian's hand between both

of hers, rubbing and patting gently until she became aware once again of the hot summer evening, buzzing of insects and tinkling of wind chimes, and the soft. rippling shadows of the old weeping willow near the porch. Lillian forced a quick smile and gripped her hand before turning back to the screen.

Even more subdued now, the soft voices of Brenda Ann and Muriel continued.

'Daddy said the officers seemed like gentlemen, and believed they were telling the truth when they said their only intention was to use the house for shelter on that cold, rainy night. He sent them over to the Heights, the Barkley's Cardinal Heights, and true to their word, they left the place standing when they left two days later. The day after the fire, Daddy went in and found Miz Leah and they laid her to rest in her vault in the family cemetery.'

Though Brenda Ann was telling the tale, she continued to pat Muriel's hand. Muriel, the little girl in the vision. Lillian could see the resemblance even after seventy years and when she spoke again, Muriel's strong, almost strident voice was also subdued.

'It surely was a grand place, the grandest in the county. Even from the ruins, you can judge that plain enough. Such terrible waste.' Muriel uncrossed her arms to pull a large white handkerchief from the pushed-up sleeve of her cardigan. She wiped her eyes and blew her nose loudly.

The two women were quiet for a moment, and the young man gently changed the subject, 'And after the war? How did you all get along?'

'Struggled hard, and it took a lot of work to get the gardens and crops growing again. They had some help from some of our folk who returned after the war and were willing to work for food and shelter until there was money enough to pay wages. Finally, they were able to build this house in the seventies.'

'In exchange for their help around Laurelton, Miss Amelia Hall taught the lot of us kids from the time we were about five or six to whenever we needed or wanted to stop,' said Muriel, giving a rare smile. 'We never did, which is why we both went on to become teachers.'

'Mister Wilson Hall, Miss Amelia's brother, became a lawyer after the war. He was a great friend of my daddy's just as he'd been a great friend to Mister Brendan. After the war, he lived in Wilmington with Aunt Sarah Bonneau while he got his start. After she died, he moved closer to home and worked in Camden. It was he who would help sell off parcels of land or trade in the gold for Daddy.'

'Gold?'

Brenda Ann nodded. 'At the time he deeded the property, Mister Brendan left my father with some, but there was no way he dared use gold outright. He would've been beaten or even lynched for his trouble. Mister Wilson made the transactions for him."

"Wasn't that demeaning for him, as a free man?' the interviewer asked.

Brenda Ann and Muriel exchanged looks again. "You're not from around here, are you, young man?" Muriel's words were polite, but the tone couldn't hide the old teacher's opinion that he should don a dunce cap and sit in the corner.

'If Daddy was more proud than smart he might have felt demeaned! No sir, free on paper isn't the same as free. People knew that well enough then, just as we know it today.'

The interviewer glanced at his watch and

back to his notes.

'A place like Fleur-de-Lys must have been filled with treasures. Was everything lost or did the family hide the valuables before the army arrived?'

A worried expression crossed Brenda Ann's face.

'Goodness, Brenda Ann, go ahead and tell! There's no one to care anymore, and I bet it's a sight more interesting than most of the other stories this youngster has heard.'

'Young Mister Brendan returned from the war not long before the end, on leave from his duties on a blockade runner, and stayed long enough to make sure his family were all cared and provided for.'

'Not quite the *saint* Brenda Ann makes him out to be, mind you! If you had ever heard old Amelia Hall— '

Brenda Ann scoffed, 'Mama said it was one peck under the mistletoe…'

'Well,' continued Muriel, skeptically, 'all I know is she carried quite a torch for that handsome young man for years, brokenhearted he never returned.'

'You intimated not all was lost?' Clearly, the interviewer wanted to hear the more intriguing speculation about the riches of Fleur-de-Lys.

'There was talk, mostly old Miz Leah, but a few others in the county were happy to spread the gossip, that young Mister Brendan stole most of the valuables from the house before he returned to duty on his ship.'

'The Confederate Navy?'

'He was an officer in the United States Navy before the war, and he refused to switch sides when secession came. Daddy told me once that Mister Brendan was in a terrible fix before the war started. He would not fight for the Confederacy because he had given an oath to the United States and also because he didn't believe in slavery. He wouldn't take up arms to fight against his family, friends, and neighbors neither, so he became an officer on a blockade runner.'

'A wealthy planter's son not believe in slavery?'

'Attitudes were changing even then, young man!' Fully recovered now, Muriel snapped at him, again as though he were a naughty schoolboy giving the wrong answer. "The Halls, where I was born, and both of the younger Bonneau children and their father all wanted to free their slaves, but the State of South Carolina, along with many other southern states, would not permit manumission.'

Again, Lilién's diary was being confirmed in this amazing documentary, Lillian thought, glancing at Miranda, who, like everyone else in the room, was completely enthralled.

'My mama and daddy did say there were things missing,' Brenda Ann continued with her story, 'but they were sure, *if* he was the one to take them, it was only to safeguard. Of those who knew him, only his mama was willing to believe the worst of him.'

'And was he successful?'

'No, well, that is to say, they never knew. He died in the last days of the war and was never able to return the belongings or declare his intentions.'

The interviewer looked disappointed and glanced again at his tablet. '1886. The big earthquake? Do either of you remember the—'

The expression on both faces changed

immediately. Even Muriel was laughing heartily along with her friend.

"Most folks seem to think that a pretty frightening experience,' the young man said reproachfully, as Muriel wiped tears from her eyes once again.

Brenda Ann shook her head, still smiling.

"We were attendin' a revival over towards Winnsboro. Muriel's Auntie Zelda thought the earth movin' under her feet was the Holy Spirit come over her! She only prayed louder, standin' there a swayin', eyes closed, hands raised up to heaven!'

'Oh, Lord!' Muriel gasped, still quivering with laughter, 'She thought the cries and hubbub around her were folks praying along with her until things started crashing down from the ceiling and the whole congregation, old Deacon Bailey in the lead, ran screaming out into the night!'

'The Lord's own revival,' said Brenda Ann, 'for He surely got all of us, white and colored, praying that night!'

Over their chorus of laughter, the young man said his thank yous. The screen went back to salt and pepper and then to black.

CHLOE *WAS* SPENDING THE night to help Miranda keep a watch for spirits. A convenient excuse, the girls didn't want to be separated for their last hours together.

Neera's husband Gilley came home early to meet his new in-laws and was very interested in the stories and handwritten family tree the girls had drawn on large sheets of butcher paper. His own heritage was mixed and his appearance striking, with the black hair and gray-green eyes inherited by his sons. With no idea where his family lines originated, he said he was happy to be ensconced in the middle of such a distinguished line.

Counting back generations on the family tree, Chloe and Miranda had discovered they were fifth cousins once removed, giving them even more to talk about, if such a thing were possible.

Standing over the sheets of paper spread out over the floor, Neera held little Drew on her hip, reading the names in funny voices, trying to get the teething baby to laugh.

"We're all there, little guy," Neera said, finishing with his name, "right there in black and white."

After two seconds of pin-drop silence, Miranda and Chloe looked sideways at one another and burst out laughing. Drew took a drooly fist out of his mouth to point at them and began to laugh, too. Confused, Neera was soon the only one in the room not laughing.

Now as sunset neared, the ruins were in shadow, insects and pollen dust flitting in and out of the rays slanting through the trees.

She smiled, thinking about the many times through the day she was about to tell Neera or Althea what she had seen in the chapel, and now wished she would have done so before hearing Jenny and Althea's stories. instead of her own tale being corroborated, it would probably seem as though she were highly susceptible to suggestion. Still, it was enough to know she was not alone in her experience.

She thought it would never happen, but the girls had finally stopped talking. Now that it was quiet except for the crickets, she couldn't quiet her own mind.

She stood in the kitchen, looking out into the darkness towards the tall pines, inviting the energy, willing it back by standing quietly at the counter, her fingers resting lightly on the old, work-worn surface as though it were an Ouija board planchette waiting to spell out a message. But visions of the cold winter fog and disorienting sensation of déjà vu did not return.

TOM MADE IT THROUGH his visit to the Cherrington estate

without once going inside the old house, a good compromise, and made him appreciate the cottage, cove and other things he *had* missed. On their last night, they were invited to the Reynolds' for dinner, which had often been like a home for him.

Little Cherry Reynolds, Alexander's five-year old-daughter, reminded Tom of his old friend, Jake, her great-grandfather, in looks just as Alexander reminded him of Jake and his take charge kind of attitude. She sidled up to Tom and stayed close through dinner, and even afterwards when the other kids couldn't get back outside fast enough.

"Why were you away for so long?" she asked, petting the wiry, white hair on his arms for a while before slipping, less unobtrusively than she seemed to think, onto his lap.

That was it, he thought, the heavy, ripe-wheat blonde hair she kept flipping out of her eyes like he always used to, and she had also inherited his straightforward approach to just about everything and was always full steam ahead.

"Well now…I was a sailor. For a long time my work kept me far away and out at sea."

She tossed her hair back again and continued to look steadily up at him with those gray eyes. She obviously wasn't buying it.

"And then it was just a lot of bad memories that kept me away for the rest."

"Why did you come back?"

"Cherry," her mother scolded, "don't plague Mr. Cherrington with all your questions—"

"That's my name," she said.

"Cherry? A pretty name—" Tom stopped when she shook her head.

"Cherrington. My name is Cherrington Elizabeth Reynolds."

The room grew even quieter as Tom tried to find his voice again.

"Well, Cherrington Reynolds," he finally said, rather gruffly, brushing the hair away from her eyes, and chucking her under the chin. "To answer your question, I came back to make some good memories. And by Jove, this one's a first-rater."

LILLIAN HAD LEARNED, HAD experienced, so much more than she could have imagined when her father had suggested she journey south.

"When have I ever steered you onto the wrong course, girlie?" he had said when she and Miranda had given him the highlights of the day. Hearing his voice as he asked questions about their discoveries, it was difficult to imagine he was the same man who had scoffed at the importance of family history. Even more than the clues to Brendan's fate that had inspired the trip, Tom's delight at finding out about these new-found relatives he could claim, or that would claim him, as he put it, was even greater. Another legacy, perhaps not as tangible as deeds and diaries or as delicious as Althea's sweet potato pie, but every bit as valuable was the total lack of prejudice she heard in her father's voice.

Lillian knew her own acceptance by the Bonneau family stemmed from the actions of Charles, Brendan, and Lilién long ago. Her color, her lineage, had not been an issue for any of them … well, except for James.

James had listened to Jenny's narrative and returned for the video but hadn't said much afterwards when the talk centered on what they had heard and speculation about what happened to Brendan and the treasures he may have removed from Fleur-de-Lys.

"I thought you'd like to use this tonight." Neera, serving coffee with Althea's sweet potato pie, had served Lillian's in a special teacup.

"Oh!" she said, recognizing the Bonneau family coat-of-arms. "Are these original?"

"Found in the old summer kitchen after the fire, and we use them only on *very* special occasions. Grandma," she added, loudly, "how about you, do you want to use the other?"

Althea smiled and shook her head, "Not with my shaky old hands, child, and I like my old mug better anyways."

Tracing her finger along the tiny, golden fleur-de-lys around the rim of the cup and plate, noting the crackle patterning in the old porcelain, she didn't know James had come in and sat down at the table until she heard his deep voice next to her.

"I'll use it."

Lillian smiled, thinking of Althea's triumphant look when their eyes met.

The stories she had heard about her family, just in the last few hours, had given her a new perspective, especially about the summer kitchen where she would sleep again tonight, just as Leah and Sarah had done those dark, cold months during the winter of 1864.

Before they left tomorrow, she would visit the cemetery again, and she would go inside the ruins once more to leave a flower for Leah.

But still, there were mysteries to solve. She needed to find out what happened to all of those long missing treasures of Fleur-de-Lys. Most of all, she needed to find out what happened to Brendan.

PART VIII

BRENDAN

Wilmington, North Carolina to St George's, Bermuda

December 1864

"Charles Maxwell Allen was to spend the next four years attempting to thwart the blockade-runners and reporting on their activities in detail to the government."

Charles Maxwell Allen was the United States Counsel at Bermuda, 1861 – 1888

from: Dispatches from Bermuda
Edited by Glen N. Wiche
Kent State University Press, 2008

Chapter Twenty-Two

The Promotion of Seaman Crawford

"PERMISSION TO RETURN TO duty, sir," Brendan said, saluting.

"Welcome back, lad," Captain Shaw gave his casual half salute but then gave Brendan a second, more assessing, glance. "A successful trip, I take it?"

"Aye, aye, Sir," Brendan answered with emphasis and a smile that raised one of the captain's wiry eyebrows. "You've already promoted Hudson?"

"Just as easily knock him down a rung," he shrugged, unconcerned. "Steams up and we're off as soon as cargo's secured."

"Aye, Sir."

Brendan took out his logbook to make notations of the weather and crew activity. 'Ship hauled into the stream at 2:00 p.m., steam ordered 3:00 p.m. Deck cargo loaded 5:00 p.m.' He finished and watched the last bales on the aft decks secured and covered.

Three cordons of Federal blockaders between New Inlet Bar and St. George's blocked their passage. Even past the third cordon, cruisers patrolled the Gulf Stream and it would be six days of constant tension once they passed out of range of protection from Fort Fisher until they reached the neutral waters of Bermuda.

In the hours it took them to reach Smithville, where the hold would be fumigated to extract possible stowaways, the night had grown dark and calm.

Brendan accompanied Shaw, Sanderlin and company

agent Tilford when they rowed over to Fort Fisher, both to pay their respects to Colonel Lamb and to be advised on the whereabouts of the Admiral's flagship and movements of the squadron.

A small area around the *Malvern* would go unpatrolled and the *Kendal* would, if all went according to plan, slip through this gap in the first cordon just after midnight and out to the open sea where their chances of outrunning pursuers were much better. *Kendal*, built with her mission in mind, was one of the finest runners in service and had a good supply of hard, clean-burning anthracite in her hold. With a sea speed of nearly sixteen knots, she could be pushed to nearly twenty.

But the *Malvern* had once been the blockade-runner *Ella and Annie*, captained by Frank Bonneau, Brendan's own, though distant, renegade relation, and was now a fast, fully-outfitted warship with enough firepower to blast the *Kendal* into splinters.

IN THE GLOOM AND mist surrounding their small skiff, Thomas looked puzzled as Brendan rowed away from the *Kendal*. Brendan held a finger to his lips and shook his head. Finally, he stopped and rested the oars.

"Before we go further, Thomas, I must tell you a few things," he whispered.

Thomas tossed the hair out of his eyes. "I'd be much obliged if you would, Sir, 'cause beggin' your pardon—ain't we goin' the wrong way?"

Brendan smiled at the easygoing tone of voice, which given the circumstances, said a lot for the young man. Once his galley duties were complete, Brendan had ordered Thomas to report with his knapsack to the starboard aft deck. Young as he was, Brendan knew he was honest, dependable and would be loyal, to Brendan, not the misguided and futile Cause. "Your instincts and internal compass are sound, Seaman Crawford."

Thomas leaned forward. "Beggin' your pardon again, Sir, but I'm just the mess boy. Slop boy, if you're listnin' to the cook."

"I'm promoting you, Thomas. Field promotion to Brevet Seaman for duties you are about to perform." He paused briefly, but Thomas was now sufficiently flummoxed to remain silent.

"The first of which will be to report directly to Admiral Porter aboard the USS Malvern," he paused, nodding toward the shadow of the blockader, "and then to Captain Everleigh in Annapolis."

Twenty minutes later, after the bemused youngster had twice repeated his orders back to Brendan without error, he ordered Thomas to light a lantern and raise a gold and white standard on the mast of the small boat. While they waited for their signal, Brendan gave Thomas funds enough and furlough papers granting him leave and freedom to travel. As they approached the Federal flagship, Brendan leaned over and whispered an urgent addendum.

"Thomas—your promotion? That would be in the *United States Navy*."

THE *KENDAL* STEAMED HER way quietly towards New Inlet Bar and the first cordon of blockaders. At his post, Brendan sat looking out into the blackness, praying the newly commissioned Seaman Crawford would reach Annapolis and Easton safely and that he and the cargo stowed beneath his berth would reach St. George's.

Brendan could detect the faint outline of the bow against the black water of the Atlantic. The wind had shifted during the last hour, blowing in from the northwest, bringing in clouds that obscured the stars and promised a rough beginning to their passage to St. George's. Brendan searched the darkness for any distinguishable shape, any movement and listened for sounds beyond the rhythmic stroke of the engines and slapping of the paddles.

Near midnight, *Kendal* slid quietly into the safe zone around the flagship. Brendan repeated Shaw's whispered commands to the helmsman. Waves slapping against the hull of the anchored ship helped mask the slow stroke of the paddles.

Brendan could hear voices of Union sailors aboard the *Malvern* and see the outline of the hull and rigging of the ship. As they passed by the stern, the faint sounds of a guitar being played in one of the forward cabins drifted past and knew an alarm would not be raised, not by the sailors aboard the *Malvern*.

He wondered how young Thomas was coping with this unexpected turn of events.

Shaw kept the speed up. Within minutes they were well past the first cordon, the Bar and the shallows of the coast. By dawn, they were very nearly past the second cordon before hearing the call from the lookout, "Sails in sight!"

For the next three days, Brendan's time was split between his duties on deck, writing in his personal journal and keeping the logbook filled with notations on wind speed, weather conditions, and headings as the *Kendal* sped towards Bermuda. Their course changed as they maneuvered to evade two federal gunboats from the third cordon, who had started their pursuit just before sunrise.

> *December 27, 1864. A narrow escape this time and I fear it will be the last trip we make through the Wilmington blockade. Fort Fisher was shelled after I left Wilmington for Fleur-de-Lys, and most share the opinion that it was but a warning of much more to come.*
>
> *I was gratified by the crew's reaction to my return, although in hindsight I believe it has more to do with preferring me to serving under Hudson. Hudson, unfortunately demoted back to 2nd, could have shot me on the spot.*
>
> *Our young mess boy, Thomas Crawford, is absent without leave. Last seen aboard sometime prior to midwatch, he did not report for duty this morning. A search of the ship revealed his absence and that of his personal belongings. Seaman Carter reported Crawford had received news of his sick mother just prior to departure. It was the consensus of all that his anxiety overcame his devotion to duty, and he left the ship at Smithville to venture back to his home near Vicksburg.*

As we had left Smithville some hours before and were well past the first cordon, there was nothing we could do. He's a good lad, and I wish him well.

Narrow escapes from both the second and third cordons this trip. I believe it was almost retaliation for the ease in which we slipped past Admiral Porter's ship last night. Carter sighted the first from the cross-tees and has earned his extra dollar. I regret to note, however, Paulson was not so observant. During his watch, Captain Shaw himself sighted sails to the southwest, so he will have five dollars docked from his pay this trip.'

Brendan stopped writing and stood up and stretched in his cramped cabin. Weak afternoon sunlight struggled through the light fog and nearly opaque, salt-stained glass to provide minimal light for his writing. A quick glance through the porthole made him hope Paulson, on duty again as lookout up in the cross-tees, would earn back one of his dollars today.

'Only two nights away from Wilmington and I am impatient to see Arabella again. I admit it was not a conventional, nor, I daresay, gentlemanly way to make my proposal but, along with her admission that she has considered herself my wife for some years, she accepted with such abandon I have no doubt as to her feelings. We know Jems would approve, as Old McRae did, enjoying the story of my search and discovery mission most heartily, with typical wriggling of his bushy eyebrows.

The war cannot continue much longer, the blockade closing tight around each harbor, even the meager support we bring to the country will be halted. My love for the sea is unchanged, but after these last seven transient years, I am ready to return to Fleur-de-Lys—whatever remains.

When I left home to join the navy, it was in the knowledge Louis Charles would be master one day and there would be no room for me and my views. Now as heir in this new world the war has created, I feel as though I will truly be useful. With everything I have saved over the

*last four years, and with the help of Mother and Aunt
Sarah, Gabe and Jenny, and of course, with Arabella at
my side, we will be able to begin again.*

*I owe it to Father to reclaim what is ours. But
in part, it is also the sense of belonging I had never
experienced before. Perhaps I simply took for granted
Fleur-de-Lys would always be there, but to have seen the
destruction visited on other areas of this land and to know
what may lie ahead for our own home was almost too
much to bear.*

*My cargo this journey is not the usual cotton
bales. The three steamer trunks, which were intended to
hold Lilién's trousseau on her wedding trip, now carry
some of the Bonneau legacy, or at least a few tangibles of
great importance and great sentiment, all I could manage
to carry with me. One has already been sent with a trusted
courier north to Lilién, though I dearly wish I could have
delivered it myself.*

*With God's blessing, before tomorrow's sunset,
we will see the western shores of Bermuda.'*

His eyes grew heavy, and Brendan closed the ledger and
stretched out on the hard, narrow berth. His next watch would
begin at dusk. Although Shaw and Chief Engineer Ramsey
refused to sleep for the entire journey, except for the briefest
respites, the captain insisted on shorter rotations for the crew to
help keep their senses alert.

Every person left behind was dear to him, and in the
same predicament so many Southerners had lived through these
long years of the war. In harm's path, but where could they find
refuge? There was no place free from danger, from want. It was
true Laurelton would not be as likely to draw attention, and the
small house would give them both companionship and shelter.
Gabe would bury and hide provisions to see them through the
possible destruction brought by Sherman's army.

Shining through his cabin window, the sun warmed him
through the wool of his uniform, rekindling the memory of
holding Arabella in his arms.

While she dozed, he studied every feature, every curve and angle of her beautiful face and her strong, young body, wanting to commit each detail to memory, to sustain him during their separation.

Long auburn curls spread out across the pillow in a tangle. He brushed a strand from her cheek and her eyes opened and contemplated him quietly.

"What are you thinking about?"

He smiled, as his hand caressed from her shoulder to breast.

"What a vile hypocrite I am. Setting out to rescue you from the baser instincts of man, and I have proven to be every bit as bad."

"And didn't even have to pay," she finished, wrinkling her nose at him playfully but blushing, too. Again, the delightful contrast he had seen earlier.

"I will pay, every day until death us do part. Will you marry me, Bella?"

A shadow passed over her face, and she raised her left hand where the gold and sapphire ring sparkled in the firelight.

"We are married, Brendan," she had whispered. "All you need to do is come back to me."

The ship turned, light and warmth faded. Brendan shivered, pulled the blanket up around his shoulders and slept.

WAITING FOR CLEARANCE TO enter the harbor at St. George's tried Brendan's patience. After three frustrating days, permission was granted and they finally cleared Ordnance Island and docked at Hunter's Wharf. Cotton, turpentine, and tobacco would be unloaded and transferred onto one of the big steamers leaving for Liverpool. Funds from their sale would go towards stocking *Kendal* for her next run. If there was to be a next run.

The interminable wait at least allowed Brendan the opportunity to write the letters to his Aunt Sarah, as well as to Lilién, explaining what he had done.

Rain fell in heavy, drenching sheets as Brendan made his

way down the gangway and walked along Hunter's Wharf. Pulling the collar of his oilskin higher, he headed down the alley towards Jake Holland's freight warehouse. Under an awning over the warehouse door, Brendan shook off some of the water from his hat and around his collar.

"Remy!" he said, turning around as someone nearly walked into him.

"What, oh! Hey Brendan!" he stammered, looking over his shoulder at David, his usual partner in crime, who rounded the corner of the building on his heels.

"What the hell are you two up to now?" Brendan asked, amused at the sight of them literally scampering around the corner.

"Just finishin' a job for someone," Remy said, ducking inside, gesturing for Brendan to follow before he faded into the shadow of the interior. "What're you doin' down here?"

"I need a favor," Brendan said, stepping cautiously into what appeared to be a large broom cupboard, where Remy was lighting the squat nub of a candle stuck into an old wooden yarn spool. From the candle's perch on a rough stone ledge, the dim glow revealed the outline of lengths of rope, casks, crates and various tools scattered across the floor.

"Say the word."

"Can you help me out tonight?" Brendan paused and continued when he saw the two men nod. "I need a good hiding place."

PART IX

LILIAN

Annapolis, Maryland & Hamilton, Bermuda

*Safely in harbour
Is the King's ship, in the deep nook where once
Thou call'st me up at midnight to fetch dew
From the still-vexed Bermoothes, there she's hid.*

*William Shakespeare –
The Tempest, 1610*

Chapter Twenty-Three

Kindred Spirits

"I THINK IT'S TIME you planned another trip, missy."

"We've only been home a little over a week. Trying to get rid of me again so soon?" she said, setting down the newspaper and unfolding a new, third, card table for their expanding collection of genealogical research.

"You bet."

"I can't help being worried, Dad."

Her father had read the paper first and only reluctantly handed it over to her, still turned to the page with a photo of Duncan and Victoria taken the day before.

Somewhat jaded, the columnist nevertheless wrote about the Scotts' reconciliation. Nancy resolutely maintained the three pictures of Duncan with other women were proof he was as much of a philanderer as his spouse. In the latest, however, they were together, and there was no mistaking real affection in Duncan's eyes and Victoria's, who was quoted to say she was looking forward to spending an extended period aboard the *Fleur-de-la-Mer.*

"And I waved the white flag about Duncan a while ago, remember?"

Her father cocked an eyebrow at her.

She sighed. "Where to this time, pray tell?"

"Bermuda. A bit hoity-toity for me but you liked it well enough, at least when you were twelve or so."

"Bermuda?" She laughed. "I emailed the archives in Bermuda and the Bahamas for information about Brendan as soon as we got back from Columbia. I don't need to spend the time or the money to go to Bermuda."

"Well then, I won't remind you about your position on the need to go South."

"*Touché.*" She rolled her eyes as she reached into the drawer behind her for a fresh pair of the white gloves always kept within reach before moving photographs and letters to the new table. "Why Bermuda? Do you think I might find another branch of the family?"

"Several times now, we've read Brendan was in Bermuda during the war. You could go while the kids are up north with their dad."

She rolled her eyes again, remembering Aaron's comment when he told her about the planned weeklong stay with his parents. "I really just want the kids long enough to see what you do the next time they're out of town. More intriguing media coverage?"

There was no question the kids would go, though; they would love a week with their dad and his huge family. Still, she had given him the look, which had taken the smile off his face.

"I know Brendan was in Bermuda, Dad, but as a Confederate naval officer all of his records would have been held in Richmond during the war."

She had already tried a search through the National Archives and Records Administration for Brendan, assuming he had transferred, if not his loyalties at least his commission to the Confederate States Navy and found nothing.

She washed her hands and joined her father at the table, wondering if she had been wrong not to search Brendan's United States Navy record, but they already had proof of his academy graduation and resignation from the service after the Battle of Hampton Roads in Lilién's diary.

Her father set the black diary between them and she once again stopped herself from moving away, reminded again of a movie scene where a face emerged screaming out of an old black leather-bound book. Since reading the early entries, she felt as though there was something just as terrifying waiting for her inside the bindings and had followed her instincts and let it be.

"I'm not so sure Brendan was a Confederate naval officer, honey." He opened the diary, where an envelope was glued onto one of the last pages. He pulled out three letters, faint echoes of Lilién's handwriting across the faces of the envelopes, two of which were black-edged.

"Oh!" Of course, Brendan was dead; he was only the bright-eyed and cocky young sailor forever in the old tintype, looking down at them from his place of honor on the wall.

"What do you mean, not in the Confederate Navy? Brenda Ann said he was serving on a Confederate blockade runner during the war," she paused, thinking back to the evening on the shady porch of Petit Fleurs, "at least, I assumed he would be in the Confederate Navy…"

"Just a hunch, more than anything, but it occurred to me he might have been on a private runner. We've read how loyal he was, how he refused to relinquish his commission… look here at the date and postmark."

Annapolis, April 7, 1865.

"Put the pieces together, Lily. Why would there be an official notification from *Annapolis*, unless Brendan was still commissioned in the United States Navy?"

"A spy for the Union?"

"Makes damn good sense if you think about it. Bright, honorable young officer with mixed loyalties? Might have been his way to serve both sides…"

"Have you read them?"

Tom shook his head."

He watched as she gently removed the envelopes from the book and the pages from each envelope and spread them out on the table. "Slogged my way through the last few pages of the black book last night. It didn't give me bad dreams, honey, but sure left a bad taste in my mouth. She was a very unhappy woman during those years. Worse than unhappy, hopeless. But, no, not the letters."

"Why not?"

"I've seen the way you handle things so gently, I didn't

think you'd take kindly to me ripping them out of there."

"Maybe I'll even get you to use these "damnable" gloves someday."

Addressed to Lilién Cherrington, all were dated 1865. After all the discoveries they had made, seeing her own name written in another time still sent a chill down her spine.

The letter sent from Annapolis was an official notification of death from Captain Everleigh, so short and so impersonal Lillian sensed there was much more this man could have said. Perhaps her father was correct, *again*. When Everleigh penned the letter, the war was still being fought. He could not have revealed the truth even had he wanted. The second letter was signed by Brendan's commanding officer aboard the *Kendal*, Captain Shaw.

> Glendevon House, St. George's, Bermuda.
> Dear Mrs. Cherrington,
> Although I know you will by now have received a letter from Captain Everleigh, I wished to convey my own sympathy for your loss.
> First Officer Bonneau's strong principals and conscientiousness made him a fine naval officer, and a good friend to those he served with aboard the *Kendal*. He will be greatly missed by all who knew him. Though our service together officially ended with the fall of Fort Fisher and we were very soon to be traveling for opposite destinations, I grieve knowing such a vital and wholesome presence is no longer amongst us.

Although both letters expressed sympathy for the loss of Brendan, they did nothing to illuminate his actions any further than Lilién's diary.

The last letter was in a heavy parchment envelope, torn raggedly across the back, but still with a broken wax seal impressed with the familiar fleur-de-lys. Wrapped in a piece of rough muslin was a trunk key, and a medal. A Saint Michael's medal. After gently unfolding the heavy cream-toned paper, she immediately turned to the last page.

"From Brendan!"

Finally, she thought, Brendan's own words and not just the opinions, good or bad, of others. Tom gestured for her to read.

> *Glendevon House, St George's Bermuda,*
> *January 9, 1865*
>> *"My dear little sister,*
>> *If for no other reason, I feel relieved your marriage has removed you from the immediate dangers of war and the desolation I recently witnessed at home. I trust this letter finds you happier with your life than last we met those three long years ago. I will come to you at my earliest opportunity and should you wish to bring your child home to whatever remains of Fleur-de-Lys, we will find a way.*
>> *This war must end soon; the Confederacy cannot continue now Federal forces have closed Wilmington. I must admit my mind now turns to the future.*

He explained what he did and why, confirming Jenny and Brenda Ann's narratives, and Lilién's own affectionate regard, but the few details of the trunks and deeds were almost incidental to the paragraphs involving a young lady named Arabella Barkley and his impatience to return home.

Lillian could almost hear the "vital and wholesome" young man explaining his actions, all of them taken with the very best intentions.

> *You will by now have received your trunk of belongings, thanks to my special envoy. Seaman Thomas Crawford. He is a dependable young man and very loyal to me. I hoped you were not deceived by his outer appearance and rough manners. Enclosed is the key I neglected to send with Thomas, which no doubt you have long since realized. Also within you will find my Saint Michael's medal. Aunt Sarah has given me Father's, a special bequest only she knew of. I want you to have, and to wear mine. A small token of a much grander protection.*

"Poor Brendan," she whispered, tracing her finger over his bold signature. "He freely admits taking everything," she said, glancing at the envelope with its Bermuda green and white stamp bearing the image of Queen Victoria, the postmark smudged and date undecipherable, "but nothing here to tell us what happened to them after his death."

Tom turned one more page, "I *have* read this."

Lillian recognized a page from one of Edward's journals, ripped along one side, and folded over twice, the faint transfer of Lilién's handwriting crosswise along the page. Tom opened it and read it aloud.

"My contact has confirmed that Bonneau is dead in Bermuda. Sometime in early March and something hush-hush about it, no doubt information pertaining to traitorous and avaricious Rebels is still limited at this juncture. I will say nothing to Lilién, not until I trace his activities to know where he has concealed the remaining wealth of Fleur-de-Lys, which is now mine by rights.'"

Tom's voice was cold reading his great- great-grandfather's callous words about the tragic death of someone so profoundly important to his wife.

"Poor Lilién," she whispered. "After what we've already learned about Edward Cherrington, for him to speak of Brendan, of anyone, as being traitorous and avaricious is…."

"I think the man was a psychopath," Tom finished, gruffly.

LIFE HAD GROWN A bit dull for all of them after a month of historic discoveries, international intrigue, and cool house guests. Even Tom was feeling better enough to be restless and grumpy. Her suggestion to take a few days to sail to Easton and around the Bay seemed to raise everyone's spirits.

Nearly midnight on the night before the trip, her cell

vibrated and lit up the room.

"Hello, Lillian."

"Mark! How are you?" she asked, "I've missed you after that last very interesting week."

"I've missed you, too," he said, "and I need to talk with you."

"Oh?"

"I'll be in town tomorrow. Dinner?"

SHE MADE A COMMAND and highly presumptuous decision by inviting him to stay and sending her family off on their sailing adventures without her. A doctor's appointment, she said the next morning, that she had scheduled several busy months ago and forgotten. She arranged to meet up with them in Easton the next afternoon.

"Actually, they're all out sailing," she said, as they came into the quiet house and Mark asked where everyone was. "I'm meeting up with them in Easton tomorrow."

"Oh?"

At the odd tone in his voice, she turned to look at him.

"What is it?" Afraid she had presumed incorrectly, she put her hand gently on his chest. "I…wanted to be with you. I thought you would want…"

Still, he didn't smile or reach for her as she expected. She looked up into his face and saw his jaw tighten. She began to draw her hand away when he took it gently in his and raised it to his lips.

"You took me by surprise, Lillian. Surprised and sadly unprepared *again*, but of course, I want you." He pulled her into his arms, his mouth meeting hers passionately, almost roughly.

"Well, then," she said, pulling away just enough to whisper, "it's a good thing *I* am."

The familiar wicked smile was on his lips as they met hers again.

LILLIAN WAS FEELING FAR less presumptuous several hours later when they prepared dinner together, Mark clad in only boxers and she in his castoff dress shirt, the long sleeves rolled up to her elbows.

The house was dark and quiet, the kitchen illuminated only by under the counter lights, and they talked about what had brought him back to Annapolis.

"I've been placed with an antiquities dealer in Kingston, a man named Phelan Conrad. He has stores on several islands but is an American, expatriate American, he says, although I have never heard *why* he's an expatriate. He has been suspected of small-time antiquities smuggling for years," Mark paused, lowering the heat under the boiling pot of pasta, "and when he had his feelers out for an independent maritime antiquities expert, NCA knew about it. I was able to insinuate myself rather easily into his Kingston operation soon after I left—"

He looked up at her short laugh. "Yes, somehow I can imagine …"

"—therefore, was on the scene when he heard from one of his contacts at the Bahamian Archives in Nassau about your email."

"That must have surprised you," she said, lighting candles, setting the table and pouring the Chardonnay while he cooked, sautéing shrimp and scallops in a buttery herb and garlic sauce. After bringing bread and salad to the table, she leaned against the counter, watching as he tested, drained and tossed the pasta in the sauce.

"At first, I thought it had to do with the Andrastus connection and tie-in with Scott, so I was surprised—and hugely relieved—to see it had nothing to do with that at all." He brought the still simmering pan to the table.

As they ate, he asked about their trip to South Carolina.

She started the tale with Miranda's confession, pleased to find out her daughter had at least been truthful in reporting her ambush of their houseguest.

While telling him about the experience of seeing Leah's spirit in the ruins of Fleur-de-Lys, the candle guttered in the breeze from the open window and sent chills down her back. At his expression, she asked, "Do you believe me?"

"My home's foundations date back to the Plantagenet's, of course, I believe you." He poured more wine into both of their glasses, adding, "What did you learn about Brendan?"

She told him about the family lore verified by the Federal Writer's Project testimonies, and the black-edged death notices and Brendan's letter. "But we still don't know the truth about how, where or why Brendan died, so near the end of the war. Or, besides those he sent to his sister, what could have happened to the family treasures taken from Fleur-de-Lys."

After dinner, they had gone to their familiar mid-watch post on the living room sofa. The breeze from the open windows cooled her skin and made the candle's flame dance.

"Seeing your credentials in your email, Conrad asked if I knew you. I had to admit we had worked together. Instead of being suspicious, he was thrilled," he paused, kissing the top of her head. "I am to find out what you know."

"So, I'm an assignment? Again?"

"And how very fortunate for me." He reached for the folded paper on the coffee table. "Conrad was familiar enough with the name of Bonneau from this, which at least solves one of your mysteries about Brendan."

He handed the paper to her, smiling at her expression as she leaned forward to hold the paper to the light.

The Royal Gazette May 19, 1865, CAPTAIN of the BLOCKADE RUNNER KENDAL REVEALS SECRET MISSION

Retired Royal Navy Captain Roderick Shaw returns to his quiet life in rural Inverness after twenty-four successful trips through the North Atlantic Blockading Squadron. The only runner to cross the squadron successfully after the fall of Fort Fisher, Shaw admits to a secret mission up the James River near the Confederate capital of Richmond only weeks before the surrender of General Lee at

Appomattox.

Lillian paused, remembering her father's supposition that Brendan may have been a spy for the Union. What could have taken him up the James River in a Confederate blockade-runner?

Willing to reveal the mission but not their purpose, nor the magic used to travel unmolested through long-held Union territory, he admits during our interview that the ship carried both inbound and outbound cargo, as well as passengers bound for Nassau.

'Kendal', built in 1861 in Greenock, Scotland and owned by MacGregor and Buchanan of Edinburgh, is unique among the dozens of other blockade runners that once traveled from St. George's to Confederate ports during the war. Not only in her successful record of runs but the company's aims were always to provide for the civilian population. No armaments, munitions or at the other extreme of the mercantile scale, luxury items despite high demand and higher profits.

Kendal's good fortune lasted long enough to see them free of the blockading squadron, until a Union patrol, a spring tempest and the illness of Shaw, and a passenger, the wife of a Confederate official, perilously close to her confinement, forced the acting captain to alter course to St. George's, there to founder on the northwestern reefs.

Their mysterious cargo, all of which was safely discharged before the ship was destroyed, has since disappeared, causing rather sensational speculation.

"Acting Captain Bonneau's orders were to have the lot shipped to Nassau. I have no doubt he followed my orders to the best of his ability. However, due to the actions of Jack Hudson, we may never know."

Shaw's departure from Bermuda has been delayed due to the murder trial of Jack Hudson, former second officer, arrested for the murder of Shaw's first officer Brendan Bonneau shortly before the completion of their mission, Acting First Officer and Acting Captain respectively due to the illness of Captain Shaw on the inbound journey.

Hudson is also suspected in the murder of two local dockers. Rémy St. Clair and David Blythe, conscripted by Bonneau to assist in the transfer of the cargo in question, were discovered dead on the lane leading to Glendevon House, island residence of Kendal's senior officers.

At the trial, Shaw testified that in his long career he had never met a finer officer or a braver man than Bonneau.

Asked if he will miss the adventure of blockade running or warmth of the tropics, Shaw shook his head, sadly, "No, I just want to go home."

"'No finer officer or braver man,'" she quoted softly.

"Quite the *épithète*." Mark gently wiped the tears from her face.

"Thank you, Mark. This is wonderful." She set the article aside and leaned forward for a kiss. "But I don't understand why he's so interested in my search or this particular ship, is it something to do with Brendan's Fleur-de-Lys artifacts? To help Mr. Conrad increase his inventory of antiques? If there *is* something, I admit it might have value to a simple antiques dealer, but certainly not enough to risk an established smuggling network!"

"Conrad's not after artifacts, Lillian, not as such, nor is he a simple antiques dealer. He's looking for gold."

"Gold?"

"Not just any gold, either. He believes the *Kendal* has something to do with part of the Confederate treasury which went missing during the last days of the war."

"*What?*"

"Conrad has been on this hunt for years. Decades. He has a *serious* obsession with the lost treasury gold, and his antennae are always out for clues. When he found out about your request for information about Brendan Bonneau, he told me everything, how he has thoroughly searched not only Bermuda, the Bahamas, and Cuba, all transshipment points used during the war, but every place in the reunited States and the United Kingdom connected with the officers and crew of the *Kendal.* He is convinced the gold was moved to Nassau on another runner after the *Kendal* hit the reefs. I knew your search and our investigation were dovetailing—"

"I'm sorry."

"I am absolutely *not* sorry. Any other time and you might have been completely vulnerable to this lunatic. As it is, there is a chance to stop him and possibly to even help you."

"Oh?"

"Do something for me?"

She raised her eyebrows.

"Not that, well, not yet." He smiled, pulling her back into his arms. "I want you to write once again to the Archives in Nassau for more information. You might include a note stating requests to sources in Bermuda yielded no useful information, and I will be telling Conrad, quite honestly, you did not have any information about Brendan's last mission or his fate. His contacts at the Bahamian Archives will inform him you've been unsuccessful."

"All right," she nodded, remembering from her research that Nassau was the primary transfer point for most of the blockade runners, being well over a hundred miles closer to the Confederate ports than St. George's "Throwing him off no scent?"

"For the sake of the current operation, and above all, for your safety, it's best if he and his cohorts stay in Kingston."

They lay quietly, his hands moving down her back over the thin fabric of his shirt.

"Thank you," she said again, turning in his arms and looking at him thoughtfully before adding, "Something seems…well, different for us this time, or is it just me?"

"I think it *is* you."

"Oh?" she asked, propping an elbow on a cushion, she looked down from the new vantage. His face was half in shadow, half in candlelight, emphasizing his striking features and illuminating the gold in his hair.

"I rushed you into our first and tricked you the second. At the cottage we were, it seems, influenced by some ethereal presence – which was *brilliant*, by the way," he paused for a long, lingering kiss. "But today … it was you."

"I did *want* to be with you, you know, all those times…"

"But you felt hesitant, didn't you, unsure of yourself, even a bit frightened?"

"Maybe," she said, smiling uncertainly, remembering how insecure she was their first time after fifteen years of marriage.

"Today, *you* contrived for us to be alone, *you* led me to your bedroom by my tie and didn't even draw the blinds."

"I spent years feeling so…well… inadequate. I suppose that takes a while to get over. But now, after everything *we* have been through, I guess I just trust you."

His eyes moved over her face, taking in every feature slowly, from her eyes to the neckline of the loosely buttoned shirt.

"The finer points of your intelligence, talent, and uncanny instincts as a scientist, your generous and nurturing spirit towards your children, parents and friends may be too far beyond your ex-husband's intellectual spectrum to appreciate, Lillian," he reached up and gently cupped her cheek in his hand, "but, you can trust me when I say that any inadequacy that might have existed in your relationship was not yours."

DUNCAN SAT AT THE console, finally putting into words the letter he had been drafting in his mind ever since he had received hers. He could not put off the reply any longer.

> *Thank you for your letter, Lily. By the delay in my response, you'll know that I'm trying not to let go either, and I don't intend to. You were right to send your written letter through Mariah, I'm not trusting email or phones for anything I consider private right now.*
>
> *I've known for some time my marriage is an*

emotional and physical sham. After the night we met on the LilyRose, I have learned it is legally, as well. I will tell you all when I can, but with Victoria on board, I wanted you to know it is for her and her step-sister's safety, nothing more.

My plan, after Jupiter's last trip, was to tell you everything and propose marriage. Ironically enough, I believe my thought was 'before anything else could happen.' Now that you are aware of the danger, I hope you can understand why I distanced myself so abruptly.

I love you, Lily. Please don't let go of me yet.

Duncan

LIFE HAD BECOME ROUTINE again when it was almost time for the kids to spend their summer week with their dad at his parents' place in Pennsylvania.

Her own father had not given up trying to send her on another field trip, and after they had finished reading through more letters and journals one evening, Tom had reached into his pocket.

"This is for you," he said, handing her a check for four thousand dollars, made out to her from the Cherrington trust account. "Reynolds assures me it is a very reasonable sum for a week in Bermuda—airfare and hotels, taxis and restaurants, tee shirts and key chains, not to mention greasing the palms of malleable government officials."

"But Dad…"

She started again but paused. She had not told him about Mark's visit or his revelations about Brendan or Phelan Conrad, and would not, not until Mark's assignment was complete and could not be compromised. She had done exactly as he had asked and written to the Bahamian Archives, twice, with specific questions showing her complete ignorance about Brendan Bonneau and the last cargo carried by the *Kendal*, whatever it might have been.

"You know, honey, it's damn rare that a man as old and

stubborn as me gets to find out just how wrong they've been, or have the chance to set things right, even to try. We're onto something here, Lily. Clues have led us closer to the truth about what happened to Brendan, what happened to this family, and the closer we get, the more important it feels to me, as though we're kindred spirits, somehow linked together by this mystery." He paused, annoyance flashed in his eyes as his strong voice wavered. "Besides," he added, gruffly, "hasn't it been an awfully long time since you've been able to have a real vacation, do something you loved without work and worry attached to it? This will be the best of both worlds."

Her father looked at her as though he was sizing up weather on the horizon. "You've been on tenterhooks for weeks, ever since you got home from Easton that morning. But you can't do anything for either one of them right now, and they wouldn't want you to." When she began to interrupt, he put his hand on her shoulder. "Go to Bermuda, Lily. Find out what really happened to Brendan Bonneau."

Chapter Twenty-Four

Between the Devil and the Deep Blue Sea

LILLIAN CLOSED HER BOOK as the plane banked for its approach. Through a thin veil of wispy clouds, she was looking directly down onto Bermuda, all twenty-two miles from St. George's to the West End. While the view from a sailboat was as beautiful in its own way, there was nothing like seeing the full map spread out over the Atlantic Ocean, framed by pink sand beaches and water in varying shades of vivid greens and deep blues.

After the initial shock of heading off into traffic on the left side of the road, she enjoyed the sea-level drive over the Causeway and around Harrington Sound towards Hamilton. Vines laden with morning glory blossoms in shades of bright blue, periwinkle to deep purple draped limestone walls, and parks, front yards, and window boxes were bursting with color. Like cupcakes topped with seven-minute frosting, most buildings were painted in the traditional pastel pink and aquamarine, topped by tiered limestone roofs.

Shining through palmettos along the short circular driveway to Leighton's Guesthouse, the early evening sun cast striped shadows on the large, pale yellow bungalow. On a wide, square-columned porch, several people sat at tables grouped at either end and as Lillian got out of the cab, one of the women stepped down to greet her.

"Mae Leighton. You must be Lillian?" The ruddy-faced, buxom blonde held out her hand and gave Lillian's a firm shake. She took hold of the suitcase and nodded towards the house. "Come on through—and don't mind this crowd. It's just happy hour on the front porch tonight!"

Through a chorus of friendly hellos and welcomes, Lillian stepped into the main entry and followed Mae down a long hallway with highly polished wood floors and mint green walls leading to the guestrooms in the newly renovated wing of the house.

Brass plates on the doors had names such as Coral Sands and The Tempest, and then Mae stopped in front of a door with a nameplate "Outer Reef."

Walls painted a deep cerulean blue created an immediate sense of coolness and tranquility. White sheers luffed at open windows framed by draperies bright with tropical flowers and foliage. Dark mahogany furnishings enhanced the British Colonial look.

"I've seen that look before," Mae said, laughing, startling Lillian out of her reverie, "usually directed at the pool guy!"

"It's…perfect."

"So is he!" Mae laughed and walked through the room, indicating the amenities. "You have a full bath in here, fresh towels in the hall closet if you need extra for poolside, and the notebook on the table has more than you'll ever want to know about the place. Now, I'll leave you to get settled and if you're the daring, adventurous type, come out and join us."

Lillian set her bags on the stand near the door and took in the details of the room. Not a large room, but big enough to accommodate the queen size bed, a chair and ottoman, dresser and desk. Draperies, coverlet and throw pillows were the same vintage barkcloth; a nubbly-textured cream background vibrant with palm fronds, crimson camellias, and clusters of tiny flowers of the same deep blue as the walls. A small desk faced a window and looked out on the pool.

Beautiful.

The other guests were all in one group from Connecticut, in Bermuda for a week of business meetings and training courses, sneaking in the occasional afternoon at the beach and round of golf. Their most important tip, however, after plying her with wine and HORS D'OEUVRES, was that Mae's afternoon teas were not to be missed.

LILLIAN WAITED PATIENTLY AS the young customs agent looked over the letters.

"I'm not quite sure how we can help you, ma'am," said young agent Chadwick, over the noise of the copy machine and ringing telephones. "The records in this office only date back to the early 1900s. But wait here, please. Let's see if Agent Jameson can recommend something."

Oh Lord, I'm going to have to explain it again, she thought, as Chadwick turned to catch another agent in mid-stride. Even with the name of a contact, this was the third office she had been to in the building, and the novelty of good-looking men in gold-braided uniforms was beginning to wear off.

Holding up one hand to cut off Chadwick's question to no avail, Agent Jameson was obviously on his way out and looked to be in a foul temper. After a moment, he took the paperwork with an expression that sent Chadwick back to his desk. He put on glasses and glanced over the letters as he walked slowly towards Lillian.

"You say you traveled here from the States to find these 'personal belongings' mentioned in a one hundred and fifty-year-old letter on the recommendation of someone in *this* office?" Neal Jameson looked down over the top of his glasses directly into her eyes. She had a feeling that his Irish brogue was more pronounced when he was annoyed.

"No, and not just because of the letter," Lillian explained, indicating Brendan's letter, the page ripped from Edward's journal and the corresponding report by the private investigator, which her father had found in another box several days later.

"And how is it you believe the customs office can be of service?"

"Well, we know neither he nor his belongings returned to South Carolina, but if any left Bermuda legitimately, we hoped there might be a record on manifests, permits, anything that may have specific descriptions." It had all been so plausible, but the bureaucratic runaround and Neal Jameson's skeptical expression now made this part of her search seem foolishly impulsive.

"The agent I spoke with on the phone," she continued, "Agent Krystof, said I might be able to review manifests of the ships sailing from Bermuda in the months following the war, but Agent Chadwick said your records only date back to 1900?"

Jameson acknowledged that with a nod, and she continued, "We truly don't care so much about the items and certainly don't expect to find them intact, but we are hoping to find evidence about what happened to our ancestor."

Jameson ran a hand through his hair. "This wouldn't be the place to start. The Archives—"

She interrupted, but with a smile, "I'm on my way there now."

"Good, and I might be able to put you in touch with someone—" his own expression had lightened, briefly, until he was interrupted again by Agent Chadwick handing him a message, "Christ, Chadwick, what now?"

"Don't shoot the messenger, sir," he answered with an apologetic grin towards Lillian as Jameson scanned the message, "please."

"I have to leave," he said to her, stuffing the message in his pocket, "but I think I know who might be able to help you. Where are you staying?"

AT THE ENTRANCE TO the Bermuda Archives, Lillian stopped. And sighed.

If she had her way, comfortable, high-backed, brocaded chairs would nestle beside solid oak tables, dark with age and scarred with use. Warm, golden light would emanate from polished brass lamps, or sunlight, properly filtered of course, would pour through high, diamond-paned windows along with the sounds of horse's hooves and ship's bells. Thick, midnight blue carpet would hush footsteps, and from high on wood-paneled walls, portraits of haughty, unsmiling subjects would keep their arrogant eyes on the activity below. Enriching the air would be the provocative scents of Bermuda cedar and a hint of salt spray. And, she thought wistfully of the hours ahead of her, uniformed servants would deliver plates with cucumber sandwiches, currant scones, and perfectly brewed Earl Grey in delicately painted, gold-edged china.

The fantasy bubble burst.

Reality was gray Formica tabletops, thin gray and tan mottled carpet, and walls covered in bland characterless paneling, all topped by a ceiling which may have once been white. Harsh fluorescent lights leached what little color there was out of the room. The only redeeming feature was the artwork; several framed photographs and maps were displayed throughout the room.

'No Food or Drink Allowed' signs were about as personable as the sour-faced archivist Lillian first approached to ask about their collections. After receiving a perfunctory greeting and a minimal introduction to the archives, the woman left Lillian on her own.

She had hesitated to ask directly about either Brendan or the *Kendal*, fearing it would get back to Phelan Conrad and disrupt Mark's investigation.

From previous research, many of the names of the blockade runners and anecdotes about them were familiar and yet still compelling. Supercargo, or company agent, on the *Banshee*, Thomas Taylor, described with such vivid detail and excitement how the captain coolly skirted past the Union flagship *USS Niphon*, just as though they were one more ship of the Federal squadron—until they were discovered. Under fire, they still managed to evade capture and Lillian could easily imagine the young man moving excitedly from the lookout to bow to stern, pushing bales of highly valuable cotton into the Atlantic to lighten the load and increase the runner's speed.

The crew of the *Robert E. Lee*, on a return run to St. George's, employed one of the more resourceful maneuvers of her captain, John Wilkinson. Feeding the boiler with turpentine-soaked cotton fueled their escape from the blockader *USS*

Iroquois. When clogged flues threatened to slow her down before nightfall, he ordered coal dust shoveled into her boilers to create heavy black smoke to shield a sudden change of course.

Beyond routine entries in a book of compiled manifests, there was no new information about the *Kendal*, not even the 1865 article from the Royal Gazette Mark had shown her.

Hours later, discouraged, hungry and cold, she found a passage written by Wilkinson, about the fall of Fort Fisher in January 1865:

> *"As we turned away from the land, our hearts sank within us, while the conviction forced itself upon us that the cause for which so much blood had been shed, so many miseries bravely endured, and so many sacrifices cheerfully made, was about to perish at last."*

"Are you crying?"

"Probably," Lillian said, smiling up at her.

"We don't get a lot of that in here. What are you looking for?"

A lull in the usual archival activity had left Kimberly, the energetic young research assistant, very bored, curious and at Lillian's beck and call and Kimberly's eyes lit up at the mere mention of the words "blockade-runner".

"I've wanted to show someone ever since I found out about it a few weeks ago! Did you tell Delilah what you were after? Come back to the reading room!"

She led the way to the small climate-controlled room, and each of them donned a fresh pair of the white cotton gloves.

Kimberly brought out a large book, covered in a utilitarian royal blue fabric. "Chief Officer's log of the blockade runner *Talisman!*" she said, happily, setting it with a gentle sort of flourish in front of Lillian. "It might not have the answers you're looking for, but so cool your ancestor had the same job, don't you think?"

"Very cool," Lillian agreed, opening the book and inhaling the scent of age and history.

She was immediately captivated. Entries were dated in

early November of 1864, and she knew that each of these log entries were the same kind of notations, in the same kind of book Brendan Bonneau would have used aboard the *Kendal*. As an experienced sailor, Lillian was very familiar with the notes about wind direction and course headings, readings of latitude and longitude by observation, by account and by chronometer. The first recorded a departure from Wilmington.

"Commenced to take in cargo. At 10 PM filled up the hole." "Hauled ship into the stream and took on deck load." "At 630 got under way and proceeded to sea over the Western Barr at 7. 1 shot fired but did not hit the ship. At 9 Bald Head Light N NE to dist. about 8 miles." "At 10 PM William Brown, and John Carpell found drunk and stealing ship's stores, were put in irons until was clear of the blockading fleet." "Hard squall with rain." "Strange steamer in sight, high astern under a full head of steam all said at 2 PM. The chase continued eastward any advantage the Yank watching every movement and doing all he could. The Talisman was not pushed as hard as she could have been. At Sundown, Yank gave it up and went to the south. Talisman proceeded on her course."

The words "swear" and "so help me God" were crossed out in most entries, and although the destination noted might be Havana or Nassau, the course heading was northwest. At first, Lillian thought it was simply an error, but every page was the same.

"Kimberly?" She beckoned the assistant over, and asked, pointing to the crossed-out entries, "What do you know about this?"

The young girl's face clouded, her brow wrinkling as she scanned the book, but quickly lit up again and she pressed a hand against her heart.

"Oh my God, it's just the most romantic thing? The officers were *lying*, see, they said they were going to Nassau, but they weren't, so they couldn't swear an oath to God!

"That is…romantic," she agreed. Shocked she had never heard that interesting tidbit before, she read with a new awareness, looking for more peculiarities in the ledger, but also, absorbed in the excitement of the scenarios, imagining such perilous circumstances when a shot fired into a heavily laden ship could mean immediate disaster.

Once Lillian reluctantly finished the Talisman's log book and left the reading room, Kimberly industriously supplied her with books, microfilm, and other material relating to blockade running in Bermuda during the American Civil War.

"I'm tired just watching you."

Lillian jumped, startled out of the yellow fever epidemic of 1864.

"That's the third roll you've gone through! Aren't you dizzy?"

"Totally immersed and fascinated, but a bit disappointed I haven't found anything specifically relating to Brendan yet," she answered, stretching and yawning. "This chair was sort of comfortable when I sat down, now it feels like a board."

"How long are you here?" Kimberly asked, and Lillian explained her itinerary while they gathered up the films.

"You should go to the Rogues and Runners Museum in St. George's. Delilah didn't mention that, either? *Everything* there has to do with Bermuda and the American Civil War."

LILLIAN LAY ON THE chaise lounge, amused by the ponderous buzz of a pollen-laden bumblebee as it struggled along a vine laden with purple passion flowers. *You don't know when to quit, either, do you*, she thought, as it left the vine and bumbled over the nearby teacart on its way to a fat, red hibiscus blossom.

Asserting she was Devonshire born and bred, Mae Leighton said she took the tradition of afternoon tea very seriously. She had delighted in introducing Lillian to warm scones piled high with thick clotted cream and her homemade strawberry jam.

The swimming pool sparkled in the bright sunlight, the afternoon's heat tempered by the breeze and soft shade of a flowering jacaranda. Through its veil of lavender blossoms and the white columns of the limestone railing, Lillian could see a sailboat out on Hamilton Harbor and thought of her father.

His usual hearty self when she talked with him the night before, but as anxious as she for answers. Even here in Bermuda, hints about Brendan were elusive.

There were notations, anecdotes and news reports about every other runner that ran the blockade during the war, so why wasn't there information about the *Kendal* in all of the Bermuda Archives, she wondered, as she let herself drift off to the sound of the bees.

Sunlight was golden, and the shade had deepened and cooled when she opened her eyes. Now the buzz came from the voices of other guests around the pool. She turned her head when she heard steps on the patio nearby.

"Hello," said Neal Jameson.

"I'll be right there with more tea," Mae called from the kitchen window.

"Oh, hello..." Lillian said, sitting up and pulling her shirt on over her swimsuit. "Mae is very serious about 'er afternoon tea."

"So I understand," he said, sitting in one of the wicker chairs, "And I seriously approve."

Mae hurried out with a fresh tray.

"You're going to help Lillian find her ancestor, are you, Inspector?" she asked. Not waiting for an answer, she bustled back inside. When more guests arrived at the front entrance they heard Mae's enthusiastic greeting, "Oh good, you're just in time for tea!"

"Milk?" Neal asked, with the small pitcher poised over her cup.

"Thank you," she accepted the service with a smile. "Now, I haven't had all that many afternoon teas, but you look like you know what you're doing," Lillian said. Had Agent Chadwick ever seen this side of his superior? The regulation jacket was gone and the open collar and rolled up sleeves of his white shirt revealed a golden tan and a trace of sunburn. The gold on the epaulets on each shoulder glinted in the sunlight.

"I worked in London for a few years and have had my share of West Country teas," he said, spooning jam over the top of the scone. "I apologize for this morning."

"Oh. You don't need to," she said, surprised. "I could see I came at a bad time, with a very unusual request. I don't *really* expect to find anything." As Neal consumed his scones and tea, she explained more fully about the family legend. "I know it all sounds very unlikely, but if you knew my father, you would understand why I have to try."

"I do have the names of two local historians who have studied Bermudian history from the inside out and off the beaten track," said Neal, reaching in his pocket and pulling out a slip of paper. "Shelby-Jones is bonafide if it makes a difference; retired from Oxford some ten years ago. The other is considered a historian only because of his age, I think. Hollis has lived in the same cottage in St. George's most of his life and is ninety if he's a day. If anyone knows anything about the hand-me-down tales from the blockade running days, it'll be him. He's difficult to get a hold of, but suggested two o'clock on Wednesday, if that works for you.

"Both men have been on the island for a long time and will know the stories of old-time smuggling hideaways. They are also people you can trust not to take advantage of you."

"Take advantage...?"

"You must know, dealing with artifacts the way you do, there is thriving illicit antiquities trade, black and grey markets, from small-time con artists to complex organized crime networks. If this story is true and there is some volume of artifacts in a sort of time capsule, it could be very valuable to any number of collectors, many who don't care how they were obtained."

"Yes, of course..." Lillian answered, wondering if he was referring to Conrad.

"Any antiques that are being *openly* exported are investigated to some degree, to determine if the articles relate historically to Bermuda or if their ownership is questioned—as you know, our laws govern the export of Bermudian antiquities. If your ancestor brought something in that doesn't ordinarily belong here, we would have no jurisdiction and it wouldn't even need to be smuggled. Anyone who knows its historic and monetary value would be well versed in those same regulations."

"I'm ashamed to admit the possibility never crossed my mind. I suppose I've been thinking that whatever may exist, its intrinsic value would be more sentimental than financial."

He raised an eyebrow at her, reminding her of when she stood on the other side of the Customs Agency counter that very morning. Now, however, a hint of a smile lurked in the tiny lines framing his mouth, and in his eyes as well.

"So, your ancestors came from a dirt-poor farm, and packed away their family Bible and an old blanket?"

"One of the richest plantations in South Carolina before the War," she admitted.

"Well then, time to tackle this more as an artifacts conservator and less like a daughter." Neal drained his cup and set it gently on the tray. "Be careful not to give too many specifics and watch out for anyone asking too many questions, or someone who turns up too often where you're searching. A familiar face in an unfamiliar country, it's time to get suspicious."

"I've heard of a Civil War enthusiast, a Mr. Conrad?" Lillian stood with him, watching his reaction to the name. "It was suggested he might have some information."

"Conrad?"

"You know of him?"

"We do. Conrad is an antiquities dealer, not a historian," Jameson's relaxed demeanor had become guarded. "From Jamaica, though he divides his time between many of the islands. As I said, just be very careful who you trust."

THE NEXT MORNING AT the Archives was no less interesting, but, at least by Kimberly's lunch hour, no more productive. The girl had been running all morning, finding articles, journals and diaries with obscure, curious little references, fully illuminating Lillian's knowledge of blockade running out of St. George's during the American Civil War, but did nothing to shed any light on Brendan's presence on the island. Lillian invited Kimberly to lunch at the nearby pub as a reward for her diligence and resourcefulness.

On their way out, Kimberly, reported in with her "nightmare of a supervisor", to let her know they were walking down to the Hog Penny Pub. Kimberly also asked for suggestions about where to look next. Lillian watched the exchange. Delilah, possibly because a patron and tourist to Bermuda was standing nearby, was polite yet still wore a somewhat truculent expression. "I'll see what I can find."

"I JUST DON'T UNDERSTAND." Settled at a booth in the pub, as the waiter walked away after taking their order, Kimberly's frustration bubbled over. "This is the first time I haven't been able to find *anything*—" She stopped abruptly looking towards the door.

Kimberly leaned forward and whispered, "Phelan Conrad."

She had asked Kimberly about the antiques dealer when she mentioned the other men recommended by Agent Jameson. The girl said she knew of him and his shop but there had been an unnatural reticence when she answered. Now, taking a second glance, Lillian was surprised to see a man much older and benign in appearance than she had imagined.

Dapper in a typical island business suit of emblazoned jacket and plaid Bermuda shorts, he had thinning gray hair and a florid complexion. As he scanned the darkness of the pub, she saw him wave and smile at someone beyond her

When she turned back to Kimberly, the girl's eyes widened in alarm.

"Ms. Harvey!" Conrad stopped at their table, beaming down at the young woman. "Miss Brooke tells me you are doing wonderful work at the Archives!" He pretended to notice Lillian sitting across the table. "My apologies for disturbing your lunch…miss…?" he paused, looking between Lillian and Kimberly, clearly expecting an introduction.

Kimberly obliged, and Lillian wondered if the man rehearsed the pleasantly surprised expression, but she was almost positive his appearance at the Pub today was no coincidence.

"A vacation," she said cautiously, "under the guise of pursuing a rather fruitless search for a long-lost ancestor. We believe he may have had something to do with blockade running during the War Between the States.

"Do we share an enthusiasm for the history of the American Civil War?"

"It is fascinating, and tragic, of course. What are your specific interests, Mr. Conrad?"

"Mostly, ma'am, my interest stems from being a proud son of Virginia," he answered, drawling out the last words pleasantly enough, his eyes observing her intently as he handed her his card. "I'm always happy to talk to a fellow enthusiast, from either side of the Mason-Dixon Line."

Watching as he walked away, she saw a young man with golden hair, also in a blazer and dress Bermuda's. Mark looked her way and smiled at her, as though seeing her here was no surprise to him at all.

Chapter Twenty-Five

A Different Sort of Bermuda Triangle

"BERMUDA?"

In *Fleur-de-la-Mer*'s dining mess, Duncan had swung around to face Vera so fast his morning coffee flew from his cup. Victoria had looked up from her magazine and simply raised an eyebrow, but poor Helena startled like a wary little rabbit.

"My God, what's wrong with Bermuda —" Vera jumped out of range, laughing until she saw his expression. "Duncan? What is it?"

"When?"

"Her email said—Duncan!"

He started towards the crew quarters.

"What's going on?"

"I need to know exactly what she wrote, Vera. *Now.*"

Moments later, seated in front of Vera's laptop he scanned Lillian's lengthy email, swearing profusely with every revelation. Finally, he sat back and looked up at her.

"You know Duncan, I've always wanted you to talk dirty to me, but this is not quite what I had in mind," Vera said, without her usual humor, adding as he headed out the door. "Where are you going?"

"Bermuda!"

HOW COULD SUCH A small island have a road so interminably long? The little pink bus made countless stops along the way and she was beginning to regret declining Mae's offer of one of Leighton's scooters for the trip out to the west end.

A midday haar settled over the island, the hovering fog and dull gray of the sea made her feel anxious, almost claustrophobic. Part of her anxiety was simple, straightforward fear that her presence in Bermuda was playing havoc with Mark's investigation. Several times she had taken out her phone to call and ask if she should leave the island immediately, each time putting it away.

Conrad, even aware of their professional link, hadn't said anything about recognizing her name, and Mark had only gestured from across the pub. She didn't know what to do and would just have to trust him to contact her if there was a need.

During the long ride to her appointment with Professor Clifford Shelby-Jones at his home on Somerset Island, she wrote a thorough accounting of what she had accomplished and who she had talked to over the course of the previous days.

In Somerset, she walked to the retired historian's home, Loquat House, a small, modern sixties-era home looking west over the open Atlantic. Lillian was greeted and shown into a small study and introduced to the elderly professor by Mrs. Shelby-Jones, who came and went through the meeting, delivering lemonade and shortbread cookies.

Clifford Shelby-Jones was very tall, very thin, and very proper in a three-piece suit with glasses hanging around his neck as though ready for his daily lecture. He glanced over the documents and listened to Lillian's explanations with a thoughtful expression.

"You do realize, Ms. Cherrington, there are many reasons, if indeed it ever existed at all, the belongings described here would not have survived," he said, an apologetic wrinkle to his brow. "Our island climate, many of the old buildings wantonly destroyed over the course of time. These traveling chests, described here, may have been destroyed along with the building they were hidden in, the contents used up by some lucky finder, perhaps even smuggled out of Bermuda long ago."

Discouraged, she walked back to the bus stop and hoped her interview with the historian in St. George's would be more illuminating.

The sun was beginning to break through the fog by the time she boarded the bus to continue on to the end of the road and the National Museum of Bermuda, though she wouldn't have time to see the museum itself. Once through the entrance, she crossed over a moat and passed King Neptune's sculpture on her way to the Upper Grounds and the two gray stone buildings that were the Artifacts Conservation Lab.

Although the door to the first building stood open, no one was about. At first glance, it appeared that, just like Prentice House, this lab had its own budget constraints and the conservators forced to be creative with their use of space. Old metal shelves and cabinets, one shelf listing slightly to starboard from the weight of boxes of supplies and protective gear, and a few Bacardi rum cases now holding a different type of solvent.

Still, this lab had a reputation for excellence and Lillian thought the old-world shabbiness added to its charm. She peered into several tubs of different shapes and sizes which covered most of the countertops, and it all made her nostalgic and wondering when she would ever work again.

An old dehydrating unit, x-ray machine, and refrigerator were at one end of the building, and at the other, several tubs set up with electrolysis units connected to various metal objects. Peering in, she saw streams of tiny bubbles flowing to the surface from all, except one, and automatically reached to readjust one of the clips.

At the sound of footsteps, Lillian turned to see an older woman in a sober gray business suit. Her pageboy hairstyle was severe, as was the look in the eyes over the rim of blue cats-eye glasses right out of the 1950's

"I'm so sorry. I'm afraid it's an automatic response, after so many years in a conservation lab," Lillian said, laughing and introducing herself. The woman's stern features relaxed with a welcoming smile as she shook her hand."

Dr. Lee Harewood was the senior conservator. "I understand and am likewise tempted in other labs. I was just leaving for another dratted meeting, but I have a few minutes.

Let me show you around our facility."

Lillian followed her into the second building and introduced two conservators working on large memorial stones. The woman looked up briefly in greeting from her painting and nodded. Lillian thought she looked somewhat regal for the grungy surroundings and paint-covered lab coat. Tall and slender with skin like polished mahogany, her gold and green headscarf was the brightest spot in the room. Dark hair and eyes were about all she could see of the other, an intern from Texas A & M University, who nodded and smiled politely from behind his respirator and goggles.

"What brings you to Bermuda?" Dr. Harewood asked, as they left the lab and walked together towards the administrative building.

Lillian told her about her search. Harewood shook her head when Lillian mentioned her visit to Shelby-Jones.

"Fellow's as dry as a piece of old parchment, but I can't imagine why he would be so negative about the chances of your family heirlooms surviving. That doesn't agree with investigations I've been on personally. We know very well how some artifacts can survive, given the right circumstances. There are still a few old houses with a lot of hidey-holes and secret rooms, built back in the eighteenth-century days of pirating and rumrunning."

"I can't imagine that anyone with an old house wouldn't know all of its secrets," Lillian said, when they paused at the crossroad that would take her to the ferry terminal.

"Yes, but you and I are in the business of history. There are those who could live in an old house and never venture into their cellars and attics, simply take for granted that nothing hides beyond the walls!

"IT'S NOT TIME—" DUNCAN started to answer Neal about the prudence of contacting Lily about the detour her search had inadvertently made through the middle of their investigation.

"If not now, when, for God's sake?" Seaton said. "She

needs to know. Today."

"We can watch George and Nick, but we don't know who else is involved!"

With Seaton at one end of the office and Duncan at the other, Neal and Cal were watching their exchange like spectators settling in at a tennis match.

"I get the fact you needed to protect her with distance at the beginning of this mess, but this is different. Conrad is the one in control now, he's looking for the same thing she is, and he'll only stand back and follow her progress from a safe distance for so long."

"We're tracking every move she makes."

Cal glanced at the screen in front of him, "Dockyards."

"This is an *obsession*," Seaton cut the security man off impatiently, closed the distance between he and Duncan and lowered his voice, "not just a money game. He's not only every bit as evil as George and Nick, he's *barking*. He would toss that phone into the harbor and hurt her and use her in any way that gets him what he wants. She needs to know what the hell is going on and have someone with her *constantly*. Or whether she likes it or not, together, we meet her at the dock, take her to the airport and put her on the next flight home."

"The problem is," said Neal, "if her search stops, more than likely Conrad's does as well. This is keeping him focused and in one place."

Duncan turned on him, "Lily is not bait! I don't care how long you've been after him—"

"*Lily* needs to get out of here," Seaton resumed, ignoring the interruption, "If you won't tell her what's going on, then as her friend, I will."

"Just *friends*, are you?" Duncan said, annoyed.

"Of course," said Seaton, meeting his eyes with a challenge and not a small amount of humor. "We had a very friendly goodbye before I left for Kingston."

Cal didn't bat an eye at the glare Duncan shot his way. "I told you I don't tell on those who kiss, unless I'm paid to, and you weren't paying me for that."

Duncan wanted to punch Seaton's face, again. "I told you—"

"You didn't tell me one thing I didn't already know. Should I have refused a thoroughly beautiful woman I care about when she wanted me, needed me? Not bloody likely." Seaton stepped closer, all trace of humor gone from his eyes. "Interested to know what we discussed for afters—?"

"After*math* is more like it," Cal muttered, obviously impressed during his last night of surveillance outside Lily's house. Distracted, Duncan never had a chance to avoid the fist Seaton used to punctuate the answer to his own question.

"*You!*"

INSTEAD OF THE LONG bus ride back to Hamilton, she caught a late afternoon ferry which would take her right to the terminal only blocks away from Leighton's in a fraction of the time. Trying to enjoy the scenery and formulate a plan for the next day, her thoughts kept drifting.

Miranda and Ryan were having a great time being spoiled by their grandparents, having fun with their cousins, riding horses and hanging out around the pool.

Her father reported that not only did the doctor say he was beginning to "come about" and respond to the new chemotherapy, he was also beginning to use proper nautical terminology.

Another sailor in the making, Lillian had joked, but the prognosis made her wonder if it wasn't letting go of the toxic past that was helping her father's body begin to fight the cancer.

An e-mail from Vera two days before with news about the salvage operations and the latest discoveries included the news that Duncan, Victoria and her sister were still aboard, and that Vic and a friend named Sophie were visiting, as well. Did he now believe others were in danger?

What is going on, Duncan?

And Mark? Was it only the legitimate business interests of Mr. Conrad that brought them to Bermuda, or her search for

Brendan and Conrad's obsession with the Confederate gold?

It was time *someone* told her *what the hell* was happening, she thought, the now familiar anxiety pooling in her gut. An uncharacteristic paranoia made her want to look behind her, to stand with her back against the bulkhead.

Like Brendan, perhaps, on his blockade runner, she thought wryly, but stubbornly refused to leave the wide-open space at the ferry rail.

LESS THAN AN HOUR later, Duncan followed as Lily walked along Par-La-Ville Road, up the shaded stairway and through the old limestone moon gate that led into Queen Elizabeth Park. Moon gate arches were supposed to bring good luck to couples who pass through, he thought, would it still work if they passed through…separately? He remained in the shade behind an obliging palmetto frond, holding the cold water bottle to his left cheek, watching as she continued in the direction of her guesthouse.

The island heat put a rosy flush in her cheeks and made her skin glow. When she passed through the dappled shade of a tall, spindly cedar, she was close enough that he could see the sleeveless blouse she wore, a shimmery peachy sort of color, enhanced the chestnut and gold highlights in her dark hair.

Last night, Seaton had staked out Leighton's. A contact of Conrad's in Bermuda knew when Lily had arrived, where she was staying and for how long. Conrad was very well informed, but unfortunately, Seaton had not discovered who the informant was, yet.

She stopped, and turned towards him, but only to shade her phone before answering. He ducked behind the wide palm but watched as she smiled and spoke to the caller. She hung up almost immediately and began her walk toward Leighton's again. Tonight, Cal would provide surveillance.

Tomorrow, he would see her and tell her everything. He would not leave her side until she was safely leaving Bermuda, no matter what happened between them.

AS SHE WALKED BACK to Leighton's from the harbor, Neal Jameson had called and kindly offered her a lift with Agent Chadwick to her appointment with Hollis Walker in St. George's, as the young agent had business at the east end of the island in the morning. Arriving early would give her a chance to tour the Rogues and Runners Museum, as well.

Ryan called to say goodnight, well before bedtime, something he did when he was homesick. No matter how much fun he might be having by day, at night he was a homebody.

A bit homesick herself, disappointed by another day passing without finding anything about Brendan and still anxious about Mark, Lillian was not holding her own in the polite conversations with other guests and said goodnight early. She lay in bed for a long time, admiring the bright halo around the moon before finally drifting off to a restless sleep.

THE NEXT MORNING, MARK was leaning on an ornate, wrought iron lamppost outside the Customs Office when she arrived, and sans Bermudian businessman's attire, he looked more himself in a black tee shirt and worn blue jeans. He gave her a somewhat formal nod, which did not stop her from giving him a quick hug and kiss.

"You're in a British Commonwealth now. I'm not sure if your American demonstrativeness is acceptable on the streets of Hamilton."

"Too bad," she said, relieved to see him. "I hope I haven't gotten in your way."

"On the contrary," he said, then stepping closer and lowering his voice, added, "Our investigation is progressing quite well. Still, you need to be very careful of Conrad—"

"I wanted to call you a dozen times yesterday to ask if I should leave, but I was afraid for you, afraid I'd catch you at the wrong time."

"*I* wanted to sneak into your room at Leighton's last

night."

She knew, after Duncan's letter, that part of her and Mark's relationship was at an end. Still, she winked at him and said, "At least that would have meant some luck for me on this trip."

He laughed, and apparently no longer concerned with demonstrativeness, drew her into his arms. She felt herself start to blush as his hands very slowly slipped under her shirt to caress her bare back. "You have a few more days, don't you? Still a chance for all kinds of luck."

She felt a chill from a sudden, heavy gust of wind from the Sound and Mark reached up and brushed a strand of hair from her face.

"What happened?" she asked, taking his hand and looking closer at the grazes on his knuckles. When he didn't answer, she looked back up into his face. "Mark…?"

Before she could say more, he kissed her goodbye and walked away as Chadwick pulled up to the curb.

Chapter Twenty-Six

"Bermoothes is a Hellish Place for Thunder, Lightning and Storms"

BUILT AT THE END of the seventeenth century, the distinctive peach, black and white building on St. George's York Street had once been a governor's mansion, a private residence and finally the Globe Hotel.

During the Civil War, Confederate Agent Major Norman Walker used the upper floor as his headquarters. Appropriate, thought Lillian, it now housed the Bermuda National Trust Museum, more colorfully and controversially known as the Rogues and Runners Museum.

Lillian paused at a display case containing the uniform of an ordinary seaman. "Too bad there isn't one for a first officer," she said, almost to herself, thinking of Brendan, while Esther, the ancient docent, walked her through the exhibits.

Esther told her about their extensive collection beyond the glass cases "We do have several other uniforms in the back. We change them out to clean and alter the displays from time to time. I believe there is a commander's coat. Would you be able to come back?"

"LILY?"

She was sightseeing on a narrow, cobbled lane in St. George's, on her way to her appointment with the historian. One of the last voices she expected to hear when she answered her phone was Duncan.

"Duncan?"

"Can I see you tonight? I promised to tell you everything soon, remember?"

His voice sounded different to her, possibly because it was filtered through her disappointment at being a thousand miles away from home.

"I think our bad timing curse is still upon us. I'm in Bermuda."

"Our curse has lifted, Lily, I'm in Hamilton, right now. Just tell me where and when."

Eight o'clock at Leighton's.

In the center of the fortunately traffic-free street, phone still to her ear, she came back to awareness while gazing blankly at the storefront of a trendy Somers Wharf boutique. She was kindly taken in, plied with jasmine tea and essential oils, and then two clerks and several other customers critiqued an impromptu fashion show.

A classic Von Furstenberg wrap in dark blue, high heels, silk lingerie and sandalwood essential oils completed her ensemble and prepared her for almost any contingency. Ten percent of her trip's budget and one hour later she was on her way to her appointment with the historian.

HOLLIS WALKER GREETED HER at the door of "This and That", the little antique store in the front room of his tiny pink cottage, and he was so small and so jovial, with rather a mop of gray curls, she had to stop herself from looking for hobbit feet.

"How do you do? How do you do!" he said, shaking her hand when she introduced herself. "Mrs. Cherrington, did you say? Lillian! A lovely name. Well, Lillian, I'm happy Neal sent you out! Come in, come in. Only thing not for sale is the TV," said the old man, one hand on a battered cedar cane and the other gesturing toward what appeared to be a 60's era console with crinkled aluminum foil wrapped around a single antenna. "Have a look at my treasures and I'll be right back with a treat.

It's not every day I have such a beautiful visitor, you know!"

Even if she learned nothing about Brendan Bonneau, this at least promised to be a very interesting and enjoyable visit, she thought, wandering around the little shop.

At first glance, she saw a collection of bric-a-brac and novelties on several rows of shelves covering the rough-hewn limestone walls around the top half of the room. Colored glass fishing floats and antique medicine bottles caught the dim light from the two small windows that could not have been washed in at least a decade, cut crystal door knobs and decanters, tarnished but unique silver service pieces and even a sculpture. Could that possibly be a Moreau bronze, with every bit of its surface so clumsily painted in a glossy Chinese-dragon red? She shuddered but could not resist looking closer at the full-wigged, scantily-clad French courtesan, and, glancing at the price tag, decided it could not possibly be authentic and would be her farewell gift to Mark, red lacquer and all.

Several dining chairs of various qualities and vintage, a chipped and scorched Formica table, a pair of Depression-era lamps and many other larger pieces were arranged along the lower half of the room. Lillian was examining a chair she thought might be seventeenth-century Bermuda cedar when Hollis returned.

"I took the liberty to pour you a bit of something special to warm your bones on a cool, breezy day like this," he said, the cane tucked neatly under his left arm as he leaned on a small serving cart bearing a bottle of Goslings black rum and mismatched crystal glasses. "Of course, it works on a warm day too, you just add a bit of ice. Tea and rum, two of the best drinks there ever was!" After parking the cart in front of two brocaded wing chairs near the electric fireplace, he turned on a floor lamp that cast interesting shadows around all the various and sundry pieces in the room. "To history, my dear! Cheers!" he said, taking a robust drink.

Remembering a long-ago encounter with black rum, well-disguised in a pretty glass with fruit juice and an umbrella, Lillian sipped more cautiously and explained her father's request.

"Oh, my! You don't say! Goodness!" His enthusiastic responses peppered her story and when she presented Lilién's diary, he rummaged through the papers and playing cards on the table next to him for a magnifying glass and a pair of cotton gloves. With each exclamation, Lillian realized it was one of the few times she had explained this implausible situation to someone when they did not look at her with a thinly veiled impatience or amused disbelief.

"Look at this! Now isn't this fascinating? Who did you say wrote this, your great-grandmother?" he asked, missing a few greats, but was pulling on the gloves and leafing through the delicate pages of Lilién's diary, reading passages here and there.

"And this is your ancestor?" Hollis looked at the picture of Brendan intently. "A bit of the rogue in this one, I should say! You mentioned other sources you've talked to, my dear?" he asked, setting the picture back inside, closing the diary gently and handing it back to her.

At the mention of Shelby-Jones's name, he reacted with a puckered expression, evocative of the other historian's condescending demeanor. "I don't know if he's always chewing on a sour loquat or is unfortunate enough to appear all prune-faced naturally." He reached for the rum and after pouring more for himself, he held it out to offer a refill. She hurriedly placed her hand over the glass and shook her head with a smile. "Did he tell you all of this was nonsense?"

"Not in so many words, but he did cite damaging environmental conditions, as well as the probability of anything that might have existed being found long ago.

"The other person, and I'm not sure how he heard about me, was an antiques dealer named Phelan Conrad," Lillian paused, observing Hollis's reaction, a subtle lift of an eyebrow, a grim line to his mouth not there before. "I didn't contact him, but he happened to be at the pub where the assistant archivist and I were having lunch yesterday," she added. "Agent Jameson didn't exactly warn me away from him, but he and Kimberly both reacted like you when his name was mentioned. What exactly is the deal with him?"

Hollis hesitated and then shrugged and smiled, "A well-established antiques dealer in Hamilton, Nassau and Kingston since the eighties, and successful. Perhaps more successful than might be justified by even a thriving *legitimate* antiquities trade?" he wriggled his eyebrows at her, "and he's a bit of a fanatic about ... treasure hunting. But whatever the deal is with him, be assured your caution is quite prudent.

"Now to tell you the truth, something is niggling at me, I might have heard something ..." He sat quietly for a few moments, sipped his rum and stared into the amber glow of the old electric heater. "Mind you, stories of hidden treasure in Bermuda are easy to come by..."

"I want to believe it exists," she said, "mostly because finding information about the artifacts from Fleur-de-Lys would, I believe, confirm his honorable intention to return them to his family after the war. But I am trained in the science of artifact conservation, I know about groundless myths and legends, and I know what a climate like Bermuda's *can* do to things over time."

"You'd be very surprised, my dear, at the finely preserved state of some of the trinkets we've found, some quite recently," he said, settling into his chair a little more. "During some work beneath one of the old warehouses on the wharf, while just trying to shore up the old foundations, they found a hidden room at the back of the building, lined with cedar and sealed up tight."

"What was it used for?"

"What else? Smuggling! That building went up in the late eighteenth century. Now, you would think the damage would just be rife, but along with several crates of rum, they found some old furniture, old bottles, ragged and stained old work clothes, a pouch of tobacco and a stack of newspapers from the 1870's, all preserved quite well. And I've always wondered, who was the very last person to be inside?"

Lillian smiled at him, recognizing a kindred spirit.

"Shall we go see it?"

"Now?"

"Certainly! No time like the present!"

Before leaving, Lillian purchased the statuette, trying to

argue Hollis up to a reasonable price.

"If this *is* a Moreau, Hollis, I will send you a check!"

He chuckled. "Send it to the Bermuda National Trust," he said, opening the door for her, "I paid ten dollars for the thing at their annual jumble sale! No end of the treasures people don't realize are treasures. Who am I to tell them?"

In his vintage Morris Mini, they whipped along the incredibly narrow alleys and around tight corners. She held on to her seat as he told her about other treasures and unusual bits of this and that he found at jumble sales and auctions, and about finding everything from bits of pottery to gold coins in so many unusual places Lillian couldn't be sure if the stories were true. Still, she was an appreciative audience and he plainly knew the history of the island.

"In the case of Brendan's trunks, I have two ideas," he said when he slowed as they neared the town center. "One is a private home used for a time by one of the Confederate agents during the War Between the States." He saw her make notes in her journal, and added, "I'd like to have a word with the owners first. I sent a person off with too much information once and lived to regret it!" He returned her smile as she snapped the notebook shut. "The other is abandoned, on the edge of town just below Fort Albert. I've had a cursory look around a time or two but always wondered if there might still be a mystery to solve! With talk of a new hotel and the possible re-opening of Fort Albert, both on the hill above, the entire area is overdue to be widely developed," Hollis added, pulling up near a loading platform behind a weather-beaten old building. "This may be the last chance to be the one to discover its secrets!"

She followed Hollis to the building, noticing the wind and how the day had grown darker as the clouds had thickened.

"This was nothing but run down, neglected warehouses until a few years ago," he said, indicating the new mall of shops and restaurants fronting the area. "But there are, believe it or not, still one or two buildings on Bermuda that have not been turned inside out with renovations, like this one is soon to be. This was one of the many warehouses used during the blockading days, a place the supplies came and went from."

"Warehouse?" Lillian asked, with a smile. The building's peeling aquamarine paint and graceful columns suggested a more distinguished past.

"And that is what it will be again soon, or so they say. Tourist shops! How many more places to buy beach towels and pastel prints do they think our little island can handle!" He handed her a flashlight and put on a battered old miner's helmet as he led the way to a small door beside the loading bay. "But this will show you exactly why I think something could very well exist in reasonably good order…Sammy usually leaves a key…here" he said, looking behind the address number plate for a hidden key. As Hollis pushed open the door, she noticed an old-fashioned milk bottle hanging nearby.

"Hollis, what is this?" she asked, having seen a few such decorations on fence posts and door frames on the island. The liquid inside was a mixture of a lovely transparent gold with an opaque white sediment rising up in a ghostly swirl.

"Hollis?" she repeated more loudly, her voice echoing when she stepped inside the brightly lit, cavernous space. A noise behind a partition drew her to where he searched for something between the cracks in the limestone block of the wall.

"Ah ha!" He gave the rough wooden handle a firm tug and a panel opened in the wall. Hollis turned on his lamp and stepped inside the absolute blackness.

A flutter of panic rippled through her chest, but Hollis was already inside the hidden compartment, describing the interior, his voice growing fainter. She clicked on the flashlight and followed his fading voice until she saw him descending to a lower level.

"… this room, in particular, look at the cedar-lined walls, all sealed up tight on the leeward side of the building. *Cases* of rum in here when the room was discovered, and they reckon it must have been here for well over a century, if not two! Now, see here, my dear," he gestured towards a nearly invisible line in the wall, "where the goods were moved to and from the building…"

Her claustrophobia faded as she followed, caught up in his excited monologue. For the first time since she arrived, Lillian began to believe the answers they were searching for just might exist, perhaps in a room very much like this one.

Hollis pulled away a cedar panel to reveal another deep hollow, also lined with cedar. "See here, this would have been for small things like gold or currency..."

"Any idea who that last person was, and why they never came back?" she asked, examining the tight, tongue-and-groove cedar and built-in nooks and crannies.

Hollis's eyes twinkled. "That's the real mystery, isn't it, my dear? Who was the last person to close the hidden door and leave? Many people had to be involved loading and unloading the goods, why didn't they come back to sell off, or at least drink, the last of that lovely liquid contraband?"

When they finally stepped back into the light of the warehouse, they were met by the sound of rain drumming loudly on the roof high above. She waited while he locked the doors and saw that the liquid in the jar was now a milky white.

"Hollis, what is this?"

He looked up from hiding the key. Surprise, followed by concern, showed on his face.

"A barometer. A shark oil barometer," he said, beckoning her to follow.

"There was just a little swirl of white in the gold when we went in," she had to yell over the noise of the deluge as they ran to the car. By the time they were inside the mini, they were drenched. "I've heard of shark oil barometers before but never seen one. How does it work?"

"It's really rather a mystery, that," he said, reaching into the backseat for a towel and handing it to her. "Some say the oil responds as the shark responds to a change in weather. A shark dives down into deeper waters, and in the glass, the oil swirls and the sediment rises. If a hurricane is coming it will even have a funneled appearance—isn't that something? And I must apologize, my dear," he added, starting up the car, "if I had observed the one on my own house I would have sent you on your way back to Leighton's immediately! By the look of conditions, not to mention that barometer, I'm afraid this fast-moving little tempest will only grow stronger and hover over the island for a while. Certainly, you will not be traveling back to Hamilton tonight!"

"But—" Despairing disappointment flooded through her, dousing the pleasant tingles of anticipation she had been enjoying all afternoon. "Surely a taxi?"

Hollis shook his head, gesturing through the rain-blurred window towards the palms whipping in the wind. "You don't want to get caught out in this, not out over the Causeway, in fact it may even be closed. For tonight, it would be best if you didn't venture too far. I know a very nice couple just up the hill with a spare room. You'll be safer, and nearby, so we can get an early start on our adventures tomorrow!"

A weary sadness drug her down like the change of weather had the barometric pressure. "Thank you, Hollis, I'd be grateful," she said, sighing, knowing there was no help for it.

Hollis regarded her with concern and she felt the need to explain.

"I actually thought the curse had lifted. Maybe this is another sign." She smiled, but her voice wavered just a bit.

"Well, my dear, I can understand your disappointment, but you're much too clever to be seeing signs in inclement weather! You can at least be sure he's not getting away from the island tonight, why, it's quite probable he's away from Hamilton himself and similarly stranded! I'm sure it will be more important for him to know you are safe."

He pulled a phone from his jacket and punched in a number. "Oliver? Hollis here. Say, I have a young lady visiting and she's been stranded by the storm and can't get back to Hamilton…You do? Wonderful! We'll be right along." He snapped the phone shut and back in his pocket it went.

Ragged old windshield wipers flapping frantically to keep up with the rain, they seemed to mimic Hollis's gesticulations, hands off the wheel more than on, as he zipped through the high-walled alleys and told her about the house at Elliott Cove, where he hoped to find cellars connected by secret tunnels.

"Is that a common set up in the old buildings on the island?" she asked, discreetly gripping the ratty armrest, trying not to reach out and brace herself against the dash.

"I've seen it once before on the island, and it makes perfect sense, given the layout. I'll just bet underneath that place are enough hidden passageways and rooms to hide a good many interesting things. I've fancied a look for years but couldn't get past the dear old battleax who owned it. But she's gone now and it's still vacant, so this is my chance!"

"And the other place, you said it was abandoned? Who do you ask about going there?"

Hollis looked surprised at the question and shrugged. "If the local kids can run amok there by night, we should be able to poke around the foundations by day!" He stopped the car and gestured towards a large limestone arch, beyond which she could see a large and well-lit villa-style structure. "Weather permitting, I shall pick you up at …say… eleven o'clock?"

ONCE OUT IN THE wind whipped rain, Lillian knew Hollis had been correct about traveling back to Hamilton. As she ran up the path, she saw the sign swinging violently in the wind above the doorway, pleased to see that Hollis's friends with the spare room were the proprietors of the Rosecrest guesthouse.

Innkeepers Oliver and Rose welcomed her warmly as she stepped inside. Oliver closed the door against the wind and ushered her into the house, taking her soaked jacket while Rose presented her with a dry towel from a fully stocked shelf near the door.

"You're in time for our evening wine tasting. Have you had your dinner?" Oliver asked in his cultured Bermudian accent. "I would think not if you've been talking history with Hollis."

"Well, no, actually, the afternoon got away from us, rum and history proving a dangerous combination. I should probably pass on the wine-tasting," she added with a smile, feeling like an intruder as she walked into the large open living area where several guests were seated in clusters around the room.

"Not to worry, with the weather turning on our guests and keeping them inside tonight, we have our emergency rations at the ready."

"You have plenty to take care of already," she said, glancing down at the crowded sitting room before following Rose upstairs while Oliver went back to the wine tasters.

"Always room for more," Rose said, smiling, opening one of the doors. "This is our Bermuda Blue Eyes Room, one of our more romantic rooms. Normally it is always full, but last night's guest had to leave unexpectedly."

"I do appreciate the hospitality — oh, how beautiful," Lillian gasped, walking into the room. "As my father would say, this is quite the port in a storm."

FINALLY ALONE, SHE FELL face down on the bed and allowed self-pity to triumph. Not even able to cry, simply numb from disappointment, she lay still, just listening to the rain and wind, muted conversation and laughter and the far-off rumble of thunder.

Separated by fourteen miles and one tropical storm.

Laughing at herself, even if she were the type to succumb to self-pity, it really wasn't the time or place for a meltdown. Cell service was down so she couldn't even reach Duncan. She called Mae with the guesthouse phone, who promised to tell Duncan if he was able to show up for their date and not similarly stranded.

She wondered why the lovely room was called Bermuda Blue Eyes until she saw accents stenciled around the door and window frames, tiny blue flowers of the Bermuda Blue Eyed grass, the national flower. All the furniture was black with a faint white leaf and vine patterns to lighten the severity. The huge, four-poster bed was nearly as high as the ceiling, gauzy white curtains embroidered with the tiny blue flowers were draped at each corner. Though she usually avoided the confined space of a canopy, claustrophobia would not be a problem in this bed.

Above the bedside table was a delicate pastel print in a scrollwork frame, where the tall flowering grass bloomed against a classic Bermuda-pink cottage, behind which an azure sea sparkled in the distance.

Light from a small desk lamp was reflected in a tall mirror, and in a small alcove two high backed wing chairs were grouped in front of windows with a view to the gardens. Floodlights on either side of the house showed the flowering shrubs buffeted by the wind and driving rain and with each gust, the curtains fluttered at the old windows.

The day's weather *had* changed quickly from the morning's high clouds and errant sprinkles to tropical storm conditions, but regardless of the distraction caused by Duncan's call and the fascinating historical research with Hollis, she felt foolish for being caught unawares. Years of sailing taught her to be better prepared and should have made her more observant.

After a quick shower to both refresh and wash away dust and cobwebs from her trip into the smuggler's hold, she slipped on one of the terrycloth robes hanging on the back of the bathroom door, and towel dried her hair. At least the small bag of essentials she kept in her backpack and her shopping spree meant she was prepared to join a large party of complete strangers for dinner and small talk, as much as she might want to hide away and sulk.

The color of the one-piece teddy camisole was called champagne, and the shimmery, golden silk was the sexiest thing she had purchased for herself in years. And, by far the most expensive undergarment she would *ever* purchase, she thought, removing the price tag.

Worth every cent, she thought, a moment later, looking in the mirror and then sighed and slipped on the dress and tied it at the waist. She tucked in the Saint Michael's medal she had put on a long chain and worn since her father had discovered it hidden in Brendan's letter, and the finishing touch was a dab of the essential oil, which was guaranteed to either revive *or* calm.

Toilette complete, she considered her reflection. The silk jersey fell with a casual elegance and felt like a second skin, and the blue was the same shade of the Bermuda Blue Eyes. Rose had mentioned on their way upstairs this was considered one of their most romantic rooms and hinted at a story. Well, whatever it was, Lillian would not be adding any chapters to that book tonight.

Oh well, she said to her reflection just as the lights flickered and died, a flash of lightning catching her fleeting expression like a photograph. If she had been describing anyone else, she would have said the eyes were sad, almost hopeless. Impressed in her mind by the penetrating white light, even the return of darkness couldn't dispel the image.

Was it only the day's disappointment or something more? Did others see it, she wondered, had Mark before he said goodbye and kissed her that morning? Is that why Vera always pestered her about her love life?

She turned away from the mirror as the lights flickered back on, and, not quite ready to go downstairs, she sat in the little alcove and updated her journal with the events of the day.

She pulled her research and Lilién's diary from her bag and glanced through the material she had been able to collect. Pathetically little, which meant that Conrad was not only collecting information, he was somehow controlling its retrieval from the Archives. If that were true, how had the man acquired that kind of power?

Drops and rivulets of rain sparkled on the windows, lightning flashed, and thunder rumbled as she sat writing notes about her visit to the museum, Esther's offer to find the first officer's uniform, and Hollis. Hollis was an especially delightful surprise, she thought smiling, including in her notes her triumph of drinking Gosling's Black Seal rum, neat, without choking. Personal notes about shopping sprees and star-crossed lovers she omitted and ended with the description of the old warehouse, plans for the following day, and the meteorological accuracy of halos around the moon and shark oil barometers.

Downstairs, in the large open lounge, the gas fire was lit, and candles burned along a buffet table covered from one end to the other with food and drink. Baskets of rolls and bowls of salad were at one end and on either side of a large bowl of pasta were two kinds of sauce simmering gently in warming pans. Emergency provisions, indeed.

"Hello," said one of the guests as Lillian entered the room. "Are you our refugee?"

"Yes, that would be me," Lillian said, smiling as she accepted a plate from Oliver.

A very friendly and diverse group of guests sat on couches, chairs, and footstools scattered throughout the room, chatting in small clusters. A couple from Wisconsin celebrating their fiftieth anniversary, and three single friends, two from California and the third from Paris who met in the middle. For two couples, the visit was both business and pleasure; a visiting biologist from an Alaskan aquarium and her husband, and a novelist from England with his wife researching a thriller set on the island.

The living area was somewhat insulated from the effects of the storm until it drew nearer. Finally, lightning flashed at windows on both sides of the house and a booming crash caused the crystals in the chandelier to quiver before the electricity flickered out once again, leaving the room dark except for firelight and candles on the buffet table.

"What brings you to the island?" the biologist asked her, while Oliver and Rose lit extra candles and hurricane lanterns.

After telling them the highlights of her search for Brendan, Fran from California asked, "Where *is* the American archeologist we saw here this morning? I bet he'd have some good ideas—"

"...and If he doesn't, I sure do," said both Sharrie and Fran at the same moment, laughing.

"Can't take them anywhere," Sylvia said, winking at Lillian, "but he was a handsome devil. A bit of a rogue, too, had just the hint of a black eye." She brushed a finger under her left eye. "I asked him to tell us all about it, but he only smiled and said he'd walked into an Englishman."

This morning? Lillian thought, closing her eyes, remembering a certain Englishman with freshly grazed knuckles and his mysterious comment, *still a chance for all kinds of luck…*

"Sorry ladies," said Rose. "Urgent business took him to Hamilton. I think you're out of luck tonight."

Out of luck, Lillian thought, *yep, that's me.* She excused herself and escaped upstairs.

Chapter Twenty-Seven

Safe Harbor

TO DISPEL THE GLOOM, not to mention the oddly strobe-like effect of the wind-whipped palm fronds through the glow of emergency floodlights, Lillian lit candles in the decorative wall sconces, tapers beside the framed watercolor above the bureau, and one small lantern on the table where her research waited for her attention. She sat, but only sighed and watched new shadows when the candle flames guttered gently in the drafts from the old windows.

There was a quiet tap on her door. "Lily?"

"Duncan!"

Not cursed, after all, she thought a moment later, somehow off the floor and in his arms and breathing deeply of his scent. His kiss, his lips cool with salty raindrops, sent a searing streak of warmth through the center of her body.

"What are you doing here? *How*?" she said, her feet on the floor again but still in his arms.

"Looking for you, of course," he said, smiling, still holding her in one arm. With the towel he'd brought from downstairs, he swiped his face, shirt and hair before tossing it aside. "After everything we've been through, you didn't think a little Bermuda tempest would keep me from our first date, did you?"

Her breath caught with something between a laugh and a sob. He *was* dressed for a date, but his silvery blue tie and black silk shirt were rather bedraggled despite the blotting, his dark hair tousled and falling into his eyes.

"And, for a castaway, may I just say that you ..." he

kissed her lips, her cheeks, her neck, punctuating his appraisal, while his hands moved down her back, warm through the thin layers of silk, "look, and *feel,* simply stunning."

After he'd dropped his bag and left his squelching shoes and soaking wet socks in the corner behind the door, Lily took his hand and led him into her room. He wondered if it was the dress or the high heels that gave the somewhat hypnotic effect to the sway of her hips and had him almost pausing mid-step more than once. Candlelight glinted in the golden highlights in her hair, and the classy dress had a belt tied invitingly at one hip, like a big, blue ribbon on a long-anticipated gift. He wanted to tug on it. Now. He'd imagined this moment so many times, in fantasies so intense they alternately relieved and increased his frustration, made him feel guilty for using her and more determined to have her. He couldn't rush her, though, not after everything they had been through to be here, finally together.

"Would you rather go downstairs, Lily, or shall we sit here and talk—?"

He stepped towards the chairs set in the little window alcove as another flash of lightning lit the room.

"No!" she said, as thunder cut off the rest of his sentence. "I don't want to talk."

"No?"

He might have believed she was angry if it weren't for the way she wrapped her arms around his neck and pulled him down for another kiss, a deep kiss, their mouths fitting perfectly, their tongues caressing, tangling and savoring with all the passion of their first, but without the anger or desperation.

"I do," she answered, breaking the kiss for just a moment, her voice husky. "Of course, I do. And we will, but not yet."

A thought struck in sudden, almost adolescent panic. This. Was. It.

He was with her. With Lily.

My God, he thought, watching her through narrowed

eyes, what did Lily want? What did she like? Except for their brief and ill-advised moments of physical contact, all these years of wanting and waiting had been devoid of opportunities to talk, flirt, tease or practice, and he was so seriously out of practice.

Her long, dark lashes trembled against her skin, and through his own lashes he saw the little pucker of tension on her brow just before he heard and *felt* her moan and press herself against him. He'd meant to tell her everything, meant to propose and see his ring on her finger before this moment happened for them. But he wanted most of all to please her now, to be everything to her.

Clouds obscured the heavens and a storm raged tonight, but this woman had been his North Star for years. Now, all he had to do was hold his course.

Tonight, Duncan allowed desire to show in his eyes, in his voice and in the slight tremor of each touch, a vibration humming through him, through them both. His mouth fit, perfectly, as it moved against hers tenderly, not the way he had kissed her that night at the lab with such fierce, probing intensity.

Until she had told him she didn't want to talk and pulled him down to her again, unwilling to wait. Until she licked his lips and his mouth opened over hers, until their tongues met. An urgency for their love to move beyond hope and fantasy to reality ached, pulsed in her womb and down her inner thighs, her body in harmony with her heart's need for something far more than their certain sexual gratification. *Was* it simple desire, or her feminine intuition heightened by so many other recent experiences?

Duncan, finally, in her arms, moaning her name when her mouth moved to his neck where she inhaled the musky, salty scent of him. His hands moved over her back as she removed the medal and hung the chain on the corner of a frame near the bed, along her arms as she untied his tie, rested on her hips while she slowly unbuttoned his shirt and pushed it away from his shoulders. Lightning flashed, and thunder cracked and rumbled

on into the distance as she ran her hands over his skin, her thumbs rubbed his nipples and her fingers dipped into the hair on his chest.

Duncan pulled off his shirt and tossed it aside, and with the belt of her dress he tugged her toward him.

"Beautiful wrappings, Lily, but I can't wait any longer to see *you*," he whispered raggedly, pulling, first one blue silk tie and then the other. The dress fell open, and he ran his hands over her shoulders and down her arms, caressing the dress from her body until it fell to the floor. Duncan groaned out a choked kind of laugh against her skin, kissing the inner swell of her breast revealed by the deep neckline, sliding his tongue under the edge of lace to tease and taste.

While still conscious of practicalities, Duncan removed the small square case from his pocket and tossed it onto the bedside table before quickly shedding his slacks and boxers, so that there was nothing between he and Lily but her glowing little wisp of lace-edged silk. Lily's hands moved down now as their mouths met again, and stilled at his hips…. her hands on his bare skin was, God, how much longer could he wait? Hell, seeing her reflection in the mirror, *all* of her reflection from tousled hair, to silk-clad derriere and down her long legs to the high heels, he would probably come if she sucked his tongue again.

He turned her around in his arms so they both faced the tall mirror across from the bed. Lily looked into his eyes as he cupped her breasts, full and perfect in his hands but he had to see them, now. He pulled the narrow straps off her shoulders, and by anticipation-heightening gradual degrees, the fabric slipped down.

My god, he thought, Lily Rose, indeed. Her skin was like a Bermuda lily, her nipples a dusky pink rose, hard under his palms, her back arching as he began to rub lightly, pinch gently. He studied the delicate arch of her eyebrows, the heightened color in her cheeks, fullness of her lips, skin glowing in the golden light. Her body trembled, and she moaned as he smoothed one hand down over the curve of her waist and hip and slipped his fingers between her legs.

He wanted to kiss her but couldn't seem to look away from their reflection as he caressed her, gently. She moved against his hand, her back arched again, and from some distance he heard his name when she reached behind her and began to stroke him.

His vision blurred as candlelight danced in the drafts, reflected in the mirrors, picture and window glass becoming a hundred tiny flames, imbuing the room with shimmering layers of shadow and light. The room went dark at the edges, her skin absorbing the warmth and glow and color of candlelight until Lily was the only flame.

The sexy high heels hit the floor when he lifted her in his arms and laid her on the bed. He knelt over her, his knees on either side of her hips as she stroked him and helped him slide on the condom.

He fought the impulse to close his eyes. A primal need gripped him to see her, to *see* her feel him inside of her for the first time, to witness that exquisite ache of pleasure. Lily's eyes were closed, and she cried out his name in a whimpering, gasping sob and wrapped her legs around his as he pushed slowly, deeply inside her. They lay motionless for several moments.

"Lily," he whispered.

Lily opened her eyes and met his. She reached up with both hands to cup his face as they began to move together in the shadows of the curtained bed.

Duncan. His face above hers, looking into her eyes, his voice whispering her name, his body against her, inside of her. Their legs were entwined, her smooth skin against the coarseness of the hair on his, the bare skin of their bellies quivering with heart beats and heavy breaths. Tears filling her eyes again, she reached up and touched his face as they began to move.

No one else in the world could possibly be doing this or could know this secret. She'd had the thought before, all lovers did, didn't they, but it was true tonight. In the middle of a vast ocean on this small island, the storm raging around them and the shadows of candlelight dancing against the bed curtains, this man above her, inside her, moving with her. Unique, and a universe apart.

Duncan felt the pressure of his orgasm building, surging deep, beyond the base of his cock, gradual but powerful. He finally closed his eyes and let other senses rule, kissed her mouth, her neck, suckled her breasts and she moaned words of pleasure he couldn't quite comprehend. She took him even deeper when she shifted to wrap her legs around his waist, and, my god, it was the scent of her…his head bowed to her shoulder in surrender…he *had* to move faster and thrust harder, powerless to slow time and make this moment last forever.

Lillian's fingers tangled in Duncan's hair as he kissed her lips, her neck, her breasts. His hands slid beneath her, pulling her even tighter against him. Tendrils of pleasure, sparked like plasma filaments far beyond their joined flesh, igniting an intense longing ache deep within, where joy soars and heart meets soul, until they cried out together, their climax quieting the storm and making time stand still.

IN THE SMALL ALCOVE, the lantern still burned on the table covered with her research. Wind buffeting against the windows and rain cascading from the guttered roof to the limestone patio outside were the only other sounds as he quietly told her about the events of summer, his marriage and instant freedom granted by Victoria's stunning revelation.

"I was angry and wanted out, but she not only wouldn't give me a divorce, she threatened to lie to her father about me. I wasn't worried he would believe her, but you were still married so I just went away on one assignment or another, putting off legalities until …well, until I found out you were divorced."

She looked at his face, earnest and intense in the candlelight. "But… the baby?"

"There was a baby, but not mine, Lily."

He explained his impulse to see her that night and how he had been turning away from the lab when he had seen her with Mark. "I was angry and jealous, but I should have–"

"Trusted me with the truth?" She stood up and went to the window. Looking out into the wind-whipped garden, she remembered the elation she had felt at his attention, the name of the ship, and her confusion and hurt knowing his wife was expecting his child.

"Until I received your very recent letter, I had convinced myself there was no possibility of a relationship with you—"

"Lily—"

"…while you were living in some romantic, Chauvinistic fantasyland, deciding the little woman is safe from the bad guys by being tucked away and lied to."

"I'm sorry."

She turned back to him, arms crossed, searching his face to see if he was mocking her with the apology.

"I had no idea what I was in the middle of, Lily—"

"Why not tell me everything the night on the *LilyRose* when I passed on Mark's warning? I already knew about the smuggling and 'forewarned is forearmed' remember?" Sitting down, facing him again, she asked, "Why now, tonight? Why show up here of all places?"

"Among many other things, I want to talk about what brought you to Bermuda."

"About Brendan?" she asked, confused. "What do you know about that?"

"Until the other day, only what Vera told me. But we've recently found a significant connection with the Andrastus smuggling network and a man named Phelan Conrad."

"Conrad?" she asked, remembering Mark's caution about the man that very morning— "*Oh. My. God*! Is that why *tonight*, Duncan? Because you saw Mark kiss me this morning!"

"You think it's funny?"

"No—I think it's appalling!"

"Do you love him, Lily?"

"You really need to ask me *now* if I love someone else?"

"I would've asked you earlier, but if you remember…" he quirked an eyebrow at her, amusement in his eyes.

"That's when I thought *you* were the one to do all the talking," she raised her eyebrow right back at him, "and was I in any way unclear about my feelings tonight?"

"I know you love me."

"Why are you asking me about Mark?"

"We drank to the truth, remember?"

"Mark and I have been lovers."

"I know. I'm asking if you love him."

"And if I say yes, you'll think I can't possibly love you, but if I say no, it means I'm some kind of slut?"

He knelt in front of her and took her hands in his. "I would *never* think that of you, Lily."

She hesitated, still angry but his voice held no judgment. His eyes met hers, searching for the truth and his hands gripped hers tightly. On his left hand, there was nothing but a thin band of white on the tanned finger.

"I do love him." She looked up when his muscles tensed at her admission. "I *care* for him very much, and he's been a good friend to me, Duncan. But we've both known our relationship was meant to be… ephemeral. He has a life in England he wants to get back to, and he's known since, well, ever since he took the assignment that I'm in love with you—"

Duncan pulled her into his arms, barely allowing her to finish, holding her so tightly she could feel his heart beating against hers.

Thank God. That morning, when he rounded the corner near the Customs Office and saw them once again in each other's arms, he had not been as jealous of the kiss as of the ease and comfort of their intimacy as they stood in such a casual but close embrace.

Still holding her, in the interest of full disclosure, he told her about the night on the Fleur-de-la-Mer, after the accident, after he had read her letter telling him goodbye, when he and Gail had…what? Made love? He still wasn't quite sure how to categorize what happened but told Lily everything.

"We've both had more than our share of secrets and lies in our lives, Lily. I want, I *need*, our time to begin with complete honesty." Finally pulling away, he asked, "Are you smirking, and are those sympathetic noises for me, or for Gail?"

"I think they're for me. Honestly, if I thought I could have gotten away with a bit of heavy petting, your visit to my house might have ended with more than a few friendly kisses and a sea shanty."

"*You* couldn't have gotten away with it, Lily. You don't know how close I was to —"

"I do," she whispered, now stroking his back, his arms, fingers running through his hair, "That was weeks before you found out about the smuggling, Duncan, why not tell me then?"

"Would you have made love with me?"

"Yes."

"As wonderful as it would have been, you would have been ashamed to be in a relationship you couldn't share with your family and I couldn't fully be a part of your life. I had no idea how long it would take me to be free and that's not what I wanted for us." Holding her close, their foreheads touching, he asked, "Please marry me, Lily?"

She heard the vulnerability in the whispered proposal but waited to answer until she could steady her own voice to say the word gamboling around her heart like a ball in a pinball machine. Pulling away just enough to reach out and hold his handsome face in her hands, she answered, her voice surprisingly steady.

But her hands shook as she opened the small velvet covered box he gave her. Deep, midnight blue velvet, the plush softness still damp from his rain-drenched jacket.

The rose cut sapphire was in a white gold, Art Deco setting and was, "beautiful… perfect," she whispered, as he slipped the ring onto her finger.

RESTLESS, SHE SLIPPED OUT of the warm bed. Not only

should she *not* be restless, she should be comatose given her state of emotional and physical satiation. Something hovered at the edge of her thoughts and kept her from drifting off to sleep. She slipped on the white robe again and went to the alcove where the lantern still glowed on the table.

Removing the copy of Brendan's picture from its hiding place in Lilién's diary, she looked at the handsome young man with the mischievous glint in his eye that so resembled her father. She searched his face and tried to will answers from him.

What was *Kendal's* mysterious cargo, she wondered. *Could* it possibly have been part of the Confederate Treasury? Since Mark had given her the article, she had read so many accounts about the Treasury, from how much remained in Confederate coffers to speculation about its eventual disposition, it was impossible to know what to believe. Whether Brendan was involved was still very much a mystery.

"Can't sleep?"

She felt the kiss on the top of her head and looked up. Duncan was pulling on the other bathrobe against the chill of the room.

"Thinking," she waved a hand over the paperwork spread out around her and told him of her father's suspicions about Brendan, and the article Mark had copied for her.

He read the article, handed it back to her. "What do you think about the possibility? Close to Richmond, near the end of the war?"

"I'm no expert about who had control of what territory in the Civil War, but I'm sure the eastern end of the James River was in Union hands not long after the Battle of Hampton Roads…" She shook her head. "A Confederate blockade runner, traveling up the James River just before the end of the war … just doesn't seem …possible…"

Her unfocused gaze blurred the golden fleur-de-lys of Lilién's diary glittering in the lamplight. Lillian reached for it, turning to the pages written in early 1865, and scanned the entries quickly, a frown creasing her brow.

"I remember, distinctly, an entry about Thomas

Crawford, the young sailor sent by Brendan, who brought the trunk from Fleur-de-lys. Thomas said 'the last time I saw the Commander, he was raisin' a funny flag and deliverin' me into enemy hands. Gold, looked just like that ring you're wearin', ma'am.' Lilién told him it was her fleur-de-lys ring."

"Told him?" Duncan smiled at the Southern accent which crept into her words but faded as she held out her right hand, with an uncharacteristically dramatic flair, as though seeing the ring on her own finger. "She wrote out a complete conversation?"

"It's not here," she said, running a bare finger over the pages, "why can't I —?" her voice rose as the now familiar breathlessness came over her, that contraction of her diaphragm stronger than ever as she stared blankly at the page, *remembering* what young Thomas looked like, *remembering* how he had flipped his long, dirty blond hair out of his gray eyes as he looked into her own so frankly—

He had looked at *her*, *into her eyes*, eyes that she knew were now wide with terror, waves of gooseflesh prickling painfully over her entire body.

Gasping for air, she flung the diary out of her hands as though it was charged with electricity.

"Lily! What is it? My God—" Duncan was again on his knees in front of her, cupping her face with his hands. "Breathe, Lily. Breathe!"

Breathing was impossible, a viselike band around her diaphragm only tightened until her vision blurred.

When she could see clearly once again, it was a hand drawing back in a slow, casual manner just before pain exploded behind her eyes, and then she was standing at the little beach of the cove in the gray, bone-chilling mist.

She woke to a long, rolling rumble of thunder and opened her eyes to see Duncan's worried face above her.

"What happened?" she whispered. He put his hand gently on her shoulder when she started to sit up. A candle on the bedside table illuminated the gauzy curtains around the bed with warm golden light.

"Rest, sweetheart. Just relax." She closed her eyes, swaddled in the warmth and snugness of the blankets pressed down by his weight beside her, comforted by the gentle strokes of his hand along her arm and his lips resting against her temple.

"Tell me?" she asked.

"Something frightened you so badly you fainted, and the only good thing about that is you started to breathe again. You were cold as ice and as white as your robe."

She reached up and felt her cheek. "Is there a bruise?"

"I'm sorry, I was just trying to—"

She shook her head and told him of her experience at the cottage after reading the diary entries of Lilién's pain and anguish.

"I ... *I* felt the pain in my cheek. Edward had hit her, hard, he often did but she never wrote about it! *I* saw Thomas's gray eyes—*beautiful* dark gray eyes, and dirty blond hair, so long he kept flipping it out of his eyes—I *know* I heard his voice, and it was cold that morning, a bitterly cold winter day—and the cottage wasn't there! The cottage wasn't there, Duncan! *I've never seen the Cherrington estate without the cottage—*" Fear returning, a hysterical pitch rose in her voice and the high canopy closed in on her.

"Lily!" At the sound of his calm but firm voice, she opened her eyes and forced herself to take deep breaths while he continued to stroke her hair. "I believe you."

She felt Duncan move away and then heard him pouring a glass of water from the bottle on the bureau. When she opened her eyes again, he helped her sit up against the pillows he propped behind her.

"I've seen you look at something ... a silver locket, with rubies, wasn't it?"

"Garnets."

"Vera and I watched you have a kind of out of body experience. Somehow you knew *facts* about it, facts which proved out over time, didn't they?"

She shrugged noncommittally, watching as he went into

the alcove and picked up the diary from the floor. He sat next to her again, holding the book gently.

"I don't think I have to ask if you believe in spirits, Lily. You work at investigating the past, especially as it's connected to things. There isn't a shipwreck I've discovered that didn't involve the deaths of many, sometimes hundreds of people, who died looking at, wearing, clinging to the artifacts you conserve.

"I know what this discovery of family means to you. This woman is your ancestor; you were holding her thoughts and feelings, recollections of important events in your hands and in your mind. Did any of it make you cry, laugh, angry?"

She nodded again and set the glass on the table, looking away from the diary.

"You experienced her emotions, while on the land where she lived, in misery from the sound of things. While you slept, maybe there was, I don't know, a connection, a kind of vibration from the past? Maybe Lilién's spirit and yours are furnishing details no one else can see yet or will ever be able to see."

"My kindred spirit?"

"Quite literally," he held out the diary, waiting for her to accept it, "and, I don't think, one you need to be afraid of."

Holding the book in both hands, she no longer felt the fear or foreboding. What had so vividly been her own memory was now vague, like any other faded dream. The book was simply her great-great-great grandmother's old diary, with its yellowed satin and flaking fleur-de-lys.

"I DON'T SUPPOSE CONRAD would back off if I told him I'm not searching for the gold of the Confederate treasury?"

Out in the inn's tiny parking lot, she watched Duncan drying off the motorcycle. The air was warm, muggy with humidity, with puddles along the driveway and water still dripping from the waxy green leaves and fruit clusters on the nearby bay grape tree.

"If he was your run of the mill treasury fanatic, maybe, but from what Seaton says, he's far from that *and* he seems to have some hold over George which worries the hell out of me. As the Captain would say, this is the big league. I'm glad you're going home tomorrow."

"The afternoon with Hollis should prove to be a safe enough adventure for my last day."

"I'm glad I'm going with you; sounds like this Hollis might be serious competition—" his phone rang, finally signaling the return of cell service.

After answering and listening briefly, Lillian saw his expression cloud. "What? Here, to Hamilton? Okay. I'll meet you there."

"Trey's been hurt," he said, disconnecting, "a fall, apparently. Hugh and Josh are bringing him to the hospital and they'll be here soon. Hugh seems to think he'll be fine, but, I'm sorry, Lily, I need to go."

"Of course, I'll go with you. I'll cancel —"

He shook his head. "You don't need to. Wait here for Hollis. I'll make sure Trey's all right and meet up with you later." Reaching for her before putting on his helmet, he pulled her close for a last, long kiss. "Will you be where you're supposed to be tonight?"

Without opening her eyes, she whispered, "Conditions seem favorable. Why?"

"I'll come looking for you again."

After watching him drive down the lane, she turned toward the inn where guests Sharrie, Fran, and Sylvia were standing on the porch.

"You were right," she winked at them as she passed by, "he had lots of good ideas."

After answering several rather impertinent questions from the three ladies over continental breakfast, she escaped back to her room as her own cell rang for the first time since being out of service the night before.

"Hey Dad!" she answered joyfully, tossing her few belongings in her backpack.

"Hey yourself! You sound perky. Having any luck?"

"Ah…well…"

PART X

BRENDAN

James River, Virginia
March 1865

"Let us have faith that right makes might,
and in that faith let us, to the end, dare
to do our duty as we understand it."

Abraham Lincoln
Cooper Union Speech, February 27, 1860

Chapter Twenty-Eight

Final Voyage of the Kendal

DEPARTMENT OF THE TREASURY

February 18, 1865

Hon. Jefferson Davis
President of the Confederate States
Richmond, Virginia

Sir,

We have received news of the burning of Columbia today. All indications are that Sherman's troops will advance through North Carolina, and into Virginia. Richmond will soon fall, and this will occur not within months but weeks.

Amidst the chaos and anxiety of evacuation, which causes conflicting loyalties in the hearts of even the staunchest supporters, is not the time to act to protect the pitiful remainder of the treasury which supports this government. Such as it is, our friend Mallory is quite correct in summarizing such cargo as 'a very troublesome elephant.'

Given my experience previous to the honourable appointment in which I now serve, I recommend that the bulk be removed by blockade runner as promptly as possible from these Confederate States where it is vulnerable to Union forces advancing rapidly from North and South. As much as I might wish to recommend the services of a government vessel or one contracted by Fraser, Trenholm, and Co., this is no longer possible. I believe it is in our best interest to acquire the services of the blockade runner owned by Buchanan and MacGregor of Edinburgh. We have spoken previously about the Kendal, which, in three years of service has had extraordinary success with twenty-four runs safely through the blockade under the command of Roderick Shaw. A trusted source in Wilmington reveals that a goodwill mission is being undertaken, to deliver food and medical supplies (that will otherwise continue to degrade in warehouses in St. George's) to the now conquered Wilmington under a flag-of-truce, for distribution through Federal forces there, to the hospitals and churches for local citizens. My source has intimated the utmost confidence in her officers and assures that Kendal will continue north to our own designated rendezvous location if she can be of service to the Confederacy at this critical time.

Sir, my recommendation is to remove a fair portion of the treasury, as much as half, to Bermuda and from there to Liverpool with one or more trusted agents to act as "supercargo", finally to be deposited safely on account for when our capital relocates in a more secure location. The remainder should serve as payment as necessary for officers and troops, as well as your own escort when the time comes for evacuation from Richmond. We may also consider utilizing the Mexican silver to decoy false shipments so as to deflect attention from other methods of securing treasury assets. Final hour umbrage or suspicion expressed at this discovery will most certainly dissolve in the relief knowing the primary assets are safely invulnerable to any approaching threat.

Regrettably, time is of the essence. Please reply at your earliest,

I am, Sir, your obed't, serv't,
G. A. Trenholm
Secretary of the Treasury

THE EVENING SUN HAD finally broken through the clouds, turning the pale new birch leaves as gold as the daffodils blooming along the banks of the obscure little cove off the James River. Two vehicles sat next to the old farmhouse, a delicately framed but mud-spattered waggonette and a battered old freight wagon at the end of a narrow, deeply-rutted trail leading from the north end of the Petersburg rail line not yet been destroyed by either army.

Leaning against a tree, not approaching the man everyone, except perhaps Captain Shaw, regarded as some kind of god, Brendan hoped the contempt he felt didn't show on his face. Proud as he was to do his duty, and of old McRae for concocting the outrageous plan, he could have shot the old man on the spot after learning of the mission for which *Kendal* had been commissioned.

The academy officers who escorted the shipment now unloaded boxes and casks from the wagon, some obviously heavier than others by the grimaces and groans of the men.

As he followed the men back to the freight wagon to lend a hand, he heard laughter from the wide porch of the old farmhouse. Not a farmer in sight, Brendan thought, only politicians, naval officers, and a few cavalrymen. He looked up and met the eyes of Jefferson Davis.

In that instant, he remembered his father, Josiah Barkley and Edgar Hall, all working urgently to reach a compromise with other planters to end slavery and keep the State in the Union, their plantations intact and their land producing.

He also remembered kneeling in the mud beside his father's grave under the old oak tree in the Fleur-de-Lys cemetery, his stomach clenching and a wave of anger washing over him. He knew this war was not the fault of one man, but this one man represented those who made the decisions leading to its dreadful result. Davis leaned over, pale eyes still boring into him, and talked to Shaw. The captain glanced towards him and beckoned him over.

ONCE THEY WERE UNDERWAY, Shaw retired to his cabin.

Brendan raised the Union flag once again, amused at the thought of what the sight must be doing to Davis and his cabinet as *Kendal* sailed away with a large portion of the Confederate States Treasury in her hold.

"Damn convenient," Hudson muttered, as he passed

Brendan.

"Hudson!" The man paused but didn't turn back.

"Regardless of your personal contempt for me and my methods, you will accord proper respect to my rank at all times!"

Hudson turned and answered grudgingly, "Aye, *Sir*," adding with a smirk as he nodded towards the flag, "too precious for anyone else to touch?"

Brendan weighed his answer. Common as the practice might be, he personally did not approve of the ruse. He knew it was sometimes absolutely necessary and at the same time felt it dishonorable.

"*Le ruse de guerre*, Hudson, a trick I learned from old Maffitt on the Dolphin."

"Why *not* old Maffitt or Wilkinson for this mission, *Sir*?"

Brendan shrugged. "*Kendal's* record speaks well for all of us. But, if not for my methods, my flag, and my old uniform, we would *not* have been chosen for this honor. Now, prepare passengers and cargo for sea. We'll be at the Roads soon."

Passengers. Understandably, several of the cabinet members were frantic to remove their wives and children away from the expected Yankee invasion. A dangerous combination. Vulnerable civilians on board and a cargo of such high value to the Confederacy, he hoped no one would believe it would be sent by blockade runner.

"Sir?"

Brendan turned to see Thomas standing near the wheelhouse, looking pensive.

Thomas had rejoined them in Wilmington and presented himself to Captain Shaw for punishment, with a letter written by his most grateful, and apparently newly-returned-from-the-brink-of-death, mother. Brendan was relieved to see Thomas back and healthy, and, when they were sure of privacy, had enjoyed hearing about the boy's adventures, his time with Lilién, and meetings with Everleigh in Annapolis. Everleigh had sent Thomas back to serve as a sort of aide-de-camp for Brendan, obviously trusting in the lad's abilities and discretion.

"Captain's real sick, sir. Wants to see you and Hudson in

his cabin."

AT TWILIGHT, SOON AFTER Acting Captain Bonneau signaled for lights out, Thomas threw back the tarpaulin covering the hatch and called out in a fierce whisper, "Trouble below, sir! Hudson's drunk and into the stores!"

Brendan and Carter were through the tarpaulin and down the ladder in an instant, enveloped in the stifling heat of the closed-off hold. In the gloom, Brendan found Hudson in the galley, on his knees in front of the pantry in the company of a half-empty bottle of Shaw's favorite apricot brandy and loudly resisting Paulson's efforts to remove him.

Brendan thought of their proximity to the cordon of Federal blockaders and knew they must silence him immediately.

"Hudson!" Brendan ordered, wresting the bottle from his hand and passing it to Paulson. "You are confined to quarters. Carter, see that Lieutenant Hudson remains in his quarters until morning, so he can sleep it off."

"Here's something to sleep off!" Hudson shouted, stumbling to his feet, fist raised, only to stumble again as the *Kendal* rose on a gentle swell.

"Paulson, you and Carter get him in his cabin and guard the door," he said, turning towards the ladder.

"Sir!"

Brendan saw the flash and heard the report. The shot whistled well over Brendan's head and through the bulkhead just above the waterline. A beam of light pierced the darkness and the acrid odor of gunpowder filled the hold as Carter threw himself onto Hudson and Paulson struggled to wrest a revolver from the drunken man. Simultaneously, the engine room door and hatchway cover were thrown open and through the churning whir of the engines and haze of coal smoke, Ramsey and Sanderlin both shouted, "What the hell's going on?"

Face down on the floor, Hudson was still struggling and shouting obscenities as Carter pulled his arms firmly behind him and Paulson locked his wrists in irons.

"You may just have succeeded in killing all of us, you

fool," he said through his teeth, looking down into the bloodshot eyes. "Take him to the brig. And Paulson?

"Sir?" Paulson said, looking up from his attempt to pull Hudson to his feet.

"If he makes one sound, you are under orders to knock him out cold. Understood?"

"Aye, sir!" Brendan turned to make his way up the ladder.

"I will kill you—" Hudson groaned in mid-threat, collapsing when Paulson brought the butt of the revolver firmly down on his head.

"Oh, you idiot," Carter hissed, glaring at the huge form crumpled at their feet.

"I had my orders," Paulson argued, looking to Brendan for support.

Brendan gestured for the revolver, and once Paulson sheepishly handed it over, Brendan left Carter to deal with the mess. As he opened the hatchway, he heard Carter hiss, "Damn it all, now we have to drag the sorry son-of-a-bitch."

Typically blockade runners were not armed, nor were crew members. Brendan reported the incident to Shaw, omitting only Hudson's threat and the slapstick maneuvers of Carter and Paulson.

"You all right, lad?"

"Aye, Sir. Between his drunken aim and Carter's warning, he missed me by a mile."

Through the darkness, Brendan could sense Shaw's steady gaze even in his feverish state. "Another few minutes and that shot would've brought every ship in the squadron on us, no matter what tricks you have up your sleeve.

PART XI

LILLIAN

St. George's, Bermuda

"Begin doing what you want to do now. We are not living in eternity. We have only this moment, sparkling like a star in our hand, and melting like a snowflake..."

Lord Francis Bacon

Chapter Twenty-Nine

Sometimes It Helps to Swear

WAS IT JUST THE local tendency to be relaxed about punctuality, she wondered, when Hollis failed to arrive on schedule? 'On Bermudian time' was an expression Lillian had heard more than once. Landlines still down and cell service patchy, armed with directions and a map, she decided not to wait any longer and left word with Rose.

Periwinkle morning glories and orange nasturtiums bloomed together in gentle contrast, entwined and draped over limestone walls and fence rails.

Not a cloud in the sky and just enough of a fresh, cooling breeze to stir the heavy air after her walk uphill; even the feral cats lazed about on rock walls or sat like statues on the top of gateposts watching as she walked by. High thin whistles of a waxwing, flute-like trills of thrushes and wrens, coos from a pair of mourning doves competed with honeybees and the more automated buzz of chainsaws.

If it wasn't for the Bermudian utility workers and homeowners cleaning downed branches from streets and yards, the storm might never have happened. Shark oil in the barometers she passed by was now the palest gold in the sunlight.

What had happened on the Fleur? Had the heavy weather impacted the ship? She pulled out her phone to text Vera, but once again, no signal. She typed the message so it would at least be sent when service was restored.

The engagement ring flashed in the sunlight, sending colorful prisms dancing against a shadowy limestone wall, like the fragments of ideas and plans shared after, and a time or two even during, the many times they made love throughout the night. Sleep deprived and swathed in a lovely state of surreal euphoria, she found it difficult to keep her mind focused.

She was surprised Hollis had not caught up with her by the time she reached the crossroads. The gray walls of the old fort high on the hill above, and around the bend was the old military cemetery just as he had described. Up the lane behind the cemetery, she saw the house. Standing before its ruined gate, it was an ideal haunted house next to the cemetery.

The dignified old Georgian did look as though it might be haunted, with empty eyes staring out from three distinct floors and only fragments of blue paint still clung to the weathered gray stone of the outer shell. The roof and walls seemed sound, though a portion of the second story floor had collapsed, sometime in the past decade, Hollis had said.

The crumbling limestone newel post near her …meowed. She looked up to the top to see a large gray cat, sitting as still as a statue, except for the tail flipping past the single word engraved on the front.

Glendevon.

Glendevon House?

"Oh my God," she said to the cat.

Just last night, she had looked at the letters from Brendan and Captain Shaw, both written somewhere inside the neglected ruin at the end of the long, winding, weed-choked path.

With the old fort and its undeveloped acreage on two sides and the cemetery on another, Glendevon was as isolated as any place on Bermuda could be. Stepping through the sagging and rusted wrought iron gate, she ventured closer. Somewhere beneath could be the network of tunnels and cellars Hollis hoped for, and in them, answers about Brendan.

Hollis had told her everything about the place, except about its connection to the *Kendal*. Did he even know? Conrad had known all along of its link to the *Kendal* and her crew and must have thoroughly investigated the place. Could there possibly be anything here to find?

Weeds grew in profusion through cracks in the stepping

stones, and as she ran towards the house, the brilliant yellow dandelions tickled her legs and caught in the straps of her sandals and between her toes.

Its roof, the four outer walls, a wide first-floor veranda, and a ludicrously secured front door looked to be the only stable elements of the building. At each of the windows, fragments of shattered glass protruded from the brittle remains of dried and crumbling glazing like shark's teeth. Windows at the rear were higher and even less accessible.

Scrambling up a grassy embankment, she peered into what had once been the kitchen, the chimney still intact, the floor above partially caved in at the center. Moss was growing thick in dark corners, weeds thriving in cracks and crevices and a purple bougainvillea, dazzling in a narrow shaft of bright sunlight, was enclosing an interior wall bared to its wooden frames. Limestone roof slabs, fallen and shattered, had very effectively blocked the back entry.

She heard a vehicle pulling up the lane, slid down the muddy hill and ran to the gate, but it wasn't Hollis. Old Esther from the museum reached out towards Lillian even before screeching to a halt.

"Lillian! Thank God!"

"Esther?" Lillian took hold of the old lady's shaking hand.

"Hollis! They took him!" The little woman's voice started out in a shaky whisper but ended in a high-pitched squeal.

"*What?* Who took him?"

"I don't know! We're closed because of the storm but he was there at the museum checking on something—said he was in a hurry, said he was late meeting you —I was in the storeroom looking for that bloody uniform — and Hollis kept repeating eleven o'clock and I knew he meant you, and then he said something like 'Conrad' very loudly…He didn't scream or cry out for help, but I know he didn't want to go, and was trying to tell me something and then he was gone … I tried and tried to call you but couldn't get through. Should I call the police?"

"No!" On her phone, the ominous 'no service' was once

again the only message on the display. She pulled a notepad and
pen from her backpack and scrawled out Neal's number. "Call
Agent Jameson at Customs and tell him everything, but *no one
else*. Tell him I'll be inside, somehow."

"You shouldn't go in there alone!"

"If Phelan Conrad has Hollis and thinks we're on the
right track, I have to get inside first!" Lillian was already turning
towards the house. "Go, please, before someone sees you!"

Esther sped away with a grinding of gears and a shower
of gravel. Poor Esther, she thought, hopefully, the frail, wren-
like old lady was tougher than she looked.

Trey has an accident, Duncan is called away, Hollis
abducted. Of course, it had to be all connected she thought,
pausing only long enough to enter a quick message to Duncan
and Neal.

As she began to put her phone away it chimed, startling
her so she nearly dropped it onto the road. Vera, she saw on the
display.

*"What about Trey? He's right in front of me and as annoying as
ever."*

Reading the message once more, her hands grew cold.

She forwarded Vera's message to Duncan and tried
immediately to call him. Each ring seemed to stretch on for
seconds longer than normal, but his brief voicemail greeting was
cut off. Service out again.

Hopefully, little Esther would get through somehow, she
thought, shoving the phone deep in her pants pocket while
running back towards the house. She needed something…a
piece of wood or a rock large enough to break away the glass
from the windows so she could get inside.

Rattling the old gate on her way through, the big gray cat
leapt down and ran behind the house towards an old, rough-cut
limestone cottage. When the animal slipped through an empty
doorframe, Lillian followed.

In the muted light filtered through nearly opaque
windows, she saw a narrow staircase to a small open loft area,
presumably the location of the trysts Hollis mentioned, romantic

or otherwise. Here was the typical trash and graffiti. Fresh tracks in the grime hinted at recent activity. During the storm? Well, it *was* dry inside, she could at least say that much for it.

Going up only far enough to peek into the dim recesses, she wrinkled her nose at the unsavory mess of blankets and mattresses. Stubs of candles were stuck in filthy old canning jars and dusty wine bottles, and disposable lighters and flashlights of several sizes and vintages were thoughtfully piled at the bottom of the stairs to light the way for nighttime visitors.

Thick cobwebs hung heavily from open rafters and draped across windows and layers of dust, which had turned to grime in the constant humidity, coated everything.

The long workbench and rows of shelves held more old canning jars with nuts and bolts, screws and nails, most now liquefied to an orange slime or rusted into flakes. Finally, along another wall hung old crowbars, claw hammers and a strange collection of other tools she didn't even recognize, but as rusty and grime-covered as they appeared, at least a few of the crowbars and hammers looked sound enough to help her get into the house, if there was only time.

Cat tracks led beyond the stairs through what might generously be called a kitchenette, where an old Primus stove, and the gray cat, sat on a tiny chipped and stained table. An old, web-draped cabinet filled the space behind the loft stairs.

Curiosity getting the better of her, she reached in past the webs, grasped the small cut-glass knob on the cabinet and pulled hard to loosen the long, narrow door, warped and swollen by time and moisture.

Shifting slightly from its place against the wall before finally opening with a violent rattle, the cabinet contained dozens of old keys of various vintage. Crowbars would be more useful than keys, she thought, given the state of the house but one crudely made skeleton key caught her attention. She reached in to pull it off its hook, drawing her hand back immediately at the unexpected sliminess of the metal.

Rubbing her fingers together and sniffing cautiously, she realized the keys, all of them, were coated in petroleum jelly, probably the only reason all had not dissolved into rust long ago. Reaching in again, the key caught on the hook as she pulled, the eighteenth-century square-cut iron nails gave up their tenuous hold on the old wood and the entire cabinet shifted. A sudden, cold draft poured through the narrow opening.

Grasping the edge, she pulled the entire cabinet away from the wall. Steep, narrow steps cut into the limestone spiraled down beneath the cottage.

"Hollis, you wonderful little man!" she cried aloud. The cat blinked his yellow eyes, meowed, and flipped his tail at her.

She pulled her jacket out of her backpack and pulled it on, knowing *exactly* where that passage would lead and resolving to follow it no matter what. She ran back to the loft steps and stuffed her pockets with flashlights, candles, and lighters. On her way through the opening, she grabbed a handful of the greasy old keys and, wishing she were wearing jeans, not to mention more substantial footwear of any description, stepped into the passageway and pulled the cabinet into place behind her.

Ten short, narrow steps descended into a tunnel, which was, she saw gratefully, high enough for her to walk at a slight crouch, the white stone reflecting the light and helping to keep claustrophobia from clamping down on her chest.

Thick veils of cobweb and the not so subtle fragrance of a hamster cage, however, were freaking her out. She pulled up her hood and used one of the flashlights for light and the longer one as a wand to get rid of the cobwebs in her way. Some areas of the tunnel had cracked, loose, crumbling stones littered the floor nearby, but the tunnel itself seemed sound.

"Ouch!" Wasn't it only a few months ago, she wondered, breathing sharply from the pain in her big toe after tripping on the rough limestone floor, she complained to Vera about having an uneventful life? Not boring, but a bit routine, mundane with the demands of work and kids with homework, laundry, and sibling rivalry galore.

Now she was in the midst of love affairs, thieves, spies, and smugglers—ironic, she thought, since she knew one of the primary reasons her father put her on the hunt for Brendan in the first place was to distract her from Duncan and keep her out of danger. What *any* of the men in her life would have to say about this adventure she could only imagine…and try to convince herself she had *not* heard the furtive rustlings and high-pitched squeal of a rat.

The tunnel forked, and she felt a draft of fresh air, but she kept on in the direction of the house. The tunnel became larger, the limestone smoother, almost polished and ended at a large, wooden door, framed by a thick, rusted metal band. Propping up one flashlight and holding the other under her arm, she tried the old skeleton key. A loud, satisfying clunk vibrated through to the hollow space beyond the door.

She grasped the iron handle and pulled as hard as she could. The door did not budge. She looked closely along the frame for other locks or latches and tried again, one foot pushing the wall for leverage, but with not the slightest hint of movement. Rust or moisture-swollen wood, or both, were keeping it as tightly shut as if it were still locked.

Shouldn't this fear of being caught, fear for Hollis, fear of whatever the hell was going on out there be giving her that mythical superhuman strength? Cursing the lack of upper body strength which had let her down many times before, she rushed back through the tunnel.

Listening at the opening and hearing nothing except for the far-off cry of seagulls, she pushed open the cabinet and hurried into the workshop—and screamed.

AS DID THE TERRIFIED teenage girl she ran into, both stifling their screams at the same instant, with the same gesture.

Lillian started to laugh in relief, but the girl's eyes were wide with fright.

"Men with guns! Two of them! At the old house!" She clutched Lillian's arm. "One of them," she paused, her whisper so low Lillian could only see her pale lips move. "I think he might have seen me!"

From the multi-colored neon beads threaded into her

long, braided hair, to the bright pink shirt against her ebony skin, the girl would have stood out like a warning buoy. Without further discussion, Lillian pushed her towards the tunnel and grabbed the tools she needed. Running back to the cabinet, she stopped only long enough to throw the back door wide open, hoping whoever it was would believe the girl escaped up the path and into the wooded area beyond, perhaps even draw them away from the house.

Lillian made sure the cabinet was completely back in place and turned to the still trembling girl. Handing her a flashlight, Lillian beckoned her to follow.

"What's going on?" the girl said, in a trembling whisper, treading on Lillian's heels every other step in her attempt to stay close. "Who are you?"

At the crossroad of tunnels, Lillian stopped briefly and introduced herself. "When we get the cellar door open, come back here and head down this way, the opening must be somewhere down near Barry Road. I need you to call for help." she pointed down the shaft, breathing deeply of the fresher air and hurrying once again toward the house. On the way, the girl saved Neal's number in her phone, impressively proficient on the keypad scared as she was. "Agent Jameson should already be on his way, but just in case… What's your name?"

"Andromeda."

"After the constellation?"

'What—"

"Daughter of Cassiopeia!"

"*Whatever.*"

Even as they hurried through the tunnel, Lillian could *hear* the girl roll her eyes.

"Get that a lot, do you?" Lillian smiled at the familiar teenage tone and felt a pang of mom-sickness. "What are you doing here? I heard the older kids only came here at night."

"I lost my phone last night," she said, too scared to be embarrassed by the admission. "I was on the path, almost to the shed, and this guy, he just…just walked up to the door of the old house, pointed a gun and blasted it. I didn't see the other one, but he yelled, "Nick, what the fu…" she broke off, looking at Lillian, "or something like that. Do you know who they are?"

"Maybe…"

Bad news if it was Nick, she thought, very bad. Nick was a brute, no better word to describe him, even without a gun and one of the men both Mark and Duncan specifically warned her about. Hurrying along the trail of light from the dimming flashlight she wondered who was with him. Was Conrad the other man, and if so, where was Hollis?

When they finally reached the door, they propped their flashlights and she handed Andromeda a crowbar.

They wedged the tools into the wide metal lip around the door and pulled. And pulled, and pulled, with each of them losing their grip and falling back onto the hard floor, hardware flying over their heads and rattling into the tunnel.

"One of us will have a concussion long before we get inside. Oh ew!" Lillian said, reaching for the crowbar, jumping back after the beam of the flashlight found the bones of …something.

"*What?*"

"Nothing," she said, wiping her hand on her pants and brushing dirt and bits of limestone from her behind. "Let's try again. If we can't, we'll both go down the other tunnel and get out that way."

"My dad says it helps to swear," Andromeda said, rubbing her hands on her shorts.

Wincing from the blister already bubbling up on her palm, Lillian shrugged. "What the hell? Why not?"

Pulling, and swearing so much Lillian imagined Smurf blue smoke rising from either end of the tunnel, helped assuage the fear almost literally crawling up her spine. She was trying to remain calm for Andromeda, but was feeling anything but calm, especially after hearing her report of Nick and a gun. Still, if he and his cohort were forced to enter the cellars from above, they had a lot of time-consuming and noisy work ahead of them. If Lillian could get inside *now* and look around, she may have a chance for reconnaissance and escape, either out the other tunnel or into the woods behind the shed.

Her hands were burning from friction, stinging from sweat and slipping on the rough metal. The muscles in her arms and back were swearing in their own way by the time the door very slowly, very gradually began to give, finally opening with a deafening screech that echoed through the now wide-open cellar, the force of their effort sent them once again flying back onto the rough limestone, panting and still swearing.

"Neat trick," Lillian said, easing herself to her feet, "thanks."

"You swear like a little girl," Andromeda said, shaking life back into her hands.

"You swear like a sailor. If you were my kid, I'd wash your mouth out with soap."

Andromeda laughed but stopped abruptly. "Shit!" she exclaimed, obviously annoyed and scrambling to her feet, "now I have to tell my Dad he was right about something!"

"Is that so bad?" Lillian laughed, too, brushing off the sharp fragments of rock embedded in her calves and arms and elbows, and tucking Saint Michael back inside her shirt.

"Yes!" Andromeda said, her voice fading as she ran back down the passage.

Lillian was now faced with the yawning blackness of the cellar. The light of the flickering flashlight did not penetrate beyond the thick, dust-covered cobwebs still barring the door. She pulled her hood up and cinched it tight again, stepped closer and used the longer of the two crowbars to swipe them away. When she could finally see a hallway not much wider than the tunnel itself, she stepped inside.

Still brushing away webs, she followed the hallway to an open foyer with several rooms, some with doors, a few alcoves with open archways. Heavy brass lanterns hung on the wall beside each door. Several candles had fallen from a rusted out taper tin, fragments of which somehow still clung to the wall. While spiders were certainly present, rodents had not breached the outer defenses, or the candles would have been eaten long ago.

She lowered her hood and stood quietly for a moment, listening, but there was only silence. She pulled one of the wand-like lighters out of her pocket and hoped it would work.

Expecting a few sparks and a sputter, she dropped the thing when it went off like a blowtorch.

Unsure if the old taper would even light, she cleared away the webs from the outside of one lantern and then pulled the trigger again.

"Whoa, that's cool!" Andromeda said, watching as flames flared inside the cobweb filled lantern and set them ablaze. When the flames diminished, the candle inside remained lit and the shadows of the cellar already seemed less formidable.

"If we could trust the flashlights, I wouldn't risk lighting candles at all," she gestured for the girl to close the door to keep webs from drifting toward the flame. "No luck?"

"No way out of the tunnel, a gate locked from the outside and way before I ever got close to the end." Responding to Lillian's hopeful look, she added, "no signal."

Lillian ventured into the shadows with the dim flashlight while Andromeda remained within the circle of candlelight. Lillian questioned her about the gate, wondering if she should send the girl back with a crowbar but decided, for now, it might be best to remain and escape together. Talking, and swearing, seemed to keep both of them from panicking.

One wall at the far end of the cellar was made from wide, rough cut planks, out-of-place against the limestone brick, and without a door or hatch or exit in evidence. She put her ear to the wood and listened. No sounds yet from above.

Lillian pulled the skeleton keys out of her jacket pocket. "Look into any of the open areas for…" she paused.

"For what?"

"I have no idea, but let's try to do it quietly."

She tried several of the keys until finally, one slipped into place with a click, but was stiff and almost wouldn't turn.

Door number one… she thought, pushing the heavy door into the dark space. An actual wine cellar, with empty floor to ceiling racks in separate brick arches along each wall, and a wide island sort of structure in the center with wooden brackets on each side, apparently to hold large casks. But broken glass littered the floor and, well, everything, and not one intact bottle remained. Obviously, someone had emptied the room in a hurry or spent way too much time sampling the vintages.

No tidy nooks and crannies like the smuggler's hold Hollis has shown her down at the wharf, not that she had seen so far—.

"Oh my God! Oh my God! *Oh my God*!"

In the foyer, the beam of Andromeda's flashlight was making frenzied figure eights on the walls and ceiling as the girl spun around stamping her feet, the beads at the ends of her long braids clattering like hailstones on a tin roof.

"*What*?" Lillian cried out, trying to get close enough to find out what was wrong. "Andromeda! What is it?"

"A *fucking* spider the size of a *fucking* cricket ball down my *fucking* shirt! That's what!" Dropping the flashlight, she pulled off her shirt and shook it while still dancing around in her lacy pink brassiere, light glinting from a gold belly-button ring.

"Quiet!" Lillian hissed. "I'm sure there's…nothing…" she faltered, aware of a scurrying movement in the faint, undulating beam of the flashlight, rocking on the cellar floor. She shuddered at the feel of its very large body being crushed under the thin sole of her sandal.

"I'm getting the hell out of here," Andromeda was pulling on her shirt, all the while muttering an impressive string of four-letter words and their various tenses. "I'd rather deal with bad guys and guns than *FUCKING GIANT SPIDERS*!"

"*ANDROMEDA*!" Using her angry mother voice, Lillian reached out, stopping her before she could escape to the tunnel. Quiet, but still shuddering, the girl looked up at the ceiling above her and kept smoothing her hands over her head and Lillian wanted desperately to do the same. Before handing over the brighter flashlight, she waved it above them to make sure there was nothing moving nearby. "Stay here while I look, and please, *please*, be quiet!"

Grabbing up the faltering torch, she hurried back to the

plank wall and listened again, now hearing sounds from above, distant and muffled but determined thumps, and the screeching of nails being wrenched from wood.

Inside the second room, dark corners were so full of cobwebs the beam of their flashlight didn't fully penetrate. Two other arched alcoves held only remnants of building materials and empty crates and casks.

At the jarring bang against the plank wall, Lillian jumped, dropping the handful of keys. Andromeda roused out of her arachnophobia and hovered close while Lillian opened the final locked chamber.

"As soon as we're done, we go back up the tunnel, out the back door and through the woods, okay?" Lillian said. They couldn't delay their escape much longer. "I know you're scared, but *please* be careful and quiet before going into the cottage. We don't know who else might be around…"

Finally, something besides cobwebs, she thought, now hearing men's voices from behind the wall. At the center of the room, something very large and covered with a filthy, crumpled old tarpaulin. Striding in, sweeping a path through a particularly thick veil of webs, heedless of spiders, spirits, or even archeological site preservation, she flung the canvas aside, disappointed, at first, to find only dingy white, rope-bound cotton bales.

"What on earth…?"

Andromeda, shining her flashlight up into the rafters above looking for more spiders, jumped at Lillian's gasp and swung the brighter, wider beam towards the top of the bales where the clenched bony fist of a human skeleton reached out towards them, the face with its eternal grin and empty eye sockets, the skull covered with grizzled dark hair.

Andromeda, eyes wide with terror, too frightened even to scream or swear, backed out of the room and ran through the foyer. The candlelight wavered in the draft and then Lillian heard the heavy door slam against the brick wall, the girl's footsteps fading quickly as she escaped through the tunnel.

Wood was splintering under a constant barrage of heavy

blows and Lillian knew she could not put off running or hiding. But, she *knew* this man was a clue, something to do with Brendan and she couldn't leave, not yet. Gathering the two crowbars, she blew out the foyer candle, went inside the chamber, closed the door and locked herself inside.

Any human remains she had ever been near had been bared of clothing and flesh, dismantled and found at the bottom of the sea, not left for over a century in a spider-infested cellar.

Poor Andromeda, Lillian thought, propping the crowbars against the wall near the door. She said a quick prayer for the frightened girl, both that she would get out and away from Glendevon safely and remember to call for help.

Reminded of her own useless phone, she still did not want it taken by whoever was on the other side of the wall. She thrust it down the front of her underwear, hoping it was snug enough to stay in place, imagining it flying out the leg of her Capri's at some inopportune moment. But there was nowhere else, and if they found it there, well then, she'd have more to worry about than a lack of cell service.

Before moving back into the web draped corner, she saw something clenched in the skeleton's hand just as the wall into the foyer was breached with a final shattering crash. Wresting the brittle document away from its bony grasp and stepping back into the far corner, she folded the paper as quietly as possible.

Shuddering, she stuffed it down her pants along with her phone.

Chapter Thirty

Saint Michael Defend Us

"CANDLES." IT WAS A familiar voice, but definitely not Nick. "The wax is warm and soft. Whomever we saw earlier has already come and gone."

Mark!

"What the *fuck*? How the hell did they get in or out? We've been working our asses off out there for over an hour!" That *was* definitely Nick.

"More like a half hour, and there's an alternative entrance. Feel the draft?" Intense beams of halogens flashed through gaps above and below the door, and Mark's voice and footsteps faded as he walked to the tunnel entry.

"Somebody could still be in here, with the gold!"

She heard footsteps coming near and the click of a safety being released on a gun echoing through the empty space.

"For God's sake, don't shoot anybody."

Just as she and Andromeda had done, the men worked their way through each of the rooms, although now most of the doors were already standing wide open for them. Nick had an expletive for everything; the most colorful reserved for the cobwebs hitting his face. Finally, she heard them stop outside her door and inched back into the corner. With the jangle of keys and scratching of the metal in the old lock, the door opened, and the room filled with light.

"Jesus Christ," said Nick.

"Highly unlikely," said Mark wryly, pausing in the doorway, shining the light over the body and the bales but didn't enter the room. She tried to inch even closer to the wall as the beam swept through, praying they wouldn't see her and it wasn't a spider she felt in her hair. Her heart pounded so loud she was sure they would hear it if they moved any nearer.

"Who do you think—" started Nick, his light sweeping the room.

"Check the rest of the place, see how they got in here," Mark said, stepping in front of him, his words masking the whimper of fear that escaped her.

"What are you doing?"

"Searching for identification. Would you care to assist?"

Another expletive was the only answer. Nick's voice and the light faded away. Mark stood still a moment and then ventured further into the room.

"Lillian?" it was barely a whisper.

"I'm here," she breathed, remaining motionless.

He swore under his breath and closed the short distance between them, whispering urgently. "Are you all right? Have you found anything?"

"Just him" She wasn't telling *anyone* about the letter, not even Mark, not yet.

He moved away and pulled up the corner of the ancient tarp, "Get under and stay still!"

She crouched down and pulled her hood more tightly over her head before he threw the tarp over her. Now, well beyond her usual claustrophobia, she held back a moan as the dust and grit rained down on her.

She could hear Nick's footsteps approaching just as several bright flashes went off.

"There's a tunnel leading away from the place. Now what the hell are you doing?"

"A pre-disturbance survey—"

"Fuck that! Disturb the son-of-a-bitch so we can find the gold and get the hell out of here! It's not like he gives a crap!"

Lillian heard the old bones being shifted. Nick wouldn't know a pre-disturbance survey was something done on shipwrecks, not dead men in a dusty cellar, but Mark was stalling for time. Finally, she heard the sound of brittle old paper being handled and the light shifted.

"What is it? Who is he?" demanded Nick.

"Legal documents of some kind…" Mark paused, rifling through the papers. "Looks like this may be the notorious John Hudson, acquitted of the murder of… *Brendan Aubert Bonneau.*"

Lillian gasped and clamped her hand over her mouth, hearing the names of her ancestor and the man who killed him.

"But how the hell did you get down here, all alone, and what's with the bales of cotton…?" Mark's voice drifted off, as Lillian's often did when considering a historical mystery.

"*Is* it just cotton?" Lillian heard Nick's heavy footsteps stalk towards her.

"*What the bloody hell do you think you're doing?*

She heard Mark's exclamation, but before she could move out of range, she felt the body land on her. The weight of what was once John Hudson was not much, but to Lillian he might have weighed a ton for the suffocating sensations of fear, of Nick and his gun, of the cellar and its crawling occupants, of the darkness, the filthy tarpaulin and now the bones of the man who may have killed Brendan melting down around her. Mark's outburst, she was sure, was to cover any sounds she might have made if she had not been close to a catatonic state. She heard the ripping of old burlap, metal bands snapping and releasing the long-imprisoned steam-pressed cotton. The bales shifted as Nick pulled at the cotton, and she braced herself to keep from being pushed more firmly against the bones of the dead man.

"Nothin'!" Nick grumbled. "Conrad was sure there was somethin' here."

"Obviously," Mark drawled, in what Vera called his full-bore boarding school Brit, dripping arrogance and annoyance with every slowly enunciated syllable. "This John Hudson undoubtedly believed the same and you can clearly see what happened to him."

"Let's get the hell out of here," Nick repeated, walking out. "Are you coming or am I leaving you here?"

"By all means, my good fellow, please leave me behind."

"Huh?"

"I'll carry on until I have explored the mayhem you have created in the single most significant scene in this investigation to date. Please enlighten George, if, that is, you are capable of expressing or even formulating an intelligible thought, why it is you have no one but Conrad to authenticate the specie, when it *is* eventually found. You know how much he trusts Conrad."

Lillian held her breath in the long pause that followed.

"Yeah. About as much as I trust you. Ten minutes."

When Nick left the cellar back through the hole in the wall, Mark threw back the tarp and helped her to her feet.

He held her close and she took a deep breath, reassured by his strength and scent, even enhanced as it was by sweat and the musty air of the cellar.

"I'm all…all right," she whispered, "and never tell Vera I told you, but we love it when you talk like that."

He laughed softly and she felt the tension ease from his body.

"It does rather baffle the ignorant oaf."

"Nick is an oaf, but George—" she paused, feeling a tickle on her scalp, frantically ran her fingers through her hair and brushed off her clothes, tucking the Saint Michael's medal back inside her shirt. "Where *is* George?"

"He had something coming in at the airport and said he'd meet us later—"

"My God," she felt the air escape her lungs again in a panic. She reached out and grabbed his arm. "Duncan was going to the airport when he left me. Hugh called him this morning, he said Trey was injured and they were flying him to Hamilton."

Mark's eyes met hers. "When?"

"Around ten-thirty, I think. But Vera said Trey is fine and on board. I tried to reach Duncan before I found my way down here, and couldn't—"

She felt him tense before pushing her into the room and grabbing for the ring of keys half hanging from his pocket. "Mark, what--?" Alarmed by sounds of the key scraping in the lock she forgot to whisper.

Remembering the key in her own pocket, her panic

subsided until she heard a new voice.

"Well now, what's all this I hear about a skeleton?"

Conrad!

"John Hudson, circa 1865, stretched across the top of three old cotton bales. No other clues as to how or why he is here," Mark answered, the brittle documents crackling as he handed them over to his employer. "I believe we should leave, sir. We observed a girl running into a cottage behind the house and there is an escape tunnel she may have used to access the cellar—"

"Open up, I'd like to have a look at the fellow," Conrad urged, ignoring the warning.

She heard the keys jangle once more and slipped as quietly as she could behind the door while Mark made conversation and took his time opening the lock. "What about the old man? Was there anything of significance at the other site?"

Conrad made a sound, something between anger and amusement. "That wrathy little mite led us on one hell of a wild goose chase."

She knew Mark wanted her to remain quiet, but the thought of Hollis being kidnapped and even hurt made her angry. When the door opened, she stood in the middle of the room, her flickering flashlight pointed towards Conrad.

"What have you done with Hollis Walker?" she demanded.

"Bloody hell," Mark ran a hand through his hair, giving Conrad a sheepish look.

As Conrad looked between the two of them, a slow smile as affected as his Virginia drawl spread across his face.

"Tryin' to keep your lady friend from harm, verrah chivalrous, verrah commendable," the smile faded as he faced Mark, "as long as you're not trying to hide anything else from me?"

"No, sir. The remains and cotton bales, and documents were the only items discovered. No indication about the location of the Treasury. Ms. Cherrington was—"

"Tell me, Ms. Cherrington, what did *you* discover before young Sir Lancelot here discovered you?" Conrad cut Mark off once again, his phony accent slipping away along with the pleasant demeanor.

"I found the skeleton of the *Confederate lunatic* who killed my ancestor laid out across the top of three cotton bales."

"Bloody hell," Mark repeated, although Conrad was oblivious to Lillian's comparison. "Lillian…" he put his hand on her arm but she shook it off impatiently.

"You haven't answered my question, Mr. Conrad. Where is Hollis Walker?"

"Quite safe, my dear, tucked up in the trunk of my vehicle not far from here. But he's just a little minnow," Conrad paused when the sounds of struggle filled the foyer behind them, "we've caught ourselves a much bigger fish."

"Nice doing business with you, *Cousin*," George Andrastus growled, pushing someone into the room.

Duncan, hands bound behind him, stumbled in and fell to his knees.

"Duncan!" she cried, crouching next to him, feeling for the restraints. His arms trembled, fighting against tight cable tie cuffs cutting cruelly into his skin. Another set bound his ankles with just enough give to let him move. "My God, Duncan…"

"I'm sorry, Lily," Duncan said, his voice ragged as he struggled to his feet, his face bruised and bloody. They looked deep into each other's eyes as they had only a few hours before. "So sorry…" he repeated.

"No," she whispered, shaking her head. "No. You *promised* you wouldn't say that again."

George's light flashed over Lillian.

"Well, well," he said, "look who it is."

"My god," Mark said, with barely controlled anger, "you have successfully managed to introduce an entirely new level of bedlam into this situation."

"Shut up!" Nick yelled.

"I would be very careful right now, Mr. Seaton," Conrad said, turning his attention quickly back to Mark when he stepped closer to Lillian.

"She was hiding under the tarp when your inbred associate blundered in and threw the skeleton on top of her. I found her and locked her inside to keep her out of harm's way, that's it."

After regarding him skeptically for a moment, Conrad held the gun on Mark and waved the flashlight towards Nick and George. "Search the other rooms—"

"We did!" Nick said impatiently.

"Thoroughly." Conrad's tone left no room for argument and George and Nick left for the far chambers. Conrad looked directly at Lillian.

"Now, my dear, if you value the life of your…" he paused, glancing at her ring when the bright beam of his flashlight hit the stones, "fiancé, you will tell me everything you know about your traitorous ancestor's last voyage on the *Kendal*, and what he did with the Treasury of the Confederate States of America entrusted to his care."

Perhaps it was fear and desperation, but at the insult to Brendan and the fanatical gleam in Conrad's eye when talking about the Confederate States, an uncontrollable anger boiled up inside of her and the familiar breathlessness overwhelmed her. Now, however, instead of being unable to grasp hold of the feeling, it grabbed hold of her.

"Everything *I* know?" She stood, and with hands on her hips, stepped towards Conrad. "How could *I* possibly know anything? You've spent years hoarding every shred of information about the *Kendal*. Thanks to you, Mr. Conrad, *I* know nothing.

"However, *Brendan Bonneau* knows he was doing his duty as an officer of the United States Navy. His oath and that entity in existence long before the so-called *Confederate* States of America."

"*Brendan Bonneau* knows that both Jack Hudson and Cabinet Minister Perkins were responsible for the loss of the Treasury, Perkins by his petty pilfering and Hudson by abandoning their sinking ship ahead of the passengers and crew to discover where the Treasury had been hidden. Only to *murder* the only two men who knew its location.

"Greed, Mr. Conrad. Greed is what happened to the Treasury."

George and Nick pushed her aside and she stumbled and grasped the door to keep herself from falling. Her head ached, and the cursed breathlessness made her dizzy again. What had she touched? She hadn't had a vision…

Jack Hudson's skeleton was flung against the wall and the three bales picked up and ripped open with knives that barely disturbed the long-imprisoned steam-pressed cotton.

"Nothing," George said, finally. "Nothing but crap in here. Let's go."

Conrad stepped towards the door, still looking at Lillian warily and she began to hope they would simply leave them behind…so what if her keys were taken … so what if they were locked in, both Esther and Andromeda had called for help…Mark would come back when he could …

Until Nick said, "We should just kill them now, and get it over with!"

"*Just* kill them?" Mark's said, his voice icy, clipped "Are you mad? There's no need, lock them in and be done with it. We'll be gone before—"

"Shut the fuck up!" Nick was pushing his way toward Mark, "Why should we listen to you?"

"We need to leave, *now*. If you haven't already noticed, Nick, the girl we saw earlier is *not* here and has, by now, called for help. I'm surprised the place isn't crawling with police already!" Mark looked between Conrad and George.

"That was just a kid!"

"I don't care who it was. She saw you shoot the front door, for God's sake!"

Conrad glared at Mark. "Why the hell didn't you tell me when I first got here?"

"I did, sir, but you wanted to examine the skeleton, and to search for the lost Treasury gold, remember? It must be here, somewhere, you said. And, you must be correct because, after all, there is a body of one of the blockade runners right—"

"And the gold is here, too, goddamn it all to hell and back!" Conrad growled, all trace of his old-Virginian gentility gone, "I know it is!"

Conrad, she soon realized, was not simply dangerous, he was insane. He shifted gears abruptly, now unconcerned about the imminent arrival of authorities. He began raging about the War, states' rights and Northern aggressors, the treasury, and traitorous Southerners like Brendan Bonneau. Eyes bulging and spittle flying, he insisted the skeleton of Jack Hudson proved the gold existed on the premises and he wasn't leaving until he found it, no matter who was on the way, in the way, or who else had to die.

Now it was George and Nick exchanging glances, both agitated and aiming their weapons into the cellar between Mark and Conrad, squinting against the piercing halogen beam of Mark's flashlight. She couldn't see his expression, but Mark held the flashlight in his left hand and his right was in shadow, Lillian suspected, aiming steadily at one of the three in front of him. Duncan was edging himself in front of her.

Frantic for some way to help, but the crowbars, the only real weapons she possessed, were on the wrong side of the room. The only other armaments at her disposal were the dying flashlight and a finicky barbecue lighter.

And prayer, of course, the medal reminded her, glinting against her jacket.

Saint Michael the Archangel, defend us in battle… Her mind stumbled through the familiar prayer. She had always thought of the "battle" as simply a metaphor for the trials of everyday life, some of those you win and some you lose.

Until this moment, when the battle was everything and losing not an option...

In the wide beam of Mark's flashlight, she saw the gossamer strands of web float down and settle gracefully onto Nick's thick, curly black hair.

With Duncan shielding her movement, and Nick and George focusing their attention on Conrad's diatribe, Lillian moved back into the dark corner where she had dropped her backpack. She reached inside for the Moreau sculpture. In one hand she took a firm grip on the red-lacquered courtesan, with the other, she held that very aggressive grill lighter as high as she could, feeling a now welcome revulsion at the cloying, tickling mass against her skin.

She pulled the trigger.

Sparks flashed and spit, frail strands connected to thick accumulations in drafty corners sent flames bursting along the draped network of webs in every direction.

"*What the fuck!*"

Conrad's tirade ceased with a gunshot and his cry of surprise.

More gunfire, the sickening sound of impact followed by Mark's cursing.

Filaments of fiery web fell onto her hair and burned the bare skin of her face and hands. Lillian raised the statuette with both hands, smashing the base of it down on George's arm with every ounce of strength the possessed.

He roared, and the gun flew out of his hand. Before she could raise it again, he lashed out, backhanding her fiercely across the face so hard lights flashed behind her eyes and she was thrown against the brick wall behind her. The breath jarred from her lungs and pain from both impacts made her cry out.

George, right arm hanging at an odd angle, now held the gun in his left hand and staggered towards her from the opposite side of the room. Another shot rang out and toppled him back into the foyer. She started towards George's gun but stopped in mid-reach.

Flashlights rocked on the uneven floor, webs still flickered and sputtered feebly overhead. The wavering half-light, however, was bright enough for her to see Nick directly in front of her, gun still in his hand.

Lillian froze, vivid images of Miranda and Ryan racing through her mind even as Nick's hand rose, his finger moved on the trigger in a surreal kind of slow motion until Nick reeled backwards, his head hitting the stone wall with a shocking crack as Duncan, groaning from both effort and pain, tackled him fiercely, knocking the gun from his hand.

Flames once again flared overhead, thick, grimy clusters of web melting and dripping like napalm onto Nick's thick, unruly and already web-draped hair.

His screams echoing shrilly through the cellars, Nick ran into the foyer, slapping at his head, ripping off his burning shirt while drafts from two open doors fed the flames. Fire swept into other areas with him, down the hallway to the tunnel and beyond, burning hotly at arches and door frames, along the brick walls and up into the low rafters.

Lillian crouched beside Duncan, frantically brushing away the fragments of still burning web from their hair and clothing, the cellar now eerily silent, but Nick's screams still echoed in her mind. Was he dead? Had she actually killed him? And worse, where were Conrad and George? The thought of them still alive and armed troubled her far more than Nick's death. She scrambled to her feet and searched for the three guns now scattered on the floor.

Candles, in some of the lanterns she had not dared light because of the masses of webs in and around them, had been lit by the fire and now illuminated the smoky foyer in soft, flickering light. All three men lay there, Conrad writhing and groaning, and George, still and quiet, eyes wide open in surprise, blood pooling beneath him, and Nick, lying still on the threshold to the stairs.

"Lily…"

"Duncan! Are you all right?" she dropped beside him, to help shift his weight from his arms. "I need something sharp to cut this—"

"My God, Lily, that was amazing!"

"Knife…on my belt," Mark groaned from the far side of the cellar, "and …that was…*fucking brilliant*," adding his assessment with something between a laugh and a groan.

"Mark!" She stumbled over to where he leaned against one of the bales, sparks still flickering around them in the loose tufts. Grimacing in pain and as pale as the cotton behind him, she saw the blood oozing through his fingers as his hand clutched his left arm. "Are you okay? How bad is it?"

"I'll live. Here," he shifted back against the dismantled bales so she could reach the pouch on his belt.

She pulled out the Swiss Army knife and moved quickly back to Duncan, using the blade to cut through the ties.

"It was a ruse, Lily," he said, "Conrad and George ambushed me—"

"I know!" The tie snapped. Duncan groaned again as his arms fell free. He shook and rubbed the life back into them until she cut the cuffs from his ankles and then he wrapped his arms around her. A barrage of quick, reassuring kisses cut off her words. She clung to him, the fear she had felt for all of them returning with a rush.

"Where's Chadwick, Lily? He was with Hollis, and was supposed to be with you whenever I couldn't—

"Krystof," Mark said, trying to stand, but falling back against the cotton bales, pushing them further against the wall. "He's Conrad's mole in Customs. He told Chadwick there was a change in plan, just before Hollis was taken."

"I've got to go, Lily," Duncan said, after a few rapid exchanges with Mark about others involved and their current locations. He grabbed up Nick's gun, searched through George's pockets for car keys as she told him about the alternate route out of the cellar, and warned him about Andromeda likely hiding somewhere along the way. After one last, swift kiss, he left.

TURNING BACK TO MARK, she started to kneel next to him and gasped, backing away quickly from the skeletal hand of Jack Hudson raised as if in greeting. Mark looked over his shoulder and jumped as well. He lashed out with the flashlight, knocking the arm out of its brittle socket and into the far corner of the room.

"Asshole."

"My flight or fight response will never be the same," Lillian said.

"I think they're both spot on, myself." Another groan

wrenched out of him as she pulled his hand away, cut his sleeve open and looked closely at the wound, "Fuck, that hurts! But at least I'm alive, —Ah!" he gasped again, "None of us would be if you hadn't summoned the fire spirits."

"You've been hanging out with Nick too long. You never used to swear so much," she tried to tease, her voice shaking now, as she motioned for him to press on the wound again. She pulled off her jacket and ripped the buttons open on her blouse.

"What—?"

"Fucking ironic, isn't it?" She smiled at him through the half-light, tearing the thin cotton fabric into several strips. He laughed, but she was sorry she made the reference, seeing the regret again in his green eyes. His pupils were dilated, softening their effect.

"I know you didn't do it for me, Lillian, but thank you."

"Of course, I did it for you, Mark. We were all in trouble. I'm just grateful I thought of it and had that flamethrower of a lighter in my pocket."

Her hands trembling, she held the flashlight and looked closely at the wound again. From what she could see in the shaking light, the wound appeared superficial, but still had to hurt like hell, and sympathy pains streaked through her thighs at the sight. Like her and Duncan, he had several small burns on his arms, some already rising up in painful blisters.

He reached out and pulled the gold chain and directed the beam of his flashlight towards the medal, and despite his pain, laughed.

"Are you giddy from blood loss or something?"

"The day after Jameson met with you at Leighton's, Scott and I were at his office and Scott asked what he thought of you. All Jameson would say was 'Saint Michael defend us'." Holding the medal, Mark gave a perfect imitation of Neal Jameson's gravelly Irish brogue. "We didn't get the reference at the time."

Men, she thought. She smacked his hand and he obligingly dropped the medal safely down her cleavage.

"Shut up, and don't make me sorry I sacrificed my shirt for you."

"You know I am, sincerely, very happy for you both."

She remembered the look in his eyes when he kissed her the day before. "Thank you."

"Scott told me he loved you, was working on a divorce and planned to propose to you."

She felt a blush start to rise in her cheeks and was glad for the darkness. "That's the reason you avoided me the other night?"

He reached up and stroked her cheek, "The *only* reason."

"So chivalry is not dead."

"No…" She could hear the smile in the long, drawn-out word. "Not exactly dead… perhaps gasping for breath. I knew it before …well, before I came back from Kingston."

She thought back to the afternoon when she closed the door and surprised him with the news they were alone. His hand stilled and he cupped her cheek in his hand. "I'm sorry?"

"I'm not. How could you have told me or rejected me that wouldn't have hurt?" she covered his hand with her own and met his eyes, remembering.

"Brilliant, back to chivalry. A modern take on 'discretion being the greater part of valor'?"

"Truly valorous, Mark. You should be knighted," she pulled away from him to get busy on the bandage again.

"Speaking of valorous, it sounds like you finally found information about Brendan, some Conrad had not even heard, apparently."

"I did?" she asked, confused.

"You don't remember? From what you told Conrad earlier, it sounded as though you'd read letters or his journal."

"I only remember being very angry when Conrad said something about Brendan and then that strange, breathless thing happened again…"

Tying a last strip of cloth around his arm, she told him what she had learned about the connection through Lilién's diaries, her still vivid recollection of Thomas, and how it may have inspired her actions when they were at the cottage.

"I don't believe she *could* have made me do something I

did *not* want to do. I did want to, Mark, but I did not *intend* to come to you that night." Impulsively, she leaned forward and kissed him, intimately, for the last time.

"Well, I suppose I do know some French after all, don't I?" she whispered a long moment later. "We'll just say that was from Lilién."

He looked searchingly into her eyes and asked, "Merveilleux, Grand-mere?" adding something she did not understand at all.

At her suspicious expression, he whispered, "Means 'marvelous, would you like to do it again, Grandma?'"

She rolled her eyes and left him to search for the statuette. "I suppose I should be the one apologizing to you now…that is, if *you* feel used…?"

He was quiet for so long, she stopped and looked at him. Not exactly smiling, still, his eyes danced. "There are so many rejoinders I could make to your lovely query —"

"Never mind, Mr. Bond. Here," she said, presenting the Moreau, "a token for you, a very lucky token since she helped us today. I'll even restore her for you if you want."

"Good God," Mark said, and she wasn't sure if it was because of its value or the condition. "She's perfect, just the way she is. Where on earth…?"

"Hollis's shop. He said he paid ten dollars at a recent jumble sale and passed the bargain on to me, so don't feel guilty. Now, let's get out of here and find some fresh air." She gathered up the remaining strips of her shirt and stuffed them in her pocket and tucked the lucky courtesan back into her backpack. "We should check on … on the others."

Mark put his hand on her shoulder. "Help me up and I'll check, and then we'll go back through the tunnel."

They finally escaped the close company of Jack Hudson and went out into the foyer. Conrad was unconscious and breathing noisily. As they passed George, she shivered.

The old candles still burned, clean, pale yellow wax dripped down over the aged browned tapers, while one sitting slightly aslant burned more brightly, but created wisps of black smoke, adding to the acrid haze in the room.

"They must not have covered 'stop, drop, and roll' in his school," Mark crouched down to check for a pulse.

Nick groaned.

"Too bad." He wiped his hand on his pants and struggled to his feet again.

Loud scraping noises from the tunnel sent them both stumbling back into the shadows until she heard Andromeda's shaking voice.

"Lil-Lillian?"

Chapter Thirty-One

A Very Troublesome Elephant Indeed

ONLY HOURS SINCE HER descent into the cellar, but to Lillian, it might have been days. Hot sunlight felt disorienting and did little to penetrate the chill settling in her core as she sat on the low rock wall near the cemetery. Neal and local police arrived and took charge of the scene.

Andromeda had remained hidden in the cottage loft while waiting for Neal and led him down the tunnel. Already alerted by Lillian's text and Esther's call, he was already on his way to St. George's when he received her frantic, incoherent call and arrived at Glendevon just as Duncan scrambled out of the tunnel.

Paramedics arrived, the first team rushed Conrad and Nick off to the hospital and a second tended to Mark, Lillian, and Duncan's injuries before hauling George and the remains of Jack Hudson to the morgue. Firefighters went in to make sure all the web fires had burned themselves out, and not taken hold in the old wooden rafters

Duncan left it to the Coast Guard to apprehend Hugh and search the Fleur. It had been Hugh, not Nick, who helped himself to the currency on the *Jupiter* and gotten in way beyond his depth with George.

Lillian sat in the shade of a spindly flame tree, petals from its vivid orange flowers littering the lane, the grass, and headstones beneath, with Andromeda to one side of her and Esther, who somehow managed to procure a large mug of strong, hot tea for her, on the other. And Hollis, released from his hot but brief imprisonment in the trunk of Conrad's vehicle, was fine and as feisty as ever, complaining to the ladies that absolutely nothing had been found at Elliott Cove. Certainly nothing as interesting as old bales of cotton or a skeleton.

"I am absolutely jealous and so proud of you! You must come and tell me all about it!" Hollis had embellished the history of Elliott Cove, to try to keep Conrad away from Glendevon, "But, I never thought to be taken hostage!" the old man added merrily. "A good long visit tomorrow and a great deal of rum, my dear, that's the ticket!"

Soon after, Hollis and Esther drove Andromeda home to help her face her parents before she might be seen on the evening news. While Duncan was being interviewed by local authorities, Mark sat beside her, his arm freshly bandaged. The bright sunlight revealed just how pale he was.

"You should have gone to the hospital."

"They cleaned it up, said it was just a graze," he said, shrugging. "What about you? That was a nasty blow George gave you," he reached out and gently touched her cheek.

"I'm all right," she answered. "And thank you …"

"If any one of us hadn't done what we did, we'd all be dead right now. Remember that when you have your nightmares or your conscience troubles you," he said. Pausing he glanced away and Lillian followed his gaze. Neal and Agent Chadwick were approaching with a Bermudian police officer, who was removing handcuffs on his belt before stopping in front of Mark.

"Speaking of teamwork," he added, leaning close to whisper, "don't panic," before Neal pulled him away from her. She understood what was happening, but it didn't change her outrage when the young officer roughly pulled Mark's arms back to cuff him. He winced from the pain, and Lillian had seen that tight-lipped, hard-eyed look of controlled anger on his face too many times to believe it was all an act.

"What—?" she cried, jumping down from the wall, jarring every aching bone and muscle in her body, "Neal, what's going on?"

Neal didn't acknowledge her, but walked with the group to the police car, while the officer gave what sounded like a short version of the Miranda rights, citing "offenses to the Crown" and threats to the safety and security of the island.

"DAD?"

"Lily? What is it?"

She hadn't succeeded in keeping the quaver out of her voice. Duncan was still being interviewed and Mark was taken off in police custody, and she felt suddenly very alone and vulnerable. She also needed to tell him what had happened in case the events should make the evening news in the States.

My God, Lily," her father said, shaken, "I thought… I meant to send you *away* from that danger, not right into the middle—"

"I know, Dad," she interrupted, admitting to knowing more about the situation than she had told him. "I could have avoided this, but…" her voice shook, and she paused, thinking about all she had discovered on this trip, "I found something."

"What? About Brendan?"

She read the letter she had snatched from Hudson's grasp and promptly forgotten until she pulled the phone out of her underwear only minutes before.

It was a confession, signed by a jury of Hudson's true peers, four crewmembers of the *Kendal*, who knew without a doubt he killed not only Brendan but the two men Brendan had entrusted to hide the treasury. The first signature under the description of the crime, the proof and the sentence to be carried out, was Captain Roderick Shaw. An astonishing testament to the regard Brendan's men and commanding officer had for him, but no information about Brendan himself or the trunks from Fleur-de-Lys.

They were both quiet a moment, absorbing the impact of the revelations.

"Are you sure you're okay, sweetheart?" her father asked.

"I'm fine. Duncan will be done talking with police soon, and we'll go back to Leighton's…together." During her father's silence, she realized she had forgotten to mention a few significant events. Looking down at her ring, she added, "He's not married, Dad. And we are together. We're engaged."

LATE IN THE AFTERNOON, police officers finished their work, and she and Duncan remained at Glendevon, rejecting offers from the others for a ride to either Rosecrest or Leighton's. Duncan kept the keys to the Opel SUV, the Andrastus Shipping vehicle, George had used to kidnap him that afternoon, reasoning he had as much right to drive it around Bermuda as anyone else in the organization.

At Leighton's, Mae took one look at them and delivered a generous evening version of her afternoon tea, as well as her first aid kit, to Lillian's room.

The scent of lemon body wash would always remind her of their first shower together, where they gingerly tended to one another's wounds; she to the raw grooves around his wrists where the cuffs cut so deeply, he to her cuts and scrapes and burns. To hide the distress, she joked about his black eye looking roguish, just as the ladies at Rosecrest had described him the night before. When he gently smoothed a soapy hand over her cheek swollen and bruised from George's last blow, he didn't smile or tease.

After dabbing on first aid cream and re-applying bandages to his wrists, they lay together still wrapped in towels, too exhausted to do anything beyond lie in each other's arms, talking quietly until drifting off to sleep.

INSTEAD OF FLYING HOME the next day as planned, Lillian and Duncan remained at Leighton's. With no new guests due for several days, Mae had extended Lillian's stay, pleased for Leighton's to play a role in the excitement that was more effective an advertisement than anything Trip Advisor or Lonely Planet could highlight on their website or in their annual guide.

The Royal Gazette covered the events very thoroughly. Neither she nor Duncan had noticed when a photographer had taken the picture of them which illustrated the morning news, but it immediately changed their plans regarding the kids. Not passionate, but every bit as intimate as their first published photograph, there could be no subterfuge or gradual introductions now.

In the light shade of the spindly flame tree at the edge of the cemetery, Duncan sat on the low rock wall holding her tightly, the moment they had been reunited. Hair a mess, tear tracks in the light dusting of soot on her face, burns and scrapes still red and raw, streaks of dirt, soot, and blood on the blue tank top and the once white Capri's. And the engagement ring in full view.

As she and Duncan sat poolside at Leighton's she called the kids. She introduced the subject by asking Ryan about what he had seen of the articles or pictures.

"It said you whacked somebody with a statue and started a fire, with spider webs!" he answered excitedly. "Very cool, Mom!"

"Cool?" she heard Miranda in the background and Lillian asked Ryan to turn on the speaker of his phone so she could talk to both at once. "*Cool?*" Miranda repeated. "Are you okay, Mom?"

"I'm fine, sweetheart, and you know …well, you know I'm not… that I don't normally…" Duncan, watching her and listening to the one-sided conversation, looked at her strangely, "…condone violence…that was a very …well, a *very* unique situation."

"It was still cool! They should add that spider web thing to a video game!"

Changing the subject while he still thought she was cool, she said, "I'm thinking of doing something else very cool."

"What?" Miranda asked.

"Marrying my friend Duncan."

"*I knew it!*" Lillian moved the phone away from her ear when Miranda let out a whoop. Duncan had no trouble interpreting that sound and smiled.

After a long pause, Ryan said, "Oh."

"What do you think?"

Another long pause before he said, "Grandpa likes him."

"Yes, he does." If Ryan trusted anyone's judgment, it was Grandpa's. "What happened to Miranda? Did she faint?"

"Yeah, right." The idea of Miranda fainting was comical, to say the least. "She's run off to tell everybody. Will I have to wear another dumb tuxedo?"

"A tuxedo?" she asked, startled into laughing, wishing she could grab him to her, ruffle his hair and smooch him till he squirmed. Duncan made a face and gave double thumbs down. "We haven't talked about such details yet, but it seems Duncan shares your opinion of tuxedos."

"Cool."

MARK, CLEARED OF WRONGDOING and freed from police custody, arrived with Neal to debrief while Mae served her usual afternoon tea. Neal brought along Kimberly, the enthusiastic young archivist, who had made a discovery of her own.

Continuing to search for *clues*, she told them, her persistent questions to her supervisor about Brendan and the *Kendal* only received vague, increasingly nervous answers. Suspicious, as soon as she had the chance, she snooped, as she put it, until she found the box.

The large gray clamshell storage box contained an extensive collection concerning the *Kendal* and her crewmembers, including documents from John Hudson's trial. The testimony of Lieutenants Carter and Paulson told the story of the last moments of Brendan's life.

Clambering over the starboard side rails, they stopped at the sight of Brendan fallen on the deck and Hudson standing above him, the gun still in hand. Each testified they were only saved from the same fate by the shifting of the ship on the reef and the collapse of the aft mast which sent the gun flying out of Hudson's grasp, and caught him in its tangle of rigging.

Paulson cried during his testimony, asking the judge why

the mast hadn't fallen just moments earlier. Why couldn't they have arrived just seconds sooner? The judge's words were recorded and made Lillian cry as well. *Why? The answer to why, son, is known only to God and we cannot address the Lord's reasons for our fates and destinies here. I see convincing evidence, however, of a young man bearing a hell of a burden in the most difficult of situations, endeavoring to protect passengers, crew, and cargo in his care. His efforts were undone, and his life cut short brutally and most unfairly by the forces of nature and one man's greed.*

Acting Captain Bonneau had entrusted his lieutenants Carter and Paulson to transport the crates and boxes from the ship to the rendezvous point at Barry Road. Alerted by young seaman Thomas Crawford on Brendan's orders, Remy St. Clair and David Blythe, well known as local dock hands and for their involvement in smuggling in and out of St. George's, chose the hiding place and secured the cargo. St. Clair and Blythe were found shot dead near Glendevon House several hours later. Home to the officers of the *Kendal* and also owned by Buchanan and MacGregor, the house, from attics to cellars and outbuildings had all been thoroughly searched, but except for recent violence done to the wine cellar, the report cited no sign of suspicious activity.

The search for the cargo, never specifically referred to as "treasury", was wide but discreet, the results of the trial and search were given to Charles Allen, United States Consul and the new, short-term Confederate agent, Norman Walker having left the island before the trial ended.

Cabinet Minister Perkins did not protest the disappearance of his cargo beyond a token display of umbrage. Hudson's accusation of his filching was part of the record, and loose coin had already been discovered in the shallows around the reefs, not far from the beach near Barry Road. Because he had left the ship at Ireland Island, Cabinet Minister Lowell had had no knowledge of later events. With his wife and newborn son, he left the island for England before the trial was even underway.

Hudson was acquitted of Brendan's murder as there was not enough evidence to prove he intended to shoot Brendan, the destruction of the ship and falling debris could have caused Hudson to discharge his weapon accidentally. There was nothing tying him to the deaths of the two smugglers.

The last article speculated about Jack Hudson's mysterious disappearance from the island.

"But nothing, *nothing*," Mark said, "about the location of that cargo, nor his personal belongings."

"Or what happened to Brendan himself," Lillian sighed, sitting back and rubbing her temples. "I know Hudson killed him, but where is his body? He's not in the family cemetery at Fleur-de-Lys where he belongs. If he's buried somewhere, there must be a record."

She saw Neal and Mark exchange a look, and then Neal drew one last paper out of a file and handed it to her, a copy of an old ledger for the Grenadier Lane Cemetery. One of the last names to be entered was Brendan Bonneau.

LILLIAN WAS NOT SURPRISED to see that Brendan's grave was not far from the rock wall where she had sat the day before. Leaf litter, debris from the storm and petals from the flame tree covered the grass around the old gravesite.

Even before telling her of the discovery, Neal began the process for disinterment. Which, he said, was being expedited by a government who wanted to come out in all ways as good guys in a story already gathering too much media attention for their liking.

That night she woke in a state of deep contentment. Moonlight reflecting off the swimming pool created sparkling eddies that coursed along the deep blue walls of her room as images from her dreams coursed through her mind in a confusing jumble of memories from the past few days.

Fluttering candlelight and the golden fleur-de-lys on Lilién's diary and Thomas's dirty blond hair tossed back his crystal gray eyes. Brendan, tall and handsome in his uniform. Hollis in his battered old headlamp stepping down into the dark, cedar-lined room. Wine bottles exploding as she opened the first door in the Glendevon cellar and Andromeda's screams and the rattle of her beaded braids. Jack Hudson's grinning presence, the reassuring strength of Mark's arms around her.

No, not just her own memories, she thought, sitting up. Brendan, a living, breathing Brendan in a full, formal uniform of a United States naval officer, right before the wine bottles exploded, he turned towards her, a beautiful smile on his handsome face.

White sheers luffed at the window and she felt the breeze waft gently across her brow. She knew there was a mischievous swagger in the regard of the spirit hovering near.

DUNCAN DIDN'T ASK HOW Lily woke the next morning *knowing* where the trunks were located, he didn't have to after witnessing the incident with the diary their first night together, not to mention the change that overcame her when she confronted Conrad with facts about Brendan Bonneau she could never have known. She woke him, just after sunrise, freshly showered and fully dressed, and told him they were returning to Glendevon.

Under the steady gaze of the gray cat once again on the gatepost, Lillian and Duncan went back to the little limestone cottage, through the tunnel into the cellars of Glendevon. Most of the cobwebs and Hudson's skeleton were gone, only the ravaged and scorched cotton bales and the old tarpaulin remained.

Now, in the more thorough illumination of hurricane lanterns borrowed from Leighton's, he watched her search along the walls for gaps in the mortar and behind the wooden door frame. The camp shirt with its rolled-up sleeves, blue jeans and running shoes she wore were much better suited to venturing into underground dens and warrens. She was all business, but part of his mind was still more than a little preoccupied with their lovemaking of the night before.

Armed with one of Mae's old brooms instead of a crowbar, she brushed away the last fragments of web and knocked out some crumbling bits of mortar, but no loose bricks or levers were to be found.

"*Nothing!*"

Startled out of his reverie by the anger in her voice, it took him a moment to respond.

"Impossible."

She looked up at him, a questioning smile lightening her expression.

"You don't have anyone with guns after you today, Lily, relax." He nodded towards the foyer, where he hung the lantern he carried on a substantial wooden peg stuck in one of the ceiling beams. "Tell me about your dream again."

They sat on the stone steps and she slowly and thoroughly recounted her dreams.

"Was there anything in the dream that did *not* happen, or happened differently than you remember?"

She nodded slowly, her brow furrowed in concentration. "Brendan, of course, and the only thing that exploded was Andromeda," she laughed at the memory but stopped abruptly, "… the bottles in the wine cellar were already broken…" He saw her eyes staring at the old lantern across the room as though the golden flame still burned.

She stood and went to the wine cellar. Brick niches with shelves for the bottles lined the top half of the room, while heavy wooden brackets held the larger banded, oaken casks, all empty, and shards of thick green and brown glass littered the floor.

Duncan held the lantern and Lillian swept away the remnants of cobwebs at the beams and edges where brick met wooden frames, searching for any gap in the mortar, any clue at all. Within moments she found the old lever easily, hidden behind a loose brick exactly like the one in the Hunter's Wharf Warehouse.

Duncan pulled down slowly, not wanting to jar the old mechanisms, expecting to hear or see the signs of movement along one of the cellar walls. Their eyes met in surprise when a trap door shifted in the floor nearby, broken glass and grit sifting onto surfaces below.

After sweeping the broken glass away from the trapdoor, they lifted it away. A cool draft brought the sharp scent of cedar wafting up from the hold.

Crouching next to the opening, Lillian held a lantern to illuminate the space below. A rough-cut plank ladder, rungs attached with equally rough pegs led the way down. Lillian tested her weight on the first rung.

"Careful," Duncan said, expecting rotted wood or rusted fasteners to give way after so long. The air was cool, but with no odors of damp or mildew, or even dusty age pervading the cellar above, now growing darker as she descended slowly with the lantern.

He followed her down. The room was paneled with cedar planks and was equal in size of the cellar room above but with a much lower ceiling. Small barrels, casks, and crates were stacked haphazardly against the walls. In the center was another tarpaulin draped mound.

For the sake of documentation, he began recording video before they had even opened the trapdoor. He placed his phone on a crate where it would capture everything without being intrusive.

"No cobwebs," she said, looking into a shadowy corner, "just the way Hollis described the room in the warehouse when it was found. No air flow, or, thank God, dampness."

Together, they lifted the tarp away. Two days before she had encountered a skeleton, but he knew what they would find this morning.

"Identical to Lilién's," she whispered, kneeling beside the larger two, running her hand over the wood and leather surface, tracing the tarnished brass initials for both Brendan Aubert Bonneau and Leah Desjardins Bonneau above latches firmly secured to elaborately engraved escutcheon plates. The third trunk sat slightly askew and was smaller and more utilitarian than the family chests, scarred with deep scratches and rub marks, with short handles of thick, coarse rope at either end.

"Brendan's sea chest," they said at the same instant.

Duncan crouched beside her as she paused, hands open on the rough wooden surface, the lamplight enhanced the glow of her tanned skin against the ice-blue shirt, strands escaping from her pinned up hair. The impromptu style revealed the now colorful bruise along the left side of her face caused by George's vicious backhand. His jaw clenched, and he felt the pain radiate through his own battered face at the sight.

So close, and so simple to reach out and unbuckle the thick canvas belts that held the chest closed but still she paused.

"He wanted you to find them, Lily."

"I know."

Without further hesitation, she unbuckled the belts and they opened the lid together.

On the top of a jumble of clothing and personal effects was an officer's log book. Not the large blue official record she had seen at the Archives, but black, clothbound and bulging with pages filled with Brendan's bold, scrawling handwriting, as well as notes and letters folded up inside. Lillian turned quickly to the final entry and read aloud:

> March 3, 1865, near Bermuda: If our mission had not been a triumph to now, I would necessarily classify this entire effort a debacle. With Captain Shaw ill and no surgeon aboard. I am now Acting Captain, with an acting first officer in the brig for trying to shoot said Acting Captain in the back, and very nearly alerting the entire North Atlantic Blockading Squadron to our presence behind their lines.
>
> Hudson, drunk on the Captain's favorite apricot brandy, has been kept in irons. He woke in a frightful temper this morning, a blazing hangover no doubt aggravated by Paulson's blow that had knocked him out, as well as the coal smoke and stifling heat of the hold before the tarpaulins were pulled. Shaw

will deal with him in St. George's.

In addition, indications as of sunset are for heavy weather by morning.

Inbound journey smooth. In my old uniform, running up the Stars and Stripes to pass through the Roads and up the James. I felt melancholy as we neared the embankment where Jems and my shipmates from the Congress were hurriedly interred on that night three long years ago.

Reaching our rendezvous point, we were kept waiting hours past the appointed time for the "president" and his cabinet to arrive. During this time Captain Shaw endeavored to hide the serious nature of his condition and finally, the politicians arrived.

Discovering I was a Southerner amongst the primarily British crew, I was taken to task for being a dirty profiteer and not acting for the good of the Cause. Considering we had braved traveling through enemy territory to respond to their urgent plea for assistance, I felt this reaction was remarkably ungracious.

I gave my word of honour I would keep our cargo safe, if it be in my power to do so, until it reaches its rightful place. I was astounded when he proceeded to authorize loading, his distrust of my motives, or perhaps the honour I swore upon, very clear on his face. Yet only hours later we were smuggling cargo of significant importance to the Confederate States of America down the James River and under the very nose of the blockading squadron.

Weariness and proximity to freedom, I expect, have made me incautious on this, my last journey to Bermuda, and I will write no more until our mission is complete, by which time the war will be well and truly over.

As she read, Duncan examined the crates and casks, each of them sealed up tight and extremely heavy. That it was indeed the Confederate Treasury, Brendan's journal was confirming with each sentence. For Lily's sake, he wanted to seal it back up in the cellar and walk away. Such a historic discovery would create a nationwide, if not worldwide, furor. Speculation and judgments about Brendan's character would certainly follow.

The distraction of this discovery, its potential worth, and impact on Civil War historians everywhere, did nothing to keep the goose flesh from rippling over his skin at the sound of Lily's voice. Duncan was sure she could in no way prevent this channeling, her own voice once again imbued with a softly southern inflection, a masculine emphasis on certain words, and the playful impudence of Brendan Bonneau apparent in some of his entries. He didn't interrupt her when he went to the surface to make calls.

Over the incessantly tiresome objections of cabinet minister Perkins, I made for the Dockyards to secure medical care for Captain Shaw. As a British naval officer, his best and closest care is at the hospital at Ireland Island, not to mention the urgency to secure Mrs. Lowell to land and a midwife's care quite obvious. Stoic though she was, her pains intensified rapidly, the birth of her child clearly imminent.

I must admit I am confounded as to why our changed destination on Bermuda concerned Perkins in the least. With heavy weather approaching, I was prepared to heave to in Great Sound until the following morning, but he ordered me to honour my pledge to deliver the treasury to St. George's without delay. I have sent young Thomas ahead, and he will ensure that Remy and David are at the rendezvous point to meet Lieutenants Carter and Paulson (entertainingly inept as they can often be, are loyal without exception and without question), otherwise, my not so well thought out plan will topple like so many dominoes.

Despite our best efforts and Sanderlin's capable piloting on our unusual approach to the northeast, the weather turned at precisely the most critical moment of our journey, and we soon found ourselves being pushed closer towards the reefs. The storm intensified over the course of the next two hours and *Kendal* foundered."

The last line was barely legible, scrawled as it was with too much ink sinking into the page.

I hope Thomas has better luck than we this night. I passed the time by hauling passenger and crew luggage to the port side aft deck, where Kendal rode low, jutting hard against one of the reefs holding her pinioned.

And cursing Jack Hudson with every breath. Hudson had escaped from the hold and stolen one of the lifeboats to make his way to shore. Last seen by Paulson, rowing towards St. George's in the gray, pre-dawn light, he left only one lifeboat, forcing me to order the evacuation of cargo first, something which went against all training and every instinct. Fortunately, depth was shallow, shore not far and the crew acted with a speed and efficiency rarely before exhibited, returning for our five passengers before the ship began to suffer much damage.

The only way the ship would be salvaged was in pieces, heavy gusts and churning seas pushed her hard against the rocks, the foremast now lay crumpled like paper on the deck, along with a tangle of spars and rigging that had missed me by inches.

Ducking into my cabin again I wiped the rain from my face, which alone helped me feel a bit less soaked. Would I ever be dry again? Was it only just hours since I finished writing in my log book? Now that simple routine exercise seems like a distant memory. I wanted to make a final entry before leaving the ship for the last time but remembered it was in my sea chest that went with the first shipment hauled by Carter and Paulson to be hidden away with the treasury chests by Remy and David. I will, then, make my final notations about our experiences from the comfort and warmth of Glendevon House tonight.

Where had those characters chosen to hide everything? I couldn't help smiling at their antics. Still, I know the Treasury, along with my own belongings, will be stored safely and for now, that is all that matters to me. The only clue they had given me was that I would surely know it was the place by the mess they would leave behind. I confess I am not even tempted to speculate about their meaning.

Once my duty is complete, I will report to Shaw, formally resign my post as first officer and go home. Home to whatever remains of Fleur-de-Lys, and home to Arabella. I can picture her, looking up at me with those eyes of hers... Suddenly, intensely, my heart aches for her, and I crave the warmth and light-hearted happiness we knew our one blissful night together. Even with all I have lost in the course of this war, what we have found is no small consolation. I know I am a lucky man.

I left my cabin and made my way down the passage towards the crew cabins through knee deep water. The ship tilted sharply and, bracing myself against the portside bulkhead, I waited till she settled again. A rumble, like cargo shifting in the hold, came from a part of the ship where there should be nothing to make such a sound.

As I turned to make my way back towards the cabin Cabinet Minister Perkins had shared with Sanderlin for the journey, another rumble was quickly followed by a scream that made my hackles rise.

"Who's there?" I shouted, pulling open the door.

Hudson, swearing and grimacing in pain, was pinned between the bulkhead and berth.

"Jack! What the hell are you doing here?"

I waded in and pulled the wreckage from him. Hudson wrenched away and began grasping at and rummaging through the flotsam, enraged, searching every corner of the cabin. Odd, tarpaulin wrapped bundles floated around him, hindering his every move.

"What are you doing, Jack—"

Again, the ship lurched forcefully into the reef. Both of us braced ourselves and flinched at the screech of twisting steel and splintering wood. Resuming his search, Hudson paused only to swipe away the blood streaming from a gash on his forehead.

"Time to get off the ship, Jack," I called out, trying to ignore the steadily rising water. If Hudson was back, that meant a lifeboat was back. With the rest of the passengers and crew safely off the ship, I was free to

leave.

On his own mission and paying no heed to me or the ship breaking apart around us, Hudson continued his frenzied search. I turned and made my way back up to the deck.

Dawn was now breaking and so was the storm. The wind had lessened, the sky lightened. I heard shouts and saw Carter and Paulson waving at me from the lifeboat, not one hundred yards from the ship.

"Where is it?"

I swung around in time to see the spar on the aft mast break away. I scrambled up the tilted deck, and ran forward, just out of range of the spar and its tangle of rigging. I knew the main mast would come down with the next hard swell.

"The gold, goddamn it! Where is it?" Hudson was still screaming at me, unaware of anything but the missing treasury. "What the hell did you do with it?"

"Moved, safely ashore. And only the men on shore know where it is."

"And you!"

"No, Jack. Remy and David secured the Treasury. I won't know where it is until I meet up with them." I shook my head. "What the hell does it matter? Wherever it is, it doesn't belong to either of us. It belongs to the government. Let's go!"

"Which government is that, traitor?" I saw Hudson raise the gun, and too late, I remembered Sanderlin had taken possession of the damn thing after the incident in the hold.

"Excellent time to mutiny." I stopped myself before raising my hands to the son of a bitch, but did take a step back, sorry the decks weren't loaded with the usual cotton bales I could dodge behind should Hudson pull the trigger again. The real question was when Hudson got his hands on the gun. Before the cabin was submerged meant the powder was likely dry, or after, when it was more likely to squirt seawater than fire a bullet. "I relinquish my command most willingly, Jack. The ship is yours."

Still glaring at me, Hudson did not acknowledge my attempt at levity.

"Get off the ship, Jack. The war is over, the ship is gone—just go!"

"And leave the gold Perkins has been filching from one of the crates for the entire trip to you? Where is it?"

"What?" I shouldn't be surprised, remembering the man's peevish complaints and general shiftiness. "Probably in his pockets, although it'd be hard to tell with all the flab he carries around. If you find it, by all means, help yourself."

I turned and took two steps towards the bridge. Over wind and sea, the groans of the dying ship and far off hails from Carter and Paulson, I could hear the unmistakable sound of the revolver's hammer being cocked open, and stopped, resigned and angry once again, I was caught between duty and the noble Cause, and greed, this time the selfish greed of one ignorant, jealous, drunken lout. This moron was going to kill me for a handful of gold coins just when I was finally freed from the burden of fighting two wars, days from returning home, home to Arabella and Fleur-de-Lys.

I'm sorry.

The words crossed my mind, hoping somehow to communicate to those I would leave behind, about so much I would leave undone, unresolved, unsaid. I heard Hudson screaming, heard the screech of metal and felt the shifting of the ship beneath my feet.

DUNCAN REALIZED LILY HAD not noticed his leaving or heard him return, absorbed as she was in reading Brendan's journal. He glanced down, noting the last line was an almost illegible report of the ship being driven onto the reefs in the spring squall. A common enough occurrence, Duncan thought, evidenced by the numerous shipwrecks around Bermuda. But, after reading the last entry, she remained perfectly still for a long while, her hands splayed across the pages, eyes closed, tears glistening on her lashes.

Duncan moved quietly to her side and waited until she finally moved, reaching for the dark wool uniform, creased from age and time, though the gold braid and buttons still shone brightly in the lamplight.

Still unaware of his presence, she held Brendan's coat, put her head down and cried.

LILY?" SHE FELT DUNCAN next to her. He brushed a strand

of hair away from her face and tears from her cheeks. She smiled at the concern in his eyes, realizing she must have again shown overt signs of her "impressions."

"United States Lieutenant Commander," Duncan said, "Four gold bands."

Inside Brendan's old ditty box were silk shirts and wool socks, most of them obviously worn and pulled off and thrown in the box haphazardly. She handled them gently, but they seemed to have survived the effects of age, sweat and sea water very well. A smaller box held shaving and toiletry items and sewing supplies. Tucked in the bottom beneath it all was a coarse linen bag.

Inside, in a separate oilcloth pouch, were several letters and documents. The first was a certificate declaring Brendan Aubert Bonneau a citizen of France. Lillian remembered reading that while American citizens caught aboard blockade runners would be treated as prisoners of war; foreigners were held for a short time and released. With his heritage and ability to speak fluent French, it made sense he would take that as his fictional nationality. A second, older and more worn certificate, Brendan's commissioning as a midshipman, signed by President James Buchanan in 1858.

Letters, not many, the last from his father Charles in late 1863. Folded inside a piece of coarse raw muslin was a pennant flag, and even as she unwrapped it, gooseflesh traveled along her arms, a flash memory of Thomas's Mississippi drawl and those direct gray eyes. "Raisin' a funny gold flag and deliverin' me into enemy hands." The flag itself was white, but shining braid around its edges framed a large, gold fleur-de-lys at its center.

A small red pouch jingled as she loosened the cord still cinched up tight. Inside were one gold coin and two brass keys, which obviously belonged to the trunks. She remembered Brendan's letter which had held the key not sent with Thomas. The same letter in which he had sent his Saint Michael's medal she wore now.

The coin, an 1862 Liberty Head double eagle, felt warm against her skin.

She slipped them back into the pouch and reached for Brendan's log book once again. Inside the front cover was a letter dated February 1865, an official communication drafted by the Confederate States Treasury Secretary George Trenholm to President Jefferson Davis. Lillian noted immediately the letter was written in Trenholm's hand and not through a clerk. *What was Brendan doing with this*, she thought, beginning to scan the contents.

"Oh my God!" she said aloud, finally looking up at Duncan, and then at the kegs and crates stacked against the back wall.

Moments later, Lillian heard voices in the cellar above and was not surprised to see Neal and Mark come down the ladder.

THE INEVITABLE PUBLICITY FOLLOWING the events and subsequent discovery at Glendevon put lengthy interviews and photographs of all of them on the front page of The Royal Gazette and newspapers, newsfeeds, and televisions around the world.

The amount of silver and gold discovered in the cellar may not have been much more taken through the blockade on many runners during the four years of war, to pay debts and purchase supplies, but still, the stockpile was substantial. The fifteen crates, boxes, and barrels contained a combination of ingots, bars, and coin with a current value of just over two million dollars. Far more valuable to historians would be the large collection of paperwork, which identified several Confederate spy networks operating within the Union, from the lowest tradesmen to those connected to President Lincoln's cabinet.

Ownership of the Treasury and historic archive was not a simple matter and would take time to resolve.

She knew Brendan would never have kept it for his own purposes, not to rebuild Fleur-de-Lys or to aid loved ones and neighbors. Lillian had no wish to claim it herself, but both

Duncan and Mark *told* her she would, each one suggesting causes which could be helped if she established a foundation. Even her father acknowledged her responsibility. In her control, he said, she could do a lot of good. Could she trust any other entity to do the same?

LILLIAN FELT STRANGE WATCHING herself descend through the trapdoor. The images swung wildly, causing her to feel almost seasick until the room came into focus. Lillian and Duncan were both within the frame as they uncovered the three trunks and Lillian knelt beside them.

A hazy green distortion wavered along the dark edge of the frame when she paused and laid her hands upon the sea chest. Lillian listened to herself read the journal and although she remembered reading the entries, had not noticed the subtle changes in her own voice. Lying in the big bed next to Duncan, she tried to rub the gooseflesh from her arms discreetly.

He noticed and whispered affectionately, "You *are* a creepy little thing, aren't you?"

She bit her lower lip and glanced over at him. *You have no idea.*

As she read, the camera took in Duncan's investigation, the cask he opened was in full view of the camera, his expression a clear indication that he was looking at the lost Confederate Treasury, even before he lifted a small canvas sack that rattled with the sound of heavy coin.

When she opened the red velvet pouch, the green light suddenly disappeared and a fresh wave of chills shivered over her as she remembered the 1862 double eagle, locked in a cellar for one hundred and fifty years, and yet warm when it fell from the pouch into her hand.

Chapter Thirty-Two

Eight Bells and All is Well

"I KNOW IT'S A lot to ask, sweetheart, and only if conditions permit. But it would mean an awful lot to me." Before leaving for Bermuda, so certain of her success, her father asked her to bring Brendan home via ocean passage rather than in the cargo hold of an airplane.

"They're dead. They don't matter," her father had once said about their ancestors. She knew her father now understood, and all involved believed it mattered a great deal how Brendan made his journey home and it should not be delayed for any reason.

Tom wanted to sail the *LilyRose* to Bermuda to do the honors, but the doctor declined to clear him for sea duty, especially coming on to hurricane season. "That …*yeoman*… tells me I'm still on the 'barnacle' list," he added disgustedly.

AFTER REVIEWING LONG RANGE weather forecasts, and assured that Brendan's prompt disinterment was approved, Duncan made Tom's request a reality in very short order.

The *Aurora*, a beautiful, fully stocked catamaran, would practically sail herself and with so many of the latest electronic features, Lillian didn't yet know how to operate them. She and Duncan could safely crew her alone together on a fast, three-day crossing.

They went aboard the night before getting underway and checked all equipment and rigging, despite the repeated reassurances of the hovering charter company representative, who was obviously used to less experienced bareboaters and those carrying less precious cargo.

EARLY ON THE MORNING of departure, Duncan and Mark, Neal and Hollis helped Brendan board the *Aurora*.

Brendan's mariner's presence was companionable and in no way intrusive or troubling. In an elegant teak coffin, draped with the modern flag of the United States of America, his journey home would be in a luxurious starboard stateroom, along with the two trunks from Fleur-de-Lys.

Once past the northern reefs, they hove to long enough to have breakfast and run through the safety check one more time before starting for Wilmington in earnest. She could almost hear her father's voice calling out his pre-sail checklist.

After years of forced separation, and the last days in Bermuda of nearly non-stop activity, the sail home was a welcome interval before the course of their lives took its new tack.

During the first clear, dark night they lay on the cockpit bench and searched for and pointed out constellations, and she thanked her father again for the instruction in celestial navigation. No piece of equipment could ever take its place, he told her. Now it was one more thing she and Duncan could share.

The sky was black velvet, the expanse so broad she could see the curve toward the horizon, and her father's words came back to her, *"Out on the sea at night, with the infinite power of the sea beneath you and the ultimate wonder of the universe as your rooftop..."*

Her father was not one for hyperbole. Ultimate wonder was not an overstatement, not at this moment, she thought. The stars so dense and so bright, the beauty of it all made her chest ache with gratitude for everything, *everything* which had brought the three of them to this time and place.

AS THEY NEARED THE Gulf Stream during midwatch on

the second night, high clouds to the northwest blotted out the stars and lightning began to flash in the distance. The wind increased steadily, swells grew deeper and the sea rougher.

Anticipating the possibility of weather at this point of the journey, they followed the protocols practiced earlier in the day. Duncan began reefing in the mainsail. And couldn't. Trying to extend it out or winch it in, nothing worked, and the catamaran was beginning to beat heavily against the churning water.

"I need to go out, Lily," Duncan shouted over the rain now pounding down on the hard Bimini top over their heads.

"No way, Captain," she shouted back, shaking her head but smiling reassuringly, already in rain gear, PFD, and harness and on her way to find the problem. "You're needed at the helm!"

She connected her tether to the port side lifeline and started forward with a brief prayer to both Brendan's aid and protection. Covering every possible scenario on a sailboat was not possible, but she was now familiar enough with the catamaran's rigging to know where to look for the problem.

She initially missed the movement of a traditional monohull like the *LilyRose*, however, she now fully appreciated the fact that catamarans do not heel in the wind. Even with the slashing rain and lightning flashes, the *Aurora* had lights enough to see the problem was a snag, two of the lines twisted around one another in a tangle around the mast, just within reach. Just within reach *if* she climbed onto the Bimini, braced herself on the boom, and stood on tiptoe.

Moving her tether to a stanchion at the base of the mast, she held tight and made sure of her footing while waiting through the pitch of a large swell. Between each step she waited to get her bearings, fighting a wave of seasickness and fear as the *Aurora* dipped and lurched.

Nothing can happen to me!

Not sure if it was as a prayer or command, the thought flew through her mind, knowing if anything did happen to her, her father would never forgive himself and it would once again taint the legacy of the man they worked so hard to discover these many months.

Wrapping one arm tight around the mast, she reached to pull the snagged line. Fingers barely touched, she needed to take one…more… step—

Her foot slipped.

Before she could even scream or grapple for the mast, her feet were on the deck.

And she was angry at Duncan for leaving the helm to help her, until she saw that he was still at the helm and the line was no longer snagged. By his expression, he was as stunned as she.

"I don't know!" she answered his question before he could call out to her and went to the manual mainsheet winch. Each turn now smoothly reefed the mainsail, and the turbulent pull of the wind subsided. Intending to go forward once again to check the lines, she went to gather up her tether and found it firmly attached to the cockpit bench.

Inside, the saloon was illuminated only by the running and masthead lights and soft glow of the instrument panel. Pulling off his dripping rain gear, Duncan turned to her.

"What happened, Lily?"

She slid onto the nav station bench, loosened the ties securing the hood of her jacket and pushed it off. Wind and rain buffeted against the hull and the Aurora now rode the swells almost gracefully.

She shook her head, trying to remember.

Three explanations existed, but she knew Duncan had not left the helm and she had not flown down and attached her tether to the cockpit bench stanchion.

She had felt strong hands on her waist for just a moment…hadn't she?

THEY REMAINED IN THE saloon through the storm, checking instrument readings and forecasts, listening to the weather broadcasts until the squall abated and the skies cleared once again near dawn. Duncan left Lily sleeping in the forward cabin and went out to adjust the sails and stand watch in the cockpit. Heaving-to was best during the squall and autopilot was great, but he never felt right leaving the helm unmanned for long.

Watching her absently pull off the wet hood when she had answered "I don't know…" pausing in mid-sentence with that look on her face, he knew. Tears had sparkled in her eyes, but she must be acclimating to the sensation because she didn't cry, or faint.

It had to be. There wasn't any other practical explanation.

He smiled at himself, setting his coffee down at the helm and wiping water off the cockpit bench. Duncan had heard about many and seen a few unusual phenomena in his work as an archeologist, but never what he witnessed during this week with Lily. And now he was accepting the presence of her ghostly uncle on their small crew as a practical explanation.

As long as it only happened to Lily, he thought, not so sure how he would handle having his own paranormal experiences. After a long look at the fog-shrouded western horizon, he sipped his coffee and glanced down at the instrument panel.

The autopilot was off.

He swore. Vehemently. At modern technology, at cheap manufacturers and himself. *Dammit!* They had checked everything regularly from the nav station instrument panel throughout the squall. As he reached for the helm, he saw their headings and location.

Perfectly on course and exactly where they should be, and he knew Lily's "look" was surely on his own face.

Duncan stood to attention, saluted the helm, and sat back to watch the sunrise.

Chapter Thirty-Three

Fair Winds and Following Seas

LILLIAN'S EXTENDED FAMILY AND friends old and new gathered at the family cemetery at Fleur-de-Lys to see Brendan Bonneau interred in the old mausoleum.

Mark waited in the deep shade of a tall tulip tree at the edge of the yard, taking the opportunity to watch Lillian from a distance, one last time.

By midnight he would be on a plane to London. Thank God, he thought, ready to be out of this heat and to get on with his life, his real life. At least he had been successful, which he had not believed would be possible, even a few short weeks ago.

Lillian seemed tireless in the wilting heat and oppressive humidity of the summer afternoon, wearing a dress of pale yellow matching the topaz in the necklace once worn by her great-great-great grandmother Lilién, of whom he had every reason to regard fondly.

She had wanted him to attend; in fact, she had stopped just short of insisting. It was a celebration in honor of her ancestors, ancestors she might never have known about if not for him. All said without the irony he might have expected, given the circumstances.

Even after the events in Bermuda, the fact that he had been on assignment for Britain's National Crime Agency was not public knowledge. He agreed, however, their suspicious co-worker should finally be told the truth.

Lillian caught sight of him and smiled. She took him arm

in arm and quietly re-introduced him to Vera. In the long silence that followed, Lillian laughed and excused herself. "I simply must tell Duncan that something has *finally* rendered Vera speechless."

"I *knew* there was something suspicious about you all along," Vera said, pointing a finger into his chest for emphasis. She glanced towards Lillian, adding, "Right about everything?"

He looked, too, and Lillian met his eyes for a moment before he turned back to Vera.

"Need to know, Vera."

Before she could press further, Lillian's daughter Miranda appeared to take him away and introduce him to their newly discovered family.

LILIÉN HAD MARRIED ADAM Stuart in the autumn of 1882, and at the age of forty, Lilién had given birth to a daughter, Serena. Lilién had died in 1914, at the age of 71.

At age seventy, while serving as a volunteer physician during World War I, Adam had died in England during the influenza epidemic in 1918. Neither he or their daughter were buried with Lilién in Easton. No one could be sure of her wishes, but after reading the journals and letters and learning the truth of what happened in 1861, to leave her alone in a public cemetery in Easton was not acceptable to any of them. Lilién would also be brought home and laid to rest in the quiet corner of the cemetery, to be reunited finally with her Wilson.

The day had cooled and the sun was filtering through the trees when she walked back to Fleur de Lys after she and Mark said goodbye. After promises to stay in touch, they held each other tightly for several moments. He kissed her cheek, and then he was gone.

Vera and Tony left earlier in the afternoon, on their way to a cool weekend retreat up to the mountains. She seemed somehow, well, deflated after learning the truth about Mark, so quiet Lillian was almost worried about her. Lillian couldn't help but wonder what Vera would latch onto next, with Mark out of the picture and Lillian and Duncan engaged. No doubt she would be back to her old self by the time they worked together on some future project.

Some future project at Voyages, with Duncan. She glanced over to where Duncan, Trey and her father sat talking, no doubt trading sea yarns that never seemed to grow old.

Ryan was climbing the big old oak trees near the old front entrance of Fleur-de-Lys. He'd made a friend, Barkley, about the same age and descended from another of the old local families. A handsome boy with dark auburn hair and blue eyes the color of star sapphires, he had a suggestion of that distinct Bonneau jawline. She would have to ask Neera how their families might be related.

Althea was resting at the house after the busy afternoon, and now Neera and Gilley, Chloe and Miranda were walking back to Petit Fleurs for the boys' bedtime. The way Drew snuggled in on Chloe's shoulder, Lillian had a feeling he would be sound asleep by the time he reached his bed. Taren was smitten with Miranda and had followed her like a shadow most of the day. Tonight, he was man enough to allow her to carry him home.

Speaking of smitten, Janet was near the fence near Jenny and Gabe, talking and laughing... with James. Gone was her cousin's suspicious disregard of family heritage, and if Lillian wasn't mistaken, Janet might just be added to their family tree before long.

Along with Grace. Her father had surprised them with an announcement the night before, at dinner. Not only were he and Grace to be married, when they weren't sailing the *LilyRose*, they would live in Easton, at the cottage.

So many occurrences that would never have happened if her father had not finally revealed his secrets and set her on course to discover what happened to Brendan Bonneau.

Tonight, after more of Althea's sweet potato pie, the Bonneau family would gather on the porch of Petit Fleurs and open the trunks for the first time since Brendan closed them in December of 1865.

She stopped in front of the mausoleum, looking at the new memorial plaque Gabe had installed early that morning.

Beloved Son and Brother

BRENDAN AUBERT BONNEAU
1838 – 1865

"No finer officer or braver man."

Lillian heard steps on the path and looked up as her father joined her. He set his arm over her shoulders and she wrapped an arm around his waist.

Above them, a large white pennant fluttered in the gentle evening breeze, the golden fleur-de-lys glinting in the setting sun.

His final journey complete, Brendan Bonneau was home.

Thank you for reading Brendan's Cross.

Cynthia Rinear was born and raised in Fairbanks, Alaska. She is the author of *The Family Tree* and is currently working on her next two novels, *The Rowan Tree* & *You Belong to Me.*

https://fb.me/authorCynthiaRinear

ACKNOWLEGEMENTS TO:

With utmost gratitude to my friend and "alpha" reader, Lella Mack, for critiquing chapters along the way. And, to beta readers Tina, Becky M., Julie, Robin, Becky H., Catherine, and Heidi, as well as members of the Fairbanks Community Writing Group. Feedback and new perspectives help so much.

The late-novelist Ardath Mayhar, who I met via snail mail when I signed up for the Writer's Digest Novel Writing Workshop back in 1997. Her detailed and instructive letters were direct about my weaknesses but very encouraging about my strengths, overall project, and goals.

Dr. Susan Langley, State Underwater Archaeologist for Maryland. We exchanged several emails, and she helped me with a better understanding of not only the conservation process, but tips I had never read before in all my research...like about the goldfish!

Charles Clausen, the Chesapeake Bay Maritime Museum's (1995) interim curator, who answered *very* early questions, and even provided copies of relevant chapters of one of his college texts on artifact conservation. Very helpful for getting Lillian busy in the conservation lab.

Sister Ann, at saintbrendan.org, with whom I traded several fun emails, and who answered questions about Saint Brendan's original and the more modern cross design.

Cover art: Virginia Artist Jerry Draper for the lovely image of the Saint Brendan's Cross used on the front cover. Pixabay website for the background and compass rose, and Wikipedia for the photo of the blockade runner *Ella and Annie*.

Permission to use quotes:

Farley Mowat: Susan Renouf, Literary Executor,
Farley Mowat estate 3/19/2018
Charles Maxwell Allen: Susan Wadsworth-Booth, Director,
Kent State University Press 5/3/2018

I am always interested in these details when finishing a book...

Inspiration & Research: The story has evolved beyond recognition from the first outlines. Most of the ingredients remain the same, though quantities of each have certainly been adjusted over time: A single mother with two kids, Bermuda, Civil War history, genealogical research, romance, maritime archeology, and sailing. Through many years when I couldn't dedicate much time or mental energy to writing, I was often indulging... I mean, researching. For anyone interested in such things, here are some of the best and most helpful resources on my book / video shelves:

Blockade Running:

Confederate Blockade Running through Bermuda
        Frank E. Vandiver
The Narrative of a Blockade Runner
        John Wilkinson
Running the Blockade
        Thomas E. Taylor
Never Caught - A True Story of Blockade Running
        Captain Roberts (C. Augustus Hobart-Hampton)
Blockade Days in St. Georges / About Bermuda Video
        Lt. Col Brendan Hollis, O.B.E., E.D.
Gray Phantoms of the Cape Fear
        Dawson Carr
Lifeline of the Confederacy
        Stephen Wise
The Confederate Navy – A Pictorial History
        Philip Van Doren Stern
Civil War History:
The Civil War – A Narrative
        Shelby Foote
The Civil War – a Film by Ken Burns
        Geoffrey C. Ward, Ric Burns, and Ken Burns
Team of Rivals – The Political Genius of Abraham Lincoln
        Doris Kearns Goodwin

Diary from Dixie
        Mary Chesnut
The Civil War Diary of a Southern Woman
        Sarah Morgan
The March to the Sea and Beyond
        Joseph T. Glatthaar
The Last Shot
        Lynn Schooler
Maritime Archeology & Archeology / Artifacts & Conservation:
Lives in Ruins   Marilyn Johnson
Adventures of a Sea Hunter   James P. Delgado
The Lost Wreck of the Isis   Robert D. Ballard

Bermuda:

Tea with Tracey - The Woman's Survival Guide to Bermuda
        Tracey Caswell
The Deep (novel and movie)
        Peter Benchley

Civil War Fiction:

Gone With the Wind   Margaret Mitchell
Cold Mountain   Charles Frazier
The Killer Angels   Michael Shaara
The Fires of Pride / The Sands of Pride   William R. Trotter
In the Fall   Jeffrey Lent

Online Courses:

Shipwrecks and Submerged Worlds
        Future Learn / University of Southampton
Archeology
        Future Learn / University of Reading
Antiquities Trafficking and Art Crime
        Future Learn / University of Glasgow

Made in the USA
Middletown, DE
04 January 2021

30353563R00324